Praise for the novels of Katie McGarry

"An intoxicating and unforgettable story that kept me glued to the page."
—Kami Garcia, #1 *New York Times* bestselling author, on *Walk the Edge*

"A daring love story filled with blackmail, revenge, and unexpected trust... McGarry once again creates an incredible story with two dynamic protagonists."
—*School Library Journal* on *Walk the Edge*

"A story that readers will not want to put down."
—*School Library Journal* on *Nowhere but Here*

"Highly emotional and hugely inspiring... I had an ache in my chest as I turned each page."
—*New York Times* bestselling author Samantha Young on *Breaking the Rules*

"With likable characters and a tensely building romance, this book will not disappoint."
—*Booklist* on *Take Me On*

"Sweet and sexy."
—*Publishers Weekly* on *Crash into You*

"Everything—setting, characters, romance—about this novel works and works well."
—*Kirkus Reviews* on *Dare You To* (starred review)

"A riveting and emotional ride!"
—Simone Elkeles, *New York Times* bestselling author of the Perfect Chemistry series, on *Pushing the Limits*

"A perfect choice for readers who thrive on edgy, riveting storytelling."
—*BookPage* on *Pushing the Limits*

KATIE McGARRY

LONG WAY HOME

HARLEQUIN®TEEN

Recycling programs
for this product may
not exist in your area.

ISBN-13: 978-1-335-01334-7

Long Way Home

Copyright © 2017 by Katie McGarry

Printed in U.S.A.

LONG WAY HOME

CHEVY

The instructions of the English homework I didn't do hang out from the top of my folder: *Two roads diverged in a yellow wood, And sorry I could not travel both.*

Story of my life.

According to my football coach, I chose wrongly on the two crap paths I had to face last week. I just ran into Coach on the way to English, and he ripped into me for my sorry decision-making skills when it came to me choosing to stand up for the Reign of Terror Motorcycle Club instead of a member of my football team.

I didn't just get my ass chewed out, his tirade made me late for English with no tardy note. Which is great, since my English teacher hates late students like I hate riding my motorcycle in forty-degree weather while it rains.

I round the corner, then peek through the small window in the door of my class. Ms. Whitlock stands in front of her desk in her patented white button-down shirt, gray pencil skirt and dark-rimmed glasses. From the back row, my best friend Razor meets my eyes and shakes his head. Damn.

That means she's in one of her moods where she's refusing to let anyone in.

I'm not a tail-tucked-between-my-legs type of guy, but this lady is one of the few who can reduce me to begging. If she doesn't let me in, then she'll mark me as absent, the front office will think I skipped, and that means I won't be able to play at tonight's football game.

The window rattles when I knock. The entire class turns their heads in my direction, but Ms. Whitlock doesn't. The muscles in my neck tighten. She is one of the hardest core people I know and my grandfather is the president of a motorcycle club. That says something.

She starts for the whiteboard and I knock on the door again. This time Ms. Whitlock does look my way and she grants me the type of glare reserved for people who kick puppies. I got it. I'm late. I'm the scum of humanity, so let my ass in so I can play football.

There's this guy in my club, Pigpen. He's about the same age as Ms. Whitlock, late twenties, and he's a walking hard-on for this woman even though she would never give him the time of day. He practically runs into walls when she's around because he's too focused on checking her out. I don't see gorgeous—all I see is seriously pissed off and the person standing between me and playing.

Ms. Whitlock points at the clock over her desk. She's telling me I can wait. If I'm lucky, she'll open the door after the quiz that I'll receive a zero on. If I'm not so lucky, she won't open the door at all.

Two pathetic paths and I could only travel one. Nowhere in that stupid poem did it mention there was good and bad to both paths and that sometimes it's best not to choose, but to set up camp at the fork and do nothing at all.

I slam my hand into the nearest locker, almost relishing the sting.

"Feel better?"

A glance across the hallway and I freeze. Doesn't matter how many times I see her in a day, she still manages to take my breath away. Violet leans against the lockers as beautiful as ever. Red silky hair flowing over her shoulders, a pair of ripped jeans that look like they were tailored for her curves and enough bracelets around her wrists that they clank together when she moves.

Do I feel better? Not really, but I nod anyway as I try to judge if being alone with Violet causes more pain than having my balls ripped off. "Didn't hurt."

"Yes, I can see how slamming your hand against a locker didn't hurt at all."

My lips tilt up because she got me, and on top of that, Violet made a joke. Since she broke up with me last spring, things between us have been tense. On her side and on mine. Some people, like me and Violet, aren't supposed to break up. Some people, like me and Violet, don't know how to be near each other when we do part ways. "Are we talking now?"

"I'm locked out of class. You're locked out of class. I could ignore you if that's what you want."

It's not. Her ignoring me is never what I wanted. "Why are you late?"

Violet presses her lips together and looks away. A sixth sense within me stirs. Something's wrong. I've known her my entire life. We were born only a few weeks apart and we learned to crawl on the sticky floor of the Reign of Terror clubhouse. We were friends, always friends, until one day, we weren't just friends anymore. We became more until we lost it all.

"Late's not your thing," I say. Violet's unconventional.

Marches to her own drummer, but she's not the type to be late to class. It's a respect thing for her, something her dad taught her, and Violet may never listen to another living soul, but she listened to her father. "What's going on?"

She's silent and frustration rumbles through me. Violet used to tell me everything. Used to see me as someone who could help solve her problems. She doesn't see me like that anymore and it pisses me off. I'm angry at her for making us this way. Angry at myself for not figuring out how to fix us.

"You being late wouldn't have anything to do with Stone, would it?" Stone's her brother and the question's a shot in the dark, but I don't want to miss the chance to keep conversation with her going.

"Why are you late?" she replies as a nonanswer, and my head snaps up. Guess sometimes blind shots do hit their mark. Violet was late because of Stone.

"What happened?" I push.

"I'm not talking about it."

"Vi—"

She cuts me off. "I told you how to help me and my brother six months ago and you told me no."

By running away? No again to that insane solution.

"Tell me why you're late," she says. "If you don't, then you need to stop talking, because the last thing either of us needs right now beyond missing a quiz or possibly being marked as absent is detention for getting into a shouting match. At least it's the last thing I need, okay?"

I back up to the lockers across from her and lightly hit my head against the metal. Yeah, I don't want to talk about why I'm late either. I shove a hand into my pocket and try to think of a change in subject. Telling Violet I'm late because my football coach tore into me for hitting a guy who was causing problems for the Terror, a guy who had been causing problems for her, won't help me and Violet stay civil. She's mad at the club, which makes her mad at me.

Violet's watching me, and her expression is a lot like someone trying to figure out a word problem for math. Unfortunately, she knows me as well as I know her.

"Being late is going to cost you, isn't it?" she asks. "You can't play tonight if she marks you absent, can you?"

I meet her blue eyes, and my chest hurts at the sympathy I find there. I'd willingly miss tonight's game if I could rewind back to a time where I could talk to Violet with ease and that's not the type of trade I'd normally make.

Football is my life. So is the motorcycle club. The Reign of Terror are my family—the blood kind and the bonds of brotherhood kind. I don't know who I am without the Terror, but to be honest, I don't know who I am without football either.

Lately, I've been torn between the two, just like that poem, and everyone in my life has chosen a side. Violet used to be the person I could talk to, but then she walked.

Six months ago, Violet asked me to run away with her. She was driven by grief, driven by something she wouldn't tell me about. When I told her no, that we needed to stay home, to be near our family, to be near the club, Violet returned the next night and announced I was choosing the club over her and that we were done.

Being a running back, I've taken more than my fair share of hits over the years, but I've never been as blindsided as I was that night. Never experienced the type of pain her leaving me created.

The door to the classroom opens and a sense of relief washes over me. I'll have to bust my ass to bring up my grade thanks to that zero on the quiz, but at least I'll be able to play tonight.

Ms. Whitlock steps out and sizes me up, then Violet. "I'm only letting you in if you have a note, otherwise you can head to the office and hope they give you one."

Screw me. There's no way I'll make it to the office, get a note and return in time. Right as I'm about to kick the hell out of the locker, Violet glides past me and hands in her note. "This is Chevy's."

My head whips in her direction. "It's what?"

"Yours." Violet meets my eyes. "Thanks for offering it to me, but it's not right for me to take it. I'm the one who didn't have a note, and I'm the one who needs to make it right."

She begins walking backward, and my short-circuited brain sparks back to life. I can't let her do this. "Violet—"

"Have a good game tonight," she says, then disappears down the stairs.

"Are you joining us, Mr. McKinley, or not?" Ms. Whitlock demands. Never met a person I hate as much as this lady and it takes everything I have to force one foot in front of the other.

Everyone watches me as I stalk down the aisle, then drop into the last seat in the row, the one next to Razor. He's calm, cool, blond hair, blue eyes, and he's watching me like an owl who's considering whether it wants that unsuspecting mouse for a snack now or later.

Ms. Whitlock is lost in her own world as she continues babbling about poem interpretations and people who died too long ago. I can do little more than open my folder and stare at the top of my homework.

"Chevy," Razor whispers, and I glance over at him. He points to the paper on his desk and in his messy handwriting is *You okay?*

Yes, because I get to play football tonight. No, because Violet sacrificed herself for it to happen. Hell no, because the world's messed up and I don't know how to fix it. Worse no, because I don't know if I should read more into what Violet did—if it means somewhere deep inside she still thinks we have a chance.

I shake my head, Razor nods and the two of us stare at the whiteboard. Two roads. One path. Can't take both. The guy who wrote it acts like the choice should be easy. It's not. And he also didn't mention what happens when people like Violet shove you onto a path regardless of your thoughts.

"So how many of you liked the poem?" Ms. Whitlock asks.

The entire class raises their hands. Almost everyone, except for me and Razor.

Violet

Quick—what do you get when a dentist marries a seamstress?

Don't know?

Answer: A badass man who joins a motorcycle club.

Don't get it?

It's okay, neither do I.

I'm completely lost as to why my father joined a motorcycle club. He wasn't born into the lifestyle like so many members are. My grandparents were as middle class as they come. My grandfather was a dentist with a struggling practice and my grandmother was a dressmaker.

They got married and had my dad and he lived a very normal, boring life. Even grew up in a modest two-story house with a finished basement, white picket fence, MTV playing on the Zenith, and chalk drawings on the sidewalks.

As Dad got older, he played football, dated the cheerleader (my mom) and landed a partial scholarship to college. He went on to become an accountant. Happy middle class—that was my dad. Joining an MC didn't make sense, but he did join and because of that decision he died.

As I watch the others standing in line laughing and chatting with their happy middle-class families, all I keep thinking is, that could have been me. I could have been the girl in the fuzzy blue sweater giggling with her jeans-on-dress-down-Friday-wearing father.

But it's not me, and I doubt I'll ever understand why.

The crowd on the bleachers erupts into cheers, and an air siren wails into the cool mid-October evening. The home team, my high school team, scored a touchdown. Standing in line beside me at the ticket booth, my brother, Brandon, bounces on his toes while shoving his hands into his jeans pockets as he strains to see the football field.

He's one of the many people I love so much that it's painful. He's also one of several people in my life I can't seem to stop hurting.

"Do you think that was Chevy who scored?" It's the first words he's said to me since we left school this afternoon. He's mad I dragged him into the school's office and showed the vice principal the bruise and cut on his arm caused by some jerk at lunch. My brother is a joke to most of the boys at our school, and Brandon can never understand why I can't leave it alone.

It's because of what happened at lunch that I was late to English today. Brandon was bleeding and I took him to the nurses' office. The nurse gave him the option of calling Mom and going home, but I talked him into returning to class because Brandon has to learn how to keep his head high. Guys like the ones who hurt him will keep causing problems if they believe they're getting to him. But guys like that also deserve to be punished, hence why I dragged Brandon into the vice principal's office after school.

"I asked if you think it was Chevy who scored," Brandon repeats.

"I don't know." I breathe out the ache Chevy's name creates. Chevy used to be my boyfriend. He used to be one of my best friends. He's also one of the people it hurts to love.

"I couldn't hear who they said scored," my brother continues. "Everyone was cheering. Do you think we can find out once we get in? Do you think someone will tell us? Can you ask?" Brandon scratches his chin twice, and his cheeks turn red against his naturally pale skin.

The line is long, and he's flustered we're late. The late part is my fault. Part of it on purpose, part of it beyond my control. Either way, Brandon's angry at me. It's not new. Brandon's natural state of emotion with me is anger. I'm the one who sets rules and boundaries, while everyone else in his life is bent on either babying him or having fun.

Life is not fun and no one is doing either him or me a favor by trying to act differently.

Still, I love Brandon, and I hate that he's mad at me, so we're here to watch my ex-boyfriend play football. As I said, life isn't fun. But Brandon deserves a moment of happiness, especially since there are so many people at school determined to make him sad.

It's midway through football season, and tonight our small-town team is playing a big-city school. Two powerhouses battling for dominance. Though I seem to be immune, the excitement around us appears to be contagious. A sea of blue sweatshirts, smiles and high fives.

We move up in line, and seeing we're two people away from the ticket window, I pull money out of my back pocket and offer Brandon a five-dollar bill while keeping a five for myself.

Brandon's eyes widen, and he pushes the glasses sliding down his nose back up. "What's the money for?"

"To buy your ticket." I flash a smile, hoping he'll see I'm

calm and then he'll remain calm. My brother is fourteen, a little over three years younger than me. I'm a senior and he's a freshman. While there are many things we have in common, like our pale skin with freckles, our crazy bright red hair and our father's blue eyes, there are also so many ways we're different.

Our minds tinker differently. Not better. Just differently. Brandon's a little slower on some things, a lot faster on others, and he's often very anxious around people and in social situations.

"Can't you do it for me, Vi?" Of course I'm Vi to him now, meaning I'm officially out of the doghouse, and I almost consider folding.

Almost. My brother needs to learn how to handle simple situations on his own.

"You can do it," I encourage. "Just hand her the money, ask her for one student ticket, and then she'll hand you your change along with the ticket. The whole exchange will take seconds."

Brandon shrinks, and even though he's as tall as me, he reminds me of when we were children and I held his hand as we rode the elementary bus because he was scared.

"I don't like the way the lady at the ticket booth looks at us. I've seen her around town and she makes me feel like I've done something wrong when I haven't."

My heart sinks, and my fingers play with the bracelets on my wrist. "Any dirty look she gives is for me, not you."

That's only partially true. The woman working the ticket counter enjoys giving both of us her evil eye. I could claim that's her resting bitch face, but when she doesn't notice me or my brother, she actually smiles.

We live in a small town. Brandon's the weird kid, and after

a picture of me making out with a guy made the rounds on social media, I'm the town whore.

Before the infamous picture, I had forever been labeled a child of the Reign of Terror Motorcycle Club because my father was a member. I can't decide if in the ticket taker's eyes whore is better than Terror spawn. She probably assumes the two are related.

"Vi," he starts again, but my muscles tense as my patience wears thin.

"It's just a ticket." This time the calm in my voice is forced and so is the smile. "I need you to be able to buy a ticket."

Brandon's shoulders slump forward, and I hate that I snapped, but if he can't buy a ticket to a football game, how can he buy himself food when he grows older?

There are months remaining until I graduate from high school, and even if I figure out how to take him with me when I leave, I won't be around to take care of him forever. He needs to learn to take care of himself. It's what we all have to learn.

The people in front of us walk off with tickets. A mom, a dad, a brother, a sister. Middle class and grinning from ear to ear. I seriously hate each and every one of them for being happy. I know, that makes me bitter, but sometimes bitter happens.

"You can do this." I take Brandon's hand in mine and give a reassuring squeeze. "I know you can."

Brandon swallows hard, but nods. A combination of nervous energy and pride rushes through my veins as he grasps my hand in return and fists the cash in his other hand. He's going to face his fears. The lift of my lips is genuine now. My brother believes in himself, and I believe in him and maybe we're both going to be okay.

Right as Brandon takes a courageous step forward, two

black leather vests slip in front of us and staring back at me is a half skull with fire blazing out of its eye sockets.

The world surrounding me turns red, and my blood begins to boil. "There's a line and you just cut."

Eli, one of my father's once best friends, glances over his shoulder and winks at us as he pulls out his wallet. Like always, he has dark hair cut close to his head, plugs in his ears and a huge grin like we should be glad to see him. "I got you covered."

Fabulous. Here comes the Reign of Terror Motorcycle Club riding in on their black Harleys determined to save the day of people who really need to learn how to save themselves.

"No, really, we got this," I insist.

I try to muscle my way past to pay, but Eli's right-hand man, Pigpen, plants himself in front of me like the towering sack of testosterone and annoyance that he is. Then he's on the move and I somehow find myself away from the ticket booth.

"Surprised to see you here, Violet." Pigpen is in his late twenties and thinks he's all handsome with his blond hair and big muscles. Because he was a Navy SEAL or Army Ranger or something outrageous like that, he also thinks he's awesome, but he doesn't impress me. "Surprised you're here, but happy to see you. You haven't been at a game all year."

"I've been busy," I say.

"Is that what you call avoiding anyone from the Terror? Busy?"

"Works for me."

"Hi, Pigpen!" Brandon is lit up like a firefly who was convinced the rest of his species was extinct. Eli, of course, enjoying the role of savior, has his arm around Brandon's shoulders as they join us.

"Hey, Stone." Pigpen calls my brother by the stupid nickname the club created for him. "How's it going?"

"Good. They bought our tickets, Vi!"

"Yep, they sure did, because little ol' me couldn't handle the big ol' ticket booth on my own." Heavy on the sarcasm and then a hard glare at Eli. "Brandon was going to buy his own ticket."

Eli rolls his neck like he's the one who owns the right to be annoyed. "Most people say thank you."

"You're missing the point."

Eli pats my brother's back. "Why don't you head in with Pigpen? I'd like to catch up with Violet."

Brandon bounces like a damn puppy dog given a treat and then rushes off into the stadium, leaving me with Thing Two. And to think my brother called me Vi. The little traitor.

"Pigpen," I call out. "Don't leave him."

I forced my brother to tattle today, and while the football game will make him smile, I'm also taking a calculated risk that the people he told on won't be here. If they are here, I'm betting they won't mess with Brandon as long as I'm around.

"You worry too much," Pigpen answers without glancing back.

When it comes to my brother, they don't worry enough about the right problems.

Eli watches as Brandon and Pigpen go into the stadium. Instead of taking a left for the bleachers, they go right for the concession stand, and I'm contemplating how to stab Pigpen in the jugular. Concession food brings my brother into a near state of euphoria, and because of the crappy day my brother and I had, I wanted to be the one who made him happy with a hot dog, nachos and a slushy.

Motorcycle men around the world, as far as I'm concerned, can just plain suck it.

Eli turns to me, and my heart aches. Good God, he reminds me of Chevy. An older version, but still the relation is clear. Like Chevy, Eli's a McKinley. Chestnut hair, dark eyes, broad shoulders. I've often wondered if Chevy will be Eli's clone when he grows older. Eli is Chevy's uncle. It wouldn't be a bad thing if Chevy resembled Eli as he aged, but it's the fear of Chevy becoming the warrior and convict that Eli is that drove Chevy and me apart.

Eli eyes me warily as he pulls on the plug in his ear. Still, the man has that grin he uses to try to convince people he's easygoing. But I don't buy it. Not even God could count all the demons dancing in his soul.

To be fair, Eli used to be one of my favorite people, but he and I haven't gotten along very well since my father's death. In fact, I haven't gotten along with anyone associated with the Terror since Dad died a year ago.

"Hi, Violet."

"Brandon was going to buy his own ticket." I work hard to keep my voice steady. "You can't keep swooping in and doing things for him. He's got to learn how to fend for himself."

"It's good to see you, too," Eli says like I never spoke. "I'm glad you brought Stone. I know how much that kid loves to see Chevy play."

"Maybe you didn't hear me, so I'll try to be a little more direct," I say. "Stop butting in with my brother. You don't help. None of you help."

"How's your mom?" Eli continues, once again like the conversation on my end isn't happening.

"Moping around like always. Know what would help her? A job or a hobby or a purpose. None of which she will get as long as you guys keep popping in and taking care of her." I'm sensing the theme, but doubt Eli will. Logic complicates his thinking process.

The glint of frustration in Eli's eyes gives away that he hears me, yet he keeps up the charade. "Tell your mom me and some of the guys from the club will be over to help with the house. Mow the yard. Pay the bills."

A dangerous anger curls within me. "I'm tired of explaining to you we don't need the Reign of Terror's help. In fact, we'd be better off without any of you."

"Is it impossible for us to talk without fighting?" Eli snaps.

And there it is. Eli finally showing his true colors. "This isn't a fight. My voice hasn't risen high enough to draw a crowd, and I have yet to say fuck, so we're still in the land of civil."

Eli opens his mouth to respond when his cell buzzes. He reaches for his phone, checks the text, and a shadow falls over his face. I've seen that look hundreds of times growing up and that expression means whatever is going on in his precious club is more important than me, more important than staying.

It's the look my father had right before he left me for the last time.

Why don't I want the club involved in my life or Brandon's? Because Brandon doesn't need people who promise they're going to stick around to take care of him but then abandon him the moment their cell pings. My brother deserves better than that. I deserve better now, and I deserved better when Dad was alive.

"Gotta go?" The bitterness drips in the singsong sway of my voice.

The black gaze Eli shoots me is his confirmation. "This conversation isn't over."

Yes, it is. "I've got to take care of my brother while you guys go off and play."

I walk away from Eli because someone in Brandon's life

has to be responsible. Someone has to be the grown-up, and considering the other people in Brandon's life are determined to stay irresponsible, the burden falls to me.

CHEVY

Damn if I understand why girls like getting flowers, but their faces light up, their lips will tilt upward and their eyes will glow as if you handed them the world. Hell, maybe it's only the girls I've been around who react this way. Maybe their lives are so messed up that the idea of any guy offering them anything without expectation of payment blows their mind.

It's sad, but it's true, and I don't mind being the person who can bring them one second of happiness.

Shamrock's newest employee accepts the two daisies I "magically" made appear. I stole them—two tables down from a bouquet an army boy's holding. Guess he plans on giving it to one of the cocktail waitresses. He didn't notice I swiped the flowers and neither did anyone else. Fast hands, a distraction, and the world belongs to me.

"Thank you." She glances away and my heart drops for her. She's pretty. Early twenties. Could do well working here at the bar, but with that attitude, she won't make it through the night. There's no room for modesty or shyness or emotion in order to make money at this joint.

"Pretty girl like you," I say with a wink, "will knock 'em dead."

"Do you work here?" she asks.

The bar's manager and Mom's best friend smacks me on the back of the head before I can answer no. "Stop flirting with my girls." Brandy gestures at me while looking at the new girl. "Watch out for him, he thinks he can con anyone into loving him."

"You love me," I say.

"And I regret it most days." But she says it with a smile. Brandy then offers her hand to her newest employee. "Come on, let me show you where the real magic happens."

"My magic's real," I call out, and Brandy's only response is a loud laugh. I can't help but chuckle with her because she's going to be pissed in a few minutes when she realizes I lifted her watch...again.

The new girl waves as she glances at me over her shoulder. I nod in response. The twenty in my pocket says she won't be here when I pick Mom up later. Being a waitress here requires an iron shell.

With a thud, Mom props her overly large purse on the bar, slides off my leather jacket and hands it to me, revealing her low-cut tank and what she refers to as her jeans-that-make-her-money. She asked me to drop her off early, since the other bartender called in sick.

I usually drive Mom in her car as she hates motorcycles, but her already pieced-together Ford from the 1980s died again this morning, and I haven't had time to figure out what broke.

Mom sighs heavily when I slide Brandy's watch to her. "Will you please stop stealing from people?"

"It's not stealing if I give it back." I grin, then grin wider when Mom's lips twitch. Everyone's born with a gift. My gift is fast hands. Too bad my only career options with it are street magician or thug pickpocket. Some days, my feet are as fast as my hands and that's what makes me one hell of a football player.

"Tonight should be a moneymaker." Mom uses her phone to check her makeup.

I case the dimly lit place that's occasionally brightened by the beams of colored lights bouncing off the dance floor and the stage where the DJ mixes music. Being near the army base is great for business, but can bring in a mix of a crowd.

Because it's too damn cliché, the place crawls with army boys. Most of them too loud, too cocky and too lonely. A gang of boys with frat symbols on their T-shirts take up three tables near the stage. Odds are they're under twenty-one, so that's why they drove the forty-five minutes from their school.

The bouncers don't give a rip who's here as long as they pay to get in and pay for their beer. All those guys watch the girls on the dance floor. Most of them like starved wolves in search of raw meat.

Friday and Saturday nights make me nervous, so I offer to drive Mom, and when she doesn't accept, I don't give her a choice. There's a lot of psychotic bastards in the world and most of them seem to gravitate to bars late at night in search of those who drank too much and are easy prey.

"Why do you do it?" Mom leans in so she can hear my answer over the pounding music. It's nearing ten, about an hour before this place will be wall-to-wall shaking and shim-mying bodies. "Why do you always give the girls around here flowers?"

Because they often walk out of here with a vacant ex-pression and hollow eyes. Exhausted from being on their feet and having to pretend they're someone's fantasy so they can make more money from tips. "Question should be, why don't more guys do it?"

Mom goes into one of those blinding smiles that reminds me how young she is—early forties. If she wanted, Mom could still marry and pop out a new, normal family. Create the American dream of two kids, a dog and a white picket fence. That is if the American dream means working at a bar and already having a soon-to-be eighteen-year-old son.

She grabs hold of my chin and guides me down to her short height so she can kiss my cheek. "You're one of the good ones, Chevy. Never forget that."

Mom sees enough bad ones to know the difference. That's why I drive her to and from work on the weekends. Why I don't just drop her off, but also come in and get the lay of the land. I eyeball a few guys so they can spread the word to the others who might be thinking of going too far with my mom that I'm their personal grim reaper.

"Hell of a game tonight, Chevy!" Mike, the bouncer, bellows from across the room. A round of claps and cheers from the locals and then an echo from people who have no idea what we're celebrating.

"Nobody plays like my boy!" Mom shouts. She's been to every game I've had since I started in third grade.

I'm a running back for my high school team. Scored three touchdowns tonight, took a hell of a lot of hits, and I got a bruised shoulder to prove it. It's October and we're halfway through regular season games. With the team kicking ass like it has, we've got a decent shot at going to state. I don't miss the fact that the reason we won, the reason I played was because Violet made a sacrifice.

My cell pings twice and Mom's proud smile morphs into a frown. From the number of pings, she knows it's from Eli, my uncle, my father's brother, and the most respected man in the Reign of Terror Motorcycle Club.

Eli: You need to stay off the road tonight. Confirm receipt. This is my third text about this. Don't make me text you again.

Not what I need. I crack my neck to the side. When the club thinks there's trouble from a rival club, they warn me off of being visible.

I'm a senior in high school and not yet a full member of the MC, but being a child of the club, I often get crap from people in town and can have a target on me from other MC's. But no way was I letting Mom drive herself. No way was I leaving her to be on her own.

"Club stuff?" Mom asks like she's not pissed as she rifles through her purse. The Reign of Terror and my mother have a complicated relationship. Between her and them, I'm constantly the knot in the middle of a tug-of-war rope.

"Eli's checking in." I shrug my jacket on and dig out the keys to my motorcycle.

"Sure he is," she mumbles, then goes behind the bar. Mom's black hair falls forward when she places her purse in the safe. When she stands, she tucks the strands behind her ears, showing off the hoop earrings I bought for her birthday last month.

Mom and I don't look much alike. She's short with a small frame and has an olive complexion, while I'm built like a McKinley: tall, strong shoulders, brown hair and eyes. According to pictures, I favor my father. Mom never says much about him. The MC thinks he's a saint. I do my best to stay neutral.

Across from me, Mom taps her finger on the bar. "Have you thought about what I said?"

The muscles in my back tense. I'm reaching a tipping point in the tug-of-war game. When I turn eighteen, the MC will expect me to continue the blood legacy of the Reign of Terror and become a prospect. Eli's a key member of the club, my grandfather is the president and my father before his death was on the fast track to being a board member.

There's no doubt the board will take me, but there's a rhythm to becoming a member and I'm expected to play along. My prospect period is the initiation time frame where the club decides whether or not I should be a full-fledged member. It'll be a lot of me cleaning toilets and doing whatever the board says when they say it.

"There's no reason to rush this," Mom continues. She's asked me to push off becoming a prospect for the MC until I graduate from high school. "Once you're in the Terror, you'll always be in the Terror. Why not be a normal high school kid for a few months? Find a nice girl. Go to prom. Go to keggers like other boys your age, not clubhouses. Let me live the fantasy of being mom to the jock who has the high school sweetheart. If you're bound and determined to hang out with outlaws, at least have the decency to be arrested for cow tipping the first time I have to bail you out of jail."

Haven't told Mom yet the football coach is unhappy with me over the Terror. After that monologue, I'll keep it to myself indefinitely.

"Last I checked, it's his life," comes a familiar gravelly voice. "Not your life and not your call on how he makes his choices. And to clear up any misunderstandings, the club decides when we offer prospect, not Chevy."

My grandfather and president of the Reign of Terror, Cyrus, sidles up beside me at the bar. Mom tenses like a cat on the verge of attacking, and Cyrus merely strokes his long gray beard as he looks at me. "Club's been trying to reach you."

"Must have never turned my phone back on after the game," I lie and try to balance the power struggle between Mom and the club and that means deflection. "Everything okay?"

"Yeah. Just some bumps. Heard you had a hell of a game tonight."

I nod. If Cyrus heard I had a good game, that must mean something major is going down. Like Mom, he's always there, unless something with the club is about to go to hell.

"I heard Violet was at the game with Stone," he says, and my head pops up. Despite knowing better, there's a flicker of hope within me. I've got to cut that crap out or my heart will be hurting again.

"Don't guess you knew that," Cyrus continues.

No, I didn't and it's hard not to glance over at my mom to gauge her reaction. She, more than anyone, is aware how the breakup with Violet has gutted me.

Cyrus tilts his head to the exit. "Why don't we go back to the cabin, and you can fill me in on what I missed. Some guys might be at the clubhouse. Bet they'd want to hear about the game, too."

"Or he can go home," Mom butts in, and she twists a dish towel as if she's imagining strangling his neck. "His home. The one that has his room. His bed. His things. His home."

I hitch my thumbs into my jeans and wish I could disappear. Give me a mirror, the fine art of distraction, and I could make you believe I did fade into the nothingness, but right now, I've got nothing. "Give me a few minutes with Mom?"

Cyrus is as big and bad as they come. Sixties. My height. Monster of a man. He proudly wears the Reign of Terror leather cut on his back: the half skull with fire blazing out of its eyes and balls of fire raining down around it.

My grandfather scares the hell out of most people, and he's put me in my place more than once. He's raised me, just as much as Mom. Half my time has been spent with him. Half my time with her. I love him, just like I love my mom.

He walks away, and before Mom begins to revel in her win, I lean onto the bar and say, "He's right. It is my life and it is my call."

She slams her hand on the bar and sets her hardened green eyes on me. "Then start acting like it. You can't keep walking this line between the real world and the club for much longer. It's one or the other, Chevy. Turning eighteen, you know it means you can't have both."

My jaw twitches. Before his death, before my birth, my father didn't choose her. He slept with Mom, had some sort of relationship with her that neither she nor the club will talk about, but at the end of the day, he never claimed Mom as his girl and, because of that, my mother remains an outsider.

Because of my blood, I'm an insider. The club, it's a legit club. They don't sell drugs, guns, or dabble in prostitution. Yeah, they color outside the lines at times, work well in gray areas, but we do our best to stay away from flat-out illegal.

The club owns a legit security company that travels alongside semi-loads of expensive goods to guarantee that the truck makes it to point B from point A without any problems. People don't know it, but trucks being jacked for their loads happens more often than one would think. The security company is a ride-along bouncer.

Most of the members of the Terror work for the security company. Other members, they work "normal" jobs within the community, but Mom's right. Members and family members of the Terror, we stand out and we are our own world.

As long as I stay underage, I've been able to walk the line, and when my birthday hits, I don't know what I'm going to choose.

"Chevy," Cyrus calls near the entrance. "We need to talk."

Damned knot in the tug-of-war rope and I'm starting to feel frayed. Mom doesn't blink as she waits for me to say something. To tell Cyrus he can wait. To tell her what she wants to hear. But as much as I love her, I'm also drawn to the club. She's right, I do want both.

"I'll be back to pick you up later," I say.

Mom throws the towel she had expertly throttled into the sink behind her, walks to the other side of the bar, and the strobe light casts a red haze around her. If I didn't know her better, I'd buy the flirty smile and the way she giggles in happiness as she leans on the bar to take a drink order. But that's not her real smile and that's not her real laugh. It's part of her job, part of her act, because that's what working here requires—performing.

With a kick to a bar stool, I head for the exit. Cyrus walks out into the night and I follow. Once outside, Cyrus turns to me and his warm breath creates a cloud in the cool night. "We've had some trouble tonight with the Riot."

The Riot would be a motorcycle club north of us in Louisville. They're pissed at the Terror for myriad reasons, the main one being we're a legit club and they deal in illegal. They're also angry at one of our main members, Eli. They feel he stole their daughter and granddaughter from them. Eli didn't steal a thing. Can't call someone's free will in walking away from crazy a crime.

Life sucks for the Riot and I'm fine with that. "Everything okay?"

"Yeah. Everyone's safe, but we've had word that they've ridden past the boundary lines we set with them a few months back. It's all rumor and no one on our side has confirmed it. Could be someone's overactive imagination, but I'll feel better knowing you're off the road."

I'm under eighteen, still a kid to him. Cyrus used to act this way with my two best friends, Oz and Razor, but both are eighteen and full members of the club now. The babysitting twists my gut, but then again, I'm not ready for the decision eighteen will bring. "How about Violet?"

"I'm on my way now to look for her. She's also not answering her cell."

Yeah. A lot of that going around. "If she took Stone to the game, she would have headed straight home. I'll check on her on my way to Mom's if you want."

This gives me the excuse I need to see Violet. Because I won't be able to sleep without knowing she's okay. So I can thank her for what she did for me with the note. To gauge whether or not Violet is waving the white flag.

Cyrus lays a hand on my shoulder. "I'd appreciate that. I need to head back to the clubhouse to take care of some business. I'm serious about what I said, though. Me and a lot of guys would love to hear about the game."

I know they would and I'd enjoy being with them, but Mom's already sore that I walked out on her to talk to Cyrus. "I'm beat. After I check on Violet, I'm crashing."

Cyrus gives me a fast pat and a hug. We both mount our bikes and start our engines with a growl. My grandfather takes the lead and I follow him as long as I can before taking the path that leads away from him and toward where Violet lives.

Violet

Dad's cross dangles over the engine of his Chevelle while my other necklaces stay tucked inside my shirt. I'll admit, I don't have a clue what I'm looking for and using the flashlight app from my cell has done nothing to help. Maybe if I stare at the inner workings of the car long enough a magic fairy will pop out and tell me to smack this, turn that, jump in a circle three times naked and then the engine will wondrously rev to life.

I'd perform the act if that would make Dad's car run again. Who am I kidding? I'd do it if it would make anything in my life work again.

Behind me, Brandon paces and the rocks crunch under his footsteps. We're two miles from home and off to the side of a quiet country road. Thank God there's a full moon as my brother can be terrified of dark places. Dad used to tell Brandon that a full moon is nature's night-light. I'm banking on Brandon remembering that tidbit of fatherly wisdom because, unless steam rising from my engine means my car is about to evolve into some next generation of superpower vehicle, we're stuck.

"We should call the club," Brandon says. "They'd come. They'd help fix your car."

With strings made out of spiderwebs. The Reign of Terror would suck us in and then suck us dry. It's how they work. You don't get something for nothing with them. "If you remember, Eli and Pigpen tore off from the football game because they had business to take care of, meaning we wouldn't be high on the priority list. Besides, Mom's on her way."

She's put out, but she's on her way. Mom will take her time to prove how annoyed she is with my "careless behavior" of driving at night without the protection of a man. That's how Mom thinks. Girls, to her, are the weaker and fairer sex waiting for a man to save them, and Mom is constantly annoyed that I don't play up my femininity.

Yeah, that's complete bull.

I straighten and the bracelets on my wrist clink together and hit Dad's bulky Rolex. It's one of the many things Mom was mad about today. She tolerates me wearing Dad's cross, but she's adamant that I leave the watch alone. Dad always wore the cross and the Rolex, and today I needed both so I could find the strength to keep breathing in and then out several times a minute.

If I was alone, I'd head home on foot, but Brandon walking along the woods in the dark could cause problems I'm not giddy to deal with. At least he feels somewhat safe next to the car.

"Are you hungry?" I ask. "I didn't eat all my popcorn at the game and you can have what's left. I should warn you, most of it is burnt."

"The club would send somebody if you called," he mutters. "If you called Chevy, he'd come. At least he'd come for me."

Knife straight to where I'm weak, and I lose the ability to breathe. Yeah, Chevy would come, but what girl wants to play damsel in distress and then be saved by her ex-boyfriend? "I can't call Chevy."

It wouldn't be fair to Chevy, and it wouldn't be fair to me. The love I had for him was consuming and powerful and raw. I briefly close my eyes as memories of Chevy's hands on my body and his lips on mine cause warmth to curl in my bloodstream... Even when we fought, we never had problems with attraction.

My breakup with Chevy hasn't only hurt me, but my brother, and I'm not sure if he'll ever forgive me. I'm not sure if a lot of people will forgive me, but none of that matters. My single goal in life is to get as far away from this town as I can, as fast as I can. Graduation. That's my town of Snowflake expiration date.

A motorcycle rumbles in the distance and it's weird how my heart still flutters at the sound. When I was younger, I used to sit at the window in the living room and wait for that beautiful growl. The moment I heard Dad's motorcycle, I used to skip through the house telling my mom and brother that Daddy was home.

I'd burst out the front door in time for him to swing off his bike and then he'd catch me and toss me into the air. I'd squeal, then end up in a fit of giggles as he would tickle me in his big, crushing hug.

Those days are long gone.

The motorcycle engine grows louder. A single headlight breaks over the hill of the road that leads to town. Most sane people would be terrified at being alone on the side of the road at night with an approaching motorcycle, but I'm annoyed and slightly relieved.

If someone from the Terror wants to stumble upon me and help make Dad's car move, I'll suck up the animosity long enough to get my brother home. But at the same time, accepting their help will only make them want to go dictator over everything else in my family's life.

Anything offered by the Terror comes at a price. My father paid with his life.

I step back from the open hood and the motorcycle slows to a stop behind my car. I blow out a rush of air. Why does my life have to continually suck? I would have taken Eli or Pigpen over this. But I didn't get Thing One or Thing Two. I got my ex because I'm that incredibly unlucky.

Chevy slips off his bike and grimly assesses the car. More than once he's been under the hood of this Chevelle. Chevy and my dad were close. A part of Chevy was also destroyed when Dad died.

"Mom's on her way," I say. "You're fine to move along, since she'll be here soon."

Brandon rushes past me so quickly that his arm smacks mine. He doesn't bother looking back to confirm I'm still standing; no, my brother is too busy welcoming Chevy like he's a hero.

Brandon is all words, most of them tripping and running into the other, as he attempts to express his excitement and undying love and loyalty. "We were at your game and Pigpen bought me a hot dog and Eli bought my ticket and I didn't see your first touchdown, but I saw your second and third and you plowed right through that line and I'm so glad to see you."

Because Chevy is patient, more patient than most grown men, he stands in front of my brother with his thumbs hitched in his front pockets and that sexy slouch of his like he's prepared to listen to every single word Brandon could ever say or think to say.

As long as I've known him, Chevy's kept his hair trimmed, but today strands of his dark brown hair slightly cover his forehead and it's incredibly endearing. The type of style that's teasing and begs to be swept away.

A wave of unwanted jealousy rages through me. I used to be the one who could touch Chevy. Last I heard, I'd been replaced with a revolving door of girls who have lined up to spend the evening with the school's star running back and waterfall of muscle.

Brandon's still gushing, Chevy's still listening, but then, as if our relationship had never been interrupted, his gaze strays in my direction. Eyes straight to mine and I can't breathe. Returning his gaze is a lot like coming home after a long night and falling into bed.

I fell into way too many things with Chevy. The suck part about falling is that eventual crash landing. I tear my eyes away and force air into my aching lungs.

Thank God, Brandon's still going. "Dad's car broke down and Violet wouldn't call you, but I said we should call you. I told her that you'd come—at least you'd come for me. I told her to call the club, but she wouldn't."

Twice in one night my brother decides to go traitor. See if I take him to a football game again.

"Did Violet bring you to the game?" Chevy asks.

Brandon's forehead wrinkles. "What?"

"Did Violet bring you to the game?"

"Well...yeah."

"Then you should be grateful she did. Not all sisters care."

My bracelets clink together when I shift, uncomfortable that anyone is taking up for me, even if it is Chevy. Since

Dad died, Chevy joined the ranks of people thinking I'm the devil because I'm trying to break free of the Terror.

"Your car's broke." Chevy glances in my direction again, and there's a softness in his eyes that I hate and love. It's the same unguarded look as when we whispered our most intimate thoughts into each other's ears.

I hold his gaze for as long as he can handle. "Thanks for the update, Captain Obvious."

Chevy mimics tipping a hat that isn't on his head. "My pleasure."

The right side of my mouth edges up. Damn him for being so charming.

"Stone," Chevy says. "Have you made big plans for tomorrow?"

"Tomorrow?"

"Violet turns eighteen."

Chevy and I had so many plans for eighteen. Spent too many nights in each other's arms planning out how we were going to celebrate this year. Dinner out of Snowflake. Prom. Laughter with friends. Midnight and dancing on a blanket in our field.

"Mom's mad at Violet and she said we might not do anything because of Violet's attitude," Brandon blurts, and he scratches his chin twice. "Violet cut class and the school called Mom to tell her. Mom's really angry. She yelled. A lot. And Violet wouldn't yell back. Violet always yells back, but not this time."

Chevy's adorable smile falls into a frown and it's really a shame. Brandon looks over at me for confirmation that I'm not mad at him for spilling about my fight with Mom, because I've reminded him several times that personal conversations should stay personal, and I step toward him, then briefly squeeze my fingers around his wrist.

My brother isn't trying to tattle, he's nervous being out in the dark and upset over the fight Mom and I had before we left for the game. He has a problem with letting negative emotions go. They circle his brain like vultures do with roadkill.

Headlights shine in the distance, and my shoulders relax. Last thing I want to do is get into a discussion with Chevy as to why I didn't tell Mom that I handed Chevy my note. This has been an awful day, and I'm ready to pull the covers over my head and stay in bed for days, maybe weeks.

I step out onto the road, and using the flashlight app, wave to signal Mom. This isn't the first time Dad's car has broken down, and unfortunately, it won't be the last. Mom has passed us before. Though I'm not convinced those times were a mistake as much as Mom attempting to teach me another lesson of how unsafe I am in the world.

Footsteps against the rocks and Chevy eases beside me. The car weaves in and out of the center lane, and my arm hesitates in the air as unease tiptoes through me.

Chevy places his hand on my biceps and forces it down. "That's not your mom's car."

It's not. Mom would never drive like that and those aren't the headlights of a minivan. Those belong to something with some muscle. A scary sixth sense creeps along my skin.

Growling engines, then three single beams appear. Motorcycles. Those motorcycles aren't chasing the car, they're following. My stomach lurches as I stumble back. Chevy steps forward and he draws his knife out of the sheath.

I swallow as my hands begin to shake. The Terror never come from this direction unless they're driving to see me and none of them have a muscle car they would be following. "Brandon, get back in the car."

"What's wrong?" he asks.

My internal warning system blares like a foghorn, and instead of slowing down, the car picks up speed. I grab Brandon's arm and I shove him toward the passenger side. "Get in the car, lie down on the floorboard in the backseat and don't pop your head up until I say."

Brandon moves with me and slides in when I open his door, then close it behind him.

"Get in there with him, Violet," Chevy demands. "In the backseat, on the floorboard."

"They've already seen me," I hiss. "Odds are they didn't see Brandon. We have to protect him."

Chevy glances over his shoulder at me, his expression that of the grim reaper ready to take someone's soul. "Then in the front seat. Doors locked and call the club."

"Chevy," I begin, about to ask him to join me, but he cuts me off.

"They're looking for someone and I'll be it. I'm the first wave of keeping them off Stone. You're second. Call the club. Get me backup."

Absolute fear seizes my body. I can't leave Chevy to stand on his own. For the same reason I gave him my late note today. I care too much for him.

"Get in, Violet," he demands.

But as the headlights draw closer, I remain cemented to the ground.

"You and I can't take them alone. I need help. Get me help."

That, I understand. My pulse races as I dash for the driver's side. The engine of a Camaro roars as it pulls in front of us. Half of the car sticks out into the road, the other half blocks us in as if my car could actually move. The grille of the Camaro so close that the heat from the engine slams onto my legs.

I open my door as two doors on the Camaro open and two looming figures emerge. Nervous adrenaline crashes into my veins and I curse as I frantically roll up my window. The hand crank type, made in the '70s, and it doesn't go fast enough. By pure will alone, the window rises with a whine, and when mine is finished, I glance over to Brandon to reassure him we're safe in the car, when terror seizes my lungs. The passenger-side door is unlocked.

The car shakes as the open hood crashes down. A towering man with weathered skin slams his hands onto my car and stares straight at me. He has on a leather vest, and I briefly close my eyes at the patches. Nausea roars through my gut and I fumble for my phone. This is the Riot Motorcycle Club, and we're in serious trouble.

"Get out of the car," the man shouts.

Chevy protects the passenger-side door and he's surrounded, but he's not backing down. His arms are stretched out wide, knife in his right hand. Fighting past the fear, I select the contacts on my phone, and right as I'm about to press Eli's number, there's a crash to my left.

My hands cover my head as a man takes a lead pipe and hammers it against my window. The glass cracks and he shoves the lead pipe against it again. Brandon whimpers, and I suck in a breath as I try to refocus on the cell, and it's hard to do as shards of glass rain down over my head and into my hair. I push the call button, praying Eli answers.

"Get out of the car or we'll drag you out!" the man in front of my car yells.

A scuffle, someone springs toward Chevy, his knife slices in their direction, but then two more guys join the mix. My eyes fall to the unlocked door, and I lunge. My fingers brush along the lock as the door swings open. Fear shakes through me when big meaty fingers shoot in and grab me. From the floorboard in the backseat, Brandon seizes my hand, and my heart pounds when I spot the horror in his eyes.

It's going to happen again, and I promised him it wouldn't. Months ago, bullies from school beat him until he could no longer lift his head. These men—they're going to hurt him over something neither Brandon nor I have control over. Over politics of a club we have never belonged to.

They are going to hurt him, not like the bruises from earlier today, but like what happened to him months ago or maybe worse. Like those bullies, these men are going to make him bleed, and I promised him he would never hurt like that again.

The man pulls at me, and I release Brandon, my only hold to staying in the car, and drop my phone next to him. Without Brandon grounding me, I'm yanked from the car, and as I struggle with the man, I kick the door shut.

"Get on the ground!" a man shouts.

I struggle, wrenching myself from side to side. My arm breaks free and I swing hard. My fist connects with a face and there's swearing. Pain through my knuckles, then pain from my scalp as my head is pulled back by my hair.

I gasp and fight to not make a sound and then scream when my legs are kicked out from under me. A blinding white lightning strike to my kneecaps and my vision doubles. Snapping, and then another wave of revulsive agony.

My shins hit the ground, and my heart beats frantically as I glance up at the older man with the weathered and dirty face. He has a blue bandana on his head and a gun in his hand and I can't decide if I'm scared or numb.

Don't find my brother. Please don't find my brother.

On a warrior's shout, Chevy strikes one man with a punch to the face and then Chevy is moving, pushing off two people, and my blood grows cold when the man with the blue bandana points the gun at me.

"I'll shoot her." The man doesn't yell it, but he says it loud enough that the scuffles stop.

My mouth runs dry, and I find just enough courage to peek out of the corner of my eye to see Chevy hold his hands up in compliance. His knife is gone. Not sure if they took it or he lost it in the fight. Guess it doesn't matter. Maybe none of it matters. Maybe Chevy should still be trying to fight his way out. Maybe they're going to kill us both anyway.

Chevy looks at me and I tilt my head, worrying my forehead. *They can't get Brandon. We can't let them have my brother.* I will Chevy to hear my thoughts, to understand what I need. As if he can read my mind, he moves his head a fraction of an inch in agreement. Chevy voluntarily goes to his knees.

"You're Reign of Terror," Bandana Guy says to me.

My tongue feels too swollen to speak, but I shove out the words regardless. "I'm not Reign of Terror."

"She's not," Chevy says. "I am. Leave her alone and deal only with me."

"I know who you are, and I'll be dealing with you soon. We only dish out the best for a McKinley." A smile twists his lips as he keeps staring directly at me. His patch indicates his road name is Fiend, and I bet he's real proud of his title.

With two other men standing on either side of me, Fiend crouches and I resist the urge to shudder with disgust as he pulls on a lock of my hair. "And you're Frat's girl. Red hair, crazy eyes. You have a brother. Where is he?"

Defiance swirls into my bloodstream, and I raise my chin. "He's at the clubhouse."

Fiend studies me. "Is he?"

Frat was my father's road name and people used to tell me when he was in difficult spots, he was insane. When I was younger, I used to beam with pride at the idea of my daddy being the man who could look fear in the eye and laugh.

As I got older, I lost some of that appreciation, but in this moment, knowing my brother is in the backseat of the car, knowing a gun could be used to settle a score I have nothing to do with, I smile. A crazy-ass smile that could probably rival any level of insanity my father could have had. "Why don't we go to the Terror's clubhouse and find out?"

Fiend chuckles. "Nice try. Cuff them and let's go."

No. The guys around us move and my heart explodes, beating so rapidly I can barely breathe. A calloused hand on my wrist and I flinch, attempting to roll away, attempting to hit and kick. Another man joins the mix, grabbing hold of my other arm, pinning my head to his chest, and I dry heave at the smell of body odor. Tears prick my eyes and a million horrible thoughts crash in my mind. I'd rather die than have them rape me. I'd rather die.

Cold metal against the flesh of my wrists and then I'm pulled to my feet, my knees giving at the weight of the situation. I'm being pushed forward, to the car. A man opens the backseat door and he exerts pressure on my neck to force me in. My head whips around, my eyes so wide the wind burns them. "Chevy!"

"Hurt her and I'll fucking kill you." There's a coldness in Chevy's tone. He's on the other side of the car. His biceps straining as his body leans in my direction, but the men surrounding him are shoving him past the door and someone pops open the trunk.

My face heats and my palms grow clammy. Dizziness overwhelms me as I realize we're being taken, and we're being separated. That I'm being kidnapped. "Chevy?"

His dark eyes meet mine. "It's okay. We're going to be okay. Keep your mouth shut. Say nothing. I promise it will be okay."

He can't make that promise. No one can.

CHEVY

They stole my knife. Swiped my cell. The handcuffs I can ditch in thirty seconds. The trunk of the car—I could have open in less than a minute. But leaving Violet behind unprotected isn't an option. Escaping just isn't the goal—the endgame is to escape together.

Dark doesn't bother me. Neither do cramped spaces. What's drilling a hole in my brain was Violet's expression as they shoved her into the back of the car. It was the impact of her struggles hitting against the seat, it was her screams for them to stop.

To stop what? My gut twists, and I breathe out to try to gain some control in the madness. I got my wish. Violet stopped struggling. She stopped screaming. Turns out the silence wasn't what I wanted. Violet safe—that's what I wished for. Silence doesn't mean safe.

The car slows, and I brace myself to keep from ramming into the walls of the trunk. We've been driving for too long. An hour. Maybe more. I tried counting, tried to gauge how far from Snowflake we were taken, but worrying over Violet killed my concentration.

The engine shuts off, and the stillness causes my skin to crawl. They hurt her, I'll hurt them. Doesn't get much simpler than that. I gave up earlier to save Stone, to save Violet. Gun to the head ends all debate, especially when that gun's on Violet.

Doors squeak open. The car shakes. Doors slam shut. Movement outside, but nothing else. Beats of time pass and my already strained patience is on the verge of snapping. I angle to my side so I can reach my belt. I've got a small lock pick hidden there. It's not normal, but it's how I roll. Fast hands sometimes need assistance.

Footsteps and I return to my back.

"We're going to open the trunk," comes a deep voice. "We've got a gun trained on you, and we'll shoot, so be slow as you get out."

The trunk opens, and a spotlight shines in my direction. My eyes snap shut, and when I attempt to open them, all I see is black spots. I'm blinded. Fingers on my arm and I'm pulled out. My feet hit the ground, and no matter which way I turn my head, the light follows me. Smart bastards. With the dark night, the spotlight keeps me from seeing my surroundings, from identifying additional faces, how many people will be thwarting my attempt at escape.

We go forward, into a building; the door looks like one that could belong to a house. Inside, it's pitch-dark, and I drop my head, studying the floor to keep the light from continuing to blind me. The flooring is linoleum, like I would find in a kitchen. White squares with black diamonds in the middle.

Pushed and we're heading down stairs that groan. Wooden ones with no backing. The air temperature drops with each step, and the stench of mold and mildew fills my nose. At the bottom, my boots land on concrete and then men fall away as I'm being pulled ahead. We stop. A hesitation. And then I'm released.

The light turns off, darkness engulfs my vision, rapid footsteps. I pivot on my heels to find a way to escape, and a door is slammed shut. My heart beats in my ears, and I glance around as I blink to adjust my eyesight, but there's only darkness. No natural light.

A rustle in the corner behind me and I spin. "Violet?"

"Chevy?" Shifting of fabric. "God, Chevy, I'm here. I can't see. They blindfolded me."

"Not much to see. It's dark. Keep talking so I can find you."

"My hands are still bound," Violet continues. Never knew so much relief could be found in hearing her sweet voice. "I'm sitting. In a corner. Felt safer that way. I can stand if you want."

"No. Stay sitting." I keep blinking, an instinctual movement so my vision can adjust for light, but there's only the black hole. The tip of my boot comes into contact with something solid, but with give. "This you?"

"Yeah."

I crouch, then lean my back against the wall beside her, letting my hand brush the exposed skin of her arm. As a gesture of comfort, to reaffirm I'm here and she's safe. Violet's cold to the touch, and she trembles. She's in shock. Why the hell wouldn't she be? I rap the back of my head against the concrete wall. Fuck the Riot. Fuck them for all of this. "You okay?"

She inches closer to me and our legs touch. So do our arms. I move my head in her direction so I can inhale her scent. Violet smells like honey. It's a perfume her father bought her for her fourteenth birthday and continued to buy for her every year after that. Until this year.

I purchased it for her the other day, but I wasn't sure if I would have the guts to give it to her. We've been like two rabid dogs trapped in a cage. I was afraid she'd throw it back in my face and wasn't sure I could stomach more rejection.

The perfume sits on my dresser stuffed in a birthday bag. Somehow, in this moment, my lack of courage seems pathetic.

"Violet?" I'm slow asking because I'm not sure I can control my reaction if she gives an undesired answer. I'm already walking a tightrope, and I'm not the kind, at least when it comes to her, who can keep my balance. "Are you okay?"

"Yeah."

Fear she's lying whirls inside me. "You were screaming and then you stopped. I need to know if they hurt you." I need to know if I'll be able to sleep again.

Silence on her end. Each quiet second that passes causes my body temperature to rise with the growing rage.

"Violet," I urge, barely able to keep the anger from leaking out in my voice.

"The guy in the backseat backhanded me," she says in a small voice, as if that confession is something *she* should be ashamed of.

I'm going to kill them. I'm going to kill every single one. "How bad?"

"Are you okay?" She attempts to drag the conversation in another direction because she knows me. Knows I'm on the verge of losing my mind.

"Violet."

"He hit me and we've been kidnapped," she snaps. "Isn't that bad enough?"

No. They hurt her. No part of me is okay with that.

"Are you okay?" she asks again. "They hit you. I saw it." And I hit them back. "Yeah, I'm good."

Violet's entire body quakes in a small fit and the stream of air being pushed through her lips as she tries to control herself is audible. She's killing me, and she needs to know she's not alone. Not physically. Not mentally. "I'm sorry."

"It's not your fault. The club's maybe, but not yours. This is what the Terror is, Chevy. This is why I walked away."

This is the Riot's fault, not the Terror's, but I'm not in the mood to argue. "I'm sorry I didn't protect you better at the car."

"You did exactly what I wanted you to do."

She's referring to protecting Stone. Violet shakes again, and I edge closer to her, wishing I could comfort her more. "I promise I'll protect you now. I won't let them touch you again."

"I know you'll try."

I can do more than try. I lean forward, fish for the lock pick I'd stuck in my leather belt and begin the task of freeing myself from the cuffs. Can't remember the first time I picked a lock. Cyrus said I was breaking out of baby gates and jimmying safety latches before I was two.

"Can you do it?" she whispers, so quietly I barely hear her. She's probably frightened someone's listening. Won't lie, I'm itchy wondering the same. The rest of this dark room seems empty, but I won't feel good until it's fully explored.

"Give me a few." I work at the handcuffs. There's something about how my mind ticks and how my fingers move with the puzzle. The way I can hear the metal shifting. The gentle vibrations a lock gives right as it's about to pop.

And it does pop and a much-needed adrenaline rush floods my veins. I slip off the cuffs, careful when setting them down not to create noise, then gently move my fingers until I find

Violet. I make contact with her knee first, and she flinches as if that caused her pain.

Damn bastards. I skim up her leg, up her side, her arm, then to her face.

Material is wrapped around her head. I lift it off her eyes, then press on her shoulder for her to angle forward. She does, and with steady hands, I pick the lock, then set her hand-cuffs on the floor.

Violet's hand catches mine and she squeezes. I thread our fingers together, lower my head and nuzzle her hair until I find her ear. Memories of doing this hundreds of times flash in my mind, but each of those times was a moment to be cherished. This—this is comfort, but it's also survival.

"Stay here," I whisper into her ear. "I'm going to move around the room, make sure we're alone. See if I can feel a way to get out."

Violet reaches up, her fingers caressing my cheek, and a pleasing shiver runs through me when her lips brush against my ear as she speaks. We haven't been this close in months. Not even in the last few weeks of our relationship. "Let me help."

"I want to make sure we're alone. I need you to stay still and silent. Two of us moving around won't help."

She sags, resting her forehead against my temple. Can't understand the chaos inside me. Can't give names to the swirling emotions, but the one thing I do comprehend is the instinct to survive, the instinct to protect her. The need to gather Violet in my arms and carry her out. Yeah, I gave in earlier, but they'll have to take me down before they reach her again.

I bunch her hair in my hand, kiss her forehead, then pull away.

There's a buzzing under my skin as my fingertips slowly

inch their way across the wall. A sense that I'm being watched. That the hourglass has been tipped and I'm running out of time. My fingers slide up and down the concrete, searching for a window, a tool, anything I can use to defend us or for a way out. With each centimeter searched, any hope I had of busting out evolves into desperation.

My heart stalls when my fingertips collide with cloth. I press and beneath it find something solid. It's barely above my height and I run my hands along the length, then width. Excitement grows within me. It's a window. It's a way out.

I yank at the fabric and it tears as if nailed in, and the more I pull, the more of it gathers into my hands and falls to the floor. A tiny ray of light leaks from a crevice. Between me and freedom are wooden shutters.

A simple latch lock. I flip it, draw the shutters open, dim light floods the room and I curse as I lower my head. Bars. There're fucking bars on the window. I grab hold of them and shake, but there's no give. We're stuck. Fucking stuck, and when I rise up on my toes, all I see are bushes.

I round and survey my surroundings. Hoping for another window. Hoping for another way, but all I see are two concrete walls, two walls made of drywall, the door and Violet still huddled in the corner.

She's watching me, expectation and hope fighting on her face over the reality of our situation. Violet's praying I have a solution, and when I meet her eyes, I mash my lips together and shake my head. My heart shreds as she lowers her head into her hands.

My fists tighten at my sides and the urge is to pound the wall, but that won't help Violet. Won't help me. I gotta stay smart, gotta fight the emotion. Logic is what's going to keep us alive.

With a roll of my neck, I cross the room, slide my leather coat off my arms and offer it to her.

Violet glances up at me and my entire body seizes. Her lip is fat and blood is smeared across her cheek. Some of it from her mouth, some of it from her nose. If there was more light, I bet her cheek would be bruising. She told me she was backhanded and I was somehow able to compartmentalize that, but now...

"It's cold in here," Violet says, "and the jacket is yours."

It is cold. The bitterness already biting at my arms, but I'll be damned if I'm warm and she's not. To avoid the argument, I drop beside her and toss the jacket like a blanket over her shoulders.

"Chevy," she starts, but I cut her off.

"Just take it."

Silence on her end and I feel like a dick for snapping at her. I raise my knees to rest my arms on them and stretch my fingers like doing so could release the anger, then tension. "I couldn't stop them from taking you. I couldn't stop them from hurting you, but I can keep you warm. Let me do this. It's not much, but it's all I got."

Violet slowly turns her head in my direction, and it's damn hard not to stare at her damaged lip. The light falling into the room is weak, but bright enough to highlight a strand or two of her red hair. I try to focus on that and how I used to lie with her and run my hand through her hair for hours. Better times. Happier times. What I sure as hell hope we can find again after we escape.

"I was going to say we could try to share your jacket." She hesitates. "That I don't mind being close to you."

My brain freezes, and I hear more than what she's saying. Hear her fear, hear there's more to what happened in the backseat of that car, hear that she needs me.

I straighten my legs and Violet eases into me. Her shoulder, leg and arm pressed to me as she attempts to cover both of us with my jacket. I wrap my arm around her and briefly close my eyes at how soft she feels. It's been a long time since I held her, and each night without her has been torture.

Violet rests her head on my shoulder, and she reaches up to try to make my jacket stay on my other shoulder, but it falls. "You're not covered all the way."

She's covered and that's all I care about. "I'm okay."

"No, you aren't," she whispers. "You should be home. I should be home. We should be nowhere near here."

She's right, but instead of replying, I lean forward, slip my arm under Violet's knees and gather her onto my lap. Violet stares at me, eyes blinking, a bit bewildered, and I shake my head slightly to let her know I'm not fighting with her. I'm not claiming some stake in our future. I just need her, maybe more than she needs me.

She exhales. It's a long one and then she lifts her hand. I stop breathing when she brushes her fingers along my cheek. "They hit you. You're bruising. Everywhere."

And I'd go through each and every hit again to protect her. My only regret is that we ended up here.

"I'm sorry," she says. "I didn't know how else to protect Brandon."

"We did what we had to."

Violet rests her head into the crook of my neck, and when she raises my jacket to my shoulder again, it stays. I weave my arms around her and rub my hands up and down her cold arms, almost like I'm trying to convince a dying fire to stay burning.

"Why is this happening?" Her breath tickles my neck, and I wish we were anywhere but this damp, cold prison.

"I don't know." Yeah, Cyrus had warned us off the road,

but I don't know why they would target Violet. Why they would target me. Odds are it's me. My grandfather's the president of the Terror and my uncle is the man the Riot hates the most. The Riot feels Eli stole their daughter and their granddaughter even though Meg and Emily left Eli, too.

Maybe the Riot decided to play out an eye for an eye, and I'm the closest Eli has to a blood child in the state. "Guess it was me they were after and you were caught up in it."

"The Riot hasn't kidnapped anyone before."

Beat the hell out of members of our club? Yeah. Killed people belonging to our club? That, too. But I agree, at least from my limited knowledge, kidnapping wasn't their style. "If they wanted us dead, we would be."

She snorts. "You need to work on your comforting skills."

My lips slightly turn up. "Noted."

She settles further into me, her arm curving around my body. "What do we do now?"

Not much. We stay alive and... "We wait."

"For?"

She's not going to like my answer. "The club will figure this out. Eli and Cyrus will get us."

The way her body tenses under mine is a confirmation of her disbelief that the club will make the situation better. I want her to have faith in them. I want Violet to be part of our family again.

"Waiting is its own form of torture, isn't it?" she says. "I'm not sure if waiting and thinking of all the horrible things that can happen is worse than what will actually be done."

I cling tighter to her as my own demons and nightmares awaken. The what-if's messing with my mind are the torture she speaks of. Anything happening to me isn't the problem. I'm plagued with thoughts of what will happen to her.

Fear.

I've never been scared by much. Never believed in bogey-men living under the bed. Magic and sorcery belong to people like me who have fast hands and can deceive the human eye. It's hard to believe in evil locked in closets when you realize at an early age it's all made-up stories to explain what people think is unexplainable.

It's not unexplainable—only mere men manipulating shadows and mirrors.

But there's a bitterness in my mouth now. A metallic taste I don't like much. A coldness in my blood and a freezing in my bones at the thought of what the men outside that door could do to Violet.

"I'm scared," she whispers.

Me, too.

I strain to hear anything beyond her breaths and my heartbeat in my ears. Occasionally there are footsteps overhead. Muffled voices. The sound of the ascending and descending of the old wooden staircase. Violet curls closer into me whenever there is movement outside the door, and I keep up a steady caress up and down her arm.

My gut tells me we're in here for a while. Tells me that they want us to be tormented by our own thoughts before the next round.

"Do you think Brandon's okay?" she eventually asks.

I pray he is. I pray harder he kept his courage and called Eli for help. Faster the club gets involved, the faster we'll be out of this mess. "Yeah. Your brother is a fighter."

"No, he's not. He's scared of the world and most everything in it."

I know, and Violet loves him more than she loves anyone or anything else in the world. Family first is a priority I understand. "He's all right. You saved him tonight."

"We saved him."

We. It's not a word Violet has used in a long time for us. It's a soft kiss and a ripping of a Band-Aid at the same time.

"They took my bracelets and my necklaces. They also took Dad's watch."

I hug her tighter. The bracelets and necklaces—it's not their worth that means something to her, it's who gave them to her, the sentiment behind the gift. Some from me, some from Cyrus, most of them from her father. Losing them and her father's watch would be like losing a part of her soul.

"We'll get them back."

She doesn't argue, but doesn't agree either. "You think it's after midnight?"

After midnight. Damn. This isn't right. None of this is right. "Happy birthday, Violet."

"Eighteen," she whispers.

We had so many plans. "Eighteen."

"I want to go home."

"We will." I'll walk through hell to make sure it happens. "Why don't you try to get some sleep?"

"I'm not sure I can."

"Try anyhow. At least doze. We both know you can be awake and asleep at the same time. Do that. There's no telling how long we're in this for and we have to keep sharp."

Violet nestles into me like she might try to sleep and I move my hand from caressing her arm to rubbing her head. That always made her sleepy, always made her fall asleep in my arms.

"Thank you for sacrificing yourself for Brandon," she murmurs. "He loves you."

"I know." A lot like he loves her. A lot like I love her, too.

Violet begins to sing. Not loudly, softly, under her breath. She has a beautiful voice. When I was a kid, I used to think that's what angels would sound like. Violet used to sing all the time when we were younger, but less and less as we got older.

Last time I heard her sing was the night her dad died. I held her that night, too. We lay in her bed, her head on my chest, and she sang in a soft tone until she fell asleep.

Broke my heart then. Breaks my heart now. But like then, I'm helpless and do only what I can, hold her and pray.

Violet

The beams of sun warm my skin and I stretch lazily on the blanket. I'm at my favorite place on earth—the back field of my house. Walk long enough and eventually I'd wander onto Cyrus's property. Dad would let the grass grow high here and he'd have it cut several times throughout the summer and sell the hay, but he would leave this small portion untouched for me.

I loved the wildness of free-growing grass, trees with long limbs and branches heavy with leaves. Beside me, Chevy's propped up on one elbow and he's watching me. Chevy always watches me.

"I'm dreaming," I say.

He smiles, shifting from fourteen to seventeen, then back to fourteen. Can't decide which one I like better. He's handsome either way, but at fourteen, Chevy couldn't make up his mind on whether to hold my hand. Confused about how he felt, since we had been raised to love each other as siblings, but we were more than brother and sister, more than friends. The two of us always shared a special connection.

At seventeen, he broke my heart. I blink and Chevy is sixteen and I loved sixteen. He did way more than hold my hand then and we were light-years away from him shattering my soul.

I've always been able to do this. Be aware when I'm dreaming, but there's a cost to it. Sometimes I become paralyzed. Powerless to move my body. My mind awake, my muscles asleep and I'll panic at the thought of never being in control again. To never speak or walk or run.

I hope this isn't one of those dreams. To be sure it isn't, I focus hard and I'm able to twitch a finger—not in the dream, but in reality. Coldness rushes into the heat of the day and I pull back from my conscious mind and return to the dream, but a sense of dread washes through me.

"We aren't safe," I say to Chevy. "I shouldn't be asleep."

"I first kissed you here," he replies like that's an appropriate response, but it's a dream and I go with it.

"We did a lot more than just kiss here." Happiness swirls within me at the memories of stolen moments I thought would last forever. We did a lot of firsts in this back field. Too many to count. None of it rushed. All of it slow. Teeny, tiny baby steps because I was never ready for too much too fast and Chevy was patient, always patient as if he was just as scared as I was to go any further than we had before.

Chevy's smile widens and it's that mischievous dimpled one that continuously dared me to go along with one of his crazy schemes. Smuggling hot cookies out of Olivia's kitchen when we were seven. Lifting Cyrus's Reign of Terror cut when we were ten. Pickpocketing Eli's keys so we could go joyriding in his truck before we had our licenses.

Can't take much credit. Chevy was the mastermind with the fast hands. I was the lovely assistant who helped with the distraction, but I loved being part of the action.

I reach out, stretching because I miss touching him so much, but his smile fades and his expression darkens. "Violet, wake up."

Fear seizes my lungs as storm clouds gather in the sky. Chevy grabs ahold of my arms and yells, "Wake up!"

My eyes snap open, a haze of morning light barely lightens the basement room and the air is knocked out of me as I'm being shoved to the concrete corner. Scuffed black boots in front of me, and when I look up, Chevy has his back to me, arms out, the handcuffs dangling from his fingers.

Nausea races up my throat. They're returning and this is all Chevy has for weapons.

I push off the floor, and as I stand, Chevy presses back so I'm flush against the wall. "Stay behind me."

I rub my eyes to wake myself as four men enter the room. All of them from last night. Fiend marches in behind them like a victorious general. Two men fan to the left, the other two to the right. Fiend stays near the door in the middle and sizes Chevy up. "I heard you were wily, but I had bet you couldn't bust out of cuffs. Guess I was wrong."

Chevy says nothing and Fiend makes a show of leaning as he looks at me. "Have a nice sleep?"

I don't break eye contact as I follow Chevy's lead on staying silent.

Fiend hikes up the waist of his pants. He has a belt on, but his gut is overbearing. "This is how it's going to play out. McKinley, you're coming with us. We need to talk about your club."

"I'm not a member, and even if I were, I don't speak for the Terror."

"Your grandfather is the president of the Terror. I have faith you can handle this negotiation."

"Nothing I do or say holds any weight in the club."

"I disagree. President's grandson does hold weight. Especially when it's his life on the line."

"You got something to say, say it," Chevy spits out. "But I'm not leaving her."

Fiend's eyebrows rise. "You mean Violet? We know who she is and who her father was to your club. Just like we know who you are and what she means to you."

My gaze snaps to Fiend's and he catches it, then winks. Chevy shifts, obviously uncomfortable with the exchange. Uneasiness gathers in my stomach in rolling waves. In the car, Fiend kept reaching over like he was going to pull down my shirt. Twice he almost succeeded. He stole my bracelets. Stole my necklaces. Stole Dad's watch. Touching parts of me I wished he hadn't in the process. I suck in a breath in order to contain the dry heave.

I went full-on crazy when he touched me and I kicked the hell out of him. Then Fiend hit me. Several times. I tried to fight back, but he was bigger than me and I thought he was going to keep going until I died, but the man in the front seat barked an order at Fiend to back off, for me to shut up, and the asshole retreated to his side of the backseat and went silent.

It's funny how my body throbbed, but I felt no pain. How blood trickled against my skin, but there wasn't an ache. I don't know what any of that was about, but I do know both men scared me, I'm still scared and I want more than anything to go home.

I didn't tell Chevy all that really happened. He's already sacrificed enough to save my brother. I'm not sure if I'll ever tell Chevy. Not sure if I make it out of this I'll ever tell anyone. I just want to leave here and pretend none of this happened.

"This can be easy," Fiend says. "You come with us and she

stays here. If it becomes hard, it's because you made it hard. Anything that happens to you is by your choice."

Such a bullshit answer. "My choice is to leave."

Fiend offers me a fake sympathetic shrug. "Not my call to make. But I'll tell you what, if it makes you feel better, I'll stay behind to keep you company. Finish what we started last night."

Heat rushes to my face, dizziness overwhelms me and, this time, I bend over when I can't contain the dry heave. An arm around my waist, and when I glance up, dark concerned eyes meet mine. It's Chevy, and as he takes in my reaction, stone-cold anger replaces the concern. He quickly returns his attention to the men who stepped closer at the lowering of his defense.

"I'm okay," I whisper and shove him away from me. To protect him. To protect us.

"Let's go, McKinley," Fiend demands.

Chevy stretches out his arm again. "No."

Fiend nods, the men are in motion and Chevy backs up, pinning me to the wall again. Fiend reaches to his back and all the air rushes out of my body. There's a gun in his hand and he's pointing it at us—at Chevy.

"Move or I'll shoot you," Fiends says like he's bored. "That leaves her alone with us. Your choice."

My pulse pounds violently in my veins. Chevy promised to protect me, but I don't want him dead. "Go with them."

"No."

"Go with them, Chevy," I say through gritted teeth.

"I'm not leaving you alone."

And I need him alive. If he cooperates, they'll let him live. It's obvious they have a message for Chevy to give and I'm just the person they're using to control him.

The guy to the left lunges at Chevy. He raises his arm to

fight, leaving an opening, and I watch as Fiend keeps the gun trained on Chevy, but aims it lower, to Chevy's leg. Maybe Fiend's going to injure Chevy, ruining his chances of walking, playing football, and if that doesn't bring him to submission, Fiend will then torture me to make Chevy break.

I'm stronger than this. Bigger than this. If this is how it's going to be, I'll go down fighting. I'll be the wild and crazy girl my father loved. My throat burns at the thought of him. At the thought of leaving behind my mother, my brother. Not sure how the two of them will exist without me there to push them along.

The club will take care of them. The club might never let them learn how to survive on their own, how to be their own person, so my mother and brother will never thrive, but they'll eat, they'll sleep and I hope to God the club will learn their lesson from what happens to me and Chevy and they'll protect the people I love the most.

Chevy's throwing punches and they're throwing punches back. He's losing, he's bleeding and he grunts in pain. Chevy hits a man so hard that he falls limp to the ground, but then two other guys tackle him and Chevy's head hits the concrete. His head rolls forward with the impact and there is red streaming from his skull.

The blood drains from my face, but I push my feet forward, toward Fiend. Hoping somehow I'm faster. Hoping somehow I can turn the tables.

Fiend's eyes widen as he realizes I'm heading for him, and he turns the gun—in my direction. Chevy screams my name and right when my eyes close, as I understand I'm not going to be fast enough, there's a loud bang and I suck in a breath.

Then oddly I let out that breath in the silence. My heart beats in my ears. Again and again and again and I inhale, the air feeling cold in my lungs. I reopen my eyes and look down at my body. Expecting to see blood, waiting for the pain, but there's nothing.

"What the hell is going on?" a raspy voice demands. An older man with gray hair, a real-life Mack truck with legs, barrels into the room. He heads toward another new man with a scar on his face who has Fiend pushed up against the wall. His hands around Fiend's throat like he's willing to crush the life out of my enemy.

The gun is out of Fiend's hand and the man with the scar offers it to the older man.

The old man points the gun in Fiend's direction like it's a finger and not a loaded weapon. "Did you just shoot a gun at her? Are you insane? She's Frat's girl."

My feet become strangely planted while my head floats as if it's curiously light. As I turn my head to find Chevy, the entire room spins. Is the enemy of my enemy my friend?

"Let him go," the old man says.

I throw my arm out, searching for a wall to stay upright and instead discover a warm hand. A solid arm around my waist and then there are beautiful dark eyes. "I got you."

My hand goes to Chevy's face and I gingerly touch his eye that's swelling, the bruises forming on his face, the blood flowing near the corner of his lip. "I'm sorry."

This is my fault. Maybe we gave up too easy at the car. Maybe we should have run into the woods. Maybe I should have yelled at Chevy when he stopped his motorcycle to help. I should have pushed him away then. I should have known that I'm cursed and that I'm only capable of hurting everyone I love.

"Get him out of here," says the old man.

The guy with the scar lets Fiend go and the two men who were fighting Chevy grab Fiend and drag him away. I blink several times and lean into Chevy's body as my mind has fractured.

"What's going on?" I whisper to Chevy, but he only shakes his head. His fingers tap twice to my side and I straighten. Two fingers tapping. It's a childhood code. He's telling me we're in danger, and considering the past few hours, it scares the hell out of me that we've somehow fallen into a deeper hole.

The old man hands the gun back to the guy with a scar on his face, then scans me and Chevy as if he's perplexed. His blue eyes tell me he sees all, knows all—a god to many in his world. "I'm going to apologize, but I know it won't sound like much. I'm—"

"Emily's grandfather," Chevy cuts him off. "You're the president of the Riot."

Realization causes me to curl my fingers into Chevy's shirt. This is the man whose daughter, Meg, left him to be with Eli when she fell in love with Eli over eighteen years ago. The man who has tortured the Terror since the day Meg left. Then when Eli's life in the club proved too much for Meg, she left Eli for good as well, taking their daughter, Emily, with her. This past summer, Emily and Eli reconnected, and Emily and my best friend Oz fell in love. Those newly cemented relationships burn the Riot up and they're holding a grudge.

The old man cocks his head. "I am. The name is Skull and I know who both of you are. There's been a gross misunderstanding, and I only learned that you had been picked up by Fiend about thirty minutes ago. Came straight here when I found out. I had no idea about the conditions you were taken under or how you were being held. Again, my apologies."

I don't believe him and obviously neither does Chevy. "Then let us go home."

"We will," he says. "But why don't we get you upstairs first. Let you clean yourselves up, get you some food and then me and you will call Eli together. How's that sound?"

Sounds like heaven, but by the way Chevy and I grasp each other, we're both aware that we're mere steps away from descending into hell.

CHEVY

My entire body throbs, but I ignore it as I watch Violet enter the bathroom. She's slow going in. Shuffling her feet. Most of it in reluctance to face what's waiting for her in there, also could be because they kicked the hell out of her last night by the road in order to make her kneel. She has a limp and I can't help but wonder if they did damage to her knee.

I don't think she notices. I don't think she feels any of the pain from the bruises on her body. Too much in shock. Too damn headstrong. What the hell was she thinking gunning for a man ready to shoot her? I rub the back of my head, feeling my own head wound. I know what she was thinking. She was trying to protect me, trying to take on the world on her own...again.

Violet's knee gives, she trips and I shift to the balls of my feet to catch her, but she remains unaware, recovers and keeps moving. Not sure if I'm grateful Violet's numb to the pain or if that scares the hell out of me more. If we survive this, how are either of us going to snap back mentally?

Violet looks behind the bathroom door, then hobbles to

the bathtub and peeks behind the light blue curtain. We're upstairs now, but there's no window in this bathroom. Still no escape.

She glances at me to let me know that, at least in the bathroom, she'll be safe.

In the basement, Violet dozed in my arms, did that thing where she dreams but stays somewhat conscious. Could tell by the way she jerked and murmured. Even with the semi-nap, the circles under her eyes are black against her pale skin and the bruises are overpronounced.

"You can take a shower if you want." The president of the Riot, Skull, is by my side, acting like we're out-of-town guests. "Towels are under the sink. You're safe now."

"Take your time," I say, meaning if there's a lock on the door to use it, shatter the glass of the mirror and use it as a weapon and hide in the bathroom until help hopefully arrives.

"I'm not taking a shower." Violet holds eye contact with me. "Just using the bathroom."

"Take your time," I repeat, and Violet nods before shutting the door. There's the click of a lock. Good girl. Got to admit I could pick that lock in seconds, but it's better than nothing.

Skull inclines his head down the hall, away from the bathroom. "Why don't we go in the kitchen? Give her a few minutes to regroup, get you some food."

Considering we were kidnapped, he should be offering to call the police. I'm not stupid enough to mention that. Not stupid enough to think this scenario is over. There are no pictures in the hallway. No personal touches in the kitchen we passed on the way here. No color to the walls. This place is nothing more than a dump house—a place to lie low, a place to hide, a place to take people you kidnap or want to kill. "I'm staying here."

"Come to the kitchen and we'll call Eli. Faster we make that call, faster you two go home. You and I both know she's not coming out unless she knows you're on the other side of that door."

I want ten-foot-thick concrete walls between Violet and the Riot. For now, a door will do. I knock on it. "I'm going to the kitchen. Stay in until I come back."

"Okay," comes her muffled response.

Skull goes first, I follow and weigh my odds of making it out of here with Violet if I were to knock the hell out of him from behind, but figure there's a wall of cuts surrounding the house. We enter the kitchen and I'm surprised when no one else is there. House feels too empty and that's eerie.

"Take a seat." Skull pulls out a folding chair from the cardboard table.

I choose to lean my back against the corner that leads to the hallway so I can keep an eye on Violet. "I'm good."

He shrugs. "Your choice. Before we call Eli, there are a few things we need to discuss."

Skull looks over at me as if waiting for my permission to continue, but I say nothing. He eases down at the table in the compact kitchen and kicks out his legs. "Look, I did send out my guys to find you, but they misunderstood my instructions. I told them to tell you that I needed to talk to you. To convince you to come with them. Not kidnap. Just for us to talk."

My eyebrows rise and the action causes a slice of pain. "We don't have anything to talk about."

Skull sighs, then leans forward, drawing his legs in and rubbing his hands together. "Son—"

"Don't call me that."

"You turn eighteen soon," he talks over me, ignoring my response. "And the way you've been groomed, I'm betting you'll have the shortest prospect period in the history of your club or you'll have a full-blown cut on you by the time the clock strikes midnight on your birthday."

Not seeing how that's his concern.

"Before that happens," he continues, "I only felt like it was right to let you know some pertinent information. There's a detective from Louisville who has been digging into our past and he seems intent on talking to your club, too. Because of that, I think you should know before your club does. Give you a chance to protect yourself."

He's talking in code, in circles, verbally waving his right hand to keep me from looking at his left. My eyes flicker down the hallway and the bathroom door is still closed, light still peeking out from the cracks.

Some of what he's saying is true. There's a Louisville gang detective who's been trying to nail the Riot MC and the same detective talked to some members of the Terror in hopes of us being able to supply them with information. I'm in the dark on whether or not the Terror can or have helped.

"I liked your father, Chevy, and for what he did for us, you deserve to know the truth before you have the Terror's colors on your back."

Did for them? There's a ringing in my ears as my world narrows in on him. My dad died before my birth, and I'll admit to not knowing much about him other than family ramblings about Thanksgivings and Christmases, but I know my father was Terror through and through. "What the hell are you talking about?"

"Your father may have had Terror colors on his back," says Skull, "but he was loyal to the Riot."

Violet

Chevy wanted me to stay in here, but each second of silence is maddening. I sit on the edge of the bathtub and my hands shake. I don't know why they shake. The rest of my body feels oddly calm, sort of like I'm drunk, but I haven't drunk in weeks.

I'll admit to getting wasted more than I should have this past summer. Upset over some pictures some idiot guy had taken of me at a party, upset he blackmailed me into dating him—because that's the way to make a girl care for you—upset that my dad wasn't alive to protect me from the real-world monsters.

But the pictures are no longer an issue, and neither is the guy. Razor's to thank for that and the only thing he asked of me in return was to stop drinking around people who weren't the Terror. I decided to stop drinking, period. The drinking didn't help anyhow. Didn't make me forget like TV and movies said it would. It only made my crazy emotions crazier, made the sadness sadder, made me fall into dark places when I already couldn't see daylight.

I roll my neck and try to focus. Try to make out any sounds outside the bathroom door, but it's been hard. My mind keeps wandering. Goes to random places, but then returns to the way my heart slammed in my chest as I ran for the gun, the way my stomach sank when I heard the bang, the bullet that missed, and then my thoughts wander off in weird directions like to this past summer and how I'd give almost anything to push rewind and get a second chance.

A second chance—will I have one going forward? Will Chevy?

Focus!

I suck in a deep breath and try to listen, but I hear nothing. How long have I been in here? Seconds? Minutes? Hours? Did they take Chevy out of the house? Are they hurting him? My eyes burn and I quickly stand, not wanting to let visions of him bruised and bleeding enter my mind.

I stare at the door and will it to open. Will Chevy to be standing on the other side, offering me his hand and telling me that we're safe and that we can leave. But nothing happens. No noise. No turning of the knob. Nothing.

My entire body quakes. He's been gone too long, and I need to find him. I need to know if he's okay, but what if he's not okay? What if I open the door and there's another gun pointing at me?

I shake my head. What if there is? If I'm going to die, I'm going to die. At this point, it could be a relief compared to thinking of how this is all going to end.

The three steps to the door are the longest of my life, and when I turn the knob, I quit breathing. The hallway right outside the bathroom is empty. I step out, I turn my head and Chevy's down the hallway, leaning his back against the corner of the kitchen, and he swings his head in my direction.

I blink. Something's wrong. This whole situation is wrong, but his expression…

"Kenneth's talking with Chevy on some club business." A woman appears to my left. She's older, in her sixties maybe, but she has blond hair, blue eyes, jeans, a purple sweater, pearls in her ears and a gold cross around her neck.

My hand goes to my father's cross. It should be buried beneath my shirt, pressed against my skin, but Fiend stole it along with my bracelets, Dad's watch and my other necklaces.

"Sweetheart, do you hear me?" she asks.

I died. I died and I'm in some sort of hell.

"Kenneth is Skull," she continues. "My husband. I'm Jenna. We're both sorry about how you were treated. I'm sure Kenneth explained it was a misunderstanding."

Sure it was. "Then let us leave."

"Chevy and Kenneth are calling Eli now. We'll figure out how to get you home safely without entanglements."

She means police. If what she says is true, I'm not sure why she thinks we won't call the police the moment we're free, or why Eli wouldn't call the police if he hasn't already. We were kidnapped. Me and Chevy. Two people who haven't blood-pact-pinkie-sworn to be part of an MC.

"Why don't you come in here and give Chevy and Kenneth the time to work out details?" She waves her hand toward a bedroom diagonal from the bathroom and farther away from Chevy. "I have something to drink ready for you. Tea. It's warm and can help calm your nerves. There's also something to eat in there if you'd like."

As if I could eat, but I swallow in an effort to ease my dry mouth. I follow her, and once I reach the doorway, I jerk back. The man with the scar stands in the corner with his arms crossed over his chest.

"Don't freak," he says. "If you remember correctly, I'm the

one that kept that bullet from going into your body. And as a public service announcement, I'm not into seventeen-year-old girls nor am I going to hurt one in front of my mother."

The scar across his face—that's from Eli. I've heard about this my entire life. Eli fell in love with this man's sister, Meg. Meg left with Eli, had a baby with Eli, and when she refused to return to her family, this man tried to force Meg to come home and Eli came to her rescue. The bad part of the rescue is that Eli became so violent, he almost killed this man and Eli went to prison for attempted murder.

Scarred Guy's mother sits on the bed and crosses her ankles. "See? Justin confirmed you're safe."

They aren't using road names. They're trying to make me feel like they're normal, like I'm safe. I glance down the hallway at Chevy again and he looks as lost and bewildered as me.

Chevy cocks his head to the kitchen, then gestures with his chin for me to remain where I am. He returns his attention to whoever is speaking to him. He's okay and he doesn't want me to be a part of what they're talking about. If he's okay, maybe I am, too, for the moment.

I rest my shoulder against the door frame of the room.

Jenna and her son share a look because—shocker—the kidnap victim isn't cooperating.

"I'm ready to go home," I say.

Jenna mashes her lips together. "I'll tell Kenneth."

She leaves, goes down the hallway to the kitchen, and then I hear the door to the outside open and close. Funny how I didn't hear her make a peep to Kenneth.

Scarred Guy Justin still stands in the corner, still has his arms crossed over his chest, still watches me. Chevy wants me to stay here and I don't.

"Let's cut to the chase," Justin says. "We weren't after

Chevy. It was you we wanted to talk to, but our guy got out of control. He thought he had you alone, he was ordered to convince you to come talk to me or Dad. Fiend didn't know Chevy was going to be there when they pulled up, and when that kid started swinging, our guy lost his mind."

"Well, gee, I guess that makes everything okay."

His lips edge up but then fall back down. "Fiend will be punished, so there's no need for you and Chevy to go all crazy and cause legal problems for us later."

"I feel so much better," I say drily. "Besides, you're full of crap. Chevy's the one with the possible power play, I'm nobody."

"We've been watching you for a while," he continues. "You're the one that brought Emily to us this past summer."

I readjust as the need to shed my skin overwhelms me. I did bring Eli's daughter to Louisville, but in our defense, neither of us knew at the time that her grandparents were Riot royalty. She thought she was meeting her long-lost normal grandparents, at a time when she really needed some normal and some answers in her life.

"You lost your dad, and I'm sorry. Frat was a good man."

Anger wells up in me from the tip of my toes and then explodes out of my mouth. "You know nothing about my father."

"Untrue. Your father was the one reason why the Riot and Terror never went *Apocalypse Now*. He had a steady head. Smart as hell. If he was still around, none of what happened this summer surrounding Emily would have happened. He would have figured out a way for Eli to see her, for us to see her, and she wouldn't have been caught between us, trying to figure out who's good and who's bad."

Easy. If I had to pick, they're both bad, but the Terror are annoying-little-brother bad and the Riot are serial-killer bad. No-brainer.

"Your father wanted peace more than anything else. Did you know he was on his way to meet me when he died? Once every three months, he met with me and he listened to our list of grievances with the Terror and he'd tried to explain how we somehow had done the Terror wrong."

I straighten away from the door frame. "Are you saying you killed him?"

Justin's face screws up. "Fuck no. I respected the hell out of Frat, regardless of whose colors he had on his back. He wanted peace. Our club wants peace. His death was an accident. Trust me, we looked into it just as much as your club did. We weren't sure if your side was trying to take him out because he was the one person who was able to see both sides and tried to keep us all from killing each other."

I roll my eyes and Justin catches it. "You don't believe me?"

"No. I may not know much, but your club is the one always pushing on the Terror to pay for riding through your territory and your club is always the one hurting Terror members." I hold out my arms in a "hello."

"There are rules, ways things are done, and the Terror think they're above it."

Maybe they do, maybe they don't, but regardless... "Your politics have nothing to do with me."

"It does."

He's delusional. "It doesn't."

"All that stuff I mentioned, we could possibly get past it, but what we can't get past is Eli. He took my sister, turned her against us, and because of him she's not in our life. My niece isn't in my life."

Emily is the one person I envy more than anyone else.

She's a blood child of the Terror and the Riot and she grew up far, far away from both clubs.

My temples begin to throb. I'm tired and I'm ready to fall to the floor in exhaustion. "Why are you talking to me?"

"As I said, we've been watching you. You're not happy with the Terror. You're not happy with Eli. What if I could offer you an opportunity to do what your father always wanted? What if you could bring peace to the clubs? What if by doing so, we'll help you get the Terror out of your life and help get you out of your town?"

I'd be lying if I said he didn't have my full attention. "If you want peace, all you have to do is leave the Terror alone."

"We will leave the Terror alone, once we have Eli out of the way. He's hurt too many people we love for him to be around. We can't kill him. My mother still has hopes Emily will want a relationship with us someday. If Eli dies, she'll blame us. But if Eli happens to be caught doing something illegal, caught betraying his club, caught by the police in the process and sent to prison, then we'll be happy and we'll pretend the Terror never existed."

My blood freezes in my veins, and I shake like I'm having a seizure. "Why are you telling me this?"

Justin looks straight into my eyes. "I want to frame Eli. Make it look like he's been embezzling money from the club's security company and from their clients."

Eli may not be my favorite person, but… "No one will believe that."

"Leave the belief up to me, but in order to frame Eli, I need account numbers. The club's account numbers, the clients' account numbers, as many numbers as I can get my hands on."

The throbbing in my temples increases. "What is it you think I can do?"

"Your father was the accountant for the club and for the security business. We've heard how your mother is having a hard time dealing with his loss—not moving on very well. Even heard his clothes still hang in her closet."

There's a burst of painful fear in my chest and it steals my breath. He's been in my house. This man has been in my house.

"I bet everything of your dad's is still where he left it. If you search hard enough, you could find something. Some old files. Maybe search around on his computer."

A cold tingling in my bloodstream. I may be mad at the club, but I'm not a traitor. "Why didn't you just look for it while you were there?"

Justin smiles and it's the type that causes you to fear the devil. "Me, in your house? That would mean breaking and entering. Plus, or so I've heard, your mom doesn't leave the house very often. I'm hypothesizing here, but it would be hard to get things done when she's around."

Bile rises in my throat.

"Just to make this situation move faster rather than slower, if you're wondering if the Terror clubhouse is a place where little birds can't see, you'd be wrong. Birds have a way of looking through all windows. Even ones that belong to the Terror. Hiding there brings vultures to your doorstep. Your home—it's like hanging out with songbirds."

Dear God, I'm not safe anywhere.

"Think about it, Violet." He uncrosses his arms and uses my name as if we're friends. "You can bring about the peace your father always wanted between our clubs. You want out—we'll help you get out. Help pay for college, help you find a job—whatever you need. All you have to do is keep your mouth shut to the police about this whole misunderstanding, search around the house for some numbers that really mean nothing to you and then sit back and watch your father's lifework come to fruition. What do you say, are you in?"

My stomach cramps, and when I look down the hallway, Chevy's nowhere to be seen. Eli is like a father to Chevy, he used to be my father's best friend, but he's also brought so much heartache to the club. It's because of his past garbage that I'm standing here today. It's because of his past garbage my dad was on the road that night.

But still, am I capable of being a traitor? "What if I'm not?"

Justin slides his hands into his pockets and his blue eyes go cold. The hairs on my arms stand on end and I rub at the bare skin as if that would grant me warmth. "Just so we're clear, I wasn't there last night when Fiend took you. Because if I were, I would have put a stop to it. We all have our boundaries and I don't kidnap kids, but let's say I heard things.

"I heard how you had an argument with your mom in your house and then left with your brother to go to the football game. Heard how you had a fight with Eli outside the game over tickets and how you wanted him and the club out of your life. Heard how your brother was with you when you broke down and how the reason Chevy probably didn't kill one of my guys was because your brother was in the backseat of the car and you two were protecting him."

"You heard this?" I shiver while heat flushes my cheeks. This man, he was there, and he saw and knows everything.

Justin walks closer to me and stops on his way out of the room so that our shoulders touch. "As if I was there watching, but as I said, I don't kidnap kids. It would have been a shame if Fiend hadn't taken you on the side of the road. Maybe waited until you were tucked safely in your bed, entered your home and took you and your mom. Would have been a shame if Fiend had known about your brother in the backseat and brought him along for the ride."

My head ticks to the side. "Are you threatening my family?"

Justin smiles as he tries for mocked shock. "No, because I don't do things like that."

Then he winks. A small part of me wishes that the bullet had hit me and I was dead because then he wouldn't be using my family as leverage over me.

"We'll find a way to stay in touch," he says. "After all, we know where you live."

CHEVY

My brain's fogged. Like I was plowed on the football field by a two-hundred-pound linebacker. Like I slammed my head on the ground and I wasn't wearing a helmet. The world's fuzzy and I'm having a hard time registering Skull's words, but he's talking and I'm trying to listen.

I'm sitting at the table now. Skull's sitting, too. He's been explaining that my father didn't get along with Cyrus—the man who's raised me as one of his own. That my father, James, joined the Terror because he didn't feel like there was another option and he later regretted it.

Cyrus told me Dad often felt trapped by Snowflake, so he would go to Louisville and stay for long periods, but he never mentioned Dad being at odds with him, with the Terror.

Skull has a different version. That Dad had a place in Louisville, that he had a steady girlfriend in Louisville, that he hung out and worked with the Riot and they trusted him because he gave the Riot information on the Terror.

My lungs hurt like I'm drowning. If what he's saying is true? My father was a traitor.

No. My father was no traitor. This asshole is messing with me. "My father was loyal to the Terror."

"No, he wasn't." Skull has the nerve to look at me like he's sorry to be breaking the news.

"There's holes in your story. Dad didn't do steady with women. Even I know that." From the club and from my mom. A rare moment of information verified on both fronts.

"He didn't, but the woman he had in Louisville he cared for. Called her a friend, let her live with him after she had run away from home. I can give you her name if you want. Meet her. She'll confirm everything I'm telling you. In fact, I hope you do. There's things about her you need to know. Things, as a man who values family, that I think you need to know."

Probably because he paid her to tell me what he wants me to believe. "You're full of shit."

"If I were in your shoes, I'd think the same thing, but it doesn't change the truth. That Louisville detective figured it out recently. Won't be long until he's going to try to use that information against the Terror…and against you."

I slouch in the seat. "The Terror's legit and anything my father did or didn't do doesn't affect me."

"Maybe, maybe not. Way I look at it, how well do you know your club? What is it that the Terror are hiding that the son of the president traded sides? Other question to ask yourself is how the other members of Terror are going to treat you once they find out your old man was a traitor. Are they going to be wondering how far off the tree that apple falls?"

Footsteps down the hallway and the man with the scar emerges. Violet limps in behind him. I stand so quickly that the legs of the chair bounce against the floor. She glances over at me and the lost expression on her face is worse than any punch.

Nausea twists my gut. She was alone with him and I fell for it. Skull waved his right hand in order for me to lose focus on his left. "You okay?"

She nods.

"Did he hurt you?"

Violet shakes her head and it bothers me she's gone mute.

I set my sights on Skull and make it perfectly clear we're done talking. "Call Eli now, get us home or I swear to God I'll make each of you bleed before you get a chance to put a bullet in my brain."

Skull laughs like I told a joke, but stands, pulls his cell out of his pocket and slides it to me. "Once you get ahold of Eli and tell him you're okay, give the phone to me and I'll tell him where to pick the two of you up."

Violet

I'm blindfolded again and I'm handcuffed. The car is different, but my placement in the backseat isn't. This time it was Chevy who placed the cuff on my wrist, then folded the bandana over my eyes. He did both with such care, touching me like I was on the verge of shattering, looking at me with such tender eyes that I wanted to weep.

The blindfold was a "request" from Skull, but the one wrist handcuffed was Chevy's idea. He didn't trust them to blindfold us and keep us together. I still don't trust that they're taking us to Eli, that they're taking us home.

Before Chevy did either, he whispered, "Do you trust me?"

Of course I did. Trusted him to be the first boy to hold my hand. Trusted him to be the first boy I kissed. Trusted him to be the first for so many things. Did I trust him with my life? I held out my wrist, then stepped closer so I could allow him to blindfold me.

More than the car is different. The backseat doesn't smell of rotten food. The material of the seats isn't torn. The en-

gine doesn't roar. This ride is quiet. No radio. No one talking. The engine barely a purr.

This time Chevy sits with me in the backseat. Our legs
are pressed tight together and he hooked one of his fingers
with mine. He continuously slides his finger up and down
in a reassuring caress. Not too fast, not too slow. It's like a
heartbeat.

A promise.

We're going home.

He's here with me.

It's going to be okay.

I want to believe him, but I'm not sure if I can. There's
a nagging sensation that we're reaching the end and not as
in the they-all-lived-happily-ever-after, but as in the tragic
finality of a nightmare.

My mouth is dry, my blood feels funny as it courses
through my veins. Never thought much about breathing
until this all happened. How air feels so good coming into
my lungs and refreshing as it leaves. How each inhale and
exhale is a gift.

Never thought too much about how a comforting touch
from someone you care for is a blessing. Chevy is a blessing.
Breathing is a gift. My heart beats a bit faster. I could be on
the verge of losing both.

The car leaves the smoothness of a paved road and Chevy
and I jostle into each other as the car dips and rocks. We're
on a dirt path. A knot forms in my throat. Not good. Not
good at all. My stomach flips, and I breathe out to try to
calm my nerves, but it doesn't help.

Chevy shifts, his head near mine, his breath warm on my
ear. "You and me, Violet. We're going to get through this.
Just do what I say when I say it."

I nod. Together. We're going to survive this together.

The car slows to a stop, a door opens and my heart beats in my ears. Chevy fidgets next to me, leaning forward. There's a click, and a loosening of the handcuff and then the blindfold is lifted from my eyes. I blink at the brightness and snap my head in Chevy's direction when his door opens. Both of his hands are free, the handcuff still on my wrist, but I'm not bound to anyone or anything anymore.

Chevy slides out and I scramble across the seat to follow. Frantically, I glance around, searching for Eli, but besides Justin, there's not another living soul. Trees. Lots of trees. Trees full of colored leaves and the sunlight filtering through the thick branches, but no Eli.

They lied.

A hollowness in my stomach and the world tilts. Chevy grabs my hand and yanks me. "Run, Violet!"

He shoves me away from the car, away from Justin, away from him, but instead I reach out for Chevy, to force him to come with me. I will not abandon him now.

"Eli's at the other end of this road," Justin says in such a calm way that it's frightening. "A half mile. I didn't bring you out here to kill you, I'm sending you home."

I grab on to Chevy's wrist. He readjusts, taking my fingers with his.

Justin sets his hard glare on me. "I already explained we want peace. Me and Eli in the same breathing space means war. Safer for both of our clubs to drop you off here."

"Then get in the car and leave," Chevy says.

Justin glances over me, as if he's trying to judge whether or not I'll do what he's asked. As a reminder of what they could do to my brother and mother if I don't.

Without another word, Justin returns to the car. The world has an unreal quality to it, as if I'm watching a movie, as he U-turns and drives back the way he came.

We're free.

Yet the adrenaline coursing through my veins doesn't feel like relief. My back itches like someone is watching, my entire body vibrates with the sense we're about to be ambushed—as if I'll never be safe again.

The wind blows through the trees, making a clapping sound, and the breeze is cold against my cheeks. Chevy's hand is warm and strong. We watch Justin's car leave. Rocks cracking under the pressure of the tires. Dirt blowing up as a cloud in the wind.

The dust settles, the car retreats around a bend, the sound of the rocks being driven over and the purring engine fade yet we still stare in the direction Justin disappeared. As if we're both frightened to turn our backs and tempt fate to drag us back to the basement prison.

Chevy pulls on my hand. "Let's go."

He steps forward, I walk with him and unbelievable pain shoots through my knee. I falter, clinging to Chevy as I try not to fall to the ground. The pain then leaks into my blood and every bruise, every cut throbs in agony. I gasp, confused how I had gone from no pain to sheer torture.

Chevy steadies me. "You okay?"

I nod, but I'm not, and from the sympathetic way he looks at me, he's aware. With a sturdy arm around my waist, we go forward. Each step causes my muscles to twinge, my knee to give, bringing me to a new level of exhaustion, but each of those steps brings me closer to home, brings Chevy closer to home, and he needs to be home.

He needs stitches for the gash on his head, he needs a doctor to look at the eye that's so swollen I'm sure he can barely see and he needs to be safe and secure and as far from the Riot as possible.

We hobble up a hill and that's when we see them—Eli,

Cyrus, Pigpen and a whole group of men. They're leaning against their motorcycles, but the moment they see us, they straighten and some of them are on the move in our direction. Chevy's grip tightens on me and I lean into him. My eyes water and it becomes too blurry to see. We made it. We're going home.

Chevy starts down the hill, but this time when my knee gives, I go down with it. The hard ground is honestly a blessing and my fingers touch the grass and dirt like it's a pillow and a bed. I don't hunker down, but I consider it. Dream of resting my head and going to sleep. Then I can begin to pretend this was all just a bad dream, an awful dream.

"We're almost there." Chevy crouches beside me.

I'm too tired to talk. Too afraid if I do, then I'll discover that this part of the nightmare—the part where it might end well—was a dream. I'll twitch my finger, awaken and be back in the basement. I glance up at Chevy and the sun beaming behind him hurts my eyes.

"I'm not going without you." Chevy slides his arms under my knees, along my back, and lifts me, cradling me against his chest as he walks toward his family. I'm too exhausted to argue. Only have the strength to slip my arms around his neck and rest my head in the crook of his neck.

"We're almost there," he says again. "Almost home. They see us and they're coming for us now. We're going to be okay."

Okay repeats in my head, circles over and over again. Somehow I don't think Chevy and I will find a way to be okay again.

CHEVY

The nurses separated me and Violet in the ER and I'm about to lose my mind. Being wheeled from place to place, IV in my arm keeping me grounded most of the day, too much time wasted in an MRI machine searching for a concussion that didn't exist. Five staples in my head later and I'm wheeled back to my room with promises of being discharged.

The nurses are pissed Pigpen gave me a fresh pair of jeans and a T-shirt to change into. The hospital gown wasn't cutting it.

I did allow the staff to numb my head for the staples, but I've refused pain medication. Don't need my brain fogged. Need to think straight. Need to be in control.

I'm seventeen, which means pediatric ward, and I'm having a hard time digesting pictures of clowns holding kittens. I've had a gun held on me by an illegal motorcycle club. While having the hell beat out of me, I caught glimpses of the only girl I've ever loved running into the line of fire... for me.

When that bang reverberated against my skin, my soul

crumbled because I thought she was dead. I thought I was dead. And if I wasn't dead, I wasn't sure how I could go on living without her. Kittens and clowns don't make sense to me anymore. Feels abnormal in dark reality.

The aide turns the corner and outside my room are men in Reign of Terror black leather cuts and my mother. From the way she's shaking her head and finger, black hair swinging from side to side, she's furious and she has a right to be. I went missing, I scared her and Mom doesn't handle scared well.

"I want you out of his life." Mom points in the direction of the elevators. "I want you gone. I want all of you gone."

"I understand you're upset, Nina." Cyrus holds up his hands in an act of submission. "But I have every right to be here."

"Right?" Mom's eyes bulge from her head. "You have no rights."

Not in the mood to play referee, I place a hand on the tire of my wheelchair. The aide looks down at me and I say, "That's my dysfunction in the hallway. Mind leaving me here for a few?"

He's a young guy, probably in his twenties. With an expression of you-would-have-fared-better-being-born-to-wolverines, he backs me up without the beeping and offers me a weak fist bump before heading to the nurses' station.

I'm angled so they'd have to really search to see me, but I can watch them.

"He was kidnapped!" Mom leans into Cyrus like she's willing to punch him in the gut. "Do you even understand what that means? He was held against his will. My son had an MRI performed, is getting staples in his head because a rival motorcycle gang you have a problem with took him against his will and hurt him. As far as I'm concerned, you lost the *right* to see him the moment they laid hands on him."

"He's my grandson," Cyrus states calmly, and I swear Mom's hair stands on end.

"And he's *my* son. Not yours. You lost yours and don't you forget I know why you lost James. Not many people in town can say that, can they? But I know and I will not make the same mistakes you did. Leave now or I'm telling the police to shove you out."

The area near the staples in my head pulses. James. My father. The Riot said he was a traitor. The pulse turns into a pound and I rub at my head, trying to avoid the cut. What did Skull mean by traitor? What does it mean for me, if anything, if he was?

Thinking of what Skull told me about my father, my mind wanders. I've never questioned anyone on my father's relationship with Mom or his family. Felt the tug-of-war strings being pulled at an early age, so I decided to stay neutral. Bringing up my father meant inviting people to make me choose a side.

"Excuse me." A nurse in Hello Kitty scrubs who couldn't weigh a buck twenty wet enters the fray and cracks a clipboard against the wall to gain everyone's attention. According to her name tag, her name is Becky. "All of you need to either take this outside, away from the hospital, or stop. This is a hospital, a children's floor for that matter, not a bar."

I wince on Mom's behalf.

Nurse Becky scans Cyrus, then my mother. "I don't have a problem calling the police on either of you." She then surveys the rest of the guys in the hallway. "Or on any of you. That was your first and only warning."

Becky walks away, Mom and Cyrus communicate through glares and my aide returns. "That help?"

Yes. No. "For the short-term."

"Pain meds, bro. It's the way to handle the long-term."

The aide wheels me back around the corner and this time Mom, Cyrus and the rest of the crew hanging in the hallway notice. Most of the guys offer some sort of greeting, my grandfather looks at me like he's proud and my mother smiles in sadness.

They create a clog my aide won't push through and I'm stuck in the hallway. Mom on one side. Cyrus on the other. Tug-of-war.

"You okay?" Mom's face turns an ugly shade of gray as her eyes wander over my head. On top of scared not being her thing, neither is blood.

"Yeah. Where's Violet?" Not being near her is a crazy itch that needs to be scratched.

"They're taking a look at her knee," answers Cyrus. "Running some tests. Eli's promised to stay with her. You did good looking after Violet. Let us take that burden now."

Mom coughs in disgust, Cyrus's eyes narrow on her and I push the wheelchair forward on my own. Mom and Cyrus are smart enough to move out of the way.

Footsteps follow me into the room and a glance back verifies that Cyrus, Pigpen and Mom are the only ones who come in. Good thing they're also smart enough to stay away as I stand and then sit my ass back onto the hospital bed. One more person tries to help me and I'll be throwing punches.

Outside, the lamps to the parking lot are lit and headlights go up and down the main county road. I'm lost as to what time or day it is. Lost is a great way to describe everything.

"I want to see Violet," I say, and nobody argues with me. Nobody says shit, but nobody argues. Maybe they all went deaf. "I said, I want to see Violet."

"After she comes back from the tests, I'll see what I can do," Cyrus says.

I don't like that answer and I don't like how Cyrus paces to the window to look out, turning his back to me.

"She okay?" I press.

Like a fucked-up checklist, I go through our time with the Riot. Relive in rapid succession every hit, every punch, every slap she took—I relive the gunshot and I flinch. Everyone notices, but no one says a thing. As if maybe if they do speak, I'll explode.

Mom crosses the room and sits on my bed next to me. She wears the same clothes as when I dropped her off at work on Friday night. Same tank, same jeans, same earrings and that's when I notice she's not just gray, she's exhausted. Black circles under her eyes and pronounced worry lines.

She reaches out, brushes my hair away from my forehead like I'm a child, then takes my hand. I let her but then flip them so that my hand covers hers—so I'm the one offering the comfort. I don't like it when Mom's scared.

"Jenny said Violet's not talking," Mom says.

Jenny. Violet's mom. The pounding in my head ceases, but it's an insane silence that follows. "What do you mean not talking?"

"Violet nods and shakes her head," Mom continues. "Verifying information only through that show of a yes or a no. Violet seems to understand everything that's being said to her and she seems lucid enough through the painkillers they've given her to respond to difficult questions this way, but it's scaring Jenny."

It's scaring Mom. I glance around. Neither Cyrus nor Pigpen will meet my gaze and the two grown men wearing black leather cuts shuffle their feet. Must scare them, too. Got to admit, I don't care for the unsettling happening within me.

"The police want to talk to you and Violet," Cyrus says.

"Okay." No news there. Two undercover officers were

with Eli at the end of the dirt road. The Terror involved them from the start. We haven't been questioned yet, though, and I'm guessing that's because we were bloody, bruised, and Violet has a busted knee. "But I'm asking about Violet."

"Before they talk to you," he continues, "I need to know—with how she's acting. Did they…"

My skin prickles as a darkness rolls through me. I know what he's asking. The same thing I asked Violet in the basement.

"Did they *hurt* Violet?" Pure menace leaks from Cyrus's voice.

Cyrus, Pigpen and I talked not long after I was admitted. That dead period after the hospital figures out you're not dying but still need tests. Mom left to fill out paperwork and I told them as much as I could. The play-by-play and who was involved.

They listened, grimly nodded as I gave them the down low, but I didn't get beyond the head of the Riot showing up and explaining it was all a mistake. Mom returned and I didn't want her involved in the details. Don't want her sucked into any of this nightmare.

Pigpen readjusts on the wall he leans against. "We know she was hurt, but—"

"I know what you're asking," I cut him off. "She was alone with the Riot in the back of the car."

"Alone," interrupts Mom, and her voice has gone higher in pitch. "Then where were you?"

She doesn't want the answer and I don't want to be a witness to her reaction. Can't imagine *trunk* will go over well. I was kidnapped, now I'm home. That's all she needs to know. "I asked Violet what happened there. She said they hit her but didn't try anything. Besides for a few minutes upstairs, she was in my sights the rest of the time."

Pigpen's eyes snap to mine. "They separated you at the house?"

"After the president brought us upstairs, I put Violet in a bathroom. Wanted walls between her and them while they called you. I had an eye on the hallway almost the entire time. There were maybe two minutes with her out of my sight at that point."

Cyrus and Pigpen share a look and I shake my head. "Even with her out of my sight, I would have heard if there was a struggle. I would have heard her yell for help."

"So Violet was talking," Mom confirms.

"Yeah."

"When did she stop talking?" Cyrus asks.

I run a hand through my hair and there's a shot of pain when I hit my newly stapled gash. "Sometime after the gunshot."

The hospital bed moves as Mom jumps to her feet. "They shot at you?"

Ah, hell.

"Who were you with when you were separated from Violet?" Pigpen asks.

Mom throws her arms out to her sides. "Did anyone else hear what he said?"

But they already know. "Skull."

Pigpen studies me with narrowed eyes. "What did you two talk about?"

"Get out," Mom roars as she rounds on Pigpen. "Get out now!"

Pigpen and Cyrus both look at me for approval and I nod. That one act causes Mom to mash her lips together. "He's my son and he's a minor. I'm the one still making the decisions here. Not him and not you!"

Cyrus raises an eyebrow. An unspoken reminder that I'm weeks away from eighteen.

Pigpen pushes off the wall. "Won't be far." Which means he'll be outside the door, standing guard.

Cyrus rounds the bed and gives me a brief but strong hug. "I'll find out about Violet and your discharge."

"I'll find out about discharge," Mom snaps.

"Fine with me, but he's coming home with us." Cyrus leaves and my mother goes from exhausted gray to red.

"I hate that man."

She's never said that aloud before, but I have no doubt she's thought it a million times throughout the years. Any other circumstances, I'd be giving Mom a hard time, but it's been a tough day all around.

I lie back in the bed and close my eyes. "I think we should do it."

There's a dip on my bed as Mom sits, followed by a deep sigh. Cyrus wants Violet and me to stay at his place until the club and the police can figure out the fallout from the kidnapping.

"I've never been welcomed at Cyrus's," she says.

Not sure if it's true or not. My earliest memories have always been a separation between Mom and the club. "He told me you could stay, too."

"I sleep during the day and work at night. It'll be off from everyone else."

"I don't want you at the condo by yourself." I open my eyes and my heart rips at the wetness in hers.

Mom glances away and wipes her face with the back of her hand. "You're staying with him, aren't you?"

It's what he and the board asked of me and I don't know how to say no. Their logic makes sense, but I don't want her alone either. Not until I know the Riot are no longer a problem. Until I can protect Mom on my own again, I'll ask the club for a favor and ask them to keep it silent. To watch over my mother until I can.

"He's my family," I say. "Same as you."

"You need to cut them out of your life."

But that would be like cutting off parts of myself. An arm. A leg. "I'm okay, Mom."

Her head tilts in an effort for composure, but a single tear falls from the corner of her eye regardless. She reaches out, palm up, and I take her hand again. We sit like that, in silence, holding on to one another.

Violet

Silence.

It's weird how I crave it, and I can't seem to find it.

There's a thrumming. Like a strange background music. It's persistent and annoying and I can't figure out where it's coming from. None of the others who rotate in and out of my room seem to hear it. I don't ask, but I can tell. They don't appear as if they're ready to peel their skin off their bones.

My mother's here, beside me. Chair as close to the hospital bed as it can go and she won't stop talking. Mom talks when she's nervous. She talks when she's not nervous. Mom talks. Most of it nothing of importance. Just words so she can fill the quiet I so deeply desire.

"I hope you don't mind, but I cleaned your room while you were gone. Thought it would be nice if you came home and found it clean. I changed the sheets and the comforter. I used a new fabric softener. Smells like lilacs. I know you like lilacs. At least I think you do."

Never really thought of lilacs one way or another.

Mom braids her blond hair. It's a habit she has when she's

anxious. Mom lives in a constant state of distress. It's been worse since Dad died. I can't imagine what the past twenty-four hours have been like for her. Possibly the same fear and soul-crushing agony as when I sat next to her waiting to hear why Dad hadn't returned home.

Because of that I let her talk. It's what makes her feel better.

I'm not in pain anymore. There's an IV and there's a drip and the nurse said whatever was in the drip would take all the aches away. She was right, but it also made my head light, my body numb and my nose itch.

"Brandon and I made you cookies. Chocolate chip ones with oatmeal in them. You loved those when you were younger. We thought you would like them when you came home."

I haven't seen Brandon yet and that makes me frown. There's no reason for them to lie to me, so I'm assuming he's okay, but I'll feel better once I see him, hug him, confirm in real life he's fine.

Fine.

My heart squeezes. Chevy. I need to know if he's okay. I strip off the sheet and go to slide out of the bed. Mom's face falls, her fingers freeze on the locks of hair she was braiding, then unbraiding for the umpteenth time. "Please stop trying to get out of bed. The doctor doesn't want you placing pressure on your knee."

Evidently, I've tried this before. Time and words seem like running water.

"Violet…" Mom hesitates. "I know you answered earlier, when the nurses admitted you, but…" Mom stands, the long strands of her braid unraveling. "Are you sure nothing happened to you? Nothing that you want to tell me about?"

I blink and look down at my bruised body and my now

immobilized knee. It's in some sort of brace and the doctor talked to Mom about visiting a specialist. I raise my eyebrows. *Pretty obvious something happened to me.*

Mom touches the end of the hospital bed as if it's a protective shield between her and me. She doesn't touch me. Just the bed. "Did any man... Did anyone... Because if so, there are tests that should be run and...things that should happen."

My stomach drops. It was bad enough to answer the questions the nurse asked when it was just me and her and she was helping me out of my clothes. It was odd and awkward then. With Mom it's another level of hell. I shake my head no.

A knock on the door and I suck in a breath. Maybe it's Chevy. Mom answers and after a brief exchange she opens the door wider and Eli walks in. Rage locks my muscles.

Eli.

I hate him. Hate him so much. I hate his club. I hate the way he struts in here like he belongs, like he has the right to care. If it wasn't for his stupid club, I wouldn't have been kidnapped. If it wasn't for his stupid personal war with the head of the Riot, they wouldn't be using me to hurt him and they wouldn't be threatening my family.

"Hey, Violet." Eli stops near the edge of the bed, and unlike Mom, he touches me, my ankle, and I jerk. He immediately lifts his hand. "I'm sorry. I didn't mean to hurt you."

Little too late for that.

"Is your ankle hurting, too?"

No pain right now. It's the meds, but everything will hurt in the morning.

"Everyone's been asking about you. You've got an entire hallway and waiting room full of guys waiting to do your bidding. Just say the word, and any of us will do or get whatever your heart desires."

Mom comes up beside him and my muscles twitch when

she touches his arm. Touches him. I turn away, because since Dad died, I've been unworthy of touch.

"The doctor said she's dehydrated, bruised, and that there's damage to her knee. I'm worried. They've mentioned surgery."

Weird how important surgery seems, but how no one's mentioned that to me.

"She keeps trying to get out of bed. God only knows where she thinks she's going. The nurse told Violet to push the button if she needed to use the restroom and Violet seemed to understand, so I don't have a clue what she's doing."

Even though Mom's talking, Eli keeps his eyes on me and I don't like that he watches me so intently. My thoughts have been tough to capture, but what if he's able to read me and he knows what I've been assigned to do?

"She's still not talking," Mom whispers.

"But I bet her hearing still works," he responds.

The right side of my mouth turns up and Eli almost smiles along with me. A crinkling near his eyes, a small spark, but his expression then falls near black with seriousness.

I agree. This entire scenario is as serious as a severed artery.

"Are you purposely ignoring me?" Mom pushes down the sleeves of her red sweater. "Because if so, that's childish. I've been worried sick—"

My forehead furrows. The thrumming. It grows louder and causes a slashing pain in my head.

"She's not ignoring us," Eli says, and Mom's guilt trip magically vanishes.

Now it's his turn to lower his voice like I can't hear. "Just talked to Pigpen. Chevy's confirmed it's been a complicated few hours for her. More than we originally thought."

The air catches in my throat. *Chevy.*

"Complicated?" Mom's hand goes to her chest like the word crushes her lungs. "Complicated how?"

"I'll tell you in the hallway. I'd like to talk to you and Nina at the same time. An opportunity for all of us to get on the same page."

Eli angles for the door and I grab his wrist. He knows about Chevy. Eli turns back to me, studies my face, then the worry in his expression fades. Sort of like he had spent the past few hours trying to solve a math problem, but then the answer appeared in a heavenly glow along with a choir of angels.

"Chevy's okay," he says like that's a secret between us. "He's tough. Just like you."

He's okay. That's a start. I drop Eli's wrist and calculate how I can find him without Mom freaking out.

"Want to see him?" Eli asks.

Yes.

Eli does a quick scan of the IV leading from me to the machines. A tug of his ear and he sweeps me up into his arms. Multiple hospital sheets and all.

"What are you doing?" Mom demands, but I know and approve. "Eli, her knee. Be careful of her knee!"

"Do me a favor, Jenny, and grab that IV machine."

And we're moving. Eli kicks at the closed door of my room as a knock and the door is immediately opened by Hook. He's Razor's dad and my mind slowly feels like it's stretching after being asleep.

Razor.

Oz.

My best friends. My brothers.

I want to see them. Want to figure out if being here is a dream. My head swivels as if I can snap a panoramic picture.

Along the hallway and the nurses' station, there are plenty of men from the club, but not Oz, not Razor.

The guys from the club smile at me, nod at me, watch me as if they're grieving, angry and relieved. A strange combination. A wall of men. Most of them are men my father called family.

"Razor and Oz aren't here." Eli carries me down the hallway. "They're texting everyone in the club every ten minutes, though. And now they have Emily texting me every five minutes. They're driving me nuts. Razor and Oz are with your brother. Keeping his mind off you being gone."

Good. That's good.

"Put her back in her room!" Nurse Becky shoots in front of Eli, but he doesn't stop. Instead, he steps around her. She keeps yelling and it sounds as if someone is yelling back.

We reach the end of the hallway and Pigpen winks at me as he opens a door. My heart stops beating when Eli enters a room almost identical to mine, but instead of my mom, there's Chevy's mom and in the bed is the one person who could possibly understand the thrumming.

Dark hair, dark eyes, battered, definitely bruised, but he's still a strong, safe port in a raging storm. Chevy sits up in the bed, the pure relief on his face an echo of the unraveling of tension happening within me.

"Brought you a visitor," Eli announces, and when Chevy scrambles to move out of the bed, Eli shakes his head. "Stay put."

Eli gently lays me next to Chevy, and when our gazes meet, my eyes burn. He's okay. Chevy's okay.

"Eli McKinley!" Rebecca, Oz's mom, flies into the room. Pieces of her black hair falling from a bun. She's in her blue nursing scrubs, and she looks like she's ready to roast Eli over an open fire. "I am doing my best to keep the hospital from throwing you and this club out the door and then you go and pull Violet from her room? You can't do that!"

Rebecca checks my IV machine, pushing buttons, tracing my line and then checking where the needle goes into my skin. Her eyes flicker from me to Chevy, then back to me. She purses her lips, then she tucks my hair behind my ear. "You okay?"

I nod, and she tucks the hair behind my ear again. I like Rebecca. She understands that sometimes words are overrated. She understands a lot of things. I often used to wish she was my mother instead of Oz's.

"When are they going to be discharged?" Eli asks.

"After the doctor goes over their test results. I've told you this." Rebecca returns her attention to my IV machine. "She's on a morphine drip. You can't go messing around with the machines."

"I want them out of here," Eli demands. "I want them out of this hospital and under my roof. I don't know what the hell I'm dealing with and I don't want them here so exposed."

Rebecca glares at Eli. "Orderlies are scared to come onto this floor because of the amount of men you have planted outside this door. I think Chevy and Violet are safe."

They keep arguing. Mom jumps into the conversation. So does Chevy's mom. All loud voices with varying opinions that Eli won't listen to because he believes he knows everything.

There's a movement of the covers and my heart flips when Chevy's hand finds mine. Somehow, even though I was already lying down, I settle further into the bed, into the pillow, and the thrumming in my head becomes less severe.

It's like a buzzing now, less annoying, but still there. As if I was encased by a beehive.

Chevy laces his fingers with mine and I breathe out. It's

a cleansing breath, it's a cathartic breath, it's like slipping into a hot bath.

Chevy's hand is rough, calloused from football, from the years of working on motorcycles and cars, from the fistfights he's had over the years to protect his family, to protect my brother and recently to protect me.

It's a strong but gentle hand. One that guides our linked fingers closer to his chest, closer to his heart, and I swear to God I can feel it beating through his shirt. Maybe that's my heart beating. Maybe this is the first time my heart has worked properly since the gun was fired.

We're shoulder to shoulder in the cramped bed. His body heat drifts over me like an additional blanket, and for the first time since we arrived, my eyes grow heavy and the need for sleep is overwhelming.

I turn my head, slowly, enjoying the way the cool pillow caresses my skin. Chevy's already watching me, and if I had the energy, I'd touch his beautiful face.

"Please make them leave," I whisper.

Chevy squeezes my hand, casts his eyes in the direction of all the grown-ups who have loud voices and even louder opinions. "Everyone needs to go."

It's odd how there were so many things being said at once and how that all ended in an instant.

"We're tired," Chevy says. Simple. To the point. I like it.

"We'll be right outside." I can't tell if that was my mom or Chevy's mom and I'm honestly too tired to figure it out. Instead, I study Chevy's jaw. There's a bruise and I don't like it. I wish I could wave my hand and he'd be healed.

Shuffling of footsteps on the wooden floor, then Chevy calls out, "Eli."

"What do you need?"

"I need sleep."

So do I.

I angle my head so I can witness Eli's response, to see if he understands what Chevy's really asking, what I need to know before I can let myself drift.

"We've got every entrance and exit covered. No one's coming in here if you don't want them. You're safe to rest. Get some sleep, we'll get you both home soon and we'll take care of you there, as well."

"Thanks," Chevy says. Eli leaves and I watch as the door to Chevy's room closes.

Silence.

There's silence.

Not really silence.

There's the sound of my breaths coming in and out. The sound of Chevy's breaths coming in and out.

Chevy shifts so he's under the covers with me, moving so that I can nestle exactly where I want to be—my head on his chest, my arm around his stomach. Chevy holds me tight, his fingers tunnel into my hair and then eventually discover my temple. He starts that slow circle massage and my eyes eventually close.

"I've got you, Violet. I swear to God I've got you."

And there's no more thrumming.

Just his heat, warm covers, his heartbeat, his promise, the rise and fall of his chest and my body wrapped around his.

This. Just this. I'm finally home.

CHEVY

Violet: You look tired.

Me: I am.

Violet: Have you been able to sleep?

Me: Not since the hospital. Only when I slept with you.

Violet: Me either. There's this buzzing in my head that keeps me awake. I wish there would be silence. Everything seems too loud now. Like a TV with a broken remote.

Me: I get it.

Violet: I thought you would.

"She's quiet," says Oz. "I don't like it."
I pocket my cell, wanting to keep the messages between me and Violet private, then pick the football up off the ground. I glance over at the wraparound porch. Violet's on

the porch swing and she places her cell on her lap, but doesn't look in my direction. Doesn't let on at all that we've been chatting back and forth, sharing secrets via short words on a screen.

Her legs are propped up and she's listening to her younger brother, Stone, who is in the Adirondack chair next to her. He's telling her about some movie he and I watched last night.

In fact, he's told her about every movie he's watched while Violet and I were gone and while she was in the hospital. As long as he has her attention, he'll keep talking, and knowing Violet, she'll sit and listen. Even if we hadn't been kidnapped, Violet has always given Stone her time.

I make a mental note that one of us will have to swoop in and give her a break. "Violet's listening to Stone, that's why she's quiet. She doesn't interrupt him unless she has to."

"It's more than that," Oz says.

It's a warm day. Sun's shining. White clouds. All the poetic shit. Fall's like this in Kentucky. Rainy and cold one day, warm and sunny the next. Keeps going like this until December and then it's nothing but gray clouds and balls-fall-off freezing until mid-March.

I've been here at Cyrus's for a few days. Violet was released from the hospital last night. Right before they were about to release both of us, she hobbled to the bathroom and vomited.

Hospital kept her until she could hold food down. Some doctors thought it was a stomach bug. A few thought it was an allergic reaction. Others thought it was some sort of Acute Stress Disorder. After she got over that, the specialist kept her in for her knee. First they thought they were going to do surgery, then the MRI showed the damage wasn't as bad as they thought. They ended up giving her physical therapy for treatment.

Either way, I hated being away from her.

"Razor's quiet." I motion to our best friend, who's walking across the field, away from us. "You don't complain about him."

"He was born quiet. She was born to tell us what we're doing wrong." Oz takes after his mother with black hair, and like his father, he's tall, has fists like a brick wall, and he's a patched-in member.

He's a year older than me and, like Razor, I consider him a brother. Violet, Razor, Oz and I grew up together on this property. Slept in the old log cabin house that Cyrus calls home. His wife, Olivia, used to help us catch fireflies in this field on late summer nights.

Across the yard is a two-story three-car garage that was converted into the clubhouse for the Terror. The day is nice enough that the garage doors are rolled up. Some of the guys inside are watching the TV over the bar. A few are playing pool in the corner.

The four of us learned how to crawl on those sticky floors, played tag in the crowd during the hundreds of family dinners the club had as we grew up. Hell, I first found the courage to take Violet's hand on the picnic table Pigpen's currently sitting on as he drinks a beer.

He's been Violet's shadow since Eli left town with Cyrus a few days ago.

"Violet's talking," I say.

The look of utter disbelief is warranted. Violet is talking again, but she's not herself. Spends more time silently watching than letting her thoughts roll off her tongue. It's making every guy in the club, including me, edgy.

But then again, I only got to see her in a crowded hospital room, and since she's been home, her brother has been stuck tight to her. As much as I want a few minutes alone

LONG WAY HOME   111

with her, Stone deserves this time with his sister. He needs to know she's okay and that it's not his fault we were taken.

"Leave her be, okay?" If Violet wants to stay quiet, she can stay quiet. If she wants to run through the clubhouse like a crazy person and break every glass in sight, she can do that, too. "Violet saved her brother's life. Saved mine, too."

"I'm not coming down on her, I'm concerned. I know Violet and I haven't gotten along lately, but I still love her."

My gut twists because that's how I feel about her silence, too, but Violet's got too many people in her face hoping and praying she'll return to normal. Each hour that passes, I'm beginning to realize they want her to act normal so they can start to feel better about what happened. It's how people are also acting around me.

They smile too big. Pause for too long. Can't seem to find easy conversation. It's uncomfortable and it doesn't help this strange sensation that I've had since leaving the hospital. Like the rest of the world is moving in fast-forward and I'm creeping along in slow motion.

Fucking sucks.

Razor turns and raises his arms. Rebecca finally cleared me to start exercising. It's been driving me insane to do nothing but watch TV. The faster I can get back to football, the faster my life will return to normal.

I pull my arm back, then launch the ball into the air. A perfect spiral with a perfect arc. Razor catches it and I circle my shoulder. Every damn muscle in my body was bruised and due to the inactivity is now stiffer than roadkill.

"Looking good," Oz says.

It's not the throwing I'm concerned about. That's not my job. It's the running while plowing through a line of guys, all while catching. I hold my hands up and Razor fires it back. Like I asked, he threw it to the side and I jog the few feet. I'm able to easily catch it, holding it close to my chest.

Thanks to muscle memory, my feet automatically cut right as if I'm in a game and need to lose my defender. But I don't do a full-on sprint. Instead, I throw the ball back to Razor and pause to stretch.

The deep grumbling of multiple motorcycle engines. Cyrus and Eli have been gone since I woke up here after my hospital stay and it pisses me off that nobody's told me why they left or where they went. The group of six guys pull off to the side of the clubhouse and park. They cut their engines and the yard goes quiet.

After the last guy swings off his bike, the birds chirp again in the thick forest of trees surrounding Cyrus's property and the clubhouse springs to life as the guys who were hanging out near the bar pile out into the yard. They offer quick hugs and fast pats.

Cyrus glances in my direction. Normally, I'm a patient guy. Would let Cyrus come to me when he's ready to talk, but I must have left all my patience in that hellhole basement.

Most of the guys head into the clubhouse, but Cyrus stays behind. "Saw you as we drove up. You looked good making the catch."

Not discussing football. "Where have you been? And don't tell me on a run for the security business. We both know that would be bullshit."

Cyrus strokes his long beard and he regards Violet on the porch. "She doing okay?"

No. "Cyrus."

He settles his dark eyes on me. Cyrus is not only the head of this MC, but the head of this family. He's a McKinley, Eli's a McKinley and so am I. I don't fool myself into thinking I won't look just like Eli in twenty years and be a carbon copy of the man in front of me at fifty.

"We've been in Louisville, talking with the police."

A muscle in my jaw twitches and Cyrus catches it.

"That's it? You spent days away talking to the police? You'd think they'd want to talk to me and Violet instead of you."

His expression darkens. I talked to the police the night we got back to Snowflake, but we haven't been interviewed since. Pushing back, demanding information, that's not like me, but I'm not an idiot. They may have met with the police, but they also met with the Riot. "Did you meet with Skull? Are they going to turn Fiend over?"

"We're letting the police handle this," Cyrus says.

A nonanswer. Because club business stays within its members and I'm not a member. Even if I was, there are things some members never know. For years, I watched Razor struggle with this, but accepting my place had never been an issue for me, until now.

"I would think letting myself be kidnapped so I could save Stone and then offering myself as a human shield for Violet would be enough to get me in the know."

Cyrus places his hands on his hips, and right when I'm ready for him to try to deflect the conversation again, he tilts his head to the clubhouse. "Church. Now."

He walks ahead, I follow. We enter the clubhouse and one by one the board members watch as we pass, then also fall into line. Cyrus's hand slams on the door to the stairs and he jogs up. First door on the right and I walk into Church.

This room is a sacred place for the club, but it's not a place of worship. It's where decisions are made, problems are dissected. It's a place where whatever is discussed stays. To be in here requires trust from one person to the next.

I've been in here before. Snuck in with Oz and Razor when we were kids, but I haven't been in here in years. Cyrus tore our asses inside out when he caught us playing in here. He taught us then that we needed to respect this club and its ways.

If he couldn't trust us, he said, how could we trust them? Brotherhood, family...it requires trust.

Place looks the same as it did then. Huge black Reign of Terror banner on the wall with the half skull and fire blazing out of the eyes and fire raining down around it. The long wooden boardroom-style table is in the middle with the chairs gathered around it.

Cyrus takes a seat at the head of the table and the rest of the board members drop into chairs. Razor's dad, Hook, is in here and so is Oz's dad, Man O' War. Besides me, Pigpen is the youngest guy in here and then there's Eli. Not officially a board member, but he is the most respected man in the club.

"Did you meet with the Riot?" I ask, and all heads turn in Cyrus's direction. I don't have the right to ask that question as I'm not patched in and everyone will back Cyrus up if he doesn't answer.

"We met with the police. We meant what we said. We are going full letter of the law on this. In fact, the police want to meet with you and Violet tomorrow night. They want to show you pictures. Have you confirm the people they're looking for."

"I'm in." I'm assuming Violet will be, too. "What else is going on?"

Cyrus shares a long glance with Eli, and when Eli looks over at me, he tugs on his earlobe. "Chevy, you aren't patched in yet."

Anger kicks me hard in the chest. "Are you kidding me? I risked my life and this is how I'm treated?"

"How do you want to be treated?" Eli asks like he can't see I'm thirty seconds from flipping the table.

"With respect."

"Then you're saying you want to be part of this club? That when we hand you a cut you'd accept without hesitation, because we know how your mom feels about us and we know how you feel about her. We also know that Violet broke up with you over us. It's a shit thing for us to ask, but when push comes to shove, are you able to handle being a part of this club when the two women you love the most are going to hate you for it?

"Because when you become a member, you understand what's said in this room, stays in this room. That anything pertaining to the club stays club business. Even when doing so causes problems for you in other areas of your life. Can you handle that?"

Violet

Thanks to Chevy and me being kidnapped, Cyrus's log cabin and the clubhouse across the yard are crawling with Reign of Terror members. They flow in and out of both buildings like the busy worker bees that they are. There are men who belong to this chapter, and men who belong to other chapters. Most of them took turns watching over my hospital room, the hallway leading to my hospital room and every entrance to the hospital. I should feel gratitude, but I can't help the twinge of malice.

If it weren't for this MC, I never would have been kidnapped.

Brandon sits in the chair in front of me on Cyrus's porch and he's gone into excruciating detail about *Jurassic World*. It's not the first time he's seen it. In fact, I've lost count of how many times I've watched it with him, but he saw it with Oz and Razor while I was in the hospital and Brandon needs to feel like I didn't miss anything while I was gone.

He wants a pet raptor. Yes, he understands they aren't real, but Brandon likes to live in pretend worlds sometimes and more often than not I indulge him in stepping a toe into his fantasy realms, if only because reality is too exhausting.

I used to tell him no on the pet raptor, as if such a thing could really happen. But after this past week, I wonder if science could get on the ball, create one, and if so, how much rabies shots for it would cost. That is if genetically engineered, fictional raptors can get rabies. I bet I wouldn't have been kidnapped if my pet raptor was riding shotgun.

The front door squeaks open and Mom and Oz's mom, Rebecca, step out onto the porch. They're laughing and they hold trays full of meat and cheeses for sandwiches. They glance over at me and their giggles fade. Rebecca still smiles, but Mom's grin falters. Just a fraction, but enough that I caught it.

"Are you hungry, Violet?" Mom asks.

I shake my head no, and she frowns completely.

"Let us know when you are hungry, and we'll bring you some food and something to drink," Rebecca says.

"I'll get it for her," Brandon says. My heart squeezes, then drops. He hasn't let me out of his sight since I was brought to Eli's this morning from the hospital. "I'll take care of her."

Rebecca winks good-naturedly at him. "And you'll do a good job, too."

She goes down the stairs and Mom follows her because Mom likes to follow. Brandon resumes his description of the raptor cage.

I stopped talking after my conversation with Justin. Don't know why. Didn't plan on it. In fact, I wasn't aware I was staying quiet until the second day of my stay at the hospital. They brought in a shrink who diagnosed me with Acute Stress Disorder. I guess it's like PTSD, but they can't diagnose PTSD unless I've had these types of symptoms for a long time.

Pigpen got excited because he made me grin when he told me he thought PTSD stood for Probably There's Something wrong but Dunno what.

Amen to that.

I talked to Chevy. At least I think I did. I haven't really had a chance to see him since the first night at the hospital, at least not without an audience. I did talk to the shrink, though, and it caught him off guard that I was willing to mumble a few words to him and not much to anyone else. After not talking, it's weird to start again.

Maybe pride's in the way. People want me to talk and now that silence is present it feels like a loss to open my mouth and do what everyone desires.

Won't lie—I don't like losing. Never have. Not that this is some sort of a game or competition, but doing what the club wishes, what my mother wishes...at least this is something I can control.

Speaking.

Sounds like something a dog should do. Speak, girl. Sit. Now shake. Roll over so I can rub your belly. Do you like that? How about if I scratch behind the ears? Go fetch, girl.

I'm giving you attention now, but you're not as smart as me and won't notice when I leave you to go do something real important and you're too weak to be a real companion. Now stay here while I go. Don't move and be right here with your tongue hanging out and tail wagging when I get back.

You're such a good girl.

Speak.

Girl.

Yep, not happening.

Mom doesn't mind being a dog. She likes being told to sit and stay. Likes it when someone pats her head and gives her attention and then is fine with being left behind to sit in front of the fire waiting for her master to return home.

I imagine she'd be a labradoodle because she's fancy like that. Specifically bred to be something different than the raw rest of us. Hypoallergenic. Cute and pretty and squishable.

Like right now she's across the yard flittering about the clubhouse helping the other "Old Ladies" make dinner. It's a warm day, so the bay doors of the clubhouse are rolled back and I can see most of what's going on from the porch.

Mom wears her Terror Gypsy cut. It's black leather like the men's cut, but there's no half skull with fire blazing out the eyes on the back. Just the name of the women's support group, Terror Gypsy, and a single patch that contains the name of the member they're an old lady to. Mom's patch says Frat. Still causes my chest to ache whenever I see his name.

Even though he's dead, Mom will always be a Terror Gypsy. Just like I'll always pay for this MC's sins if I stay in this godforsaken town.

It's the old ladies' job to support their men and support the club the men love. They're woman and can never be a part of the Reign of Terror. The most respect they'll receive is that cut and a single patch underneath.

Sit, girl.

Now stay.

Speak.

No, thank you.

"Is it my fault you were kidnapped, Vi?"

My head jerks in Brandon's direction. His cheeks are flushed red and his blue eyes are watery. In the background, there's a growl of motorcycles as I slip my legs off the swing. Pain spikes through my knee, but I ignore it and grab my brother's hands. Brandon is worth speaking to. "No."

"I'm scared it is."

"It's not."

"Then whose fault is it? It has to be somebody's fault."

The crazy coiled within me unravels and I lean toward my brother. The Terror. They're to blame.

"Stone," Oz calls. "Come play with us."

Brandon lights up. He loves playing football with the guys. Makes him feel accepted, normal and loved. All things I try to make him feel, but somehow fail at providing.

Then it's like someone blew out the sole candle in the room. He doesn't want to leave me. To be honest, I don't really want him to leave me either, but I don't want him moping around over what happened. I need to be strong for him.

"Go on." I give a smile I hope appears real. "Go play. I'll watch from here."

Brandon bounds down the stairs and jogs across the yard to where Oz and Razor are waiting for him. Oz tosses him the ball and the two go off for the open field. Razor, on the other hand, hangs back and he's watching me. My forehead furrows.

Razor and I are close. Not like me and Chevy, and not like siblings who hate each other like me and Oz. We're friends. Used to be great friends, but life became complicated after Dad died and Razor fell into the realm of messy.

He's watching me, like he's waiting—because he knows me—for a reaction? I scan the yard searching for what I'm missing and then my head tilts. Cyrus, Eli, Pigpen and other guys from the board are heading into the clubhouse and Chevy's with them.

The guys from the board have been MIA. Now they return and Chevy's with them? Hell, no. They are not leaving me out of this.

Ignoring my crutches, I hop down the stairs on one foot and then half walk, half limp for the clubhouse. They've been gone about our kidnapping and there's no way they're going to talk to Chevy without me. Like him surviving, his life, is worth more.

Razor strolls up beside me. Strolls, because I'm angry-hobbling and my full throttle is his stroll. He assesses me head to toe as he keeps pace. "Where're you going?"

A glare. That's all I've got for him and it causes him to chuckle. Razor's taller than me, but not by much. He's blond hair, blue eyes, most girls' daydream in real-life form, but he's just as dangerous as he is pretty. "They aren't going to let you into Church."

Nope. They won't. Odds are I won't even make it to the stairs. They have guys whose job is to hang out in the clubhouse and appear like they're cool and calm and just hanging out, but they're there to make sure no one reaches the boardroom. Even if I do make it, the door will be locked, but I'll be damned before I allow myself to be shunned.

"Ah, hell." It's Oz, and he's muttering it from behind me. Seconds later he's on my other side. "What's she doing?"

Razor shrugs. "Ask her."

"They aren't going to let you into Church," Oz says. Seriously, when they're indoctrinated into the club and receive a cut, do they reprogram their minds to speak alike, too?

"I told her that," Razor responds.

"Then why is she still heading in that direction?"

Razor loses the humor and his eyes grow so cold I shiver. "You going to tell her no?"

Oz's lips thin out as he continues to walk beside me. We enter the clubhouse and we catch the other members' attention immediately. A few look pleased, like my voluntarily limping in here is the long-awaited prodigal-daughter-returning-home moment they've all claimed they have been waiting for since Dad died, but they are sadly mistaken.

"How are we playing this, Razor?" Oz asks.

"We say pretty please when we reach the door?"

I snort, because I can't remember the last time Razor used the words *pretty* or *please*. I'm sure that, until this moment, the combination has never been used by him before.

"Hitting brothers is out of the question," Oz says.

Razors laughs. It's brief, it's dark and it caused the hairs on the back of my neck to rise. "You worry too much about rules."

"You don't worry enough."

We're halfway through and the conversation that had been taking place in the clubhouse has died. Near the pool table, two guys straighten from the shots they were lining up.

Dust places his pool stick on the table. He's a good guy. Two years older than me, but he's one of those guys who you know is an old soul the moment you meet him. Seen too much, and from what Dad had mentioned, Dust had done too much to solve his seeing too much.

Dust's dad owned a car parts place a county over and Dust used to help my dad with installation. But when I see Dust, I'm back at the funeral home. Tears streamed down my face and I couldn't make them stop. He handed me tissues. Only man to do that. It was a simple gesture and one I'll always remember.

"Hey, Violet," Dust says. "Your mom's in the kitchen."

Nothing from me, Razor or Oz. We just keep going and he slides into our path.

"Your mom said you shouldn't be on your leg. Why don't you sit and I'll find her for you, or if there's someone else you want, I'll try to get them."

Try.

Yep, for me it's always a try.

Razor guides my elbow and changes places with me so I

can maneuver around a table to avoid Dust and possibly duck through to the stairs. In front of Dust, Razor stops, slouches and shoves his hands into his front pockets. Nothing about the way Razor's eyes bore into Dust's suggests he's casual.

"Don't want problems," Dust says, "but you know the rules. She's not allowed in Church."

I'm still going, and when the next person in line tries to block my path, Oz becomes the human shield.

Chairs crack and bar stools squeak as guys rise to their feet. Their job is to make sure the rules aren't broken. Doesn't matter if I'm dropped to the ground and shattered as long as the rules stay intact.

"Any of you touch her, talk to her or attempt to stop her and I'll kick your fucking ass," Razor says like he's ordering off a dollar menu at a fast-food restaurant. Like it's not a big deal he just risked himself for me. "She's had way too many people manhandling her for any of us to give her shit."

The air in the room is heavy with tension with each continued step of my good leg and drag of the bad. I reach the door of the stairway and I glance back. Football plays on the TV over the bar, fallen leaves scratch and scatter on the concrete outside, but otherwise it's silent.

No one is happy. I've gone rogue in their eyes, but not one man has the balls to stop me. I should be happy, but I'm not. I shouldn't have had to be kidnapped to finally earn some respect.

Another scan of the room and my stomach churns. That's not respect in their eyes. It's empty pity—even Oz and Razor.

I'm the girl who was kidnapped, the girl Chevy had to give himself up for to protect. I heard the men from the club whispering as they stood outside my hospital room door. Funny how when you don't talk, people think you can no longer hear.

Screw them all.

The staircase is longer and steeper than I remember, but I make it, and when I reach the second floor, I breathe in and out several times to catch my breath and stare at the locked door. My hand falls to my chest and the comfort I'm searching for—my father's cross—it isn't there. Just like my bracelets aren't. Just like I've lost any sense of safety and security. The Riot stole all that from me because of the Terror.

There's protocol for them to open that door and I don't know what it is. It's more than a knock. More than a series of knocks.

But I want in this room and I won't be ignored.

CHEVY

Can I handle that? I've been hurting Mom for years and Violet for months over making the club happy. Am I all in with the club? I don't know, but can I handle keeping my mouth shut so I can learn what's going on with the Riot? Hell... "Yes."

Eli does a sweep of the table and each man nods in agreement with whatever he's asking.

"Then we're trusting you," Eli says. "Giving you a chance to be your own man during this. If it wasn't for the fact I promised Mom before she died that we wouldn't patch you in until you turned eighteen, you'd be walking out of this room with a cut on your back."

"We're proud of you." My grandfather's voice is rough. "For protecting Stone, for protecting Violet, for standing strong when other men would crumble."

One by one, like dominoes on the downfall, the men gathered around hit their fists against the table. It's a show of support, a show of brotherhood, and my chest feels tight.

Too many emotions flood me and I have to lean back in my chair to keep myself under control.

This moment right here—it's what Mom doesn't understand. Doesn't get that I've watched this type of solidarity my entire life and all I've craved is to be a part of it. To be more than Cyrus's grandson, Eli's nephew, James's ghost in living flesh. More than just being a blood destiny. I've wanted to belong because of who I am, because I'm wanted…and now it's happening.

I suck in a breath and can't seem to find words to respond to their support, so instead I nod. It's short, but it happened and Eli nods back.

"Don't make us regret this decision," Eli says. "We're treating you like one of our own, so we expect you to act like it even though the cut isn't on your back yet. What we talk about here, stays here."

"Understood." Noted and written in stone.

"The Riot voluntarily talked with the police and let us in when they did it." Eli didn't even bother with a pause. Just went balls to the wall. "They're sticking with their story, claiming that the kidnapping was on Fiend, and they even went a step further."

"How's that?" I lean forward, arms on the table.

Eli mirrors my position. "Skull said after they dropped you two off and went home to clean house, he found out Fiend hadn't misunderstood anything. Fiend was upset our clubs have been trying for peace since Emily's visit and that he and a few other disgruntled members went after you to start a war between us."

My blood runs cold. This past summer, Eli's daughter— Skull's granddaughter—visited Kentucky for the first time since her mother left the state running like she was on fire in order to keep her and Emily safe from our clubs. Emily's mom didn't trust the Riot and was scared the Terror couldn't protect her and Emily. When Emily came to town because Eli's mom, Olivia, was dying, it caused a pot of anger that had been simmering between our clubs for years to boil over. "You think it's true?"

Eli gives a sloppy shrug. "Who knows, but I've been dealing with Skull since Meg told me she was pregnant with Emily. Bastard hates me. Have to say the emotion goes both ways. All the shit we've been through over the years, he never voluntarily walked into a police station and he's never talked club business with us or the law.

"The police feel Skull should have called them when he found you and Violet and they find it suspicious he had his son drop the two of you off on the dirt road."

"You don't?" I ask.

"Not thrilled with it," Eli responds, "but at the same time, police aren't the Riot's knee-jerk reaction and they did get you home quick after they found you."

All a blur, but the moment Skull found us we were up the steps, Violet in the bathroom, and the phone call to Eli happened shortly after.

"The police said they could try to charge Skull and his son, but they said the charges could be tough to make stick. They're leaving that up to us." Eli settles his dark eyes straight on me. "And we're leaving that up to you."

I hear everything Eli's saying and not saying. They'll support me if I want to lock up Skull and his son, but it also sounds like we're on the verge of harmony with a club that's caused us problems since my birth. Arresting them could kill that fragile peace.

"Can I think about it?" I ask.

"Yeah. The decision will need to be made, but you have time."

"What about Fiend and the others with him?" The temperature in the room drops thirty degrees and it's all thanks to me. That son of a bitch needs to never see daylight again due to a cell or because he's dead. Either option works for me and I'm fine being the one responsible for the punishment.

"He shot at Violet," I remind them. "Point-blank shot at her. Would have killed her if Skull and his son hadn't come in when they did. Plus the fucking asshole hit her. Multiple times. He made her bleed." He needs to bleed.

The air in the room is so charged that electricity is practically crackling around us. Each man has that determined yet faraway expression on their face. Each of us imagining how to skewer the bastard and make him cry.

Eli drums his fingers against the table. "Fiend and the guys working with him are gone. Skull seems to have no idea where they're at, but he says he's looking. We told Skull if he values this peace, that if his club finds them before we or the police do, he's to turn them over to the police. We will get justice for you and Violet. Those men will go to prison."

My body pulsates. The people who hurt Violet are free and that's not acceptable. "We've got to find them."

"We will," Cyrus says. "We're looking, the police are looking and in theory the Riot are, as well. Got to be honest, though, we have to find them before the Riot does. What they did makes them traitors and traitors don't survive in the Riot."

"Whatever you or the police need, I'll do it." Anything to make Violet safe again.

Affirmations around the table. A promise from each man to see this through, to do anything to help me nail the bastards who did the unthinkable.

"I've got a question." Pigpen flicks a paper clip he'd been

messing with in my direction. "Did Skull mention what it was he wanted to talk to you about?"

All eyes on me and the high I'd been feeling from being a part of something bigger than myself plummets. I'd been able to avoid this at the hospital because of Mom being around, but there's no dodging it now. But to be honest, it shouldn't be evaded. What Skull told me is heavy, and if these men are truly my brothers, bringing it up won't change a thing.

My grandfather's watching me. Expectant. Waiting. Patient in his own way. He's been a father to me. Doing all the crap dads are supposed to do. Taught me how to hook a worm so it won't fall off, unhook a fish, how to gut it open and fry it. Taught me how to respect a girl, open doors, treat her right. Taught me to give my all and then how to dig deeper when I don't think there's anything left.

Another thing Cyrus taught me: to spill it instead of being a coward. "Skull told me my dad was a traitor. That he worked for the Riot while being patched in to the Terror. He said the detective in Louisville recently figured it out and it wouldn't be long until he told you."

An inferno. Cyrus's face is cool, but his eyes are a raging fire. "My son was no traitor."

Don't know how to respond, so I keep going, searching the table for support from someone, and instead I'm met with relatives of the grim reaper. "Skull said he wanted to talk to me before you guys found out. Out of respect for my father. He said James was a friend of his, a good man..." And there's nothing else to say.

"Do you believe him?" Cold. Deadly. Not a voice Cyrus has used with me before.

"No." But it bothers me Skull brought it up. Bothers me he said there's a woman out there who has proof. Bothers me my father isn't buried in Snowflake. Lots of things bothering me and none of them are wise to mention.

I just survived a kidnapping. Not feeling suicidal at the moment.

Multiple cell phones chime and I jerk as if brought out of a trance. Eli pulls his cell out of his pocket, then whips his head when someone bangs on the door. Not just banging, kicking the hell out of it. The door shakes within the frame.

Man O' War shoots to his feet and Eli shows Cyrus his phone.

The banging continues, with such force I check to see if the hinges are holding. Even though no one at the table is freaking out and there weren't gunshots from downstairs, adrenaline pours into my veins.

"Open the door," Cyrus says and angles his chair so he can get a view of the door.

Man O' War pulls the door open and Violet barrels in. A flash of red and she catches herself on the wall as she stumbles. I'm out of my chair so fast it rocks, but I become locked in place. Violet possesses a superpower and it paralyzes everyone in this room, including me.

Wrath.

She wears it like no one else I know.

"Are you serious?" she spits. "You bring Chevy up to talk and not me?"

"Women aren't allowed in Church," Cyrus says. "And you know better than to be interrupting us. You were raised better than this."

Violet pushes off the wall and hobbles toward Cyrus. "You mean women aren't allowed unless they're here to clean, right? Or is this the one place you do that yourself? Know what? Don't answer. Chevy was kidnapped and so was I.

Anything you have to say to him, you say to me. I have just as much, if not more, at stake here as Chevy."

Cyrus folds his hands over his stomach. "Maybe we weren't discussing the kidnapping. Maybe we were discussing Chevy's prospect period and his eventual patching in."

Violet's eyes land on me and the pain written on her face punches me in the stomach. She then shakes her hurt away. "No, this is over the kidnapping and all of you need to pull your heads out of your misogynistic asses and tell me what the hell is happening."

Pigpen walks around the table, and as he nears Violet, she stumbles back, but he's faster. With one longer step, he engulfs Violet in a hug and lifts her into the air.

She slaps his shoulder. "Put me down, you fucking asshole!"

"She's back!" Pigpen rocks her like she's a doll and then gently deposits her back on the ground. He places his hands on either side of her face, looks into her eyes with that crazy-ass smile on his face, then kisses the top of her head. "It's good to have you back, kid."

Violet smacks his hands off her face. "Get off me."

He winks. "Love you, too."

"Are you going to let me in on this or not?" she demands. "Or are you going to continue to play your reindeer games with the Riot and let people like me be collateral damage?"

I will them to tell her. I think of how Violet fought not only for me, but for her brother. The cold loneliness of the basement. The way we depended upon each other to survive. Violet's right, and if they don't let her in, they're wrong.

Eli stands, and when he walks in her direction, she lifts her hand. "Touch me and I'll knee you in the fucking balls."

Knowing she's serious, he allows her space. "You shouldn't

be on your leg. Strutting across the yard, climbing staircases, kicking the hell out of the door isn't going to help you heal."

"Do you ever bother listening to me, Eli, or is there a translation function in your brain that screws up whatever I say into you hearing what you wish I would have said?"

Eli cracks his neck to the left. "Why can't you see all we're trying to do, all we ever try to do, is take care of and protect you?"

"Protect me? I was coming home from a football game. You know, being a normal teenager, and I was kidnapped by your rival motorcycle club. That's not safe and posting men at my door at the hospital because you're scared they'll make another grab at me isn't protecting me. That's called cleaning up your mess. The only thing that is going to keep me and my family safe is knowledge. It's up to you whether or not I'm worthy enough in your eyes to let me know what's going on."

Eli and Cyrus exchange a long glance and Cyrus sighs. "I'll talk about it with the board."

My shoulders sag and Violet turns away in disgust. That was a nice way of saying no-fucking-way. She's out the door, using the wall as a crutch, and I'm chasing after. Cyrus grabs my wrist and I pause.

"I'm worried about her," he says.

So am I. "She wants the same thing I want. To know that the bastards who hurt us won't do it again."

"We'll make sure she's safe, but I don't trust her to keep whatever she learns to herself. She's a loose cannon."

And I'm not.

"I need you to keep an eye on her. Tell us anything you think we should know."

I shift and Cyrus releases me. He's asking me to spy on Violet and report back. If I were a prospect, even a member, this would be an order. Considering how they just told me they're trusting me, this is an order. But I don't like how his request settles in the pit of my stomach.

"Do you understand me?" Cyrus asks.

I nod, then my cell pings. Damn it all to hell. Coming home was supposed to make life easier, but I traded the dark basement for being pulled apart alive. It's Mom and she's not listening to the club or to me.

Mom: Brandy called. She's down several girls and needs me to bartend. I need money and life needs to go back to normal. I'm going in. Love you. Have fun tonight.

Mom texts this like she thinks I'll drop back and let her head in on a Friday night by herself. Yeah. Not going to happen.

Violet

There are too many people in my life who drive me insane and too many people who make me feel like I should punch the hell out of anyone who comes near me.

My mother, at the moment, is one of the people I want to throttle. I don't throttle her, though. Instead, I limp across the guest bedroom in Cyrus's log cabin, grab all my shirts my mother had "thoughtfully" hung in a closet and then shove them all into a suitcase.

Evidently, my mother believed I would be thrilled to stay at Cyrus's for… I don't know…with the way that she packed she was set on us staying forever.

"You can't leave." Mom stands in the doorway and she twists her fingers. She is such a paradox. Blond hair, blue eyes, as fragile as a hundred-year-old crystal glass and she wears a black biker cut. "We're throwing a party for you and Chevy tonight."

"Do I look like I'm in the mood for a party?"

"It's not going to be a crazy one," Mom explains. "It's dinner. With all the families. Everyone wants to see you."

As long as I can remember, Mom never attended a "crazy" party. She'd be at the clubhouse long enough for the potluck dinners, but then at eight in the evening, like the good little dutiful wife she was, she packed me and Brandon up and brought us home, but Dad stayed.

Dad always stayed.

As I got older, I also stayed. Everyone believed Oz, Razor, Chevy and I went on with our lives away from the clubhouse, but we were curious, so we often circled back and watched from a distance.

My stalking days ended when I saw Dad do a body shot off some girl with no top, bikini briefs, and who was a good fifteen years younger than Mom. First time in my life I felt like someone had punched me. First time in my life I lost respect for my father.

"We need to go home."

"Please don't act this way. Especially not now. You're talking and being normal again."

Normal again. I will never be normal again. My suitcase is overflowing and I shove in the pieces of clothing flopping out. Using all my weight, I smash down the top of the suitcase and force the zipper to go around. "It's Chevy they want to see. He's the savior they all want to pat on the back."

On the dresser is my jacket. My favorite one. It's brown and leather and it's the one Dad gave me for Christmas before he died. He bought it for me because I told him once the smell of leather made me think of him. Around the same time, I had also told him I didn't like how he had been on the road more than he had been home.

Dad had written on the tag that this present meant he would be with me all the time. I pick up the jacket and lift it to my nose. An inhale in, and while it smells like leather, it doesn't really smell like him.

God, I miss him.

A hug. I can't express what I would do for his hug. To feel his strong arms around me. To hear him say my name. For the constant, throbbing, dull ache in my chest to be gone.

I try to imagine what he would say to me. What he would do. Dad loved me. That I know without a doubt, but would he have loved me enough to walk away from the club because his club hurt me? Or would he have stubbornly held on to the club's ways and rules?

"I brought it for you," Mom says. "I know you wear this jacket when you're feeling down."

"Did Dad ever talk to you about the club?" I ask. "About what he did for them?"

"Your dad was the accountant for the security company." She leaves out he was also the accountant for the club.

"Yeah, but he traveled, too. Why would an accountant need to travel? What was he doing?" I'm hunting, wondering if what Justin said was true. If my father really was the peace negotiator between the clubs.

Mom fidgets with the sleeve of her sweater, then picks lint off and drops it to the floor. "Your father didn't talk about specifics. Just that he had to go."

"And you didn't ask what he was doing? Where he was going?"

"Wasn't my place."

Of course it wasn't. That's not how Mom thinks.

Even though it's a warm day, I slip on the jacket, and when my hands run down the sides, I pause. Something's in the pocket and I'm not the type of girl who puts things there.

"Cyrus wants you, me and Brandon to stay here," Mom continues. "At least until they have this mess with the Riot straightened out."

Straightened out. Like the two clubs haven't been at war

for over eighteen years. I reach into my pocket and pull out a piece of paper. It has frayed edges, like it was torn out of a notebook. My forehead furrows. My English notebook sits on the desk along with my other schoolbooks. I flip the paper in my hand and the doodle of the flower is mine. It's what I do in my notebooks when I'm bored in class.

"I think we should listen," Mom continues. "Cyrus made a compelling argument. He doesn't mind us staying for a long time. I think he's lonely with Olivia being gone. It's like we're doing him a favor if we stay. We can take care of him and he'll take care of us."

A lot like the relationship Mom had with Dad, minus the love they shared and the way he kissed her after he walked in the house. Security. Dad offered security and now Cyrus is, too.

Tuning Mom out, I unfold the piece of paper. The handwriting, I don't recognize. The lines from the poem, I do. It was the assignment I missed in English class. I picked it up after class, thinking I'd be able to have it completed by Monday. Best laid plans...

Two roads diverged in a yellow wood, And sorry I could not travel both.

I like this poem. You probably have a lot of makeup work to do. Sorry about that. Forgot how high school sucks. Also sorry about your knee. Never what we wanted. We just want peace. Remember which path you need to travel. We'll be in touch soon.

My heart beats so loudly Mom has to hear it, but if she does, she doesn't acknowledge it. "They feel terrible about what's happened and they want to keep you safe."

My hands shake and I ball the paper in my fist, then shove

it back into my pocket. "When did you bring my stuff over? My notebook? My jacket?"

"The day you were found. Why?"

We're not safe here. We're not safe anywhere. The Riot—they're everywhere.

CHEVY

Eli's truck wheezes as I ease into the Shamrock's parking lot and I half expect it to let out a backfire shot when I cut the engine, but instead it heaves into silence. Two motorcycles rumble in behind me and park in open spots. It's Pigpen and Dust. They're part of the volunteers tailing me and Violet until the board feels we're safe.

Safe.

Not sure what that means anymore.

Shamrock's neon street sign is so bright that the stars can't be seen in the dark night. It's only seven, but feels like midnight.

"I could have driven myself." Mom glances over at her side mirror, no doubt checking out Pigpen watching us.

"You're the one who said it was time to go back to normal. Me driving you on Friday and Saturday nights is the norm."

Mom opens her purse and shifts the contents from one side to the other. "If it was a normal Friday night, you would have been at school all week. You'd be at the football game and wouldn't have been able to drive me in. If it was a normal Friday night, you'd be sleeping in your bed at home and not at Cyrus's and two members of the Terror wouldn't be here. If it was a normal Friday night, I wouldn't spend most of my shift tonight wondering if you're going to show to pick me up or if I'll walk out of here to find out someone took you again."

Mom throws her purse to the floor of the truck. It makes a thud and then we sit. Letting the weight of the past week crush us both. Can't imagine what it was like for her. Sitting at the bar, waiting. Each minute that passed upping the odds I wasn't coming to get her and that I wasn't returning home.

"I'm sorry," I say.

"It's not your fault."

"It's not the Terror's either."

Her lack of a response expresses her disagreement. Even suggests a couple of curse words she still refuses to say in front of me, but that I've heard her utter to a few asshole customers.

"After all you've been through," she says, "I don't know how to make you understand how dangerous they are."

"I'm home. I'm fine."

She whips her head in my direction. "Fine? You're not fine. The bruises may be fading, but when I look in your eyes, I don't see my son. Violet may be the one who went quiet, but you're not acting the same either. You don't laugh. You don't smile."

I curl the keys into my palm and the pain from the edges is welcomed. "It's barely been a week. Violet was just released today. What do you expect from me?"

"That you'll wake up and see that the road you're choosing is one that is going to shatter my heart." Her voice breaks at the end and it's like someone has reached into my chest and crushed *my* heart.

This is my mom. The woman who has raised me on

her own selling drinks to men who treat her like shit. The woman who has attended every practice, peewee football game, JV and then varsity game known to man. The woman who has nursed cuts, broken bones and a broken heart.

"What do you want me to do?" I ask in such a low tone I'm not sure she heard it.

"You know what I want."

A life away from the Terror. What had she said once? Football, a girl, a few high school parties, the son who goes away to college. Somebody else's normal.

"Days like today I wish I could go back and slap the girl I was in high school. Tell her to take school more seriously. Tell her to take the advanced math course over the basic. Tell her that boys weren't the answer, but really the problem. Maybe if I had taken my life more seriously, then I wouldn't have had to rely on the Terror so much when you were younger. Then maybe you wouldn't be as close to them as you are now. I should have done better."

"You've done a great job raising me."

"Bartending, waitressing, being away from you at night and on the weekends. Just because I wanted to be the one to take you to school in the morning. Because I wanted to be the mom who brought the cupcakes on party day and then picked you up. Because it's the job that made me financially free from the Terror. But it wasn't enough. I should have been home. I should have a better job. I should have found someone else to take care of you. I should have never relied on the Terror."

I wonder if she gets tired of the same fight. "They're my family."

"But that doesn't make them a good family. Even James knew that."

Lightning strike to the chest. "What?"

Mom grabs her purse and places her hand on the door handle. "Nothing. I'm just mad."

I'm not ready to let that go, especially with Skull's accusation still hanging around me like a noose, but most wars are won and lost on timing. Pushing her on my father now, a subject she hates to begin with, would be the equivalent of charging a field full of defenders without a helmet.

"Bad things happen to normal people," I say.

"They do," she concedes. "But not like this. Never like this. Stay in the truck, Chevy. I need a few minutes by myself before I start work."

Meaning she needs to find a way to center herself before she flirts her way into tips to pay for rent. The passenger-side door squeaks open and Mom leaves. Kills me not to walk in with her. My skin crawls with the idea I'm not eyeballing the men at the bar. Scaring the hell out of them so they'll pass on to others not to mess with her.

But she needs space and I need to quiet the roaring in my head. Mom doesn't go straight in. Like a taunt she leans against the side of the building and has her head tilted up as if there's something to see. Me? I wait.

The clubhouse is so packed full of people I have to park on the grass closer to the narrow path that leads from the main road to Cyrus's place. The moonlight glints on row after row of motorcycles and here and there men stand in groups near them. To the right, a couple is doing the deed on a Harley Softail.

I ignore them and lift my chin to the guys who call out my name. Pigpen and Dust have already told me, multiple times, that lots of brothers are ready and willing to buy me as many beers as I can drink tonight, tomorrow night, forever. All I need to do is walk into the clubhouse and make my way to the bar, but I don't feel like drinking.

Before I left to pick up Mom, Eli promised me he'd keep Violet safe. I trust him, but there's a hole inside me since she left my bed at the hospital and I'm damn cold with the wind blowing through it.

The trees circling the log cabin and the clubhouse have messed-up shadows. Half of the trees still bushy with leaves. The other half skeletons extending their spiny branches like fingers into the night.

The porch light to the log cabin isn't on, but the windows have that warm glow I used to associate with Olivia. If she was in the house, the lights were on. She told all of us a hundred times that the light would be left on for us whenever we decided to return home. I always thought that meant she would be there when I stepped past her threshold.

Olivia died this summer. Her death still makes my chest hurt.

Two prospects stand guard at the bottom of the porch steps. They aren't there to keep Violet in. They're there to make sure no one takes her again.

It's a family party, and if she entered that clubhouse, she'd be hugged and worshipped by almost every guy there, but Violet's not into club parties. Most people think it's because of her father's death, but I know better.

I climb the steps, and as I reach for the door, a silhouette down the wraparound porch catches my attention. Violet sits on the bench, her leg propped up on a wooden crate. She stares out onto the field, the crowd, the chaos, the bonfire closest to the cabin.

I grew up with Violet. Played in the mud with her, caught fireflies with her, even got into a few shouting matches over bad calls at kickball. But I'll never forget the first time Violet stole my breath.

Razor, Oz and I sat on this porch, holding welcome-home signs Olivia forced us to make, when Violet's mom pulled up in the minivan. We were about to start high school and Violet had spent the summer at the shore with her mom and brother. The back door to the van slid open and I felt like I had been born.

Until that moment, the world had been black-and-white and I had never known color. And then a vibrant explosion. Her hair was longer, a deeper red than I had remembered, and the ends were curled. Her blue eyes were bright, like a calm sea, and when she saw me, Violet smiled.

Smiled.

The type of smile that men drive all night in a blinding rainstorm on their bike to see. The type of smile that keep men fighting brutal wars for years in the vain hope of seeing it again. The type of smile that made me come to my feet, because if I didn't, I'd fall to my knees.

She smiled.

Not much I wouldn't give to see her smile at me like that again. Hell, doesn't have to be at me. Just for her to genuinely smile.

The firelight dances across Violet's face and highlights her hair. She's still the most beautiful girl on the planet with those long lashes and perfect red lips. Just right for kissing.

My blood runs warm with the thoughts of all those nights we had kissed. Some nights were sweet. Some nights we could lie in bed holding each other forever. Then there was the night after our big homecoming game last year. In the backseat of the Chevelle, rain pattered onto the hood, her body was nestled under mine and we both moved, kissed and gasped to the point every window fogged.

Since the night the hospital staff forced Violet back into her own room, I've felt lost, and with each step toward her, it's like returning home.

Violet glances up at me, then at the open spot next to her. I ease down beside her, and the moment my shoulder brushes against hers, I close my eyes and take a deep breath as if I've been underwater for hours.

I extend my arm, hand up, and she laces her fingers with mine. Our thighs are locked tight and I lower our hands so that they rest on both my leg and hers. Peace. This is the closest I've felt to peace in months.

Are we together? I don't know. I'd bet Violet doesn't know either. Her father's still dead. I'm still on track to join the club. All the problems we had before the kidnapping still exist.

"How's your mom?" she asks.

The back of my head hits the wood of the house. "Fine."

"Really?"

Violet was the one person I didn't have to lie to. Even when telling the truth broke us up. She's the type of person who demands bullshit be checked at the door. "No. She's pissed."

"Want to trade moms?"

A smile spreads across my face. This conversation is familiar and familiar feels good.

"They're waiting on you," she says. "Lots of guys ready to buy you beer. Pat you on the back. Tell you how wonderful you are."

"They are."

"You should go to them."

"I will." But not now. Especially since Violet hasn't let go.

The bonfire crackles, and with a pop, burning embers dance into the sky. Violet flinches and I rub my finger along hers.

"We're not safe here," she says. "We're never going to be safe anywhere ever again."

I should tell her she's wrong. That she's safe here, surrounded by the club, but after sitting in that black, cold basement with her in my arms, wondering what the hell the sick bastards upstairs were going to do when they decided to return, I can't promise her a thing.

The night's too dark, the woods surrounding us too daunting, the knowledge I can't do a damn thing about what actions other people take a kick in the gut. Can't promise her the Riot won't make another grab, can't promise her some psychopath won't make a Crock-Pot full of nails and take her out during a football game, can't promise some nut job isn't going to take a gun to school and shoot people in the cafeteria.

I can't promise her any of that, but I can hold her hand. I can sit beside her now. I can be here, I can be with her, I can, just for a few minutes, just be.

Violet moves, a readjustment, and I expect her to pull away. But instead, she leans further into me, her head on my shoulder, and her sweet scent becomes a warm blanket.

No other place I'd rather be in the world right now. No place at all.

Violet

"Violet." Chevy's deep voice vibrates against my temple and his fingertips graze along my arm. Warmth and fantastic goose bumps. His caress calls for me to cuddle closer to him and not to participate in any activity that would lead me away.

It's not the first time he's woken me up this way. Sometimes, I'd fake sleep just so he would brush his lips on my skin, mumble my name and send pleasing shock waves through my body. I've missed his voice. Missed his touch. Missed him.

"Violet, do you want me to carry you inside?"

My mind's a fog and I'm slow as I lift my head from Chevy's shoulder. The muscles in my neck are tight, and as I move, the rest of my body protests. Tingles in my arm, and my braced knee has become stiff and pulses with a dull ache. The cheek that was exposed to the air is now frozen and the other side of my face is hot and creased with the imprint of the folds in Chevy's shirt.

I stretch my arms and his leather jacket slips from my body

and onto my lap. My eyebrow rises and Chevy sheepishly shrugs. "Air temperature dropped."

It has, but that hasn't stopped the party raging in the yard. In the clubhouse, a group of men roar with laughter and then a woman's cackle comes thirty seconds behind. That hyena giggle was too late and awkward and probably because she didn't get the joke the first time. "What time is it?"

"After midnight. Mom texted. Bar shut down early. Busted water pipe in the bathroom."

Which means he needs to pick her up.

"Want me to help you back inside?"

I run a hand through my thick mane of hair and use my fingers to comb out the tangles near the ends. The slight prick of pain from the pull helps wake me. Do I want to go back to sleep? If it means his warm body beside me in bed, then yes, but I'm not sure I'm ready for the fallout that admission would create. "Can I come with you?"

Chevy blinks. "To pick Mom up?"

"Yeah, I've gone with you before." Multiple times. I had a strict curfew with my own mom, ten o'clock, but I had a fantastic loophole—Olivia. I'd tell Mom I was staying the night with her and Olivia never cared how long I stayed out or who I was with.

You're a big girl and can take care of yourself, she'd tell me. *Your momma would let a boy run around with no curfew, I can guarantee that. No reason for breasts to be seen as a limitation, because they aren't.*

Wonder if Olivia would feel the same way now.

"I'd like that." He stands, and I grab my crutches before he has the chance to ask if I want to be carried to the truck.

I'm over being carried and wheeled around. Feels like a confirmation that Mom's been right about girls being weak. I may not feel safe anywhere ever again, but I still don't feel particularly like a damsel in distress. Girls locked in towers waiting for the knight to slay the dragon at the entrance wouldn't have survived that basement.

Halfway across the porch, I wince. Sore armpits.

"This guy on the team, after he broke his leg, taped small pillows to his crutches," Chevy says. "Tomorrow, I'll try to find something that will work."

Because that's the Chevy I fell for—the sweet guy who thinks of crutches and pillows. "Thank you."

"Anytime."

Chevy takes my crutches as I begin to hop down the stairs and the two prospects who had been frozen like gargoyles at the bottom of the steps spring to life. The taller one speaks. "Eli said the party's gotten rowdy. He saw you asleep, Violet, and didn't think you'd be coming down."

"We're not going to the party," Chevy answers. "Violet's heading with me to pick up Mom. I already texted Pigpen and Dust and they're heading with us."

"She's doing what?" Eli emerges from the darkness as if he were a mirage that took physical form and his expression proves he has a direct linkup to the demons that prance inside him.

"It's not a big deal," I say. "I'd like to go for a ride. Clear my head." Not be around so many guys from the Terror.

"You should ask your mom and she's inside asleep. So's your brother."

From this distance, I bet I could use the crutch to knock the hell out of his balls.

"Jesus, you're a wet blanket." Pigpen walks up from behind Eli and grins like he just escaped from prison. "Why are you giving the girl hell for wanting to go to an army bar at midnight? It's not like she told you she was going to kick puppies."

Pigpen winks at me. "You ready to roll? Or should I say hop?"

My glare informs him where he can shove hop. He waggles his eyebrows in response.

"It's just to pick up Mom," Chevy says. "I'll take her home, then I'll bring Violet back. I've done it a hundred times."

My chest aches. Normal. He's describing normal. A normal from before Dad died, but a normal nonetheless. It's what everyone wants, but I'm not sure if I'll feel normal again. At least not where it counts—deep on the inside where I can't even fake it or lie to myself.

"I don't know," Eli says.

"It's a good way to figure out if they're still after or tracking them," Pigpen says in a low voice. In a way that indicates he didn't want me to hear, but I'm too close to the situation for him to excuse himself. "Not many cars on the road. Won't take much to know if we see the same car repeatedly."

Eli shakes his head. "Violet stays here."

"For how long?" I snap. "A week? A month? Until I graduate? Or maybe you're going to homeschool me now. Will you let me go if I marry a club guy or will I be here until I die?"

The blank look Eli gives me tells me he doesn't know.

"Chevy was kidnapped, too, yet you're letting him leave."

"That's different—"

"How? Because he's a guy? Because he's strong and I'm weak?"

"I'm trying to protect you!" Eli roars.

"It doesn't matter!" I yell back. "I was still kidnapped. They still hurt me, and if they want to hurt me again, there is not a damn thing you can do about it! Nothing is stopping them from coming here. Nothing is standing between me and the Riot. Nothing! They've already proved that once, and if they want me, they'll take me again!"

This is it. This is my life. A constant watching over my shoulder for the bad guys. Eli wants me to tuck my tail between my legs, hobble back up the steps and stay safely inside the bubble he's trying to create, but he's not offering a solution to my problem. Just an illusion.

Eli leans toward me and smacks a hand to his chest. "I'm between you and them now."

Without breaking eye contact, I sarcastically shrug one shoulder up and then down. "You would have said you were between me and them before."

Pure anger pours from his eyes as he points at the cabin. "Inside the house. Now."

I could hop over to the truck, climb in, and Chevy won't take me because he's a club boy. And even if by some miracle he did start the truck, Pigpen and Dust would stand around it like human cement pillars. The good god almighty Eli has spoken. So let it be written. So let it be done.

Blood rushes to my cheeks as what's left of my pride is in shambles, yet I lift my chin in a silent "Fuck you." I hold out my open fingers and Chevy silently hands me my crutches.

"Do not fool yourself into thinking you're better than the Riot," I say. "I might not be shivering in a basement and I might not be bleeding where you can see it, but I'm still a prisoner."

I need to get home, find those account numbers, protect my family and then get the hell out of this town.

I turn, and because I can't catch a break, I hop up the stairs with absolutely no grace. Thanks to the Riot and the Terror, I can't even make a proper dramatic exit. I hobble into the cabin and slam the door behind me.

CHEVY

Violet: I can't sleep.

Me: You were asleep.

Violet: I know, but the buzzing is back.

Me: Did it go away?

A long pause.

Violet: Yes. But now it's back.

My heart stops in my chest. Yeah. The buzzing went away for me, too, when I held her on the porch. Me: I'll be there soon.

She doesn't respond and I don't need her to. Violet told me all I need to know.

It's three in the morning. I stayed at the bar to help Brandy and Mom clean up the water. Pigpen and Dust lent a hand. Now we're back and the party's over. Music quit playing over the loudspeakers. Only smoke and charred remains are left of the bonfires.

People still mill about. Some will head home later. Some will stay the night. I'm supposed to be staying in one of the nicer rooms on the second floor of the clubhouse, but I'm not feeling like following orders.

I trudge up the stairs and only lift my head long enough to acknowledge the new set of prospects guarding the cabin. Part of me understands what Eli's doing—protecting Violet until he knows she's safe—but I also understand Violet. She and I are beyond feeling safe.

The dark living room is only maneuverable thanks to memory and the light shining from the kitchen. Cyrus is in there, standing against the frame of the back door, searching the night and nursing a cup of coffee. No doubt he hears my combat boots thudding across the wooden floor, but he doesn't look up. He knows it's me and he knows who I'm here to see.

To the right is a room and the door is cracked open. Violet's mother is wrapped in blankets on the queen bed. Stone's arm is hanging off the twin. Across from that room is a closed door and I knock as I turn the knob.

Light's off, but Violet's face is illuminated by the flashing of color from the TV. She's under a pile of blankets, her head is propped up by her hand and a part of me warms at how her expression softens as I walk in.

"Hey," I say.

"Hey." It's a groggy voice, a sensual one. I recall her talking to me late at night on the phone using that same beautiful tone.

Since I've been home, I doze, sleep while part of my mind stays awake, but I slept deep with her in the hospital. Slept.

I'm betting Violet's the solution to many of my problems. Feels like I'm the solution to some of her problems, as well.

I enter, close the door behind me and sit at the foot of the bed. She watches me. I watch her. Urge is to climb up that bed and pull her tight, but I don't know if I have that right. In theory, Violet and I are still broken up, yet it feels like the rules have changed.

Violet throws the covers back, revealing pj's that consist of a T-shirt and cotton pants. She tilts her head to the empty spot beside her. "I want the buzzing to stop."

I immediately undo my boot laces as she doesn't have to ask me twice. "I'll set my alarm and be gone before your mom wakes."

"I don't care what she or anyone else thinks."

She never has. One of the things I love about her.

Violet's watching one of those twenty-four-hour news channels where eight million things are being scrolled at the bottom. Half of the screen shows an anchor. The other half aerial shots of what looks like a school.

I take off my boots, slip off my jacket and place it on the post at the end of the bed. Violet leans forward and I climb up and lie beside her, pulling the blankets up to cover us. Violet scoots into me, and when I hook an arm around her waist, her back becomes flush with my chest.

Her sweet scent envelops me and I breathe in deeply, wishing every moment could be like this. Mirroring her, I prop up my head using my hand and watch the TV. "What's going on?"

"Another school shooting."

Damn. "How bad?"

"It happened. That's bad enough, isn't it?"

True. "I'm sorry about Eli."

"I'm sorry for the people who died. Sorry for their families. Sorry for the ones who survived. They said that the school should open again late next week. Everyone can head back to school and be normal. Just like that. Normal by next week."

Just like we'll need to start living life again.

We're silent. Listening to eyewitnesses, watching the same footage being played over and over again. It's one of those things that once you see it you wish you never saw, one of those things that can never be undone in your mind, yet looking away never feels like an option.

"Did you hear that when Eli called the police an Amber Alert was created for us?" Violet says. "Everyone in the county knows we were kidnapped. Everyone at school will know, too."

Great. Coach ought to love this. He was already giving me shit for my loyalties being torn between the team and the Terror. This won't help.

"How do you think they handle it?" Violet keeps her eyes glued on the screen. "The people who've been through shootings before. Do you think they go back to school and everything's normal because that's how other people think it should be, or do you think they just show up and fake it, hoping one day the faking becomes real?"

"I don't know." I don't know how to go thirty seconds without replaying Violet in point-blank range of a man itching to pull the trigger. Don't know how to make my heart not pump like I ran a marathon. Don't know how to quit the twenty-four-hour adrenaline rush.

"That's what I'm hoping for," she says. "I want to fake normal until normal becomes real again."

Until normal becomes real again. Not even sure what that would feel like anymore.

Violet rolls and rests her head against the pillow. Her silky red hair fans out around it. It's tempting to capture a lock and rub the strands in my fingers. Tempting to lean down and kiss her. Tempting to try to forget all the nightmares waiting for me when I close my eyes by losing myself in her warmth, curves and softness.

Hunger darkens Violet's blue eyes and it's as if she's become a reader of not only my mind but my heart as she reaches up and brushes her fingertips along my face. Heat seeps into my veins, and as she slowly pulls away, I capture her fingers and rest our combined hands on her stomach.

"How's the buzzing?" I ask.

"Gone. But that should bother me."

"Why?"

"We didn't work the first time around and our problems didn't disappear."

They didn't, but I don't feel like chasing my tail. At least not tonight. "Can't we just be?"

"Can we?"

"Only time I feel slightly human is if I'm around you," I admit, "and I think you're feeling the same way about me."

"Are you going to patch in? Because I can't be an old lady. I can't be treated the rest of my life the way Dad treated my mom and how Eli treats me. I deserve better than that."

"Your dad worshipped your mom."

"But that didn't stop him from doing that body shot off that girl. It would kill Mom if she ever found out."

The muscles in my neck tense and I try breathing out the anger. We had this argument a hundred times, and the last time, she broke up with me. "You think I'm the guy who could do body shots off somebody else if I'm committed to you?"

"That's not the point. The point is Mom and Dad worked because she stuck her head in the sand. That's what being an old lady requires. I'm not that girl. For better or worse, my dad raised me differently than that."

He did. Frat raised Violet to be a force of nature. A hurricane that looks beautiful from space, but can be a monster once it hits landfall. Am I going to patch in? The question hangs over my head like a machete.

Violet raises her eyebrows until they disappear behind her longer bangs. "Ignoring our problems won't make them go away. We're playing a dangerous game, and I'll be honest, I don't know how many more hits I can take."

"You want me to walk away?"

"No," she says quietly. "I never wanted you to walk away. I need you, but I don't know how to be with you. You need me, but you don't know how to be with me either. Not while you still want to be a part of the club. I broke up with you so you wouldn't have to choose and I've tried to treat you badly since so you would never regret my decision."

A swirling of hurt and anger in my gut. "Why can't I have both? You and the club?"

"Besides the fact that being blood-related to members alone almost got you killed?"

I can't win that argument. Can't make her see that the blame should fall solely on the Riot.

"Because the club demands trust, loyalty and respect and I demand the same. I deserve that and you deserve someone who can be happy with the scraps you'd be willing to throw them after you swear your allegiance somewhere else."

Don't know why, but while I'm sure that was a statement meant to make me hurt, it makes me feel like I can breathe. There's hope. A small sliver, but it's still hope and I've got to offer something—a gift, a sacrifice, something for her to hold on to while it feels like we're falling through a hole so deep that we've forgotten how to stand.

"Eli met with the Riot."

Violet turns off the TV and the only light left in the room is from the utility pole in the yard. "What did you say?"

"Eli and the board met with the Riot. That's what they told me in Church. He said Fiend and the others with him went rogue. That Skull and the rest of the Riot had nothing to do with our kidnapping. The Riot are working with the police and are also looking for Fiend."

Violet blinks repeatedly. "They'd never patch you in if they knew you were telling me this."

She's right, and if I was a full-fledged member, they'd kick me out. "Are you going to tell on me?" I give a halfhearted grin and Violet's mouth mirrors mine.

"Is that a dare?"

I chuckle and she nudges my foot with her toe. My brief moment of lightness dissipates as I recall the rest of the conversation with the board and contemplate how deep of a cut I want to make on my wrist. "The police are coming to talk with us tomorrow. Going to show us pictures so we can identify the guys that kidnapped us."

I pause and the silence builds, stealing my courage instead of adding to it.

"And?"

"The board is leaving it up to me if we want the police to go after Skull and his son. If I tell them to go after them, it can cause a full-out war between our clubs. If I tell them no..." Then there will be no justice for their role. "The cops aren't sure they can prove they were involved anyhow. Can't disprove their claim that they were our saviors."

"Do I get a vote?" she asks.

According to the board, no. But... "Tell me what it is."

I expect an instant answer, but instead the bed shifts as she rolls so that she's facing me. "Maybe we shouldn't identify anybody. Maybe we should do nothing."

My eyes narrow. "You think we should let them get away with what they did? To give Fiend the opportunity to hurt us again? To hurt someone else we love?"

"This war between the Terror and the Riot has been going on since we were babies. If we go after Fiend, then maybe someone who is loyal to him will come after us. Just like you're saying why we shouldn't go after Skull."

"They hurt you," I say slowly and overpronounce each word. "Someone has to face judgment for that. Men like this, they only understand one thing—punishment. If we show them we aren't afraid—that we're willing to pursue legal action—then it'll stop anyone else coming behind them."

"So you're saying that goes for everyone but Skull."

She's got me cornered and I've got to slip right, then shift left to move the ball down the field. "You want to go after him, then I'll tell the board yes and we'll do everything possible to nail that bastard to the wall."

Violet gathers her hair at the nape of her neck, then lets it go so that it flows over her shoulder. "If there was a way to keep your mom, my mom, Brandon, Cyrus, Oz, Razor and most of the people out there in that clubhouse safe, would you do it?"

"Yeah." In a heartbeat.

"Me, too," she whispers so quietly I'm not sure if she really said it, but then says, "If I ask you something, will you tell me the truth? At least the closest to the truth you're willing to share?"

"Yes."

"What did Skull talk to you about in the kitchen? I know it was serious because I read the way you looked at me when I stepped out of the bathroom. You were warning me off."

I rub my forehead, then roll my neck. Even though I've admitted it once, it doesn't get easier saying it aloud again. "Skull told me my father was a traitor. That he was loyal to the Riot, not to the Terror."

Violet places a hand to her lips as my words soak in.

"Cyrus says it's not true," I add like that can take away the sting.

"What do you think?"

That I left that basement with more questions than there are possible answers. "I don't know." If Skull was right and my father was a traitor, then why did he trade sides? I've been raised to hate the Riot, but what did my father know that I don't?

Violet reaches over and rests her hand on my cheek. Her fingertips feathering up and along my jaw. "I'm so sorry."

Yeah, so am I. I suck in a deep breath and tell her my darkest thought. "I need to know if Dad was loyal to the Riot."

"Do you have any idea how to figure it out?"

"Skull mentioned there was a woman I could talk to, but I didn't ask for her name and he didn't give it. Might mean talking to Skull again."

Violet snuggles closer, and as she does, I sink further until my head is on the pillow beside her. I'm not just holding her now, she's also holding me.

"You need him to stay out of jail," she whispers.

I guess I do. "He probably planned it this way. Probably told me this lie to buy himself a get-out-of-jail-free pass."

"I've thought of that, but what if what they said is true? James lived in Louisville. He died there. He's buried there. I've always thought that was weird, but if I asked—"

"You were shut down." Just like I've been shut down by Cyrus, Eli and even my mom.

"Promise you'll keep me involved," she says. "Maybe

knowing what's happening, feeling like I have some sort of control over it, will help me feel normal again."

Not sure if she's talking about what the board has to say about the Riot or about my father, but I don't care. She wants normal, so do I, and like in that basement, I'm going to fight for both of us. And like in that basement, I need Violet fighting for me, too. "I promise."

"Do you remember when I first told you I loved you?" she asks.

The memory hits me like a jolt of electricity. I started my first varsity game that night, and I had scored two touchdowns. That entire night was a celebration. With the team, back at the clubhouse and then with just Oz, Razor and Violet.

We sat on the front porch laughing, talking, shooting the shit, enjoying my win because a win for one of us was a win for us all. Violet sat beside me and I memorized the way she laughed and the way her blue eyes kept finding mine. That smile she gave me when I held her gaze for longer than a second—best moments of my life.

Not soon after, we called it a night. Violet retired into this room. Razor, Oz and I to the room across the way. I waited for Oz and Razor to fall asleep and then I crept over here. I lay beside her, Violet held her hand out to me and then I kissed her.

That kiss—made the world spin. She melted into me, I fell deeply into her, and when our lips finally separated, she whispered those three beautiful words to me. Her trust in me, her love for me—rocked who I was and made me someone better.

"I remember."

"Me, too." Violet rests her head on my chest and her leg

over mine. I wrap an arm around her, keeping her close, then tunnel my fingers into her hair.

Her fingers graze up and down my arm and her touch is comforting and intoxicating. My body pulses with the need to kiss her, but also with the need to just keep her close. Slowly her caresses come at a slower rate, her body becomes still and her breaths even out.

Best friend. Violet has always been my best friend, but it's more than that. She's always been a piece of me, and without her the world was cold—a bitter freeze that cut deep to the bone.

But I'm no longer in that freezing basement. She's here beside me. Violet is warm and soft and all the two million thoughts in my mind stall out and there's finally silence. A comfortable, peaceful silence.

Violet

Physical therapy stinks.

Stinks.

Like pigs in mud.

Like milk that's gone sour.

Like dog poop stuck to the bottom of my shoe.

Stinks.

It's not like I was a huge fan of treadmills and stationary bikes to begin with. Sweating's not my thing. Also definitely not my thing? My knee being pushed and pulled and practically yanked off like it's part of a turkey leg on Thanksgiving.

My physical therapy chick must be having some problems at home and she's taking her pent-up aggression out on me. Note to self—don't piss off my therapist. The lady is freaking sadistic.

Mom pulls her minivan into the parking lot of the only diner in our small town and I slowly turn my head in her direction. "What are you doing?"

"It's early and they're still serving breakfast." Mom smiles at me when she places the car into Park. She looks very youthful and refreshed for nine thirty in the morning in her red sweater, dark blue jeans and blond hair in a very complicated bun. It's Monday and today is a teacher in-service day. Tomorrow will be my and Chevy's first day back. Today was my first physical therapy torture session.

Breakfast. With my mom. After shaking off the initial sensation that doing so would be like having my fingernails pulled off, there's a sense of excitement. I can't remember the last time Mom has voluntarily spent time with me. "I am hungry."

"Great! Eli's waiting for you inside."

Wow. I need to be tested for a personality disorder because I just went from anxiously happy to wanting to tear up pictures of cute kittens. "I'm sorry. I must have misunderstood. I thought you said I'm having breakfast with Eli."

And there it is. The Mom frown. The constant state of disappointment my mother has with me and me alone. "Please don't start. You really are being ungrateful, and your behavior—the way you've been yelling at Eli—it's embarrassing. He's gone out of his way to take care of us. To take care of you."

Embarrassing. It's so funny, I'm numb. "You know I was kidnapped, right? My knee was busted out because the guy who really hates Eli beat the hell out of me. Did anyone fill you in on these details? I mean, you were there when the police came and showed us photos. That wasn't a dating match service."

A disgusted noise manages to slip through her throat. "Why do you have to be so crude?"

Crude? I didn't even use colorful curse words. "You're the one that married a biker and then reproduced. You can't blame me for crude."

"Your father was never crude," Mom whispers.

I sigh because she's right. He was never crude around her. Dad taught me to burp the alphabet in the clubhouse and every curse word I know I learned from working on the Chevelle with him, but he was on point with Mom.

I wish he were here. He knew how to keep peace between me and Mom. He used to help me navigate between being the person he raised me to be and living in his world. Without him, I'm lost.

"Go have breakfast with Eli." Full-fledged disappointed voice. "I'm going to run errands and he'll bring you back to Cyrus's."

I open the door, grab my crutches and slide out. Before shutting the door, I lean back in. "I would have liked to have breakfast with you."

Not bothering to wait for a response, I slam it shut.

Snowflake, Kentucky, is a forgotten place. Hundreds of years ago, people climbed up and over the Appalachian Mountains and some of them settled here. There's a river, fertile farmland, and I often wonder if the people who planted roots here thought this place would become the center of commerce and the universe.

It didn't. Instead, it's stuck back in a different time. Back when towns had Main Streets with old buildings and bustling shops. Back when people rode their buggy into town and had to hitch their horses. There's a green space in the middle of the town with a statue of a Confederate war hero and nobody remembers or cares why he's there.

The buildings are now cracked and the streets look odd as parking spots were added in front of the stores. It's all out of proportion—time catching up to a place never meant to go forward.

In front of the diner is a row of motorcycles. Two prospects turn over the engines on their bikes and take off. Don't have to look to know they're tailing Mom.

The bell over the diner door rings when I hobble in. To the left, Pigpen, Man O' War and Dust are laughing in a booth with my brother, Brandon. To the right, Eli is in a booth by himself and he's watching me. Mom would be pissed if I took the left instead of the right, but I like the guys to the left a lot better than Eli.

Frost had it wrong. Two roads converged and I didn't want to travel either. Where's the poem where the person runs screaming in the opposite direction? That one I would understand.

The dominatrix at physical therapy wants me to get a walker because she wants me to put pressure on my leg. I'd rather shoot myself in the head than go around school like that. It's going to be bad enough to fit back into my hard-won old life that had new non-Terror friends with that Amber Alert. A walker will only make people think I'm weak. Crutches I might be able to pull off. Limping would be better.

Keeping my physical therapist's request in mind, I gather the crutches with one hand and slowly attempt to walk on my own. Eli jerks like he's going to jump to his feet, but luckily I reach the booth before he has the opportunity to act like an idiot in a room full of people.

"Why are you putting weight on your knee?" he demands.

"I'm having pancakes with blueberries, blueberry syrup and whip cream. I'm also having bacon and your bacon and as much orange juice as I want. You're buying. And walking, which requires placing weight on my knee, is what the lady at physical therapy told me to do." I add *asshole* in my head, but I'm pretty sure my expression said it loud and clear.

Eli pulls at the plug in his earlobe, then fold his hands together on the table. "I don't like how we've turned out."

Even though I know what I'm ordering, I open up the plastic tri-fold menu and pretend I don't have it memorized.

"We used to be close," he says.

Yep. We were.

"What happened?"

My eyes flash to his. "Dad died. That's what happened."

"In an accident." Eli leans forward. "In a stupid, fucking accident. Why are you mad at me? At the club? Hell, anyone within a two-hundred-mile radius can see you're still in love with Chevy and you left him. I don't get it, and I don't know how to make things better between us, so maybe if you explain it, I can fix it."

This man makes my head hurt in so many ways. "I've explained it to you multiple times and you don't listen."

"Try again."

"You don't listen."

"Dammit, Violet, I'm trying here. Why can't you see that?"

I fold the menu and toss it in his direction so that it smacks him in the arm. "You don't listen! That's it! You never listen. You talk over me, you talk to anyone else but me, and what's worse is when I am talking and by the rare chance you are silent, you're not even listening. Instead, you're busy formulating in your pint-size mind whatever it is you're going to say to me next."

Eli opens his mouth and I tilt my head in an *I told you so*. Sort of cartoonish how he snaps his trap shut. He drums his fingers against the table, then slumps back into the booth. "I'm listening now, so talk."

"No, you're not."

"Yes, I am."

Because Rome was built in a day. Fine. Whatever. "I want to go home."

"No."

"I don't mean this very second. I mean after breakfast."

"I know what you meant. No."

I throw my hands up. He has no idea he's proving my point.

"I'm listening," he says in defense. "I just don't agree."

"Listening would mean pausing to reflect upon any argument I might have. That would require me giving you my opinion, you listening while I give my opinion, thinking over my opinion and then you and I have a spirited discussion that may or may not require curse words until we come to a mutually beneficial decision based on friendship and respect."

Eli's eyes sparkle and it's insulting how he's attempting to hide his smile. "You sound exactly like your dad."

"I don't take that as an insult."

His eyebrows draw together. "I didn't mean it as one. Your dad was one of the most amazing men I knew and I know a lot of great guys. I miss him, Vi, and I'm sure you do, too. I know we don't always get along, but I swear we're on the same side of this war."

War. I've been asked to deliver Eli on a platter. "Are you admitting you're at war with the Riot?"

"The Riot, anyone at school who gives you shit, anyone in general who gives you shit. The world. I wish you knew I'm on your side."

His words sound pretty, but that's all they are. Something ugly wearing makeup and bows. Or in his case, a black T-shirt and ear plugs. "Then let me go home and stop treating me like a prisoner."

Eli rolls his neck and almost looks regretful. "I can't do that, and I'm not treating you like a prisoner."

"The hell you aren't."

Demons shoot out of Eli's eyes. "Do not compare me to the Riot. They hurt you. I'm protecting you."

I lean forward to explain exactly where he can shove his protection, when there's the clearing of a throat. "I think they rang the bell for the first round a few minutes ago. It's time to return to your corners."

My heart swells. It's Chevy's mom. I smile before I have the chance to remember I broke her son's heart and she wasn't particularly pleased with me. I go to cast my gaze away, but Nina leans down and gives me a quick hug and a kiss on the cheek. When she pulls away, she grabs my chin and stares deep into my eyes. "You okay?"

From the way she searches my face, she's not asking about my fight with Eli, but my time in that basement. I suck in a breath to lie like I do for Eli, Cyrus, my brother, my mom and anyone who asks, but *fine* becomes a knot in my throat.

Nina nods like she heard the truth, then kisses my forehead. "You'll make it. The strong ones always do."

Not sure if she's right. I'm starting to feel depleted of strong.

Nina settles beside me and pats my good knee as she turns her attention to Eli. "Hello."

"I thought you were hanging out with Chevy this morning."

"I am." She gestures down the narrow diner and Chevy's watching us from Pigpen's booth. "We decided to have breakfast, but when we walked in, I saw you two mixed up in a wrestling match. I don't think it would be appropriate for Violet to be reduced to throwing steak knives. We should at least have the decency to wait until she's eighteen."

Eli shrugs. "She could be charged as an adult then. Better for her to get it out of her system now."

"I could see where you would think that. Now, what's the problem?"

"She's seventeen and thinks she knows everything," Eli says while I say, "He won't let me go home."

I almost add that I'm eighteen now, not seventeen. That I left seventeen behind in the basement dungeon, but everyone seems to have lapsed about my birthday. Chevy remembered that night, but hasn't brought it up since. Honestly, I'm fine with it having been forgotten. I don't think I could stomach giving the Terror another excuse to throw a "party" in my honor and I don't feel at all celebratory.

"I see." Her eyes flicker between me and Eli before choosing to remain on him. "Why can't she go home? You said if Chevy wanted he could return home. The only reason he's still at the clubhouse is because he doesn't want to be away from Violet."

I twist my lips to the left because there are so many portions of that I wasn't aware of and don't know how to process. But of course Chevy was given a choice. He has a penis. And I was not given a choice because I'm a girl.

Eli looks like he wants to rip off his skin. "Violet's mom wants to be at the cabin so we can keep an eye on her, Stone and Violet."

"Jenny is another subject for another time, so I'm going to leave her out of the conversation." Nina understands my issues with my mother. When I was dating Chevy, she patted my hand and explained, *Your mother can do things for herself, but she chooses not to. She's very capable. I remember that about her in high school. But some women believe they need to dumb it down in order to keep a man. Eventually, they forget they were ca-*

*pable. That's what happened to your mom. Don't be her, Violet.
Never be her.*

"I believe Violet has earned the right to have her own
mind and make her own decisions," Nina continues. "If she
wants to return home, she should return home."

"She's not your kid," Eli says.

"Are Violet and Chevy at risk?" Nina continues like Eli
hadn't spoken. "Do you think they are going to be tar-
geted again? Because from the multiple conversations I've
had with you and the police over the past few hours, I was
under the impression the people who kidnapped them were
under arrest."

"They were what?" I ask, and Eli briefly closes his eyes.

"Arrested," Nina repeats. "This morning, and before Eli
has a chance to lie his way out of this, your mother knew.
Chevy didn't know until after you left this morning."

Because he was asleep with his arms tucked around me
until Mom took me to therapy.

I pick that steak knife up and Nina raises her eyebrows at
me. I drop it only because I have always secretly wished she
would adopt me.

"I was going to tell you," Eli starts.

"Sure you were."

Eli pinches the bridge of his nose, then lowers his hand.
"I was going to tell you because once the men are back in
Kentucky, we'll need to drive into Louisville. The police
want you and Chevy to pick out the guys in a lineup. They
were arrested in another state, where they are facing other
charges, but it's expected they'll be sent back here soon to
face the kidnapping charges."

A lineup. I slouch in the seat and deal with the mixture of
relief and anxiety. Fiend is caught and I'll have to finger him
in a lineup. If he doesn't plead out, I'll have to testify. The

ground beneath my feet begins to feel unsteady, like sand falling through an hourglass and I'm trapped inside the cylinder.

Peace. Justin suggested there could be peace and he also suggested he could and would harm the people I love. He never wanted the police involved and he expects me to help him nail Eli.

Eli and Nina are locked in an intense conversation, their words blending together and making noise. Justin wanted account numbers, he wants Eli to pay for taking his sister and eventually his niece away and he wants Eli to go to jail.

My throat thickens and I swallow as I look at Eli. He carried me to Chevy in the hospital, he's here to buy me pancakes, he drives me absolutely insane, he doesn't listen, he often makes me feel like my existence is worthless, but even as he's arguing with Nina he glances over at me with pleading eyes, as if to check to make sure I didn't disappear, because...

Because he cares for me.

I hate his way of caring, though. Hate how he controls. But how can you fully hate someone who does all the stupid things because that's the way he loves?

My stomach bottoms out, and where I was hungry minutes ago, I'm now nauseated.

I can't do it. I can't be responsible for hurting Eli. I can't be responsible for anyone's death, because regardless of what Justin said, they are out to destroy more than Eli's reputation, but if I don't hand over the numbers, then what will happen to my family?

"You okay, Violet?"

I lift my eyes and Chevy stands at the end of the table, concerned dark eyes boring into me. Chevy knows me too well. Sometimes better than I know myself. Once again, I dig deep for the lie, but I can't bring myself to try to deceive him. He would see through it and then start asking questions I'm not able to answer.

Justin threatened my family. He threatened me. The Riot have already proved they can do what they want. They kidnapped me. They kidnapped Chevy. I could have easily died in that basement. There's nothing stopping them from hurting us again, and if I tell Eli, will whoever slipped that note into the cabin find out and tell the Riot I'm breaking the deal?

No matter which way I go, I'm choosing wrong.

Two paths. Both lead to my emotional, if not physical, demise.

"Eli," Chevy says in a low voice. "You seem to be upsetting my girl. Don't you think Violet's been dealt enough shit?"

A flutter in my chest at being called his girl, but then those butterflies disappear. I promised myself months ago I wouldn't come between Chevy and the club. I can't be an old lady, but I also can't be the girl who makes a boy choose between her and his family.

Eli makes a show of scanning the diner and says so the entire place can hear, "Anyone else want to butt into this conversation?"

Pigpen and Dust chuckle, but the rest of the patrons take an intense interest in their food or menu. Chevy motions for Eli to move and he does to allow Chevy to sit. Not sure if this is good for me or if he'll side with Eli on matters dealing with my safety.

"With the people who kidnapped me in jail, why can't I go home?" I ask. I know why I'm not safe. I should be begging to stay at Cyrus's cabin, to be living in the clubhouse, but someone left me a note there. They found a way to slip past the wall Eli believes is impenetrable.

Eli drums his fingers against the table and watches each tap against the wood. He's contemplating the fact I want to go home and he's aware there's no reason to keep me under lock and key. At least no reason that won't piss me off. I have him cornered, and men like him don't react well when their back is against the wall. Dad taught me that.

"Men like me, we like to feel like we're in control. That we have a way out with our pride intact or we end up coming out of the corner swinging, even if that's not the right solution, even if it's with words instead of fists. It's instinct—at least for me—something born within me I don't know how to kill. Men like me, we need our pride. Take pity on us and try to let us keep it."

We were fishing at midnight at the pond. It was a humid summer night. Frogs croaked. Crickets sang. Millions of stars shone down from above. I was fourteen and thought Dad had hung every last gas-burning light in the night sky. "How?"

"You offer them a way out. One that makes a man feel like he's able to walk away with his head held slightly high. If he doesn't take that offer, Vi, he's a moron and then I say fuck 'em."

Dad assumed that trait was reserved for men, and he was epically wrong. I often come out swinging when I'm pinned in a corner, but for now, I want home more than I want my pride. "If you let me go home, if you drop the guys tailing me, I'll have breakfast with you every Saturday."

Eli's eyes meet mine, and I don't look away. I'm promising him I'll try with him and that's the biggest peace offering in over a year.

"Home maybe, but the guys tailing you—I don't know about letting those go."

And what if one of those guys is the one who left the note in my jacket? My body actually twitches as I have to physically squelch the need to raise my voice. "The guys who took me are in jail, right? And the Riot are pinkie-swearing to be Boy Scouts, correct?"

There are some reactions that are so cold I could freeze to death. That would be the glare Eli's giving me.

"I need normal." The truest words on the planet. "I need my life to go on."

The hard set of Eli's jaw tells me he's not going to give.

"We both need it," Chevy says, and there's something silently exchanged between Chevy and Eli. Whatever it is works. Eli lays his hand flat against the table.

"You can go home after the police lineup. There's no way a judge will grant them bail with both of you fingering them. I can stomach you going home with them rotting in a cell. I'll agree to no tails, but I'll have guys checking on your house. That's nonnegotiable. You were taken on the way to your house. No one else from the Terror would normally be going that direction and that doesn't sit right with me. Makes me feel like they were targeting you."

If I could hide under the table, I would, but I do my best to school my expression, my body language, to conceal what happened between me and the Riot.

"Why would they be targeting Violet?" Nina asks.

"To use me against Chevy," I say as a deflection.

"And me," Eli adds. "Frat's death hit me hard. They know this. They know I would have taken it upon myself to care for his family."

I sink lower. My dad and Eli were friends. My world is a mess.

"You gave me your word, Violet. Every Saturday—it's you and me, kid."

Yeah, I did. The waitress comes, and Eli announces he's buying for everyone. We order, one at a time, but I ask for oatmeal instead of pancakes. My stomach is twisted and feels heavy and I'm not sure I can even eat that.

I need help. I need a way out. I need options. God, I wish my father was here. He'd know what to do and he'd be able to help me negotiate the high wire I've been forced to walk.

Eli and Nina talk, I make an airplane out of my paper napkin and Chevy watches me. Keenly. Too in-depthly.

He has a way of seeing things no one else can. Picks up on the most minute movement. The slightly longer intake of air. A twitch of a finger, of an eye. The angle of a foot toward a door. He knows all. Sees all. And there's no doubt he's aware something is horribly wrong.

Chevy won't say anything now. Probably won't say anything the next time we're alone either. He'll wait because he's patient like that. He'll wait for the unassuming time, when my defenses are lowered, when he'll be able to slip past my skin and into the truth.

"You know what you two need?" Nina says, ripping me out of my thoughts. "To do something normal. Be actual teenagers."

Yeah. Sounds great. Sounds easy. Sounds impossible.

"Hey, Violet?"

My head snaps up at the sound of my brother's voice. He stands at our table with his hands shoved in his pockets and his cheeks are red. My eyebrows draw together as I try to understand why he's so upset. "What's wrong?"

He shrugs while shaking his head and shuffling his feet. "Nothing."

No, it's something. Very much something. My eyes dart to the table where Pigpen, Man O' War and Dust sit, because if they did something to make him sad, I'm going to make each of them bleed. "Do you need to talk to me alone?"

Chevy goes to slide out of the booth as Eli and Nina

glance at each other in worry, but before anyone else can join the conversation, Brandon reaches into his back pocket, pulls something out, then deposits a mound of bracelets on the table.

My heart beats hard twice. Bracelets. My bracelets. The bracelets Fiend stole from me. "Where did you get these?"

Brandon stares at the floor and rubs his nose. "On the side of the road. I saw that guy throw them out of the car... after...after he hit you...and..." His voice breaks and my heart breaks and I'm pushing Nina out of the way because I need to get to my brother.

"...and I called Eli like you said...and I'm afraid it's my fault you were taken...and you love your bracelets...so I picked them up..." He chokes on the words and his eyes are filling with tears and my vision becomes blurry as my mouth turns down. "...but I didn't find Dad's watch or cross and I know they mean more to you, so I was scared to give these back, but then Pigpen saw them and told me..."

I don't care what Pigpen told him. I throw myself into my brother and hold him tight. Brandon slowly wraps his arms around me, places his head on my shoulder and cries. Shoulders shaking, leaning down into me from his tall height, and I squeeze my eyes shut to push back my own tears as I try to comfort my brother.

A touch on my arm, and when I look over, Chevy's standing beside me. One hand on me. His other hand on Brandon's back. His eyes a storm full of pain and sorrow, as well. We stare at each other and the same question burns out of his eyes as the one that's circling my brain—will we ever be okay again?

CHEVY

Violet lives in a brick two-story Cape Cod. Wouldn't know the official name of it if Violet's mom hadn't made a big deal about it when they moved into the place when we were eight. Oz, Razor and I were in charge of lugging all of Violet's boxes into her room upstairs. Violet was in charge of ordering us around.

The guys of the club helped unpack the truck and they unloaded and repieced together furniture. It was a fun day, a great day, and it was the first time we were able to walk the woods straight from Violet's house to Cyrus's and back. It was a big hike, epic at age eight, but it was my first huge adventure and I loved sharing it with my best friends.

Typically, I'd ride my Harley to school, but I'm giving a ride not only to Violet, but Stone, so I'm driving Eli's truck. Plus Violet shouldn't be riding until her knee is healed.

Violet's mom drove them home this morning and Dust tailed them so Violet could get ready for school at home. Violet explained how her mother had forgotten some "personal" female items, and after an awkward moment where the men in the room wanted to kill themselves, Violet and Eli agreed that going home in the morning was okay.

No one, including me, wanted to ask what the personal items were.

I pull up to the house in Eli's truck and Violet and Stone walk outside.

Captivated. That's what Violet does to me whenever I see her. Her red hair is pulled into a bun that looks too good to be thrown together, but messy enough that wisps of her hair fall around her face. It's perfect and makes me want to lie in bed with her all over again.

She wears jeans with rips above the knee and a blue shirt that has a hippie look to it. Like always, as if she never missed a beat, her bracelets dangle from her wrists.

Fiend had stolen her bracelets from her when they shoved her into the back of the car and Stone had picked up each and every one as he called Eli. By himself. In the dark. Only a few of us understand how much courage it took that boy.

Violet squishes her lips to the side as she ambles down the stairs of the porch. Stone reaches the truck first, opens the passenger-side door, and Violet pulls herself up. Irritation leaks through me. Stupid. I should have gotten out and helped her in. Too late now, but it won't happen again.

"Hey, Chevy!" Stone smiles at me, and I smile back. He's a good kid who kept his head in a scary situation.

"What's doing, Stone?"

"Nothing much."

I'm a football player and a McKinley, so I take up enough room in the cab of the truck. While Stone is thin, the kid has legs like an overgrown spider and he can't seem to find a place to put himself, so he's spread out, too. Violet's got the raw end of being jammed between us, but she takes it in stride.

As if it's natural, Violet lets her thigh rest against mine and her arm brushes along my skin. Electricity shoots through my veins, and as if she felt it, too, Violet snaps her head in my direction. Beautiful. She's beautiful. Blazing red hair. Deep blue eyes. Color back in her cheeks.

Beautiful.

And I'm driven by need.

The impulse is to shove Stone out of the truck and tell him to go inside. Then I'll pull Violet tight to me and kiss her until I forget who I am and she forgets who she is. Memories flash of her in this truck, of her in my arms, of the way her hot breath tickled my neck.

Yeah, I've thought of kissing Violet, but I haven't felt these strong desires in a long time. It's a heaviness in my belly. A fire in my blood. I shift, trying to readjust and relieve some of the pressure built up in areas below, but it doesn't help. It's going to be a damn long day.

"Violet thought she was driving us to school," Brandon says.

"You did?" I glance at her out of the corner of my eye and she's looking longingly at the parked Chevelle as if she'll never see it again.

"I don't need my left leg to drive."

"No. Just to walk."

She smirks like it's painful to admit she thought I was funny.

"So." She draws the word out as I pull out onto the road. Dust stays behind to be Violet's mom's tail for the day. "This is what that long look in the diner was about? I lost the tails, but I picked up you as my bodyguard?"

I scratch the back of my head. Violet's watching me, but not with an I'm-going-to-kick-your-ass expression. That's good, because even with one leg, she probably could. "I got you what you wanted."

"Are you carrying?" she asks quietly.

"Do you really want the answer?"

"You hate carrying."

Yeah, but I love her. Never stopped. Just tucked it away as deep as I could so I wouldn't be in pain all the damn time.

Her head falls back to the seat. "Please be careful."

"Always am."

She rolls her eyes. I switch hands on the steering wheel and place my free hand on her knee. Violet rests her hand over mine. Together. This is how together feels and I missed it.

The ride to school ended too quickly, and I pull up next to Razor, who's leaning against his parked bike. Stone opens his door, slides out and waits for Violet to move.

"Give us a few?" I ask him.

With a hop in his step, he closes the door and rounds the truck for Razor. The two share a handshake Razor created just for him.

I slide my finger back and forth over Violet's thigh. Each caress makes me wish we didn't have six-plus hours of torture in front of us. "I want to kiss you, Violet."

Her breathing hitches, and when I turn my head to look at her, she's regarding me from below hooded lids.

"I'm not sure I've ever wanted to kiss you as badly as I do right now."

She licks her lips, making them wet, making them a deeper shade of red. Her pulse increases under my touch and it's matching the beating of my heart.

"I'm not going to do it now, but I want to later. You've got to figure out where you're standing on this. If all you can handle is me taking your hand, holding you at night as we sleep, being next to each other so we find some peace, then that's where I'll leave it, but I want to kiss you, and if kissing you crosses lines that are going to cause you pain, I won't even try."

"Chevy—" she starts.

"Don't answer now," I cut her off. "If you tell me yes, we'll never make it out of this truck." If she tells me no, I'll want to nurse my bleeding wounds in private.

Regardless of my words, I tuck her silky hair behind her ear, enjoying how the strands fall between my fingers, then caress the heat radiating off her cheeks. I love how her blue eyes are smoldering. Love how she's angled herself toward me. Love how her hand has wandered to my leg. It's all good signs, but this can't be the time or the place.

With a flick of my wrist, I produce a daisy. Stole it from a vase of them Mom had on the table. Violet lights up like I'm handing her the world. Damn if I understand why girls like flowers, but Violet does and I like making Violet happy.

"I never get tired of your magic," she says.

That's a good thing.

Violet squeezes my thigh once and I groan as I reach behind me, crack open the door and welcome the cold air that blows into the truck. I fall out and the little devil giggles as I help her settle her good leg to the ground.

Violet

I can't think about Chevy. I can't think about how his hand was hot on my thigh. I can't think about how his fingers against my face caused sweet tingles, I can't think about how there's this pulse in my body that won't go away after he suggested kissing.

Kissing Chevy. Once I do that, there will be no going back and that's the equivalent of throwing myself over a cliff.

There is no thinking about Chevy.

None.

Instead, I focus on surviving high school. At least this day in high school. In high school you need armor and armor are other bodies of people you can surround yourself with and that's what you call friends.

After dad died, I made new friends.

Considering we live in a town small enough that when someone sneezes you can hear the echoing *bless you* from the other side of the county, new is a relative term. They were people I had known most of my life, but I was too consumed with the Terror to notice.

Some are nice. Some are not so nice. Some need to die and be damned to an eternity of being roasted like a marshmallow. But that's life, that's people. I can't control them, I can only control me and so far I've done a suck job at controlling me.

I'm doing what my physical therapist requested and I'm slowly, steadily, on my crutches yet using both legs to walk. As if a turtle had been let loose on the autobahn. My pack is on my back, so my hands are free to drop my crutches and catch myself if I should trip. Chevy walked with me to my first class, but I'm on my own for second, third, then going into lunch.

I barely beat the bell for Business Economics, and like the first two periods of the day, the class goes deathly silent. Yep, they heard about the Amber Alert, heard Chevy and I were kidnapped, and if I'm going to be honest, if it didn't happen to me, I'd be staring, too.

Kidnapping only happens to strange people in big cities and we hear about it on investigative news programs. Even for the Terror, it's a stretch and now I'm the girl who lived.

The moment my butt hits the seat, there's shouting outside in the hallway. A scuffle. A banging of a locker and my blood pulses in my veins.

They're here. The Riot are here.

Teachers run down the hallway, a blur of white shirts, and our own teacher sprints to the doorway and he mumbles a curse. "Get in groups, read chapter twenty-four and finish the questions at the end of each summary."

He leaves, the class breaks out into conversation and my body feels like I've been put into a meat shredder. It's not the Riot. Not every sound is going to be the Riot.

The person behind me leans forward and says, "Jordan Johnson was fingered as the last guy in the picture scandal.

Twenty bucks the fight in the hall is Leeann Matteson's boy-friend beating the hell out of him for posting those pics of her changing in the girls' restroom."

I turn and blink at the sight of Addison. We're friends, but not friends. Associated, but not associated. She's blond hair, blue eyes and a cheerleader for our school. She's talented and can flip like those people on TV during the Olympics.

Some of my new set of friends are friends with her, but Addison mostly hung out with her best friend, Breanna, and this is where the association comes in. Razor fell in love with Breanna this fall, Breanna fell for him and her parents recently sent her to a private school far, far away to keep the two of them apart.

"I thought you'd want to know," Addison continues. "About Jordan."

She's right. Five guys tormented girls from our school with pictures they took of us in vulnerable moments and black-mailed us. If we didn't do what they wanted, the pictures went up on a social media account they created.

I use *us* because it happened to me, but Razor helped catch the asshole who was blackmailing me. The guy wanted me to make people think I was dating him. Honestly, he wanted more, and when he suggested sex, I threatened to kill him and he believed I would happily sit in jail with his blood dripping from my fingernails.

I tried to flat out refuse the pretense of dating and he up-loaded a picture of me. It was taken during a black time in my life. After I broke up with Chevy, after Mom and I had our millionth fight, after I didn't understand why I wanted to keep breathing.

I drank too much and blacked out at a party. Turns out boys at parties have cameras and like to play dress up with the passed-out girl. To keep any more pics from going up, I fake dated him. Had to kiss him a few times. Even though it was just kisses, I still felt like a whore.

"Why wasn't Jordan suspended like the others?" I ask.

"He was. Last week. But his daddy's on the school board and is fighting the accusations and punishment. You know, the whole—" she performs air quotes and drops her voice to mimic a man "—my son would never do such a thing. He's an angel. He was about to improve his failing grades and had told us over dinner he was going to become a rocket scientist."

I laugh, Addison cracks a hesitant grin and I turn fully around. "I hope he gets the hell beat out of him."

"Me, too," she replies. "I hope they all do. What they did wasn't okay."

No, it wasn't.

"Were you really kidnapped?" The question comes from a few rows over and all the chatter stops.

Don't know why, but I search Addison for an ally. I can tell, though, she's just as curious. Regardless of Breanna's parents' efforts, Addison's best friend is entwined with the Terror. Razor loves Breanna. I don't see signs of him letting her go as long as she wants him, so that means, in Addison's eyes, her best friend is in danger.

I can't argue with that logic.

"There was an Amber Alert and it said she'd been taken," someone else says. "So of course she was kidnapped."

"Was it people you knew who took you?" I know that voice. It's a girl I'm perfectly fine with being one of the people who burns in hell. Her name is Jana and she was over-the-top nice when I first tried to break free from the Terror. It turns out she's one of those who wants people to worship her as she kicks everyone else down.

Jana got mad at me when I told her to back off when she

informed her, in theory, best friend she was fat. Never understood why girls wouldn't stand up for themselves. But I did take a stand and I ended up tossed from her inner circle.

Boo flipping hoo.

"Mom says people in motorcycle clubs all know each other and treat each other badly," continues Jana. "I bet you knew the people who kidnapped you and you'll be mixing it up with them in a few weeks."

Mixing it up. The way her cold eyes slide up and down my body suggests mixing it up means me on my knees performing certain acts. I don't know why my face heats with shame, but it does. Like somehow this is all my fault and I deserved it. Yet I keep my head held high. "My life is none of your fucking business."

Jana flinches. "I was trying to be nice. Excuse me for asking questions. And to think I was nice to you last year when you wanted to make new friends. I told everyone not to believe you. That you would always be biker trash."

"You're such a bitch," Addison says like she's bored, and I'm shocked by the unexpected backup.

A guy in the back mumbles, "Burn," and a few other people nervously laugh.

Jana turns her little serpent head in Addison's direction. "All I did was express concern for Violet and she yelled at me. I didn't do anything wrong. She's the bitch. Not me."

The look of disgust on Addison's face is humorous—at least for me. "Nothing works up there, does it? Like your mind—it's a ghost town. Somebody else asked her about being kidnapped. You decided to get nosy, then get nasty. You're still mad because Violet made you look like a fool last year at lunch. Let it go, Jana. With the way your mind ticks, you're going to be made to feel like a fool a lot in life."

"All right." Our teacher walks back in. "I don't see enough books open or groups formed or actual work being done."

"You just dug your grave," Jana whispers to Addison.

Addison cracks a smile that's so bitter it's sweet. "What are you going to do? Talk badly about me? Go ahead. You spouting off words you don't even understand is the least of my problems."

The distant look in Addison's eyes—I've seen that before in Dust's eyes. An old soul. A soul that's seen too much, done too much.

Addison opens her book, the sleeve of her cheer warm-up hitches up and the world freezes. There are bruises on her wrist. Those are the type of bruises I had on my arm from when Fiend manhandled me. My stomach roils, and I have to breathe in to keep from getting dizzy.

People form into groups, and when Addison begins to work by herself, it hits me. Breanna, the person Addison always partnered with, is gone.

Her world is tilted. My world is tilted…and it's a terrible feeling. Like being caught in a landslide and no matter how you grasp at the mud around you nothing can keep you grounded.

I want to feel safe. Maybe Addison does, too. High school is a war zone. The people who surround you are your best form of defense. "Want to partner up?"

Addison raises her head, and as casually as I can, without being overly obvious, I pull back my long sleeve and expose my own fading bruises. Recognition darkens Addison's face and she yanks down her own sleeve in such a slow way I'm not sure she's aware she's doing it.

She finally meets my gaze. "Sure."

I go to try to turn my desk, but Addison moves hers instead. People with two fully functioning legs can do such things faster. She slides her book for me to share with her, then places her hand over the page to stop me from reading. "This doesn't mean I like the Terror. I'm really pissed at them. If they weren't around, maybe Breanna would still be here."

Yeah—"I get it. I'm pretty mad at them, too. I have been for a while."

A few beats of her digesting my answer and then she asks, "Where are you sitting at lunch today?"

I used to sit at a table that contained Jana. I sat as far from her as possible, but we still shared the large round plastic space. "Not sure."

"Want to sit with me?"

Definitely. "Okay."

The ends of Addison's lips lift, she removes her hand from the book and reads the first question aloud.

CHEVY

Coach teaches freshman geography. Multiple world maps cover the walls in his room and little else. Most teachers try to make places welcoming by adding posters of baby animals or maybe posting some sort of inspirational saying on the bulletin board. He's got none of that. World maps put up with gray tape. That's his best.

It's his planning period and I'm supposed to be an aide in wood shop—keeping the freshmen from cutting their fingers off. Parents get pissed when that happens.

I knock on Coach's door and he pops his head up from the pile of papers on his desk. "Tell me before I lose my mind. I taught you what the capital of the US is, right?"

Already knew it before I took his class. "Washington, DC."

"Thank God. These kids are morons."

Considering how many of them I've had to stop this year from losing digits, I have to agree. "You wanted to see me?"

"Yeah." He leans back in his seat, causing it to roll. "Take a seat."

The chair in front of his desk is too small for me, like it belongs in an elementary school, but when Coach tells you to sit, you sit. He's a great guy. As big as a tank. Played football in college, then a year in the pros until he busted his knee. Gentle black man when he chooses, but on the field the man morphs into a rabid wolf, tearing hunks out of us until we break.

He's made teammates of mine cry. He's run me so hard I've vomited on the sidelines. He demands respect, we give it and bust our asses to receive it in return.

"I heard about what happened to you," he says. "Want you to know that my church and I were pulling for you. We had a special prayer session for you the morning you were gone. The entire team came. I even heard that some of the guys had grouped together and went searching for you and Violet in case you had been dropped off on the side of the road. You had a lot of people thinking of you."

Didn't know any of this. Something deep and unknown inside me shifts. People said prayers for me and Violet. It's weird and welcomed. "Thank you."

"You doing okay? I heard you were roughed up."

I shrug. "About the same as playing Riverside."

Coach grins, but it's short-lived. "Listen, I'm going to give it to you straight. There are some in the school's administration who have never been happy I've had you on this team."

My skin begins to feel stretched and there's not much I can do as I balance sitting in this tiny chair.

"Some people argue the Terror are a gang and you know the school board doesn't allow anything gang-related within the school."

Son of a bitch.

"This is why I ride your back to make sure it appears like your loyalties are with the team and not the Terror. I take a lot of heat for sticking my neck out for you, but after this kidnapping...parents are scared."

"I wasn't kidnapped by the Terror." I cross my arms over my chest and dare him to push me on it.

"I know. But you were taken by a rival motorcycle club. Maybe if this was fifteen years ago, things would be different, but now with terrorist attacks, school shootings and workplace shootings... Hell, insane assholes are shooting up movie theatres. People get scared. The members of this community know you're the son of a Terror member."

"A man who died before my birth." A man who might have been loyal to the people who took me.

"And your grandfather is the head of the Terror and he's come to every parent-teacher conference and every game. People see you, they see the Terror and some parents have expressed concern that your being on the team is inviting problems."

Problems. "What the hell does that mean?"

Coach lifts his fingers in a way to indicate a who-knows. "Parents are concerned if you're on the field, a gang war will erupt and their sons will be taken out in the process."

I'm being punished and judged based on someone else's mistakes? "This is bullshit."

"I agree, but the parent making the most noise has got the ear of someone on the school board. Until the board meets again, I've been told to bench you."

"Bench me?" I repeat.

"You aren't thrown off the team. Just have to sit out games until we get this figured out."

"I'm not Terror. I'm not even a prospect."

"As I said, I know. You've been given permission to sit with the team. Wear your jersey to games. They don't want you to feel entirely left out. They said they want to do what's best for the greater good."

Fuck this. I stand, the small-ass chair banging against the floor. "Because if I dress out and play, that's when the shooting begins, but if I sit my ass on the bench, everyone's safe? How does that work?"

"It doesn't." Coach rises to his feet, his hands in the air in a sign for me to calm down. "Between me and you, this is politics, son, and it's higher than my pay grade."

Politics? I run through what Coach said and my head falls back when the answer hits me like a freight train. Some parents raised concerns, but he said there was one loud bastard with the ear of a board member. The kid who's my backup if I get hurt hasn't played much this year and his father's been an asshole about it, shouting at Coach from the sidelines at practice and during games.

This kid's dad's best friend? He's on the school board. "Ray can't catch a damn ball and move his feet at the same time. He can't remember his routes under pressure."

"I'm aware. We lost last week. Eighteen to zero."

To a team we should have easily beaten.

"Their defense knew we didn't have you and they know Ray can't play. They shifted their defense to the boys who can. Without you there, we couldn't get down the field. Our defense saw the game falling apart and they fell apart. Our team needs a leader and that's you. I need you back on that field."

"Sounds like that's not up to me."

"It's not. I'll speak to the board. So will some of the other coaches and teachers. I know Cyrus won't want to hear this, but he and the Terror need to stay clear. Them showing up will only hurt, not help."

That conversation with the board will go over well.

"What I'm about to ask requires a better man, but I'm asking because I know you're a great man." His pause causes my blood to run cold. "Chevy, I need you to come to practice and help Ray. I need you to teach him how to cover the routes. Boost the kid's confidence. We lose one more game and we lose our shot at regionals."

I stretch my fingers and resist the urge to tell him where to shove helping Ray or the team because no one is helping me.

"Don't answer now," Coach says. "Take some time. Think about it, but I have a feeling you'll show. As I said, you're the better man."

Without saying a word, I turn and walk out.

Violet

I'm jealous of my mom's happiness. I'm quite aware of how awful and bitter that sounds, but it's tough to know her happiness is due to my kidnapping. The real jealousy is that she's just happy. There's a smile on her face and pure joy radiates from her as she places the third round of hot buttered bread on the table in Cyrus's kitchen. She's plain happy and I honestly forgot how happy feels, so for a moment I wish I was her.

Found another note this morning in my math folder:

Want you to know we understand your situation. Can't expect you to get what we want if you aren't home, but we hear you'll be home once certain people are back in KY. By the way, number fifteen is wrong. You need to divide instead of multiply.

A stalker and blackmailer who is checking my math homework. My brain is slowly separating into tiny pieces and it's going to be a very short trip to become a resident in the land of gone crazy.

But my mom? My mom's happy. It's Wednesday evening and the cramped kitchen is full of hungry men in black leather Reign of Terror vests and too-loud conversations. They were all drawn in by the scent of freshly baked bread and lasagna. I've got to admit, Mom makes a mean lasagna and she bakes bread you sort of think was created in heaven.

"No one can have any more lasagna until Chevy gets in here and makes his plate," Mom announces like everyone in the room is her child.

I've eaten more than my fair share tonight, yet I'm considering the corner piece of lasagna with the burnt edges. Those are my favorite and I think I might still have room in my stomach for more. But with the way Pigpen's eyes are flickering between that piece and me, I might have to stab him in the hand with a fork to get it.

"It's mine," he whispers. "Go for it and you're going down."

Despite my best intentions, I smile and his eyes shine with the win.

Cyrus walks into the kitchen from the back door and at the same time Chevy comes in from the hallway. His hair is dark and damp from a shower and his T-shirt clings a little too tight. Butterflies race in my stomach at the anticipation of waiting for his eyes to meet mine.

But Chevy doesn't look at me—he watches Cyrus and the butterflies give way as I frown. Cyrus isn't doing anything unusual. He washes his hands at the sink, makes a few comments here and there to the guys, but Chevy is seeing something else, something no one else sees.

Finally, he does tear his eyes away from Cyrus to me and he smiles. That pirate one, the gorgeous one, the dimpled one, the one that makes me very aware he has something up his sleeve. He eases into the chair beside me, holds out his empty palm, fists it, then magically produces a coin. Within seconds, he's rolling it over his knuckles in a movement I've never been able to mimic.

Chevy's not the only one who can read people. I've known him for too long. "What's wrong?"

"Nothing."

"I can read you better than you think."

"Really?" His eyes wander along my body and I turn pink. "What am I saying now?"

I reach out to steal the coin, but it falls into his palm, and when he reopens it, the coin's gone. He waves his fingers as he waggles his eyebrows. Yeah, he's hiding something and it's not the coin.

Pigpen passes the pan of lasagna in Chevy's direction and he takes two squares for himself, then deposits the corner piece on my plate. I smirk at Pigpen and he scowls back at me.

The moment Chevy has enough salad and bread on an additional plate to feed a developing nation, the locusts descend and take the rest of the food. Mom stays by the sink and has this pride and satisfaction on her face that I once again find myself envious over.

"Maybe you should have been a cook," I say, and the guys quiet down. I talk now, but not a ton.

Mom blinks several times. "Are you talking to me?"

I nod with lasagna in my mouth, then swallow the Italian goodness. "Maybe you should have been a cook in a fancy restaurant. Your food is that good. Did you ever think about it? Cooking school?"

Mom seems surprised by the compliment and accepts it

with a good-natured grin. "I don't need a restaurant when I have all these growing boys."

Rumbles of male laughter and my own glow dies. Mom notices and her smile wanes. Why can't anything just be about her? Why does it always have to involve the Terror?

"I stopped by your practice today," Cyrus says, and Chevy, who had been absorbed in his food, lowers his fork. "Why was Ray running your routes?"

The air catches in my throat and my head turns to Chevy. In fact, every conversation ceases and all eyes are on him. Chevy mixes his salad around his plate, then uses his bread to push the lettuce onto his fork. "I'm benched."

He shoves the food into his mouth as Cyrus stares at him like he announced he has leprosy. "Why? For this week? Because you missed practice last week?"

A shrug and a drink of water. "Indefinitely."

"What happened?"

Chevy finishes chewing, then tosses his fork onto his plate of half-eaten food. "I was kidnapped."

"And?"

"The school board has decided since I was kidnapped, then I must be involved in gang activity. Until it's proven otherwise, I'm benched."

My heart stops, and I reach out and touch Chevy's shoulder. Football is his life. It's his release. It's his everything.

Guys are cursing, saying words full of malice, but all I can do is focus on Chevy, wishing he'd look in my direction, but he's locked in a stare with Cyrus. Neither of them speak, don't even blink.

Cyrus breaks first and scoops lasagna onto his fork. "I'll talk to your coach. Get this cleared up."

Chevy pushes away from the table and my hand falls from

his body. "Coach said he'll get it cleared up. No need for you to get involved."

"No way. You're family and we take care of our problems."

"Coach specifically told me he doesn't want you involved. He said you talking to the school's administration, the board, will only hurt my case, not help."

Cyrus goes red and his fork clanks against the table when he throws it down. "You're my family and we will take care of it as we see fit. The Terror will stand behind you."

"Not on this. Let Coach handle this."

"We know how to handle the school board. We know how to talk to them to get them to understand."

"No!" Chevy snaps, and I shake with his voice. He never raises his voice. Not like this. Chevy doesn't lose control. "The football team—it isn't your world. It's my world. It's completely separate from you, from the Terror, from this house. You don't get a vote on this. If I say Coach is going to take care of it, he takes care of it."

Cyrus shakes his head, opens his mouth like he's going to argue, but Chevy mutters, "Fuck it," snatches his jacket off the back of a chair and goes for the back door. It creaks open, then slams shut.

When Cyrus goes to stand, I smack my good leg against the table, rattling everyone's plates, as I struggle to get to my feet first. "Let me."

I fumble with my crutches in haste as Chevy can move faster than me when I have two working legs. The men maneuver out of my way, and Man O' War opens the door for me. I'm out, frantically scan for Chevy, and he's already halfway across the yard, moving toward his bike.

"Chevy!"

He turns, and when he sees me, he stops. I'm hobbling as fast as I can, the crutches digging into my arms. As if he realized I wasn't a dream, Chevy stalks in my direction, and when he comes close enough, I let go of the crutches and fall into him, knowing he'll catch me. My head to his shoulder, squeezing him as tight as I can. "I'm sorry."

Chevy hugs me back, in a bear sort of way, his body encompassing mine, his arms steel bands, his nose nuzzling into my hair as if he can't find a way to get close enough.

"I'm sorry," I whisper again. "I'm so sorry."

"Come with me?" Chevy asks.

I press tighter to him as if there was actual space between us. "Anywhere."

"All I got is my bike."

And my knee is bad, plus I haven't been on the back of a bike since Dad died.

"But I won't go far. I promise."

My throat knots. The back of a bike, but it's with Chevy and he needs me. "Then let's go."

The air rushes out of my lungs when Chevy leans down and swings me up in his arms. He walks fast for his bike, probably wishing that no one from the Terror is watching us. That for a few minutes, we can find a way to be completely alone in our grief.

His Harley is a beautiful piece of machinery. It's the bike his father rode and it was given to Chevy the day he turned sixteen. He cares for this bike with the same loving care he shows when he touches me.

Chevy sets me on the ground, draws his leather jacket off his shoulders, places it on mine, pulls his keys out of his pocket, and the moment he's on, he offers his hand to me.

Countless times, Chevy has given me his jacket, but I don't remember it being so warm or the rich scent of spices so thick and comforting.

I accept his hand, ease onto the seat so I don't place weight on my bad knee, then swing the good one over to the other side. Even though I haven't ridden a motorcycle in months, I'm still a biker girl at heart. Because of that, I have never stopped placing a hair tie in my pocket just in case.

I tie my hair at the nape of my neck, then wrap my arms around Chevy's stomach so I can hide my face in his back. He doesn't need to see the wince as I position the foot of my bad leg on the rest.

Chevy starts the bike, the engine rumbles beneath me and in seconds we're gone. I lift my head and enjoy the wind on my face, my hair rippling in the currents, the way my body vibrates with the powerful machine. The feel of Chevy's strong body beneath my touch is heaven and the poetic memories of freedom that only being on the back of a bike bring flood to my mind.

There's a spark within me, a jolt of hope and joy. Happiness. It's there, it's almost within reach. Chevy tackles the curve at breakneck speed as if we're chasing happiness down with all we're worth.

I rest my chin on his shoulder, then turn my head to kiss Chevy's neck. He reaches back and squeezes my thigh. *I love you, Chevy. I love you so much it hurts. I love you so much I'm not sure I'll ever love anyone as much as I love you.*

I don't say any of that, but I do press my lips to his neck and kiss him again.

CHEVY

Violet laughs as I juggle her, open the door to my home, then kick it shut with my foot. The sound is like the best buzz I've experienced. The best way to end a crappy day. The best way to end any day is with Violet in my arms.

Once inside, I gently set her on the couch and I pause as I straighten. She's beautiful. Fire-red hair, eyes that rival any clear blue sky, skin so soft it could be satin and she's smiling. Violet's smiling. She's always been the most beautiful creature on the face of the planet, but smiling, Violet is a queen.

"How's your knee?" I ask.

"Okay. Little sore, but it'll be fine once I stretch it out."

Violet shifts and lays her leg on the love seat, but her knee is still bent. The living room is only big enough for the blue love seat, a twenty-inch flat-screen on the wall and the brown leather recliner we found on clearance because of the rip on the back.

For the first ten years of my life, we rented apartments. But Mom scraped together enough money to buy this condo. Since then, Mom's spent close to eight years making this place a home with its vibrant wall colors, mismatched furniture that looks so good together it seems like she did it on purpose and a throw rug over carpet that should have been replaced years ago.

"If you want, I can take you to my room," I say. "You'll be more comfortable in there."

Violet's smile enters the realm of mischievous. "Are you trying to get me in your bed?"

I chuckle. Not intentionally. "Is it working?"

She swings her leg to the ground and grabs on to my wrist as she stands. Violet slowly walks to my room, and even with the limp, she has a sexy strut that holds my attention. Her hips sway from side to side and my blood begins to warm. Until she says the word, touching her is off limits, but not touching doesn't mean not fantasizing.

Without having to look, she flips on the light to my room and then slips onto my bed like it's hers. Might as well be. She's the only girl who has lain in it, the only girl I've kissed on it, the only girl I've held in it as I slept.

Even with our months apart, she continued to own me and I could never bring anyone else to a place that forever belonged to us.

She fluffs a pillow, takes the brace off her knee, drops it to the floor like it's poison, then stretches her hand to my bedside table and uses the remote to turn on the TV that sits on top of my dresser. My room isn't much. A full bed with a dark blue comforter and matching sheets. Football trophies and a couple of books on shelves. Colts and Harley posters on the light green wall.

I lean my back against the doorway and soak it all in. This. I miss this. I miss the easiness of Violet. The peacefulness of having her in my life. Yeah, she's a ball of fire, but when we were together, I could hold that fire and not get burned.

"I've missed you," I say.

Violet glances over at me and the softness in her expression nearly brings me to my knees. "Me, too."

My cell buzzes and I pull it out of my pocket.

Oz: Club's figuring out you and Violet split. Razor and I saw you go. They're thirty seconds to going crazy. Give me something to calm them down.

Me: Violet's with me. We're safe.

Oz: Where are you?

Me: Home. But we need silence. We need time alone.

Oz: Razor and I will cover for the two of you. If they insist Violet needs additional tails, we'll volunteer.

Me: I hear it's going to be a cold night.

Oz: It'll do Razor some good. He's gotten soft falling in love.

I chuckle and Oz sends another message: No one will come near. You've got my word.

Me: Thanks

Oz: Anytime

"Is the cavalry on the way to swoop in and save me from the dust bunnies under your bed?" Violet asks as she flips through the stations of a TV that's heavier and older than me.

"I told Oz we needed time." I push off the wall, turn off

the light and join her on the bed. I allow her space if she should need it, but she shifts in my direction. Her shoulder brushes against mine, and I won't lie, that simple contact causes my restless soul to settle. "He and Razor have our backs."

"They do," she agrees, and it's the first sign of her trusting anyone beyond me in the Terror. "I also miss them."

"There's nothing they wouldn't do for you." Nothing I wouldn't do for her either.

"Want to talk about it?" she asks, switching subjects. I'm not sure if she's talking about football or how I unleashed on Cyrus. Possibly both.

"No. I'd like to pretend the last few weeks didn't happen." She snorts. "Can we pretend the last year didn't happen?"

"Works for me." More than she could imagine.

Violet chooses a movie we've seen a hundred times, but it's one of those you don't mind watching again. Even though it's a favorite, a movie Razor, Oz and I will say the lines with while we're together, I don't watch the screen. I watch Violet.

As time continues to pass, she leans further into me. Her head on my shoulder until I move so I can wrap my arm around her. She then rests her head on my chest and places an arm over my stomach. My fingers caress the skin of her arm, and because I am pretending the past year didn't happen, I nuzzle her hair and sometimes press my lips to her head.

We've melted into each other, creating a warm bubble.

My skin tickles as Violet begins to brush her fingernails gently across the bare skin of my arm. I briefly close my eyes and bite back the need to moan. The touch is so sweet it's almost an ache. The drought of her touch has been too long and a flood of emotion breaks as her fingers trail up my arm, along my shoulder and onto my collarbone.

Violet raises her head and the smoldering look in her eyes

nearly undoes me. I know what she's searching for, what the silent plea in her expression means, but I can't. "I can't kiss you unless you tell me it's what you want."

I can't mess us up. I can't keep leading us down bad roads.

"I don't know what I want," she whispers. "I don't want to hurt anymore, I don't want to be broken, I don't want to be with you, but I can't live without you. Last thing I want to do right now is make another mistake that's going to cause me to bleed, but the only thing I do know is that if I don't kiss you tonight, I'm going to regret it for the rest of my life."

Her spirit is hurting, weak and in need, and so is mine. I don't know much either. I'm confused and blinded by the fog we've stumbled into, but Violet is real and warm and a fortress by which I fall to my knees whenever I come into contact. I need her, she needs me and tonight we just need to hold each other.

"I can't make promises," she says like we're in a church.

But I do have a promise for her. "I love you. I always have, always will. I understand the promises you're talking about and I understand why you can't make them, but I'm going to make a promise to you. No matter which way this plays out, I promise to love you and do my best to make sure whatever path we go down together or separately will be the one that hurts you the least."

Violet tilts her head as if my words hurt her while at the same time hugged her. She reaches up, her fingertips sliding across my face, and before she has a chance to pull away, I capture her hand and press it against my chest.

"I love you," I repeat.

"Please kiss me."

I release her hand, it remains on my chest, over my heart, and I tunnel my fingers into her hair. My thumb caresses the smooth skin of her cheek, and as I lean forward, adrenaline hits my bloodstream.

There's a pull to her, there's always been a pull. Violet's the gravitational force that rights my world, but this time, this kiss, it'll be imprinted in my brain, a memory that will last until my last breath.

Our mouths are only centimeters apart, and I can hear and feel her slight intake of air. When she wets her lips, I draw in closer and kiss. A light brush, a slight shake as if this is the first time, as if this is the last time.

Another press and her sweet familiar scent envelops me. I lick her lips and Violet gives, becoming liquid in my arms. She opens herself to me, her fingers in my hair, her legs tangling with mine, our mouths and tongues moving in ways that only come with years of understanding what makes the other shiver, what makes the other yearn for more, what makes the other feel as if the only way to be complete is to be of one body and skin.

Fire. Waves of flames lick through my veins and my fingers lift the fabric of her shirt in an effort to help the growing heat. We shift as we continue to kiss, her hands just as greedily taking off my shirt, helping me with hers, and then we're shedding more, touching more, remembering, retracing, re-memorizing, reliving all that was and is glorious between us.

There's a rhythm, one that had been relegated only to dreams. Holding her in my arms, feeling her caresses along my spine, her kisses along my chest, her body moving in a way that causes my mind to become fuzzy and warm, I want nothing more than to crawl inside her, to become one.

I move my hips, Violet gasps and curls further into me, but then she shakes her head, allowing her nose to rub against my cheek. "We can do things, but not that. My heart won't recover if we do that."

Make love. We've made love before, but after doing it a few times, she said she wanted to wait to do it again. That she didn't regret it, but she didn't know she wasn't ready until it was done. I told her I'd wait until she was thirty. I'd wait because while waiting we found other ways to love, other ways to touch, other ways to make her cling tighter to me and whisper my name.

So we do those things. We touch in ways that make my head spin, ways that cause her to nip at my neck, pull at my hair, press her body to mine so that we're skin against skin and bring us to a high that spirals up so fast, so quickly that when we reach the pinnacle, we both squeeze the other, then tremble in the beautiful aftermath.

There's a heat built between us, and as we struggle for breath, the first chill of the real world bites at our skin. Goose bumps form along her arm and I reach down, then pull the thick comforter over both of us.

Violet cuddles into me and I can't stop myself from feathering kisses along her face, in her hair, and I whisper the same words over and over again. *I love you.*

She holds on to me as if she'd fall off a long drop if she were to let go and I hold on to her just as tight.

"I want to stay here," she says against my chest. "I want to stay the night here with you."

"Then you will."

It doesn't take long until her body grows pliant, her breathing becomes light and she flinches slightly in her dreams. My own body is heavy from sweet exhaustion, but it's tough to let this moment go, to not fight to stay awake so I can enjoy her next to me.

Letting her go for a moment, I reach for the remote, point it at the TV, and that's when I spot the bag on my dresser. My heart stalls. Her birthday present. Violet's birthday present is on my dresser and then I run a hand over my face. She's eighteen. She turned eighteen in the basement. I remembered that night but then forgot and not one person has figured it out. All of us, including me in a way, forgot her birthday.

I look down at my sleeping beauty. See the rare peacefulness on her face, feel the way she trusts with how she's wrapped around me. Yes, I'm going to love her and I need to love her right.

Violet

Two men hold Chevy, another hits him with metal fists over and over again. Blood bursts from Chevy's nose as the blood in my veins whooshes in my ears. I scream, but no one's listening. I yell, but my words are a silent rain. They're going to kill him. He's going to die. A gun in a hand, it's pointed and then I'm running. Running toward it, running for my death and then there's a shot... *Bang!*

My eyes open, I sit up in the bed and I put my hand to my chest trying to calm my heart as I gasp for breath. I'm covered in sweat and I'm shaking. A check of the new cell Mom bought me confirms it's four in the morning. At least two more hours before we need to start getting ready for school. Beside me, Chevy's in a deep sleep. I slowly breathe out as it hurts to look at him. He almost died in front of me, and if he had, I never would have forgiven myself.

In his sleep, he seems so young. So innocent. Dark stubble along a baby face. I should tell him what the Riot wants from me. He's promised to love me through this. Maybe I can trust him like I did in the basement. Maybe this time he's choosing me.

My hands continue to tremble. I'm wired and I'm parched. Careful not to wake Chevy, I roll out of bed, pull his T-shirt over my head and slip on my jeans. The door to Nina's room is closed and a pang of guilt hits me. I didn't think about how she'd feel about me staying the night with her son. She's awesome letting Chevy stay with me at Cyrus's. No doubt she's aware it's in the same bed, but even awesome moms have limitations and I wonder if my being so overtly in her son's bed while she's home has crossed the line.

I sigh as I add that to the list of things I need to find time to worry about tomorrow.

The kitchen is off the living room and the small light over the oven casts a glow over two lumps. Oz is asleep, sprawled out on the recliner, Razor on the floor. Either of them would crush the small couch if they had tried to sleep on it.

Razor's eyes pop open as I pad into the kitchen, and from the moving of blankets, I can tell he's following. I retrieve a glass from the cupboard and fill it with water. Razor walks in, combing his fingers through his blond hair, and I have to admit, he's cute rumpled. I also have to admit, he's never been my type.

"You okay?" he asks.

I nod. "Bad dream."

"That I get." He props himself up to sit on the counter. A few weeks ago, he lived out a different type of nightmare with the girl he loves.

"When did you guys come in?" I ask.

"Chevy texted us after you fell asleep and told us to let ourselves in. Floor's a lot better than sitting on my bike all night."

"I'm sorry you have to do this."

"Don't be. Feels good to be doing something for you two instead of sitting on my hands feeling helpless."

"Helpless sucks," I say.

This time Razor nods and then he gets a faraway look in his eyes. "Can I talk to you about something?"

Considering he's been my best friend since the age of dinosaurs, I lift my fingers in a bring-it motion.

He rubs the back of his head, then crosses his arms over his chest like he feels naked. "I notice you sat with Addison at school today. Has she said anything about me? About Breanna?"

It's awful that it happens. Terrible. It's the worst thing a best friend can do, but the smile on my face is too large and I can't quite swallow the entire laugh. Razor lowers his head and mutters a curse and I do my best to sober up.

"I'm sorry," I choke through another swallowed laugh. "I couldn't help it. It's just that I was kidnapped and now I'm home and there's all this crap and all everyone wants to talk about with me is the Riot and then you ask something that's just so…"

"Pathetic," he adds.

I lose the smile and my heart is heavy for him. "No. Your question was just so…eighteen. Sometimes I forget we're only eighteen."

"Seventeen for you," he says, and I don't disagree because there's no point.

"To answer your question, yes, she talked about you. She thinks you're Satan because Breanna's no longer in town."

He bobs his head like her assessment might be right. "You're friends with Addison now?"

"We shared French fries and a lunch table. Considering how the rest of the school has treated me, that's the closest I've got to a friend."

"I'm your friend." He offers a sly smile.

"God help my soul."

He chuckles in agreement. "Think you can put in a good word for me with Addison? Breanna loves her and someday she'll be back in town. When that happens, I want to fit as good as I can in her life. The best friend is a good place to start."

Yeah, best friends can make or break any relationship. "I'll do my best, but keep in mind I'm all out of miracles. I used them all up in that basement."

"Your best is all I need." He hops down from the counter, and before he leaves, he glances at me from over his shoulder. "When you're ready to talk about what really happened between you and the Riot, I want you to know I'm around."

The way his blue eyes bore into me makes me uneasy and now I'm the one wrapping my arms around myself. "Eli talked to you, right?"

He nods his head once.

"Then you know everything."

"As I said, when you're ready to spill on what really happened, I'm here." And with that, he leaves me alone with my glass of water and my scattered thoughts.

CHEVY

Eli and Cyrus showed at six with six cups of coffee, a box of donuts and the truck to take Violet home to get ready for school. After taking a shower and getting dressed, I've run out of reasons to hide in my room. My grandfather is waiting and he's waiting in my mother's home. Hell must have frozen over last night.

Cyrus is sitting at the kitchen table, his coffee in his hand as he stares at the fridge. Mom covered it in artwork from me as a kid, pictures of the two of us through the years and a list of emergency numbers in case I need help. All of them are friends of hers and none of them Reign of Terror. She tries, but I've never let her run the Terror from my life.

I find a clean glass in the dishwasher, pull out orange juice from the fridge, pour, return it, then lean against the counter. Cyrus watches me, and I watch him. Feels like the few seconds before someone yells charge on enemy territory.

"You should have told us you were leaving last night and you especially should have told us you were leaving with Violet," he finally says.

"We wanted to be alone."

"We give you privacy at the cabin."

"We needed to be alone on our own terms. At some point, the club's going to have to give up on watching us and let us live our lives."

Cyrus strokes his beard. "You sound like Violet."

"She's got some good points and she's worth listening to."

"You've been home two weeks. Are you going to be mad at us for making sure the girl you love is safe?"

Kick straight to the nuts.

"Won't lie," he continues. "I can't imagine what it's like for the two of you. Can't imagine the demons that come along with a night like you had. Me and the club, we might not always be right, but we try. Don't fault us for that." Silence as he circles his finger around the rim of his coffee cup. "We care about you and Violet. When I heard you two were taken…"

Cyrus shakes his head and my chest hurts. He looks up at me then, straight in the eye. "I didn't want to lose you. Still don't. I've lost friends, lost your father, lost a woman who was like a daughter to me and then my granddaughter. I lost my wife. I've done too much losing for any man and my soul can't take much more. You're more than a grandson to me. You're a part of me and I can't take losing you."

A hard man. A stoic man. Taught me to tie my shoes, a tie and a slipknot for the boat at the pond. Taught me to pet a dog, make eye contact when shaking a hand and how to throw a punch. Taught me how to be a man of integrity in a world that says integrity is a relic.

I drop into the chair across from him. "The football mess—I know you want to help, but you barging in and yelling at the board won't help. It will only give them the proof they need."

"Are you ashamed of this club?"

"No."

"But you only want our help on your terms? Sorry to tell you, that's not how we work."

All or nothing. How many times has Violet said this to me? "Why can't football belong to me?"

"It can, but you've been listening to Violet too much. All we want to do is help and all I hear is you pushing me away."

"Sometimes navigating between this world and the world outside the clubhouse walls isn't easy. Some battles I need to fight on my own."

"You're not the first man to say that. In fact, your father said that to me more than a few times."

"You say it like it's a bad thing."

No response from Cyrus.

"Why did James go to Louisville?" I ask.

Cyrus readjusts in his chair and I will him to answer, not shut me down like he has for eighteen years. "The work he was looking for wasn't available in Snowflake."

"I thought he was a welder." James went to college, worked part-time as a welder to pay his way through school, got his bachelors, but after he graduated, he kept welding.

"He was." The answer simple.

A pit forms in my stomach. Plenty of welding jobs in the area. "Why not Bowling Green, then?"

"James wanted Louisville."

"Why?"

"The men who kidnapped you and Violet were brought in to Louisville last night. Eli and I will be pulling the two of you out of school early and will drive you there for the lineup."

My mind stretches in two opposite directions and it comes close to ripping my brain in half. Cyrus can talk about my father for hours when it comes to anything before his graduation from high school, but the after...he goes dead silent. The need to understand my father is overpowering, but the need to protect Violet is stronger. "Violet needs to be told."

"You can do it if you want. Eli's driving her back here so you can take her to school. We thought you would prefer that."

We would. "Thanks."

Cyrus leans forward, resting his elbows on the table. "I know you and Violet are tight again. How tight I don't know, but I want to warn you—"

"I'm being careful," I cut him off. "I'm not interested in hurting her."

"That's not what I mean. I've been watching Violet and something's got her spooked. If anyone comes up on her too fast or if she's alone, she jumps. Not a lot, but enough. And she's watching everyone and everything. Don't tell me you haven't noticed."

I have. It's not big enough that I would have guessed anyone else would have noticed, but Cyrus understands how to read people, too. "Maybe you missed we were kidnapped."

"It's more than that. She's scared. Doesn't trust where she's at."

How do I explain she doesn't trust the club? "She'll feel better once she sleeps in her own bed. Violet needs to feel normal again, even if normal is still far away."

He knocks his hand twice against the table. "She's hiding something. I know you don't want to hear it. Know you're too vested in things working out between the two of you, but I've been thinking about this kidnapping over and over again. If they wanted you, why would they be near Violet's house? If they wanted you, why would they have stopped at her car? I saw where you were taken. Your bike was hidden behind her car from their viewpoint."

An edginess sets into my muscles. "You think they were after Violet?"

"She was alone with them and she's not talking about what they said. I don't know how to protect her, you or my club when she keeps quiet. She's close to you again, and I need you to use that. Get her to talk, and once she does talk, promise me you'll tell me what she says.

"This isn't football," he continues. "This is the lives of men you consider family, friends and brothers. You want me to leave football alone, I will, but don't let your feelings and loyalties for Violet cost me any more people I love."

"You're talking like she's working against you, against the club," I say in a low voice, and there's a dangerous curling in my gut.

"The Riot went from beating the hell out of you, pulling a gun and taking a shot to letting you go within thirty minutes. Are you telling me that you wouldn't have made some sort of deal to get you and her out?"

Can't lie. After I heard that gunshot, there wasn't much I wouldn't have done. Cyrus reads my expression and nods his understanding. "Difference between you and Violet is that you trust us and she doesn't. When dogs are chained and mistreated, they'll bite any hand, even the one meant to save and feed them. Violet's no exception."

I had heaven last night with Violet, and in a matter of minutes, my mind's a mess again.

"Promise me you'll find out what's going on," Cyrus presses. "Promise you'll tell me. Think about how many people are depending on you doing the right thing."

Like Eli, Oz, Razor, Pigpen, Man O' War, their wives and girlfriends and children. It all sucks, but I love these people as much as Cyrus. Violet does, too. Our endgame is the same, even if Violet doesn't understand that now. "I'll get her to talk. I'll let you know what's going on."

The front door shuts, and my spine straightens as if I was jolted with electricity. I'm out of the chair and into the living room and Violet is leaning against the front door. She looks at me, I look at her and her expression is blank, giving absolutely nothing away.

"Eli dropped us off," she says. "Brandon's waiting in the truck and he doesn't want to be late for school."

"I was talking to Cyrus. Do you want a donut?"

Violet looks me over from head to toe. She heard. She knows I'm betraying her. "No, I'm good." Her lips lift as she jacks her thumb over her shoulder. "You ready?"

My gut twists at the smile. Maybe she didn't hear, but then again, maybe she did. Either way, we won't be able to talk about it until later tonight. After school, after the lineup, after all the other people fade away. Question is, can I lose her in that amount of time?

"Yeah, I'm ready to roll."

Violet

I wipe my cold, clammy hands against my jeans and drop into the nearest chair in the conference room the detective pointed me toward. Mom, Cyrus and Eli pulled me and Chevy out of school early and brought us to the police station in Louisville. It's Thursday and we're here to identify the men who kidnapped us.

No sweat, right? Nothing bad will happen from fingering the bastards who kidnapped and tortured us. Of course I should believe what the Riot are telling the Terror. The Riot are one million percent behind us prosecuting, in theory, ex-members of their club.

Yep, easy peasey lemon squeezy.

Doesn't help I found another note this morning in my leather jacket.

Heard after the lineup you'll be heading home. You know what to do once you get there. We don't believe it should take you long.

Whoever is watching me is on the inside of the club as Eli isn't overly talking to people about me heading home and that means I'm doubly screwed. There's no trusting the club. There's no way to ignore the Riot. There's no way to survive this situation intact.

Tonight, I'll go home, wait for Mom to fall asleep and then I'll search through Dad's computer and dig through old files to find account numbers that will secure my family's safety and Eli's place in hell. God, I want to vomit.

Chevy enters the room and sits beside me in one of the chairs against the wall. He's cool and calm and collected as always. In this moment, I find his demeanor infuriating as I feel like I'm about to spontaneously combust into a ball of fire.

"You okay?" he asks low enough so only I can hear.

"Peachy," I answer, and his body shakes with his short chuckle.

I don't know how to handle or what to think of Chevy. I overheard the tail end of his conversation with Cyrus. Some words I could understand, others I couldn't, but from what I gathered, Chevy plans on getting me to talk and then selling me out.

I should be mad. I should be furious, but I can't find the strength for so much anger. He's lying to me. I'm lying to him. I figure that makes us even.

The police station isn't really as crazy as I thought it would be. It's rather calm. Lots of random people and police officers at desks in half-walled cubicles. I assumed it would be like TV and there'd be people handcuffed to chairs and yelling obscenities. Maybe that happens in another part of the building.

Everyone's been nice. Offering us something to drink, explaining what will happen when the lineup starts, telling me that I look like I'm about to pass out and it's okay to sit. You know, nice.

"What if we do this and the Riot change their minds on being cool about us fingering Fiend and his friends?" I ask. "What if they're lying and they come after us again? What if Fiend gets out of jail and seeks revenge for what we're about to do?"

What if I don't find those account numbers? What if I do and Eli goes to jail for something he never did? What if an asteroid comes hurtling out of the sky and busts into hundreds of little pieces and hits each and every single member of the Riot?

I roll my bracelets around my wrist. Chevy places his hand over mine, lifts our combined hands, waves his other hand in a circle, and when he flips his palm over, my silver bracelet, the one he gave me for my sixteenth birthday, is in his hand.

Complete awe. Never felt him remove the bracelet. Doesn't matter how many times he does this, I'm dazzled.

Chevy flips my bracelet around until I see the inside inscription. *Forever.* My heart lifts, then sinks. At sixteen, I had believed the two of us were forever. He waves his other hand over the bracelet, claps, and then the bracelet is back on my wrist again.

"Is that your way of saying everything's okay?" I ask.

"It's my way of saying I'm right here beside you and that's where I plan on staying."

A tightness in my chest and I clear my throat to gain some control. "You could make a million dollars in Vegas."

"Nah, wouldn't happen. I don't know how to put people back together once I saw them in half."

I giggle, a little too loudly for the situation, and a guy in uniform passing the room we're in gives us a disapproving glare. Eli, Cyrus and Mom went off to talk to two men in

white button-down shirts and ties. Once again, making decisions and choices for me. "Where's your mom?"

"She has to work. She's taken off too much time and
needs the money. She's pissed she's not here, but I told her
it's not a big deal."

"Nope. Not a big deal at all," I murmur.

He bumps his knee into mine. "You want me to do this?"

"You are doing this, hence why you're sitting here next
to me."

"No, do you want me to do this for the both of us? In the
end, only one of us needs to point them out."

"I'm sure the boys in the white shirts will be happy with
that. I believe their words were something about a stronger
case with both of us pointing fingers."

"Ask me if I fucking care." The unusual harshness in his
tone grabs my full attention. "Their happiness isn't my problem."

"Then what is your problem?"

He runs a hand over his head, kicks out his legs and stares
straight out into the room. "Anything that bothers you."

I continue to watch him. He knows it, and from the way
he stays still, he doesn't like it. Yes, Chevy knows me, but I
know him just as well. Chevy's smooth, a trickster, and has
a way of bringing things up without anyone else really understanding the underlying conversation. I rode with him in
the truck on the way here and he was quiet. Mom was with
us, but still he was too silent.

"Did something happen?" I ask. "More football problems?"

"I'll tell you if you tell me why you were wound so tight
to return home and don't give me the bullshit on freedom.
I know you, Violet, and you're hiding something."

And there it is. Chevy played his cards and played them well. Waited for the moment when I'm too frayed to lie well.

"It is about freedom," I hedge.

"But that's not all. There's more and you're keeping it to yourself."

He's right, he's aware he's right and now I'm the one who's quiet.

"Someday, I hope you'll trust me again," he says softly.

I flinch. His words a knife straight into my windpipe and I can't breathe.

"Mr. McKinley?" With a file in hand, one of the officers working our case appears in the doorway. "Will you please follow me?"

The officer leaves, Chevy rises to his feet, and before he walks out, I blurt, "Be careful."

Chevy glances at me over his shoulder. "It's just a lineup."

I hold his dark eyes and wish I could find words to explain how this sixth sense crawling underneath my skin tells me that there's nothing "just" about anything involving us anymore. But there are no words and any that I could possibly think of are stuck on my twisted tongue.

I stand abruptly, so quickly my heart pounds. Chevy's forehead furrows. I don't want him to walk out this door and for this to have been the last moment alone before I go home and ruin either my or Eli's life. I don't want my last real memory of the two of us to be of a magic trick and conversation on the Riot.

I will my feet forward, practically tripping with how heavy my body feels under the burden of what's to come, and before I can overthink, I plow into him. My arms around his body, my head into his chest and I squeeze, inhaling deeply, and try to memorize everything about him. His scent of leather and dark spices, the hard plane of his chest, the sound of his heart against my ear, the heat rolling off his body.

A strong arm around my waist, another tunneling into my hair. Chevy lowers his head and kisses my forehead. The sensation of his lips against my skin causes thrilling goose bumps.

"It's okay," he whispers. "We're okay. I promise. I know things are complicated now, but it's going to get better."

It's not. "I trust you." Just him. "I do. I don't know how to trust me."

I used to trust myself. Never doubted my decisions, had the confidence that could move mountains, but I lost that. Lost myself. Way before the kidnapping, it happened after my father's death, but now I'm spiraling.

Someday, I hope to trust me again. Trust my emotions. Trust my instincts. Trust that I'm going to be able to live with the fallout of the choices facing me.

"I trust you," he says. "I always have."

He shouldn't. No one should. I lift my head and Chevy tucks strands of my hair behind my ear. He does it once, twice, a third time, and each time he brushes his fingers against the side of my neck. His light touch is warm and causes tingles that reach my toes.

"Talk to me, Vi," he says.

I open my mouth, but there are still no words. No way to explain why my pulse beats so hard and why my mind is running at a thousand miles per hour and how I feel that the world has tilted in the wrong direction and is picking up speed. "I'm scared."

"If it's the lineup, I meant what I said earlier. We'll tell them they have to deal with me being the only one doing the fingering."

Fear is clawing at me, eating me from the inside out. Fear of the Riot, of their reach, of their rage, but that's not the fear festering in me now. If I get the account numbers and betray Eli, I'll never be able to look Chevy in the eye again. Eli is like a father to him, a friend, his mentor. Betraying Eli means betraying Chevy.

If I don't fulfill my duty, then maybe I'll pay the ultimate price. Maybe I'll die, because that's what would happen before I ever let anyone touch my mother or Brandon.

The blood drains from my face and my bad knee starts to give. Chevy uses his strength to hold me up. "Violet?"

I love him. I never stopped and it's hard to describe when it began because he's always been a part of my life. Loving him was easy. It's life that's hard.

I swallow to calm the nerves. "I want you to kiss me… now."

His eyebrows rise. "We're in a police station."

"Are you saying you don't want to kiss me?"

"Mr. McKinley?" comes a questioning voice from behind, but Chevy keeps those dark orbs right on me.

"I will be there when I show. Interrupt me again and I'm walking out of this building and your damn case can crumble." Chevy says it in such a calm yet commanding tone, and he does it all while letting his fingers slide up and down the small of my back.

The caress is familiar, it's intoxicating and it takes me back to the first time he kissed me in the field between my home and Cyrus's. Chevy kicks the door to the small room shut.

"There's a window," he says. "People will see."

Though I should… "I don't care."

My blood is buzzing, the cells in my body waking after a long hibernation.

Chevy tilts my head up as he lowers his and I suddenly find it hard to breathe. But then he smiles. The endearing one. The dimpled one. That one that has haunted me in my dreams since we've been apart.

"I have never been able to understand you." His lips whisper against mine and it's like a tease and a promise of what's to come.

"Is that a bad thing?"

"Never." Chevy kisses me and my entire body hums. Hums. A sweet song, a vibration in melody. His lips are warm and his push and pulls gentle, yet a winding begins in my belly.

My hands wander along his back, along his neck, and when I tangle my fingers into his hair—fireworks.

Chevy's moving, his feet guiding me back. I follow along in the dance and he uses his arms to brace my body when we hit the wall. The edges of my mouth tilt up as we continue to kiss. I've missed all of this. The way Chevy's hands wander all of me as his lips devour mine, the way he presses his body into mine as if we share one skin, the way there's an air of reverence in how some touches are so strong and then other caresses so soft that I could cry with the tenderness.

The familiar heat in my bloodstream grows hotter and our kiss borders on out of control. We know each other, feel each other, and we know all of the buttons to push. His hands on my face, my fingers curling along his back. If I shift left and he shifts right, we'll be arrested for very indecent things.

Arrested. Police officers. There's a window.

My palm to his chest, a push and Chevy sucks in a deep breath as he backs away. Like always, after a kiss, he keeps my hand. My heart melts.

His eyes are on fire, full of light, full of happiness. If only he could always look this way. "We're not done."

I'm not sure if he's referring to kissing or to our relationship or to the messed-up conversation we were having about me being scared and what I'm hiding.

A knock on the door, then Chevy pulls me close for a hug and a short kiss on the lips. He looks down into my eyes again and I'd give anything if we could stay locked in this room forever.

"I've got you," he says.

I wish he did.

"I love you." Because I do love him. I've always loved him. Even when sometimes that love bordered on hate, I loved him. I love him and it needed to be said.

The sun rises by his expression alone. "I love you."

Another knock, Chevy lets me go, and when he walks out, he's greeted by Eli muttering, "About fucking time."

I fall back against the wall, wrap my arms around my stomach in an effort to fight off the cold that being alone again after such warmth has created. There's got to be another way to survive the Riot. There has to be another way that keeps my family alive and me with Chevy.

CHEVY

Roller coaster.

The lows have been damn low and the highs—Violet told me she loved me. Honest to God pinched myself in the hall to confirm it wasn't a dream. But the high is now evened out with the anger vibrating beneath my skin.

I just saw the men who hurt Violet. Just confirmed they were the ones responsible for taking us and making her bleed. I'm in a small room with a one-way mirror. Nothing to see on the other side anymore. I've done my job, and if Violet is up for it, she'll be in here to point out the same assholes.

It's tough to trust the system to do their job and grant Violet the justice she deserves. Even harder to not find a way past the glass and the police officers to pound the hell out of each and every guy who caused her to be scared. But this is how we're playing the game. "How long will they be in prison?"

"We're going for as long as we can get." Detective Jake Barlow is the one who answers and it's the first time I've heard him speak. He was one of the people present during the interview at the hospital, was there when Violet and I were shown pictures, but someone else always talked. He stayed in the background, hovering and listening.

He's a commanding man, even in silence, but I understand why he's stayed quiet. While he's been investigating the Riot, he was never 100 percent convinced the Terror were legit. He pushed Razor on a situation regarding Razor's mom, possibly hoping to rattle Razor into telling him something that would nail our club or the Riot. What he never expected was Razor staying true to the club.

Since the kidnapping, the Terror have shifted away from radio silence with Jake Barlow. We need him and he needs us. A mutually beneficial relationship. This guy, he's the chief of the tribe when it comes to knowledge of the Riot and that's what I need—knowledge.

"I'm fine with these bastards dying in prison," Detective Barlow continues.

Amen.

"Can we talk?" I say. "Just me and you."

He assesses me. Head to toe. The way I do to guys when I walk into Mom's bar and I'm trying to figure out who could cause problems.

The two other people in the room look to him as to what to do, but he watches me. "Your grandfather and uncle are set that they or a lawyer be around anytime I talk with you or Violet."

Yeah. They are. "I need to talk with you."

From the greedy set of his eyes, he's dying to talk alone with me. This kidnapping is a big break for him with the Riot and Eli has mentioned the detective wants more than what Violet and I are giving. Jake Barlow disagrees with the DA and he wanted us to go for prosecution for everyone involved. He wants Skull and his son's head on a silver platter.

"He's a minor," the woman in the pencil suit says.

The detective nods. "Doesn't mean we can't have a conversation. People talk all the time. No reason he and I can't exchange words."

"But it does mean you may not be able to legally use whatever he says."

"I'll take my chances." He motions with his chin to the door and the two other people leave. Once the door is closed tight behind them, he moves the conversation forward. "We haven't been formally introduced. I'm Detective Jake Barlow, but you can call me Jake."

Lowering himself to my level by the use of a first name. It's meant to disarm me, make me comfortable, make me easy to read.

I hitch my thumbs in my pockets and lean against the mirrored wall across from him. Won't make the mistake of underestimating him. The badge doesn't mean this man isn't a master of the con. Just means he cons people for the overall good. Reading people, sleight of hand, smoke and mirrors. Heading gang task forces means working people and working people well.

"I heard you know things about my father."

"From who?"

No reason to lie. "Skull."

Jake nods like he understands everything I didn't say. "Your grandfather aware you know things?"

"Yes."

His eyebrows rise a fraction of an inch. That surprised him. "What's he think about these things I hypothetically know?"

I shrug. "Believes they're bull."

"And what do you believe?"

My eyes snap to his and I'm trying to read him as hard as he's trying to read me.

"I'm in here talking to you," I say.

Jake loosens his tie. First time I've seen him do something like this. I've rattled him and that rattles me.

"Did Violet tell you what the Riot talked about with her when she was alone?" he asks.

My spine straightens. "I wasn't talking about Violet."

"No, you weren't, but I am. Has she told you?"

Loaded question. Answering means either I'm aware the Riot did talk to her or that I also believe they said something to her.

"Want to talk like men, let's talk like men," he says. "Skull shouldn't have known that I know, which means I got people who shouldn't be talking—talking. I'm not going to lie. You just gave me a ton to work with and possibly saved my ass and my case. You don't owe me this answer, but whether you believe it or not, I'm fighting for you two kids and I'm fighting hard. I've been doing this a long time and I know when people are hiding something from me and I also know when they're scared. That girl you just kissed, she's hiding something and she's scared."

I'm aware and I respect the hell out of him for being able to read someone he doesn't know. "Is it true? About my father?"

"I can't talk to you about this. The details you're asking for are part of a working case."

My body flinches with the impact of his nonanswer. Anyone else would think he's not telling me a thing, but he just confirmed there's something to be told. My father, on some level, was involved in the Riot. "How bad?"

Jake shakes his head and remains tight-lipped. I'm asking him to give me something, but he's loyal to his job. For the first time, I appreciate Violet's frustration with me and the club.

I push off the wall to leave and Jake calls out my name. I

glance over my shoulder and he rolls his neck. "We had Violet's car towed to the station after we found it. Took a ton of pictures, processed everything in an effort to help find you two. Our mechanic got the car started, but it didn't sound good. We released the car to her mom and I know the club has guys who can work on it, but there's this mechanic here in Louisville. He's good. One of the best I've met. I think you should take the car there, meet him…talk to him. He might lead you to answers."

Answers. "What's his name?"

"Isaiah Walker. He works at a custom shop, Pro Performance, during the day. A couple of nights a week, he does side jobs at a run-down garage in the south end of town called Tom's. Do yourself a favor and don't tell him I sent you."

I nod in the hopes he understands how much I appreciate this break. I go to turn the knob, but before I open the door, I say, "She hasn't told me what happened when she was alone."

It's not much, but he'll read into it exactly what he wants to know.

"Thank you," he says, and I walk away.

Violet

"If you need anything else, call me or Cyrus." Eli extends his hand to the three people who were with me while I picked out Fiend and his band of hairy friends.

The detectives said the overgrown hairballs couldn't see me. They said the men would have no idea it was me tattletaling, but the way Fiend stared straight ahead, straight at me, the way a cold sludge seeped into my veins, I don't believe them.

We're in the lobby area and my jacket is on and I'm ready to go. Chevy's arm is around my shoulders. His touch is welcome and comes close to creating a safe cocoon, but there are too many problems for me to feel completely at ease.

Mom is by my side, Eli and Cyrus on the other side of her and I'm quiet again. Don't mean to be, but everything feels so heavy that staying upright is exhausting.

Each person takes Eli's offered hand and they fake smiles except for Detective Jake Barlow. He stays serious as he shakes Eli's hand and then his eyes meet mine. He lets go of Eli and offers me a manila envelope.

"We found this in Fiend's possessions. I thought you'd like to have it back."

Nervousness descends on me. It's expected that I open it and begrudgingly I do. I peel back the lip, and when I peer inside, time freezes. It's a silver chain and attached to it is my soul. My eyes burn, my throat swells and I press the envelope to my chest. This is the closest I'll ever come to hugging my dad again.

It's his cross. The one he wore since before my birth. It's mine again. He's not home, but his cross is and I'll take this win.

Chevy brushes his fingers along my arm and Mom cranes her neck like that could cause her to have X-ray vision. "What is it?"

"Dad's cross," I whisper.

I step away from Chevy, needing room to return the cross to around my neck, and as I open the envelope again, I pause. Inside the envelope is handwriting and the first written words inform me that this is from Detective Jake Barlow.

Look at me and blink twice if you're in a situation you can't trust the Terror with and you're scared. I can protect you from the Riot, from the Terror. I can help you. If you blink twice, excuse yourself and go to the women's bathroom.

The entire world goes into slow motion and each inhale and exhale of air feels like it takes years. Two million thoughts, but I can't process a single one. A life-and-death split-second decision. I lift my gaze, meet the detective's and each blink rattles my frame like the pounding of a bass drum.

Bam.

Bam.

Detective Jake Barlow has blue eyes, like the twin flames of a blowtorch, and those eyes are zeroed in on me. He rips his stare from me and extends his hand to Eli again. "Hate to do this, but I've got another meeting. If anything comes up, any questions, you know how to get ahold of me."

Eli shakes his hand, thanks him again, and Detective Jake Barlow walks away as if he didn't just rattle my snow globe of a world.

I snap back to reality, gather Dad's cross and then notice another familiar piece. "It's also Dad's watch."

Mom audibly inhales and the guilt of losing something that meant so much to her skips along my veins. I reach in, pull it out and barely have time to offer it to her before she snatches it out of my hands. It was fast and brutal and I deserved it. Besides, I'm not going to wallow in sadness or guilt. I have Dad's cross.

I crumple the envelope until it's unrecognizable and toss it in the nearest trash can. My fingers shake as I try to clasp the cross on, but I fail and it snags in my hair.

A warm hand brushes my hair to the side and strong, calloused fingers take the clasp from me. A glance over my shoulder and Chevy's focused on my necklace. A snap, the chain becomes heavy on my neck and I close my eyes when the cross lands on my chest.

"Thank you," I whisper.

With his hands on my shoulders, Chevy merely kisses the back of my head.

"Looks good on you again, kid," Eli says. Cyrus nods in agreement and Mom's eyes fill with tears. I consider reaching out and taking her hand, but Mom steps away from me as if she could read my mind and the idea of us touching, once again, repulses her.

"You guys want dinner?" Eli asks. "Name it and it's yours."

"I need to use the bathroom," I blurt.

It came out so fast and loud that Eli attempts to hide a smile. "Okay."

I walk away, no one follows and I weave through the half cubicles, then turn the corner. A uniformed police officer stands in front of the women's bathroom, and the moment she sees me, she steps to the side.

At the far end of the three stalls, Detective Jake Barlow leans against the wall with his arms crossed over his chest. "We don't have much time, so let's cut to the chase. I will protect you. From the Riot, from the Terror, from the kid in third grade who pushed you around on the playground, but the only way I can do that is if you tell me everything that is going on. I'm going to be honest, you're a minor and I should probably have your mother in here."

"I'm eighteen."

He tilts his head. "That's not what Eli said."

"I turned eighteen the day I came home from the Riot." I don't blame anyone for forgetting. We've all been too busy cauterizing the bleeding while waltzing through a minefield.

"That changes things."

"Can you protect my family? My mom? My brother? Because the Riot threatened them."

"You've got my word. Now tell me the problem."

"When I was alone with Justin from the Riot, he told me that it was me they wanted to talk to and that Chevy was in the wrong place at the wrong time."

"It's what I thought."

"Why?"

"You're the wild card. Everyone else is too loyal to crack. What does the Riot want?"

My lungs can't draw in air. "Eli."

"How?"

"My dad was the accountant for the club and the business. The Riot want me to find account numbers. I don't know what they're going to do with them, but they said they're going to make Eli look bad with them. Bad enough he'll be sent to prison."

"Why haven't you told Eli? Anyone in the Terror? Why me?"

"Because the Riot have left me notes in my room at Cyrus's cabin—in the heart of Terror territory. There is someone who slips in and out of Cyrus's home, past prospects, past an entire clubhouse full of men, past Eli. There's a traitor and what if I tell Eli and he trusts the wrong person? I won't risk my family."

"Jesus," he mutters.

"This feud with the Riot, it has to change. It has got to end. I need it to end."

He watches me as he processes my words. "How do you think it should end?"

"With every single member of the Riot in jail."

The detective smiles and it could rival Pigpen's crazy one any day. "I can't guarantee them all, but we'll get the main ones. Got an idea of how to do that, but it's going to take some guts on your part. How do you feel about that?"

For the first time in weeks, like I'm alive. "Bring it."

CHEVY

Razor and I sit on stools at the clubhouse bar and we're both working on math.

I got in from Louisville around nine and my plan to hang and talk with Violet went wayward when she packed up and headed home. A quick hug and a kiss and she told me she'd see me tomorrow.

Too jacked in the head to return to an empty condo, I stuck around here, playing pool, playing darts, watching the MMA fights with the other guys from the club, and then when Razor settled in to do his homework, I did the same.

We've been doing this since we were kids. Papers sprawled out along the bar during quiet weeknights. There's a reddish glow on the pages from the neon signs on the wall, a low hum from the refrigerator that holds the longnecks, the background noise created by whatever sport is on TV, and the cracking of pool balls and murmur of low conversation that keep us company.

Back in elementary school, we were doing coloring sheets and seek-and-finds. Now Razor is working on college-level math. I do well in school, but don't hold a candle to him in the brains department.

Razor absently rubs at a healing wound on his arm, then goes back to his pencil flying at a hundred miles per hour. Razor's a genius at math. He's also a genius at technology, writing programs and cracking computer code. Actual life skills that will help him in the future.

Me? Razor's phone on the bar vibrates. He goes for it, stretching his arm, and his elbow collides with an open beer. It falls off the bar. In a second it's in my grasp, then back near Razor and not a drop spilled. Yeah, Razor's got brains and I've got fast hands.

As long as I was playing ball, there was a usefulness for my fast hands, but now, with football gone, I'm feeling lost in my purpose.

Razor blinks several times. "Reflexes of a ninja."

I shrug and close my math book, today's homework and most of what I missed last week now completed.

"I'm serious," he says. "You border on superhero with how fast you can move."

"Not like it helps me."

Razor's cold blue eyes flicker over my face. "What's that supposed to mean?"

To be honest... "I don't know."

I shove my math book and folder into my pack and open my English folder. Staring at me is my makeup assignment.

Two roads diverged in a yellow wood, And sorry I could not travel both. Instructions: Write an essay explaining how you've handled two roads diverging in your life. Use parts of the poem to explain how you made the decision of what path to take.

I hate English. "You do this yet?"

Razor gives a grim nod.

"What did you write about?"

He takes a slow drink from that longneck, then sets it back on the bar. "I wrote about Breanna."

Punch to the gut. It's been a few weeks since her parents sent her to a private school far from here. "You don't mind our teacher reading something personal?"

"I don't care if she knows I love Breanna. Besides, the lady hates me and probably won't read it anyhow."

"Still haven't heard anything?" Breanna's parents have forbidden them to have contact.

"The club has reached out to her parents, though. They're trying to make things work so they'll let her talk to me again." He peels at the label on the beer. "Can't help but wonder if by being away she'll figure out she's better without me. Find somebody else."

Razor's not one to talk feelings. Not one to talk much at all. He must be hurting. "I saw the way Breanna looked at you. That was love."

"Violet loved you." His response stings, but it's true.

"We're figuring things out." She told me she loved me, and for a brief minute, all was right in my world.

Something dark flashes in his eyes. Everyone in the club was cool when Violet and I started dating, but Razor was the one who was hesitant. He and Violet were best friends growing up. No feelings or attraction. Just friends, and Razor's protective of his friends, especially her.

"She's not happy in the club, so how exactly are you figuring that part out?"

"We haven't."

He rolls his neck. "Be careful with her."

"I will."

"Chevy." He waits for me to meet his eyes. "Be careful with you."

I nod. Razor doesn't want to see either me or Violet hurt.

My phone rings and my forehead furrows when Stone's face pops up on the screen. It's after eleven and past his bedtime. Quick swipe to accept, then phone to my ear. "Hey, Stone."

"Chevy?" Don't care for the quiet nervousness in his voice.

"It's me. You okay?"

Razor's now watching me like a bear ready to tear into a stranger for throwing rocks at its young. If something is going down at Violet's, he'll be in that mix alongside me.

"I tried calling Eli, but he didn't answer."

I slip off the stool and go deadly serious myself. "Eli's in Church. Tell me what's wrong."

"Eli told me to keep an eye on Violet and to call him if anything strange happened."

"Is she okay?"

Razor's now on his feet and digging his keys out of his pocket.

"I think… It's just that she's downstairs in Dad's office going through drawers. Everybody went to bed, and I fell asleep, but then I thought I heard a door open and shut. Then I heard footsteps and I was scared, but I thought of how you protected Violet, so I forced myself out of bed. Violet saw me and told me everything was okay and that she was hanging out downstairs. Then she went into Dad's office. We don't go into Dad's office. Nobody goes in there."

I wave Razor off, then rub my neck to ease the tension that had built there. "Maybe she's always gone in there and you didn't know."

"No." Stone hardens his tone. "She doesn't. Violet doesn't

go in there. Mom doesn't go in there. None of us go in there. Something's wrong."

"I get it." But Violet's expression when she received her Dad's cross broke nearly all of us. Bet she's feeling sentimental tonight, especially with this being her first official night home after the kidnapping. "I'll swing by and check on her. Will that make you feel better?"

"Yeah, it would. Should I tell her to get out of there? Dad didn't like us in there without him. That was his rule."

"Leave her alone and I'll take care of it."

"Okay."

We share goodbyes and I'm the one digging out my keys, but Razor's still on alert. "Everything okay?"

"Violet's missing her dad."

Razor sits back on the stool, pencil in hand and already figuring out a problem. "Tell her if she needs me, I'm there."

"Will do."

I've been in a cage too much lately and I've missed the wind on my face, the vibration of my bike beneath me, the feeling of complete freedom. My headlight illuminates two prospects hanging near their bikes at the end of Violet's drive. As long as Violet, her mom or Stone are in that house, someone from the Terror will be watching over them.

Using my feet, I back up my bike and park it next to theirs. It's close to midnight, lights are out in the house and I don't want the roar of my engine to wake Violet's mom.

I exchange a few words with the prospects, then walk up the long drive. The guys didn't ask why I'm here. Besides the fact I'm a McKinley, everyone, even the new guys, knows Violet was my girl. To the club, she'll always belong to me.

She will, but not the way they think. Violet is a part of my soul, but it's up to her if she wants me in her life. I've watched as man after man has treated my mother like an object. Violet's not an object. She's the girl I love.

Stone opens the front door before I jog up the stairs to the porch. He's dressed in an old T-shirt with *Star Wars* pajama bottoms and his hair points in a million different directions. With shaking hands, he runs his fingers through his hair. Now I know why it's a mess.

"Violet's still in there," he whispers, and I remind myself to keep my voice low.

Stone lets me in and closes the door behind me. Their house is exactly how I remember. Perfection. Hardwood floors, formal living room to the right with fancy furniture and fancy fragile things behind glass. To the left is the kitchen. Like it's a model home, the counters are clean and there's not a piece of paper or dish towel in sight. From there, it's a straight shot to the family room and closed double doors that lead to their father's office. Light creeps out from underneath. "Why don't you go on upstairs to bed? I'll take care of Violet."

"We have school tomorrow. We aren't supposed to have people over after nine on a school night."

"I promise you won't get in trouble if your mom wakes up."

"But—"

"Rules have changed."

"Because of the kidnapping?"

"Yeah." No use lying.

"Okay. 'Night, Chevy."

"'Night."

In socks, Stone runs up the stairs and a door clicks shut on the second floor.

I'm not worried about Violet's mom waking up. When we were staying at Cyrus's, she went out of her way to give us her approval on my staying the night with Violet. On the way home from Louisville, she went on and on about how happy she was that Violet and I are back together and that I could stay the night with Violet at their house if I wanted.

That kiss in the police station, to Jenny, confirmed everything.

Razor's right. Violet and I are still complicated, but Violet's mom is 1950s, an old-school biker wife. To her, Violet is my property, and Violet and her mom are oil and water. Jenny used to brag to people how Frat owned her. Violet would cut open my artery and leave me to bleed out if I used that term involving her.

Rebecca, Oz's mom and wife of Man O' War, is the same. So was Olivia, Cyrus's wife. Both are strong women in the club and neither would allow their men to use the word *owned* in reference to them. Neither of them would take crap from anyone at any time, but that's not how Violet's mom rolls.

Her mother's attitude used to drive Violet insane. The idea of being owned crawled under Violet's skin and it crawled under Jenny's skin that it pissed Violet off. Their relationship was rough before Frat died. Now it's got to be a testing range for nuclear bombs.

And Violet's been dealing with it alone. Not only her mom, but the problems with her brother, her issues with people at school and her grief. She pushed me away, pushed everyone away, but I'm done being pushed.

I stop outside Frat's office and memories come rushing back. The sound of Violet's laughter as she sat on her father's wooden desk, legs dangling, as he was telling her stories of him riding with the club. His office wasn't what people would associate with a biker. It was dark wood, many shelves lined with book after book and a black leather sofa where

Violet would lie for hours as her father worked just so she could be in the same room as him.

Walking into the room, I sometimes felt like a man about to face a firing squad. Violet would give me that wicked smile, then wink when she waltzed out the door after Frat told Violet to give me and him some time alone.

One time, he had caught us kissing behind the clubhouse and my hands were in places he wasn't happy about. I shuffled into the office like I had swallowed a bowling ball. Frat wasn't full of smiles and laughter as he shut the door and schooled me on how I was to treat his daughter.

She was his princess. The pride and love that shone from his eyes when she walked in the room could light up the dark. And he was her whole life. She worshipped her father like it was her own personal religion.

Frat was a great man. Taught me how to work on cars, helped me piece together my bike, and during the multiple times he schooled me on his daughter, he also spent time getting to know me. Talked to me about football, about the club, about my mom, about choices.

He always told me the choices were mine. I wish Frat was still here. He was one of the few who at least acted like he understood push and pulls. He used to make me feel like it was possible for me to come out on the other side of eighteen still intact.

Still intact.

My shoulder still aches from the kidnapping. Violet's knee is still in a brace.

Wonder what Frat would say now about surviving to eighteen.

Sadness washes over me. Violet is eighteen and my stomach drops as I remember the expression on her face when she saw her father's cross. The girl I love is in pain and I need to make her better. I turn the knob, open the door, and an ache ripples through my chest.

Violet's in the middle of the room, in pajamas consisting of a red tank top and checkered bottoms. She clutches photos, and while sitting up, she's curled into a ball. Don't have to look at the photos to know who's in them. Don't have to ask why she's alive, yet dying.

Her head snaps up and her face pales. "What are you doing here?"

"Stone called and told me you weren't okay."

"He what?" She clutches her hair and pulls as if physical pain can wipe away the devastation on her face. "Never mind. You need to get out of here."

My neck tightens and I roll it. She's trying to shut down emotionally and push me away again, but that's not going to happen. "Your mom isn't going to care I'm here."

Violet winces as she stands and places too much pressure on her bad leg. As I go to help her, she throws her hands out for me to halt. "Go, Chevy. You need to go."

"Let me help you."

When she steps forward, she slips and I spring toward her. My hand grabbing her arm, and as I look down to make sure she's steady, I spot files. Lots of files. Private documents that have the name of either the club or the security company and the papers within those files are strewn about. My blood runs cold and then I stop breathing when I spot her phone— the camera app on.

A muscle in my jaw jerks and Violet is the one now grasping. "It's not what you think."

I tower over her. The anger pumping through me so strong it's hard not to shake the hell out of her. I left her alone with the Riot. I left her alone and they let us leave. "Did you make a deal with the Riot for our release?"

"I was going through the files to search for pictures. Just pictures."

"Don't lie to me!"

"It's just pictures, Chevy. Calm down and I'll show you."

It's not just pictures. She wasn't just looking for pictures. Violet made a deal. She found a way to set us free and she's willing to betray the club to do so.

I release Violet, then run a hand over my face. Cyrus—damn. Cyrus needs to know. So does Eli. Both of them will be crushed. Screw that—I'm crushed. "Why couldn't you trust us? Why couldn't you trust me?"

Because this is a betrayal. A betrayal they'll never forgive. A betrayal I'm not sure I can forgive.

"Chevy!" she shouts. "Look at me! See me!"

I swear aloud, then do what she asks. Head to toe. Once, twice and on the third time my mind goes numb as if I was hit in the head. Violet holds two fingers pressed against her thigh. The sign we created as children that we need to pay attention. Our sign that something is wrong. Signs we made up while we played, but continued to use because the adults in our lives are often complicated. My vision blurs, then returns with a clarity that's deadly.

She's in trouble. Violet's in trouble and she's not safe.

My pulse beats in my ears and my eyes flicker about the room, searching for the threat.

"Chevy," she whispers. "Dad mentioned once he kept pictures of us in the front of his file folders because it would remind him why he worked so hard. I thought of that tonight on the ride home and I wanted to see those pictures. Wanted to remind myself why he worked hard." Violet extends the pictures in her hands to me. "I found them."

She continues to hold them out, encouraging me forward, and each step I take toward her is an echo in my mind. Violet's not safe. Not safe. For how long? Since the basement? Before the basement?

"What's going on in here?" Eli walks into the office, and while he's playing it cool with his slow stride, his glare's so sharp it could cut glass.

Violet lowers her arm, then rolls her neck. "Why does everyone think they can waltz into my home at any time of night like they live here? There's this thing called privacy. You both need to learn about it."

"Your brother called me." Eli points at the hallway, then back into the room. "And so you know, the moment you crossed the threshold of this office, you entered my world."

"This is my house," she spits.

"But those files on the floor are my property." Death. It's there in his expression and I instinctually step toward Violet to be in the line of fire to protect her.

"Really? Your property?" Violet tosses the photos in her hand in his direction and they fall around him like confetti. "Didn't see you in a single one and he called you his brother."

Violet turns her back to him and that's when I see it. Her intake of air, the rapid blink of her eyes as moisture fills the bottom rims and the slight shaking of her hands—fear. Same fear as the basement. Same fear seconds before she charged a man holding a gun point-blank on me. Same fear that has lived inside me since the moment we were taken on the side of the road.

The world zones out, then back in. She's still in that basement. There may not be concrete walls, but she's still struggling to adjust her eyesight to the darkness, still struggling to find light. Whatever the Riot said to her has kept her trapped and has her terrified for her life.

Like in the back of the car, I hook one of my fingers

with hers. She glances at me, her forehead furrows and she mouths, *Help me.*

The ache hits so low I have to work to keep from flinching. Can't remember the last time Violet asked for help. From the club, from her friends, from me.

I rip my stare away and it lands on Eli. He's looking down at the photos and it's a kick in the gut to see the pain of his expression. Each and every photo on the floor is of Frat, Violet, her mother and her brother. Each and every photo a smiling family. Each and every photo a moment that will never happen again.

"Go on upstairs, Violet," I say in a low voice. "Get some sleep."

Her eyebrows disappear behind her longer bangs at the mention of sleep, and I understand her concern. We've tried to sleep apart and it didn't work. She talked about buzzing with me not around and I couldn't relax. I lay in bed and flipped around as if I was attempting to rest on sharp nails.

"I'll show," I mumble. She briefly closes her eyes as if that's what she had been wishing to hear.

Every now and then the crazy and wild angels who occasionally watch over me and Violet produce a miracle. I expected a fight from her, but instead she squeezes my finger, releases it and starts for the door. The way she hobbles, it's obvious she's in massive pain.

"You're not supposed to be on your knee as much as you have been," Eli says.

She hesitates at the door, back still to him, and her shoulders rise and fall with her deep breath. "Sometimes life doesn't hand you choices. Sometimes the world is how it is. Sometimes you have to go down the path given to you."

"Sometimes," Eli says. "But sometimes people choose the harder path just to prove they can do it."

"Sometimes, I guess they do," she says softly, then leaves.

Eli and I wait in silence as we listen to her go down the hallway, up the stairs, and shut her door. Salvage. That's what I need to do. Need to buy Violet and myself time until I figure out what the hell is going on—why she's still so terrified.

"I'm responsible for this." Eli looks at the pictures as if the memories are of war atrocities. Broken and bleeding limbs instead of smiling faces. "It's my fault Frat died and this family is in shambles. It's my fault Violet's in pain."

It's what Violet says, but I don't believe her and I don't buy what he's saying. "It's the Riot's fault."

Eli presses his lips together, then bends to pick up the photos. "She was right. Frat kept a picture of them in each of his files. The guys used to give him hell for it, but he never cared. Frat loved his family. Loved them in a way not many people can understand and I stole that from them."

I open my mouth to argue, but he cuts me off as he starts on the files. "Go to her. I'll clean up."

"Anything important in those?" I fish.

He shakes his head. "Vending and purchasing invoices for the food and alcohol at the clubhouse. Frat was a man of many talents. Had a knack for keeping everything organized and in its place. We should have moved all this stuff by now, but no one's had the heart to look at those photos."

Bet no one's had the heart to take anything of his out of this house.

"Do me a favor," Eli says.

"Sure."

"Tell Violet… Tell her I'm sorry."

"For what?"

"She'll know. That's all that matters."

Violet

Chevy doesn't bother knocking. He walks in, shuts the door behind him, places his hands on his hips, then narrows his dark eyes on me. In the dim light of the lamp on my bedside table, Chevy's a glorious sight. He's always been sexy when he's mad. Something about his brooding expression would typically cause butterflies in my stomach. Because of how long we'd been together plus how we pushed each other during our breakup, we've had plenty of experience at being furious.

I don't want him angry at me now, but I don't blame him for being so. I lied to the club, I lied to Eli and I lied to him. Betrayal isn't something McKinley men forgive.

I'm on my bed, sitting near the pillows. My sore leg extended. This room is a beautiful place. Full of purples, hand-stenciled flowers, white sheer flowing curtains and perfection from a magazine. I remember the first time I wanted to make my room my own. I brought home a poster of a puppy from the school book fair. Mom told me no, I put it up anyway with pushpins into her perfect wall. Mom yelled at me, I yelled at her, Dad came home from work and told me to let my mother have her way.

The house is all she has. It's her identity. Let her have it.

At least Mom still has the house. I put too much of my identity into my father and now I'm lost.

"What the hell, Violet?" Chevy sounds as exhausted as I feel. "Just what the hell?"

"I've been confused by our math makeup work," I say. "Can you please take a look at it?"

He cracks his head to the side as if that action could keep him from throttling me. "Violet—"

"Please," I add.

Reluctantly, he turns to my desk, flips open my notebook, and nervous adrenaline enters my system. It's like ants are crawling under my sheets. Unable to stay still, I pick up the stuffed bear Chevy won for me at the county fair when we were fifteen and hug it tight.

I should have been the girl who threw away or burned everything he gave me after we split up, but I could never bring myself to part with the items he had chosen for me with such care. There is nothing fake about him. He's thoughtful, loyal and loves people so much that it can cause him pain.

I loved Chevy and I still do. Keeping what he had given me reminded me that the moments of happiness we shared weren't make-believe, weren't a dream…that they were very, very real.

Chevy's taking too long. What he has to read can be done quickly, but he continues to stand there, his back to me, his head lowered. Each second of silence causes my skin to feel stretched thin to the point of breaking.

He closes the notebook, slowly pivots in my direction, and his eyes meet mine. Inside that notebook are the notes the Riot lovingly left for me. I'm not safe at the clubhouse. From the conversation I had with Justin when I was kidnapped, I know I'm being watched here. I'm not safe anywhere, and I will not do or say anything to jeopardize my family and I won't allow Chevy to screw this up for me either because of his inherent need to be a caveman.

"If my father knew you were in here, he'd be angry," I say, knowing Chevy can understand subtext better than anyone else.

"Never stopped me from sneaking up."

The right side of my mouth tips up and then falls just as quickly. He's playing along, but he's also speaking the truth. The thrill and innocence of those days are sadly gone. "What do you think of the math?"

Chevy crosses the room and the bed dips as he sits. "More complicated than I remember."

"Yeah. There's a lot of that going around." I pull down the covers and wonder how much he's willing to forgive me and how badly he wants to know all the truth. "Stay with me? If only for a bit."

I'll take whatever he's willing to give—at least for now— even if he's only willing to give me memories. Memories are golden and on cold lonely nights, sometimes if I try to remember hard enough, they almost make me warm.

Chevy undoes his shoes, I turn off the lamp on my bed- side table, then slip under the blanket. Chevy settles in fac- ing me. His legs and chest are touching mine and the sweet, sweet memory of the last time he was in this bed with me heats my blood.

The day had been humid, we had been out in my field and the rain had caught us by surprise. He had taken off his shirt because it was drenched, and I took off mine because I loved the way he became hypnotized by me anytime we were alone in a room.

He was mine. Physically, emotionally, spiritually and I loved feeling needed, desired and like I belonged.

Chevy places a hand on my waist and I'm not sure if it's for comfort or from habit. Either way, I snuggle deeper into the pillows and into him, hoping what I'm about to do isn't a mistake. The venetian blinds are closed, but moonlight still filters in through the slats. He's beautiful. Oh so beautiful and he's about to become very, very angry.

Having no idea of the extremes the Riot have gone to eavesdrop on me, I'm afraid to talk in a normal tone. But Chevy needs to know and in this bed with the covers nearly over my head is the safest place I can think of. Walls between us and the world. Him tucked close to me. Me tucked close to him. Us speaking so quietly that we can barely hear each other.

"I'm being watched by the Riot," I whisper. "Here at home, at the clubhouse, in Cyrus's house. Justin told me it's been going on since before the kidnapping. I didn't know it was happening. I'm not safe. I'm terrified to be talking to you about it now. Scared of how much they know, what they see, what they hear."

A cold chill runs up my spine, and I shiver. Chevy runs his hand along my arm and his warmth is welcome. "Why are they watching you?"

"If I tell you, you can't tell Eli or the club."

His body quakes with anger. I suck in a breath to still the fear that's causing my heart to go faster.

"Is that what this is all about? Is that why they let us go? Did you make a deal with Justin to betray the Terror in order to set us free?"

I don't get self-righteous. There's no point. I would do anything to protect Brandon and my mom. I'd do close to anything to protect Chevy. "I'll explain everything as long as you give me your word that what I say stays safe with you. No one else can know."

Chevy's eyes wander over my face. I know him. He's thinking, he's weighing, he's hoping I'll change my mind. "We need to involve the club. If the Riot are watching you, then you need to be protected."

"I can't involve the Terror. If the Riot finds out I'm not doing what they want, that's when I'll be in danger."

His grip on me tightens. "So you are working with them."

I am, but not how he's thinking and I can't explain until he gives me his word.

His expression hardens as he reads my silence like a prison sentence. "If you're working with the Riot, I have to tell. I can't let you betray the club. They're our family. My family."

"Is that what I am? A traitor? When you protect your family, it's called being an upstanding member of the club, but when I do it, I'm a traitor?"

"Yes, if what you're doing hurts the people I love."

My head pitches back in anger. "Do you think I'm capable of that? Do you think I'm capable of hurting the people you love? That I love?"

The buzzing that Chevy used to quiet returns and it grows louder with each second he remains silent. As if we hadn't been kidnapped and survived together, as if we haven't held each other night after night, as if last night meant nothing. I place my hands on his chest and try to push him away. Try to ignore my breaking heart.

"Get out. Run off—tell Cyrus I'm being watched and you don't know why. And before you try going all self-righteous on me, I heard. I heard you tell Cyrus you would sell me out the moment I trusted you with anything. So go. Tell him you think I'm betraying the club. Tell him whatever you want. He can grill me, the club can grill me and I won't say a thing. Go, Chevy. Go on and finally make your choice to be their lapdog."

I go to roll out of bed, but Chevy snags my wrist. "Stop making me choose between you and them."

"How about you stop behaving like there are no choices to make? I walked away from you months ago because you aren't capable of choosing. Guess what? I'm very capable of choosing. I know what I want out of life and it's not the Terror and it's not Snowflake. I've applied to twenty different colleges. What about you? Have you applied to any? Have you even thought about what you're going to do after high school? After football season is over?"

His blank expression answers every question. "You're talking in circles. None of this has anything to do with us or with what the hell is going on."

"No, it has everything to do with you. You're terrified to choose and because of that you'll never be happy."

"I can't choose between the girl I love and my family. I get enough of that shit from my mother and I'm sick and tired of being in everyone's tug-of-war."

"You're in the middle because you don't make a choice. You know what? Go ahead, do nothing like always so once again I have to make the tough decisions when it comes to us. You want to be mad because you feel like I'm betraying you—fine, but remember, you planned on betraying me, too. Trust is a two-way street. Go, Chevy. We're done and this time we're done for good."

He jerks as if I slapped him, and this time when I go to roll out of bed, he doesn't stop me. I pull a shirt over my tank top because I need as many layers as possible to hide the blood pouring from my soul.

"Why can't you see that Eli, that the club wants to protect you?"

"Why can't you see they can't?" My lower lip trembles and tears burn my eyes, but I walk closer to Chevy so he can hear my near-silent angry whisper. "Someone in the Terror is either working with the Riot or the Riot is that good that they could slip past everyone in the Terror to reach the room I slept in at Cyrus's. Eli and Cyrus are not gods! They are flesh and blood and they cannot protect me or my family."

Chevy stands there as if I shot him in the chest, staring at me like I'm going to cave and tell him I'm not drawing a line in drying concrete. "I want to help you."

"Then stay, give me your word and I'll let you in. I'll tell you everything. I'll curl up in that bed right now, let you hold me, dry my tears on your chest and you'll know every single thought going on in my head. But you have to be with me on this. With me."

"I promised Cyrus I would tell him if there were problems with you. I promised. Way before you overheard what you did in the kitchen. Before last night. You know I keep my word."

"And you promised to love me!" I shout and then swallow to help with the closing of my throat. Returning to a whisper is difficult but needed. "You're right. I'm asking you to choose, but I'm not asking you to choose between me and the club. Stay with the club, become a member tonight, I don't care. But what I'm asking is for you to choose me this one time. I'm not safe. My family is not safe. And I have found a way to make us safe, but I cannot bring the club into this. They think they can help, but they can't. They will only make things worse.

"For the first time, can you please see I need your help more? I deserve that. I am not my mother and I am not someone who can sit by and be second place time after time. I deserve someone who puts me first, at the very least when I ask for it, and if you can't choose, then I choose to go this alone."

Muscles twitch in Chevy's face, and when he blinks several times, my chest aches as if someone took a knife and sliced me open.

"They won't forgive me if I do this. They will find out because nothing in the dark stays a secret forever and that's asking me to choose between them and you."

"You're right. If they find out, they won't forgive. But I won't forgive you either, so you have to decide which one means more to you."

His head snaps up as I hit a nerve and I won't take the words back.

"I thought loving people was supposed to be easy," he says quietly. "But it's the hardest thing I've done. I wish I knew how to love you right."

"I've told you how to love me. You aren't willing to love me how I need to be loved."

We stand there, willing the other to relinquish control, but we're too far on the other side of this war to make concessions. Like being on a carnival ride with no restraints, my heart bounces between being bruised and broken and all combinations in between.

"I still love you," he says. Chevy picks up his boots, goes to the door, turns the knob and I swear to God this hurts worse than the first time we broke up. "That will never change."

Chevy leaves the door open and each of his steps down the stairs is like a spike through my heart. When the front door closes, I sink to the floor, pick up Chevy's bear that had fallen off the bed and squeeze it to my chest as if that could keep me from falling apart.

I won't cry, I won't cry, I won't cry.

I don't cry.

My eyes press shut and I rock as I hold the bear tight.

CHEVY

It's October of my senior year and I haven't considered applying to college.

Sure, I've seen the signs in the hallways, even talked to football recruiters, have a dozen or so cards ferreted away somewhere in my room from men who would like me to consider playing for their team. Nobody big, smaller places, but still it's interest, but I have yet to show any interest in return. I haven't visited a place, gone to a website, even thought about a career beyond high school.

Violet's right, I'm not making choices. The decision I'm making now isn't the one that's going to help ease the sting of Violet throwing me out, but I'll receive honest answers.

Weekday nights are dead at Shamrock's. The customer peak is the after-work crowd of men who aren't eager to head to Little League practices or the people who aren't looking forward to heading to their place alone. Pretty sad when a dive that's lit by neon signs and smells like sweat is the better alternative.

Gotta admit, alone sucks. Cold bed, cold covers, cold heart. Cold like that basement.

The music's turned down low, but the bass still vibrates along the floor. One of the newer waitresses mops the section near the empty stage. It's an hour or so before closing and Mom leans against the bar and works on a Sudoku puzzle. Her long black hair touches the surface. She's in her favorite pair of faded jeans, a red T-shirt, and she's lost to the world as she scribbles on the paper. She loves puzzles. The harder, the better.

I drop onto the stool across from her, and when she lifts her head, her eyes widen. I only drive her on Friday and Saturday nights and me here on a weekday spells disaster.

"No offense, but your facial expression is one I see often at this bar and usually the order from that person is something hard that will get them drunk fast."

I don't respond and Mom frowns. She pulls out a glass, fills it with ice, pours water into it and then slides it to me. "I thought you said the lineup went well."

"It did." Told her about it in texts.

"Then what's wrong?"

I swipe my finger across the condensation forming on the glass. "You know I drink beer at the clubhouse, right?"

"But you didn't go there. You came here."

She's right.

"Chevy." Mom stays silent until I look up at her. "What's wrong?"

"Violet asked me to choose."

She inhales and her shoulders slump when she exhales. I'm aware of Mom's opinion. She wants me to choose, too, but I'm here because Mom knows when to keep her thoughts to herself. Knows how to be a mom. She reaches across the bar and lays her hand over mine.

"What are you going to do?" she asks.

My lips turn down, my eyes burn and I shake my head to push it all away. "I don't know."

No sense telling her Violet threw me out. I also don't want to scare Mom by explaining that one of the reasons I didn't give Violet my word to stay silent is because the Riot are watching Violet. My fingers curl into a fist and Mom lifts her hand from mine.

"Why can't Violet see the club is there to help, not hurt?" I say. "They want to protect her. They want to keep her safe and she keeps pushing them away."

"You mean she keeps pushing you away."

"Same thing."

"Doesn't have to be. From my mountain looking down, Violet has a point. You were kidnapped because of your association with the Terror."

I go to argue and Mom holds up her hand. "Chevy, do you love her?"

Without a doubt. "Yes."

"Do you think she's a capable, smart girl?"

"Yes."

"Then why don't you trust Violet to make decisions for herself? Let's put the Terror aside for a moment. If she feels her life is better without the Terror, why can't you respect that? Why are you trying to force something on her she feels is bad for her life? For months all I've heard about is how she's making you choose, but do you not realize you're trying to shove your choices down her throat?"

"I haven't chosen."

Mom's eyes become full of sadness. "Yes, you have, and by telling her you haven't, you're leading her on. By telling her she's only safe with the Terror, you're telling her she's incapable of taking care of herself without some man to watch over her. The words out of your mouth aren't the only things she hears."

The ice in the glass shifts as it melts. Mom never minces words and it's why I'm here.

"I know this may sound shocking, but Violet has thoughts and feelings, too. While you don't feel she's been fair, you haven't been fair to her either. You two are at a breaking point and that is going to require tough decisions. If you don't feel you've made decisions, it's time for you to man up and make them. If you figure out you have made decisions, it's time for you to take responsibility and accept the consequences of what you have chosen."

My stomach cramps and I readjust on the stool. "But the Terror are my family."

"No, Eli and Cyrus are your family. The rest of those men are your friends. Family and friends don't abandon you if you decide you aren't exactly like them. They love you regardless of the path you choose. Question is, Chevy—why do you doubt Eli and Cyrus so much that you don't think they could love you without a patch on your back?"

The earth stops spinning, but then it spins too quick. Unstable, I stand to find my footing in a world that has been too chaotic for weeks.

"I don't doubt them," I say, but my words sound far away.

"You do," she says. "If you didn't doubt them, you wouldn't be stuck in the middle all the time."

Stuck in the middle. Stuck in the unknown. Doubt. "Did my father choose something different from the Terror?"

Mom pales. "Yes. James wanted something different. He wanted a life away from here and Cyrus wasn't happy about it. But you already know this without any of us having to tell you. You doubt the Terror because you sense that James's relationships changed when he left."

And what happens to my relationship with them if I'm like my father? If I'm restless and choose something else… like football over patching in? "What do you know about the Terror? What is it you haven't told me?"

Mom's lips thin out and she closes her book of puzzles. "This is a conversation we need to have at home."

"Mom—" I begin, but her pointed glare shuts me up.

"Home," she repeats. "This is a conversation for home."

I can't wait for home. Mom has come close to talking to me about my father twice in my life; both times she made the promise to tell me later and I can't run the risk of time causing her to change her mind again. "Now. You tell me now."

Mom looks left, then right, then grabs my wrist, dragging me with her to the end of the bar. I loom over her and the confusion and anxiety in her eyes causes my skin to feel like it's shrinking on my bones.

"James knew I was pregnant with you."

Her words hit me like a fist to the head: "But you said—"

"Because James asked me to keep you a secret from his family."

Stunned, I brace my palm against the bar. "So you and Dad were a couple?"

"James didn't love me and it's okay because I didn't love him either. We were friends. Good friends. Through high school and beyond. He was in love with somebody else, but this woman played with his heart. He came to me when he needed the bleeding to stop. I never minded giving my body to my best friend when he was in pain and I never regretted that doing so created you."

"But Cyrus has always acted like you were…" I can't finish.

"A one-night stand? Chevy, even if I was, it's okay. I'm secure in who I am and other people's definitions don't de-

LONG WAY HOME 265

fine me. But the one-night stand—it's what James wanted them to think. They didn't know much about our friendship. He told me he wanted a life separate from the club. At the time there wasn't anything bad happening, but they seemed to fill every crevice of his being and he wanted to be himself for a few minutes and I was that person he could be himself with." The edges of her lips turn up. "Your dad and I used to read books aloud to each other. He liked horror, though, and it would give me nightmares at night. I bet you never knew that."

I didn't and I drop onto the stool next to me as I struggle with the feeling that I've been sucked into an alternate universe.

"James got me and I got him. He wanted a life away from the club even when he was in high school. I was his one friend out of the club and he wanted me to stay a secret. He was scared that if anyone found out they would try to suck me in and he'd lose me to everyone else. And he had good reason to think so—you know my home life was...lacking."

"Sounds like he loved you."

"He did once when I didn't, then I did once when he didn't, then we didn't at the same time. We were better off friends than together. Better off lovers than in love."

I wince. "Never needed to hear the last part."

Mom steps closer to me and tucks my hair behind my ear. "James left Snowflake after he graduated. He'd come home to appease his mother and see me, but he loved Louisville. Loved his job there, loved his life there, loved it all, but toward the last six months of his life, James became moody. I used to think it was because of this woman who had him tied up in knots, but it was darker than that, he became darker.

"The last time he came home, I told him I was pregnant with you. He was in shock, but he took it well. He told me he'd support me and you any way he could. Promised he'd be involved, but he asked me to move to Louisville. He told me he was breaking ties with the Terror and he didn't want them to know about his child. He wanted you to be raised away from them."

"Why?"

She shrugs. "Things were beginning to heat up between Eli and Meg at the time. The war between the Riot and the Terror was beginning. I assumed after he died it was because of that."

"But you raised me in Snowflake. You were the one who went to Cyrus and told him you were pregnant with me."

Mom slumps into the stool beside me. "I didn't go to Cyrus. He came to me. You were six months old and we were barely making it. I had worked at this bar before I was pregnant with you so I could save up enough money to go to the community college in Bowling Green. I was using that money to support us and pay for babysitting so I could work. The money was going fast. One night, Cyrus showed up at the bar asking me if it was true. If you were his grandson."

"What? How did he know?"

"He didn't say, but two days later the Riot visited me at my apartment and told me they were the ones who told Cyrus about me and you. They said that there was a war between the Riot and the Terror and they told me they would protect me and you, but in order to do so I would have to disavow the Terror, move to Louisville, and once there they would take care of us."

"Why did you choose to stick with the Terror? With Cyrus?"

She lifts one shoulder, then lets it fall. "They say the devil you know is better than the one you don't. I never wanted anyone to take care of me or you. Only person I wanted in control of my life was me. I had enough of that controlling nonsense growing up. The question I have always asked myself is how? How, when it came to James, did the Riot know something the Terror didn't?"

I close my eyes as pain rolls through me. Because my father was a traitor, that's how. When I reopen them, I'm looking at a brand-new world—or at least the world I should have always seen. "Why didn't you tell me?"

"Cyrus told me it would be safer for you if you never knew about the Riot's visit and I agreed. I thought I could take advantage of what Cyrus was offering me. Free babysitting while I worked nights. I thought you'd be asleep most of the time and they wouldn't have much of an influence on you, but I was wrong. If I could go back and change things, I would have left Snowflake the day James died and never looked back. I should have raised you on my own. It would have been hard, but at least you would have been safe."

I lean forward, kiss her forehead and hug her. So much she's given up for me. So much she's done in the name of love. Mom's right. It's time I start making choices and owning up to the ones I've already made.

One of those promises being the one I made to Violet years ago and reconfirmed in that basement and again last night. I promised to love her, I promised to protect her, I promised to be her best friend. It's officially time to man up.

Violet

My ceiling fan goes round and round. Sometimes I make myself dizzy as I try to follow one blade, sometimes I squint my eyes and the blades blend together. Numb. I'm trying for numb and I'm on the verge of failing. There's this black ball in my chest clawing to get out, and if I let it out, I'm afraid I'll never be able to contain it.

A buzz and my head jerks up from the pillow. I roll over to grab my cell off the nightstand. There are no messages and the buzzing continues. Takes my slow mind a moment to catch up, but then my heart takes off at a gallop. I spring out of bed, tripping over my own feet as my knee gives, and hit the floor with a thud.

I reach between my mattress and box spring and pull out the burner phone. "Hello."

"Yes or no answers only," Detective Jake Barlow says, "in case they're listening."

"Okay." Even though that's not a yes or a no.

"Did you find the account numbers?" This guy doesn't sleep, doesn't eat, doesn't understand anything beyond nailing the Riot. He probably doesn't understand heartbreak either.

I take a deep breath and give him the truth. "Yes."

"Bank account for the Riot?"

"Yes." In the computer. The password wasn't easy to fig-ure out and I almost didn't think I was going to crack it, but I did. It was something Dad taught me a long time ago when I couldn't think of passwords I could remember. To take the middle names of people you love the most and spell them backward.

"Account numbers for security company clients?"

"Yes." Also in the computer. I wasn't lying to Chevy. I was looking in those files so I could see pictures of Dad. I had already found what I needed at that point.

"Did the Riot tell you how to get ahold of them once you had the information?"

I huff out enough air that my longer bangs move. "No."

"Figures. We know they're watching you. They'll con-tact you soon, and when they do, you need to contact me so we can set it all up."

The muscles in my back tense. Setting it all up means being alone with the Riot again. No pressure.

The whine of a knob turning, a creak of someone plac-ing pressure on the floor. "Someone's up. I've got to go."

Without waiting to hear his response, I hang up, and shove the burner phone back between my mattress and box spring. Hands on the floor, a shove and blinding pain shoots through my knee. My butt hits the floor again hard. I slam my open palms against the carpet with enough force that my skin stings.

Stupid knee, stupid Riot, and stupid Chevy for once again breaking my heart.

A flick of the hallway light and my room feels darker than it was before. I blink rapidly and my stomach flips with the memory of being blinded weeks ago. I breathe out as my lungs tighten with the shadow in the doorway.

It's Mom. I repeat the mantra in my head over and over again. The Riot wouldn't be so short, wouldn't be so slim, wouldn't be wearing a silky robe and holding on to the door frame with one hand as though if she didn't she'd collapse.

"Violet," Mom whispers as if only I could hear and someone who broke in couldn't. "Are you okay? I heard a sound."

I sigh. No, I'm not okay. "I fell out of bed. Bad dream." That I never wake up from.

"I thought I heard Chevy and Eli."

Another sigh that leaves my lungs empty. She heard them, which means she's aware Chevy was in my room, aware he left, just aware. My thoughts return to the family who were in line ahead of me and Brandon the night of the kidnapping. Wonder if that girl's family is all safely tucked in bed. Bet her father would be yell-out-loud mad if a boy was in her room late at night. Bet her mother would be afraid for her daughter's soul. I wonder what it's like to have a normal family. Wonder what it's like to be blessedly normal.

"They left." Bet her mother and father would have already entered the room, touched their daughter and helped her back in bed. Not my mom, though. At least not with me.

Summoning my last bit of strength, I push off the carpet, use the lamp stand as leverage and haul myself off the floor. Mom shuffles forward like she might help, but hesitates just a foot short of me. In her typical way, she wrings her hands as she watches me hobble to and then collapse on the bed.

"Why do you have to make things so complicated between you and Chevy?" Mom asks, and she moves to stand at the end of the bed.

She's no longer a shadow, but the aging beauty queen with her hair up in a bun. "A boy like that will take care of you. He'll work hard, protect you, and you'll never have to worry or want for a thing. But if you keep insisting on fighting him all the time, he'll get tired of pursuing you. Boys like girls who play hard to get, but they don't like it when you take it too far."

"I'm not playing a game," I say. "And I'm going to assume that you aren't talking about marriage. I'm way too young to even think about the rest of my life."

Mom fiddles with the tie of her robe. "Your father and I were engaged by the time we graduated from high school."

Yes, they were. It happens. I can't say it doesn't. There are people who meet their true love bearing turtle doves on the second day of Christmas, and stay together forever and ever and ever, but marriage out of high school isn't my thing.

Let's pretend Chevy and I are those people who meet and stay together, though right now those odds are about negative two million to one. Marriage is still a lifetime away for me. "Well, Chevy's not Dad and I'm not you."

"I know," Mom says in exasperation, "but that doesn't make me wrong. It doesn't mean your father didn't love me and I didn't love him."

Great, guilt. "That's not what I meant."

Mom purses her lips like she has a million words to say to me, but doesn't think I'm worth the effort. She then does what she does best with me—walks away.

"Mom," I call out, but the annoyance is thick. Why can't anything be easy between me and her?

At the door, she pauses, but doesn't look back.

"Why can't you be okay with me being different from you?"

"I could ask you the same question."

I blink with her answer, then feel the need to glance down

to see if I'm bleeding. That was a stake straight through my heart.

"Your father made me happy. He made me laugh. He was the reason I smiled. I know I don't know how to talk to you. I realize you were more his child than mine, but I'm trying to help the only way I know how. You have been so sad since your father died and you used to be happy. Very happy. I want you happy. I can't bring your father back, but…" She trails off.

It becomes harder to breathe in knowing where she was headed. I was happy before Dad's death and when I was with Chevy. "Chevy can't make me better. Even if he and I could figure things out, he can't take all the sad away."

And maybe that's the frustrating part of all the men in my life. They act like their presence is some sort of a magic wand that will wipe away my pain, but that's not how pain works. Grief, despair, agony…it's shot intravenously through my veins like an unwanted drug and I'm left to deal with the ache until it runs its course. Someone wishing and talking the pain away doesn't do anything to rush it along as it creeps through my blood.

It's there and it's something I have to work through, something that no one else can fix.

"But it was worth a try," she says. "Someday you'll understand that there are some pains that make you feel like you're dying and seeing your child hurt is at the top of the list. I don't know how to talk to you, and I don't know how to fix you either. You're so much like your father. So strong, so stubborn, so independent. I understood how to care for your father, but I don't know how to care for you. Nothing I do is right. I know I fail you, but keep in mind while I do fail, I love you, too."

My throat tightens and all I want in the world is my

mother to hug me. Mom used to do that—hug me. When I was younger, Mom was the go-to person for scraped knees and sprained pride. She would almost flourish in the moment of me coming in with a trembling chin, always ready with a warm hug, hot cookies and cold milk.

But as I grew up, I shed the dresses she bought for me for blue jeans and T-shirts like my father. I turned up my nose at baking and instead became my father's shadow as he worked on the Chevelle or his Harley.

I realize you have always been more his child than mine…

My heart sinks and my hand searches for Chevy's bear to cling to, but I let my hand fall to the mattress. Dad said I needed to give a proud man an out. Maybe Mom's proud and needs an out. Or maybe Mom needs an opening and her still standing there, telling me she loves me, maybe that's her giving me an opening, as well.

"Mom." Words become stuck in my throat and I have to clear it to continue. "My knee hurts and sometimes I have nightmares, so…" Spit it out. "Can you sit with me? Just for a few minutes?"

"Yes," she says, yet she stands in my doorway like she doesn't quite know what to do with my offer. I edge to the middle of my bed, offering her room, and she crosses the room and sits beside me.

She's sort of touching me, yet not. I want her to hug me. I want all the pain to go away. "I love Chevy."

"I know."

"I hurt him tonight, but he hurt me, too. I want to be with him, but we can't seem to stop hurting each other."

Tears burn my eyes and I rap the back of my head against the headboard and it's then that something happens that hasn't happened in months. Mom's hand goes over mine, and when she links our fingers together, I choke to keep the emotion that's been building from exploding out.

"Tell me how to help you," Mom whispers. "I don't know how to help you."

She can't. Nobody can.

"I miss Dad." My voice trembles and it should be impossible to feel so much pain.

Mom releases my hand and the coldness left behind crushes me. But then she wraps her arms around me. "So do I. Every day. Every hour. Every minute. I miss him so much, and when I see you hurt, I miss him more. I wish he were here. I wish he were the one holding you."

Me, too. There's so much wrong with my life, so many things I can't control, so much grief, so much sadness, and the more I try to push it all away, the faster and harder it descends upon my chest. I breathe in and then out, short breaths, tough breaths, the sound like that of a woman in labor. The pain rolling through me like waves, but I don't want to let it out because once it's released, it'll consume me, devour me until I'm nothing.

"Breathe, Violet," Mom whispers. "Please, breathe."

"I can't." My voice cracks and I choke again.

Mom hugs me, arms around my body, her hand guiding my head to her shoulder, and the moment my forehead connects with her, the dam spills open and I sob. Tears streaming down my face, shoulders shaking, all the ugliness festering inside me pouring out.

"It's okay," she whispers. "It's all going to be okay."

CHEVY

Temperature continues to drop and the night is black against the stadium light glaring down on the football field. I'm dressed in my uniform, cleats on my feet, pads heavy on my shoulders, jersey on with my number, helmet dangling from my hand.

Both teams line up at our twenty. We have the ball, third down and we have to move on this play. The clock is counting down in the fourth quarter and we're losing by six. We need this win in order to be a shoo-in for play-off games. We lose, and we'll have to pray for a wild-card spot. It's my senior year and I've worked too damn hard to watch our winning season go down in flames.

But I watch because I'm benched. May be benched, but I'm standing, walking the sideline with my team on the field.

Better man.

Not sure what that means anymore. Allowing Violet and me to be kidnapped because we love Stone? Defying the club to tell Violet things because I think their decisions are wrong? Hurting Violet because I'm torn between promises

I made to her and the club? Starting to wonder if my goal of being like my father is trashed. Not sure if he was the better man I was raised to believe in.

This week, being the better man means killing what's left of my pride.

I did what Coach asked. Spent time training Ray so he can take over my position. He improved, but it's not enough. The kid doesn't have a fast connection between his head, hands and feet. But he does have the right connections with the right people. Has a bigger mouth to push the powers that be to give him what he wants. He and his dad are the type who if they yell loud enough for long enough everyone caves to their demands. He's shiny and looks a hell of a lot better on paper than me. Guess the old sayings are wrong. In the end, talent doesn't win.

"Put McKinley in!" someone from the stands shouts, and there are agreements and a few boos. It's been this way the entire game. Our own fans can't decide if they should be more frightened of the Terror or of losing.

The entire game, I can feel Cyrus and my mom burning a hole into my back and into Coach's. I refuse to look. I can't stand to see the disappointment and anger in their expressions. Can't stomach to not see Violet watching me in the stands.

She's avoided me since our fight last night and I don't blame her. I reached out to her last night when I got home from the bar. One text: I'm sorry. I was wrong. I choose you. Please give me another chance.

Nothing in response. Just maddening silence.

Our quarterback, Brad, scans the defense, trying to read the other team's play. Out of habit, he glances to where I should be. He's searching for a signal on whether he needs to call an audible and why. I can read subtle ways guys move.

Feet and bodies angled a certain way tips off where they're going and why. Ray can't get his own shit straight, much less have the ability to read the guys on the other side of the line.

Brad bends and two defensive guys in the back lean down and their feet are angled forward. "They're blitzing!"

Coach glances at me, then yells, "They're blitzing."

Brad can't hear me, he's in his zone and Ray looks over at us. He needs to tell Brad, Brad needs to call an audible and he needs to call it now.

Ray's paying attention to the sideline, he's not understanding us, he's not watching the line, he's not telling Brad to call an audible. The ball snaps. Ray's still not paying attention. The entire line, including the two in the back run forward. Brad's searching for Ray, but Ray has yet to run his route. Too many guys racing through our line and Brad's sacked.

I close my eyes, the horn blows, and time's up.

Cheers from the visitors' side, and our fans are stunned into silence as the rest of our team hang their heads. This is my fault. Don't know how I could have done anything differently, but I let down a group of guys who needed me. I seem to be letting down lots of people.

The other team celebrates their path to state, our team heads out. The silence doesn't last long as someone from our side calls my coach an asshole. Others join in, others yell at the people in the crowd. Soon people are booing, throwing garbage at us, and the anger pumps into my veins.

Not Coach's fault we lost. Wasn't his fault I was benched. I turn to tell the crowd where to shove it and that's when I see red hair and blue eyes. Violet's standing on the blacktop, near the fencing of the field. She's bundled in a red coat, black scarf and gloves. She's less than a few feet away from me and the entire world stills when her gaze meets mine.

A quick peek into the stands and Cyrus is in the middle of a pack of black vests. They're sitting quiet, watching me. On the opposite side of the stands is my mother, also watching my every movement. Yeah, time's up and not just on the game.

I should be heading back to the locker room to listen to Coach, but I'm done falling into line and doing what I'm told. The moment I'm past the fence, I take the right instead of going straight. My cleats click against the blacktop of the running track, but they're not loud enough to drown out the crowd.

Some people still yell at Coach, some people clap at seeing me fall out of line. As if this moment has anything to do with football and is my protest that I wasn't put into the game. I reach Violet and she's tough to read. Her arms are crossed over her chest, and she's watching me like I'm a ticking bomb, but overall she's as cool as the night air.

"Where are your crutches?" I ask.

"Physical therapist told me to do more walking on my own. So this is me walking on my own."

"Are you telling your therapist how much it still hurts and how much you've been walking on your own?"

"You're going to get in trouble for being late to the team meeting," she says, ignoring my question. "Not unless he's changed his mind after four years of forcing you to be talked to forever while I stand outside the locker room and wait."

"I'm already being punished for things beyond my control, so might as well do something to earn the benching." I pause. "You get my text?"

She inhales deeply and a puff of white leaves her mouth as she exhales in the cold night. "Yes. The only reason I'm here is because Eli hasn't swooped in and chained me to a wall yet. If you had told him what I told you last night, he would have lost his mind."

Agreed. I'm still not convinced keeping the club out of it is the right call, but… "I want you to trust me."

"You're not going to like what I have to say, and if you change your mind after I tell you and you go running to the club, I will never forgive you."

She means it. Violet doesn't blink. Doesn't look away. Doesn't even shift her footing. Her chin is tipped up, her eyes locked on mine. Violet and I are on the edge of the knife and the wrong move by either of us will slice open an artery.

"I've messed up and I'm trying to make it right. I get that this is my last chance." I hold out my hand. "Come with me. I'll ditch the pads and we'll go somewhere and talk. Let me in, Violet, and I swear you won't regret it."

She watches me as if she's the one who can read body language for the lie. Being around me for so many years, she probably can. After what feels like a lifetime of my hand in the air, she accepts it. I twine her fingers with mine, and ignoring the yells from the crowd, from my teammates and Coach and now from Cyrus and my mom, I lead Violet out of the football stadium.

Violet

The light from the bonfire dances across Chevy's face and the flames crackle and snap. Chevy's gone unusually quiet after I told him the truth about what the Riot asked of me and how Detective Barlow offered to help. I'm bundled in a blanket and he sits next to me in his jeans, T-shirt and black leather jacket. It's freezing at the pond, though the fire's warm.

The pond is the only place we could think of to go where we might be safe from prying eyes or ears. This place is so secluded we would have known if someone was tailing us, so quiet we'd hear a car or motorcycle within a mile, so remote and thick in forest and overgrowth that it would take someone hours to reach us by foot. We are alone.

Above us are billions of stars and it's a beautiful sight on the cold fall night, but the pond is a blessing and a curse.

So many wonderful memories live here. It's full of happiness and laughter and joy and I've avoided this place since Dad died. It's where he taught me how to fish, how to float and how to swim. I spent endless summers here chasing fireflies with Oz, Chevy and Razor. Spent days soaking in the hot sun on the dock. I swung from that rope hanging on the old oak so many times I should have a permanent rope burn on my ankle.

The fire roasts my front, the darkness behind me makes my back cold. It's a great metaphor for my memories. My past here makes me warm, but step away from it and my reality is harsh and freezing.

"Do you understand why I don't want the club involved?" I ask. "Either the Riot has someone who can hear and see a lot of what goes on in the heart of Terror territory or there's a traitor in the Terror. Eli and Cyrus so desperately trust everyone in the club. What if I tell them everything and they tell the wrong person? What if that means I end up in that basement again or, worse, something happens to Mom and Brandon? The Riot don't make idle threats. We both have personal experience with that. I can't do that to my family. I can't do that to me."

Dread settles in my stomach when Chevy remains a statue. His legs bent, arms lazily wrapped around them with his fingers slightly threaded below his knees. Taking a risk, I nudge him with my foot to stir him to life.

Chevy cracks his neck to the right. Fantastic. He's annoyed and he's going to snitch.

"You promised."

He picks up a twig and throws it into the fire. "It's not that. I'm pissed at myself. You told me last night you were scared and in danger—that you were being watched and all I could think about was you betraying the Terror. I didn't listen to you, not about what was important, and I'm angry at myself. I'm sorry, Violet. I'm sorry for letting you down."

It's sad how his acknowledgment of letting me down makes me happy. He's in pain, I feel like smiling. I sigh, wondering if Chevy and I will ever be on the same page.

"What's the detective's plan?" he asks.

I pull the blanket tighter around me like a shield. This is where it's all going to fall apart. "He wants me to give the Riot the account numbers."

His jaw hardens, but to his credit, he keeps his mouth shut. I've agreed to give business details involving the club to an outsider, an outsider who believes the Terror are bad.

"If the club is truly legit, then the account numbers shouldn't be a problem."

"Keep explaining."

So if he didn't like the first part, he's going to love the second. "I give the account numbers to the Riot. The police watch the accounts, and when the Riot manipulates them to try to set up Eli, they'll arrest them."

A few beats of silence, a snapping and crackling of wood. The heart of the fire burns red and the flames lick skyward.

"That's it?" Chevy asks. "We find the account numbers, we hand them to the Riot and then you're done?"

My lips twist to the side. "When did this become a *we*? Last I checked this was a me."

"It's been a *we* since the Riot pulled over on the side of the road. You don't want the Terror involved, fine, but I'm in this with you."

Annoyance rumbles through me, but at least he's trying to give, so…fair enough.

"That's it?" he repeats.

"Basically." I draw the word out longer than needed. "That and I need to wear a wire when I give them the account numbers and somehow engage them in conversation that makes them implicate themselves."

And that's when Chevy loses his mind.

CHEVY

Violet must have been hit too hard in the head during the kidnapping. Wearing a wire. What the hell is she thinking? Why doesn't she just go ahead and place a gun to her head and pull the trigger?

I make my fifth pass of stalking around the fire. Violet's on the other side, sitting there, watching the fire like she just announced we were going to make s'mores instead of...

"Wearing a wire. This isn't a movie, Violet. They figure it out and they will kill you. That basement will look like kindergarten. Have you forgotten they shot Eli this summer? Eli thinks the Riot are the ones who took a shot at Razor last month. They almost killed you. They almost killed me. These men are murderers."

"I'm aware." Violet finally raises her eyes to look at me, and I could strangle her for how calm she's acting.

She's aware. She's aware? "Do you understand what I'm saying? When I speak, is it English that's coming out?"

Violet pulls her hand out of the blanket, tucks her fire-red hair behind her ear, then shrugs. "They've already hurt me and they've already hurt you. If we don't stop them, they will continue to hurt us and they'll move on to the people we love. We have the power to end this once and for all. Don't you want to secure peace?"

Peace. I don't even know what that is anymore. I run a hand over my face when I honestly feel like clawing my skin off. "What don't you understand? I can't let you do this. I won't!"

A tick of her head. The first show of emotion and it's her building temper. "*Can't*, *let* and *won't*. Three words not to use with me. I'm not asking your permission. I'm informing you of the decisions I've made. You don't see me telling you that you can't be part of the club or I'm going to let you be part of the club or that I won't stand for you to be part of the club. You're a big boy, Chevy. You can make your own big-boy decisions and I'm a big girl and you need to learn to accept my big-girl decisions. You want a dog to order around and be obedient, I bet you can adopt one at the pound."

"Why does it always come back to the club?"

"Because that's how they treat me, and whether you realize it or not, you do a modified version of trying to control me, too. To be honest, you want to be with me and be with the club? I could live with that, as long as you learn that I am not your property, I am not a dog, that I am your equal and I deserve the love and respect that comes with that because that's what a real man does when he loves a woman."

Violet shuts her eyes like she's just poured out her soul and didn't mean for it to happen and I'm having a hard time catching my breath. The fragile foundation of understanding I had crumbles and I take a step toward Violet onto solid ground. An equal. That's all she wants and it feels sickening and strange that I never understood it until now. I thought loving her made us equal, but love doesn't necessarily mean that I listened to her. I listened...to what I thought was best for her...to what was best for me.

But to wear a wire... My throat closes and an ache ripples through my chest. She ran for the gun, and when that shot reverberated around the room, my knees gave and the pain that consumed me nearly crushed me to the point of death.

"I love you," I say. "And I don't want to live without you."

Violet pulls the blanket tighter around her shoulders. "And I love you and I don't want to live without you. Even if we can't work things out between us, I will still love you and I still don't want to live without you. If you go down roads I can't travel, then I need to know you're safe. I need to know Eli is safe, and Cyrus and Pigpen and Oz and Razor and my mom and my brother, and I don't want to be looking over my shoulder for the rest of my life.

"I have the opportunity to end it all. The war between the Riot and the Terror finally over. Years of pain and hurt and blood will end. What Cyrus's and Eli's generations could never do, I can. I won't lie, I'm terrified, but I will not let fear stop me. I will be the one to do what no one else has been able to do. I will bring peace."

The fire illuminates her face and there's an edge to her beauty I've never seen before. Violet's never been a shrinking flower. She's always been a ferocious storm, but her bursts of anger were like short downdrafts that could do damage but then quickly recede. She had the temper of a child, but now she shines with a light that only comes with maturity, with growing up, and before me is a gorgeous warrior holding her head high as she readies for battle.

"Then we do this, but I'm involved. We make up a story telling them I came to you upset with the Terror over my father and that you told me the plan to put Eli away. Yeah, you'll have to meet with them again to make the switch from you being the lead to me, but you don't have to wear a wire for that. We tell them I want to be the one to give them the account numbers because I want revenge. I'll wear the wire." I'll take the risk of death. "The Riot have been playing me, too, with my dad being a traitor. Maybe they'll be convinced I'm flipping on Eli."

"Even you have to admit how ridiculous that sounds," she says. "Cyrus and Eli are your family. You would never flip on them. The Riot know this and that's why they picked me and not you."

"I'm breaking a promise to the Terror right now."

"True," she says slowly. "But I'm not asking you to betray them."

"Eli and Cyrus will see my not telling them about you and the Riot as a betrayal."

"But it's not. We're trying to save them. If you honestly didn't believe I was doing all this to save the people you love, regardless of your feelings for me, you would have already been down the road telling Eli. But you aren't and you didn't tell Eli last night about the Riot because deep down you know me and you trust me. You know I would never purposely hurt the people I love."

"Yet the Riot chose you and they were wrong. I can convince them they were wrong about me."

Violet looks away and that one cast of her gaze feels like being hit by a car at breakneck speed. She knows something I don't. "Tell me."

"You failed their test."

"What test?"

"They told you your father was a traitor. You told the board, and you believed what they said enough to not go looking for answers on your own."

"I don't believe what the board said."

She bobs her head in agreement. "I know, but deep down you trust the club enough not to have asked for the woman's name who could in theory tell you the truth and you have yet to reach out to them for that information."

I slam my hand to my chest. "You don't think it's a problem for me if my father was a traitor? You don't think it's eating me alive?"

"I know it is, but the point is you aren't searching for answers. Your loyalty is still with the club. That's how you failed with the Riot. They won't believe anything you say otherwise."

"Don't you get it? The reason I haven't asked is because I haven't wanted to know the answers. I'm James's legacy! Who I am with the club—it's all built upon who he was, and if he was a traitor, what does that make me?"

Violet's head slowly tilts to the side as she assesses me. "Chevy..." She closes her mouth, opens it again, and a small sound comes from her throat. "Chevy, if the Riot told me my father was a traitor, I'd be devastated. But..." She scratches the back of her head as if she's struggling to get her thoughts out. "I'm not my dad and neither are you. I'll be the first to admit that Eli and Cyrus can be dense, but they aren't going to change how they feel about you if they find out James made mistakes."

My head falls forward because that's exactly what I think. "Mom told me things about Dad. She said he knew she was pregnant, but he didn't want the club to know. She said he told her he was done with the club, that he wanted something different out of life. He was going to take responsibility for me and Mom, but without club involvement."

"Wanting a different life doesn't mean he was a traitor."

"Doesn't mean he wasn't, but I'll tell you what it does mean. If my father did want a different path and it wasn't the Riot, then what the hell happened? James left town, he went to Louisville, and Eli and Cyrus won't admit it, but they broke ties with each other. Family means everything to them. If James wanted something different from the club—did the Terror shut him out? I turn eighteen next week and thanks to the wild-card slot there's still a shot that my team can make it to the play-offs and state. Becoming a prospect will be the final nail in my coffin for playing. If I choose to play football over becoming a prospect, are they going to shut me out? Am I going to lose my family because I'm not exactly like them? Because you've said it yourself—they don't forgive betrayal and will they see my choices as unforgivable?"

She blinks several times and the dawning of understanding on her face guts me open.

"You would prefer to think your father was a traitor and that Cyrus knew and has been lying to you over it rather than to find out that Cyrus cut your father off because he chose not to be part of the club, wouldn't you?"

My eyes burn and I pivot away from Violet into the dark night, but only a few steps into the woods and I turn back. I can't walk away from her anymore. I can't keep running from the truth. I blink away the blurry vision. "Yes."

Violet places her hand over her heart, then sheds the blanket as she stands. "They love you. I promise, they love you."

"And they loved James, yet I'm standing here wondering why the hell things fell apart."

Violet stumbles toward me, and when she falls into my chest, it's not me catching her, it's her holding me up. I fold her into me and hang on.

She comforts me. Her hands in my hair, fingertips up and down my back, kisses along my shoulder, along my neck, and whispers of love, as if she comprehends the only thing keeping me sane is her touch.

"I've refused choosing because I don't want to lose anyone I love," I whisper into her hair. "I don't want to lose them, I don't want to lose Mom and I don't want to lose you."

"You won't." Violet squeezes me tight. "You have me. We'll figure it out. I promise you we'll figure it out."

Violet in my arms is right. Violet holding me is peace. I love her, she loves me, and for the first time, she's fighting for me...for us. The urge is to keep her close, ignore the rest of the world and stay here forever.

But we can't. We have to move forward. We have to face the Riot, the Terror and our unsteady future. Violet's always found a way to plow forward and it's time for me to learn, like her, how to forge my own path.

"I don't want you to do the wire," I whisper into her hair.

"I know," she says. "But this is how it has to be."

I'm learning from her and I pray she's also learned from me. "But not alone. Promise me you'll keep me in this. Promise me you won't face any of this alone."

Violet pulls back and I take her face in my hand, brushing my thumb against her rose-petal skin. The sad softness in her blue eyes almost undoes me completely. "Promise me."

"I promise I won't do this alone."

The pulse thrumming through my veins is full of fear. I lost her once to her grief, came close to losing her again due to the Riot, lost her again last night because of my issues and now I feel like my chances are up. She's about to walk into the flames of hell. I've never felt so helpless.

Either we'll both walk out of hell still alive or we're both going down in flames. Either way, we're doing it together.

"What can I do to help you?" she asks.

There's nothing she can do. "I want the truth about James and Cyrus and there's no way to get it."

Her throat moves as she glances up at me. "Maybe there is a way. You said the Riot mentioned there was a woman…"

I pull Violet back into me, shaken that I had forgotten about the name the detective gave me. There might be a way and I'll need Violet's help to see it through. With the gentle way she leans into me, I know when I ask, she'll say yes.

Violet

The waitressing staff at the only diner in Snowflake doesn't bother giving Eli a menu or asking for his order. It's the same, day in and day out: scrambled eggs and bacon. They only ask if he wants coffee or orange juice because they know him so well. Today he wants coffee. I order the blueberry pancakes with two side orders of bacon because odds are I'm going to die when I meet up with the Riot, so I might as well revel in the goodness of bacon and clog up some arteries.

I tap my fingers against the sticky table and stare out the window with my head propped in my hand. Last night, I promised Chevy I wouldn't handle the Riot on my own and I have every intention of keeping that promise. Detective Barlow is on my side and I'll let Chevy in on every meeting I have with him, but when push comes to shove, I'm the only one who can meet with the Riot, the only one who can wear a wire.

The only one...

Nausea swirls around in my stomach. Maybe I should have ordered oatmeal again. No, I'm having pancakes because my days may be numbered. I agree with Chevy: if the Riot discover the wire, they will kill me, but at least then the police will have a legit murder charge they can convict them on. I'm bringing down the Riot even if it means doing so with my life.

What no man in the Reign of Terror has had the balls to do, I will. Sometimes it takes a woman to do a job men can't accomplish.

"Razor gets to see Breanna today. We worked it out with her family."

I draw my head in Eli's direction in such a slow way that the world tunnels out before focusing again. "What?"

"Razor gets to see Breanna today. He doesn't know, so I'd appreciate it if you kept this a secret." Eli sits across from me in the booth and like always he wears his black leather Reign of Terror vest over a black T-shirt. His jacket hangs on the edge of the booth.

Both of us fit in this ragtag town and diner. Orange plastic seating with tears in the cushions and a menu on the wall that still requires little black magnetic letters to complete. Half the prices are missing numbers. I understand not being complete and so does Eli.

I blink several times as I finally understand his words. Giddiness for my best friend races through me. Then I sit back in awe. The club actually pulled this off for him. "Her family is cool with the club now?"

"I'd say they're more interested in still having control over their daughter's life and we're offering to watch the relationship for them if they agree to let Razor and Breanna see each other again."

"That sucks."

Eli flicks a wadded-up paper from a straw across the table.

"Is what it is, but at least he gets to see her. What're your plans for today?"

Speaking of things that need to be done, Chevy and I need to go to Louisville today and we need to make sure the journey is Terror-free. "Chevy said something about hanging at his place and catching up on homework."

"That's it?" he fishes.

"Being bored sounds good to me." Actually, being bored sounds amazing, but I promised Chevy I'd go with him to try to find out the truth about James. Makes me a little nervous to head into Louisville, since that's the Riot's territory, but he and I need to do this...especially before I wear a wire.

Ugh, now I have nausea with flashes of heat.

"You okay?" he asks.

"Yeah." Nope. "Why wouldn't I be?"

"You look pale, plus you're quiet."

"Pretty sure I've been talking, because when I talk, you talk back."

"I don't mean like the hospital quiet and also not a pissed-off quiet. You're acting like..."

He has my full attention now, and I wait patiently for him to continue, but instead he thanks the waitress for the cup of coffee she hands him and goes to work mixing in cream.

"I'm acting like what?" I prompt.

"You look like you did the first few weeks after your dad died."

The bottomless pit that formed in my stomach after Dad died opens a little wider. "Oh."

Eli glances up from his coffee and hits me square in the eye with that patented dark McKinley gaze. "What's wrong?"

So much, Eli. So much. It would be easier to recount the things going right.

"I promise I'm listening this time," he says. "I've thought

about it, and I think some of what you said about me, you might have been right."

Stunned. This odd, disorienting, foggy feeling is stunned. "Might have been right?"

He smirks. "Don't press your luck, kid."

The right side of my mouth edges up, and Eli tips his coffee cup in my direction before drinking. "That right there. That's what I've been dying to see for over a year. Talk to me, Vi. Talk to me like you used to. Talk to me like you used to with your dad."

"But you're not my dad." I breathe through the wave of pain.

"I know, but you've got to open up to somebody, why not me?" Eli sets the mug on the table and rubs his thumb up and down the handle. "You've become friends with Emily, right?"

I nod. Emily is his daughter and Skull's granddaughter. She's also one of the reasons why the Riot hate Eli and the Terror so much. To protect Emily, her mother took her away from Kentucky when she was a toddler. The Riot blame Eli for their daughter and granddaughter leaving, but they fail to understand that Emily's mother left Eli, too.

Now that Emily is older, she and Eli are making a try at their relationship again.

"I love Emily. I always have. From the moment Emily's mom told me she was pregnant, I loved Emily. I remember how Emily used to hold her pink elephant in a stranglehold when she was scared by the loud sound of a motorcycle engine and I loved how she would hold on to me after waking from a nap and her skin was hot and sticky from sweat, but she didn't care. She'd hold on to me as tight as she could until she realized she was awake and not dreaming."

I smile slightly, wondering if my father had memories like that of me.

Eli frowns then and all the happiness in the room seems to be sucked out with the motion. "But I can't tell you who she had her first crush on in school. I can't tell you the first time she went on stage and why. I don't know what makes her cry and half the time I'm still trying to figure out what makes her laugh. Emily and I, we're figuring each other out and I'm grateful for the opportunity, but I don't know Emily and she doesn't know me, but I do know you."

My stomach sinks. Eli also has a hole in his soul left unfilled, but... "I'm not your daughter...and I'm not looking to replace my dad."

"I'm aware of both of those things and I would never insult you with even suggesting that, but what I am saying is that I was there the first time you took the stage. You were eleven and you played the bells in your school's band concert."

I snort-laugh because that was my first and last band concert. I totally forgot my parts, so I just rang the crap out of the bells until the song was over. Eli was one of only a few people who gave me a standing ovation. The other people were also part of the Terror.

"I know Chevy wasn't your first crush, but I know he was your first kiss. I know what makes you cry and I know what makes you laugh and I know I would be the sorriest replacement for your father so that's not what I'm offering. But what I am telling you is that I know you and you know me and that has to be worth something."

Worth something? It's worth a lot. More than silver. More than gold. More than he could comprehend.

"Your dad dying changed us both. Those people we were—they don't exist anymore, but I want to be here for you and I would do anything for you to rely on me again."

I rub at my face, my eyes—this is the man who carried me from my hospital room to Chevy's. The man who took the pictures of me, Dad, Mom and Brandon at my eighth-grade graduation. The man who brought me a rose from my father's casket and, on bended knee with tears in his eyes, asked for my forgiveness.

I didn't forgive him then, but I do now. I can't carry this burden of hate on my shoulders anymore. I can't blame him for my pain when he grieves just as badly. "If I hadn't made it out of the basement, would you have taken care of Brandon and Mom?"

It's a strange response to all that he's said, but it's also the most honest. Eli looks me over as he thinks over my words, and though they seem innocent, that statement is full of the trust he's searching for. It's also full of the danger he sixth-sense feels lurking outside his door. "You know I would have."

Good. "So if something was to happen to me, you would still take care of them?"

His forehead furrows and his eyes darken. "Has something happened? Are you in trouble?"

"No," I lie, then wave my hands around my head as if to explain the chaos that has controlled my mind since the kidnapping. "What happened in that basement messed me up. Makes me think of things." Like how when I die, the people I love will be grieving all over again.

"I was thinking that…" I needed to come up with something plausible. "If I went away to college next year, maybe you would look after them for me so I wouldn't have to worry. You said I could trust you, and if that's true, there's nothing I love more than Mom and Brandon, and trusting you with them…"

I fall off because the pang in my heart at the idea of leaving them behind causes me to be unable to breathe. But with all Eli and I have been through, I trust him with them and there's no greater compliment I could give him than that.

Eli's watching me, closely, like he's attempting to see past my skin and bones and into my soul. "I will always look after them. Just like I will always watch over you."

"If we're really talking and if we're both really listening, can I say something to you and have you understand I'm saying it without the intention of starting a fight?"

He nods, continuing to try to decipher me and my words.

"You enable Mom and Brandon and I understand why you do. They have been through so much and they hurt so much and you want to make something better and easier for them, but you aren't making them better. It's like handing a sobbing woman a single piece of toilet paper and then walking away because you don't want to deal with the emotional meltdown. Mom needs to learn how to take care of herself. I know Dad left her money and that if she budgets she won't have to work ever again, but that's not the point.

"Mom needs something or she will fall apart at every turn. She needs to see she is capable. If she doesn't want to work a job, fine, but she needs a hobby, she needs a focus, she needs to learn how to depend on herself for something. She can't keep putting her happiness on other people because people make mistakes, people leave, people…" Die. "People, despite their best intentions, fail, and Mom needs to learn to be happy with just being her. And Brandon…"

God, I love Brandon and leaving him behind causes my entire body to flinch.

"Brandon can function in this world. It won't be easy, but it's never easy for any of us. He's so smart and funny and friendly, but he's scared. Each and every time you do something for him because he's scared, you are teaching him to give in to the fear. Don't make him scared. Make him courageous. I'm not asking you to set him up for failure by placing him in all new situations, but I am asking you to stop doing everything for him and help show him how to be a functioning adult in a world that doesn't understand him.

"As much as you want to, you can't take all our pain away. Hurting, it's a part of life, and if you try to stop any of us from being in pain, that means you're not allowing us to actually live."

Eli bows his head, and when he looks back up, I don't see demons or charm, but a man stripped to the core. "Is that how you feel? Even before the kidnapping? That I'm not letting you live?"

I bite my lower lip, then give him the truth. "Yes. I don't know how to fit into your world while being me and I like me. I'm who my father helped me figure out I am, but I hurt you and I'm tired of hurting all of you."

"This club was meant to be a place where people can be themselves. I've failed somewhere if that's how you feel." The sting in his voice causes me pain.

"Maybe you're not the only one who's made things difficult." God, I want to peel my skin off. "Maybe I've had a hand in that, too."

Eli's now the one who grins. "Maybe?"

I kick his shin, he chuckles, and at the roar of motorcycles, I turn my attention back to the window. A large group of Reign of Terror bikes pulls into spots in front of the diner and one by one men slide off and some of them wait to help off the woman behind them. Chevy enters first and I tilt my head when he smiles at me.

Oz and Razor walk in behind him followed by Pigpen, Man O' War, Rebecca, Dust, and then I lose track. Our waitress walks up and places a huge stack of blueberry pancakes in front of me and on top of it is a lit candle.

"Chevy reminded me that we forgot something special," Eli says, "and I want you to know I'm sorry. For a lot of things, I'm sorry. But regardless, happy belated birthday, kid."

Chevy squeezes into the booth beside me, kissing my cheek, and I barely have the attention span to kiss him back as I crazily try to take in what's going on.

"How did you know we'd work things out in time?" I ask Eli.

He relaxes back into the booth, a cocky smile on his face. "I didn't. I assumed we'd be fighting and told the guys to show so I wouldn't ruin one more meeting between us."

I don't know who started it first, but soon the diner is filled with a chorus of voices, most of them singing off-key, but singing loudly and they are singing "Happy Birthday" to me.

CHEVY

"Don't you think we're going to be tight on time?" Violet asks as she plays with the radio of her father's Chevelle. It's the original radio—the type that requires turning a knob to find a station. I'm driving, she's on the passenger side and I'm not as worried about time as I am about breaking down on our way to Louisville. No way I want to explain why Violet and I aren't doing homework in Snowflake.

"Scared you're going to miss your party?" I glance at her out of the corner of my eye to gauge her reaction.

Tonight, the clubhouse is going to be full and the entire night is in honor of her turning eighteen. We're a few weeks late, but at least the club is owning their mistake. I expect Violet to frown, to go into an eloquent rant that includes curse words that would cause a sailor to blush, but instead she looks like she's contemplating the possibility of being okay with it.

"I want to hang out with you, Oz and Razor," she says. "Like we used to."

A prick of pain in my chest. Like we used to before her

dad died. I reach over and take Violet's hand. The squeeze is meant to show the way I want to love her through all that hurts her. The twining of our fingers is to keep me from turning the car around and sticking my head back in the sand. It's time to find out the truth about my dad. It's time for me to make some informed choices.

"Then that's what we'll do."

"Last I checked, when I'm the guest of honor, we don't have to sneak beer anymore or watch the party from branches in trees."

"You know you want to play hide-n-go-seek in the woods."

She laughs and the sound warms my soul. "What if I do?"

"Then we'll do that, too. We'll make Razor be it."

"He hated being it."

"That's why he's going to be it."

GPS tells me to take a left and that our destination is on the right. We fall silent as we creep past the decrepit and decaying car garage. The place isn't much, but it's on par with the rest of the area. Gray, broken and on the verge of collapse. My instincts flare. Bringing Violet was a mistake.

Instead of making a U-turn, I flick the turn signal to head back to the expressway, but Violet gently squeezes my knee. "It's just a garage."

"What if it's a garage for the Riot?"

"Then we'll tell them we found the account numbers and we'll get a jump on that meeting time the detective wants so badly."

"I'm serious. They hurt you once. I can't let them hurt you again."

"It's not a Riot garage. The bay doors were open and there wasn't a motorcycle in sight. A few cars and two people inside working on them."

With a grunt, I make the U-turn. And I'm supposed to be the observant one. "I didn't see any of that."

"No, you were too busy seeing the basement to notice what was right in front of you."

Her words ring so true that I can't acknowledge them. I pull into the parking lot of the garage and a girl with blond hair tied back into a braid straightens from over the hood of a red nineteen fifty-something Chevy. It's a beautiful piece of machinery and the girl lets her fingers slide over the car as if she's in love.

"I can see how you find this place intimidating," Violet mocks. "She screams badass."

She's about our age, in a T-shirt, but wears designer jeans and has the presence and face of a beauty queen instead of a greased-up mechanic. "Looks can be deceiving. No one would have guessed Emily's half Terror, half Riot."

"That's because Emily grew up normal and away from this madness."

Before I have a chance to edge into a parking spot, the girl waves us forward into the empty bay next to the car she's working on. I enter at a snail's pace, scanning the garage for any threat.

There's a one-room office to the side, but other than that the place is bare except for the car, the girl, workbenches and the tools. "I thought you said there were two people."

"There were, but one could have gone in the back. People do that you, you know? Normally leave one room for another. Plus you're here to see a guy, remember? Isaiah Walker. We want him to be here, or have you forgotten?"

Haven't forgotten. "Have you forgotten we were kidnapped?"

"I wish I could."

So do I. "If I ask you to stay in the car, what are the odds of you following directions?"

"Exactly what you think the odds will be."

Zero.

I turn off the ignition and Violet's opening her door before I have a chance to place my fingers on the handle. The blonde checks out Violet's car like Pigpen checks out the legs of my English teacher—like a dog in heat.

"Holy crap," she says. "I've never worked on a Chevelle before, but you shouldn't worry about that. Isaiah has worked on everything. Everything." She overpronounces the word.

"But I saw you first and I let him work on the last car, so I get first dibs. Don't let him convince you otherwise. He'll try to steal this from me. I heard your baby when you pulled in." She pets the hood of the car like it's a bleeding puppy in need of medical care. "I'm betting spark plugs. Let me guess, the engine sputters while driving? Sometimes stops working or just won't catch when you try to start it?"

Jesus, the girl's a walking car encyclopedia. Violet and I share a look and she raises her eyebrows with a faint smile. Yeah, she doesn't know what to think either.

"Yes," Violet answers. "To all that. This is my car."

I catch the way Violet's voice cracked on *my*, but I'm proud she's accepting that her father would have wanted her to feel like his car is now hers.

The blonde extends her hand to Violet. "I'm Rachel, and you are?"

Violet accepts it. "I'm Violet and this is my boyfriend, Chevy."

I can't help the smile. First time I've heard her call me that in months. Rachel beams. "I love that name."

"Thanks." The way this girl is talking, she'll have the Chevelle turned upside down, inside out, then fixed before I can get a chance to ask about this Isaiah Walker. She mentioned him, but I'd like more than a mention. I need to meet him, talk to him.

"I'm here because of a recommendation," I say.

Rachel tears her gaze away from the Chevelle and looks at me for the first time. She goes on the verge of death white. Even Violet moves toward her as she must believe the girl is going to pass out and crack her head on the concrete floor.

I throw my hands up in the air in a show of submission. "Are you okay?"

Rachel stumbles back as if I'm holding a gun and my heart picks up speed as I scan the room, then glance over my shoulder to see if someone is holding us up. There's nothing. Rachel's back hits a workbench and she places her hand over her chest as if that can help her catch her breath. "Who are you?"

With the way her gaze is locked on me, there's no doubt she's lost interest in the Chevelle and Violet. "My name is Chevy McKinley."

"McKinley?" she repeats in a whisper.

A door farther back squeaks open and a large guy comes stalking in. He's tattoos, earrings, and he tinkers with a car part in his hand. "I pulled this from one of the junk cars in the back. We're going to have to mess with it first to get it to work. Hate having to buy a new part. Logan's been short on money and—"

"Isaiah," Rachel says, and his head snaps up at the shaky sound of her voice. He's switched from relaxed to dangerous in less than a second. He now holds the car part in his hand as if he'd use it as a weapon.

He surveys the room just like I would, and when his eyes land on me, I know his stomach is dropping, his mind is stalling out and then it feels like something significant in the universe has died and we're experiencing the aftermath of the pulsating quake. I know this from the way his eyes blink, from his stunned expression, and because it's exactly how I'm feeling.

In front of me is dark hair shaved close to his head, eyes that are gray, a foreboding man of muscle and height, tattoos and earrings, but the important part is his face. Except for his eye color, this guy is a replica of my father. Spitting image of the pictures I've seen. Some of my mom sneaked into my genetics, but I'm a McKinley, and if this guy has looked into a mirror, he knows he's staring back at a part of him.

Rachel slowly walks over to Isaiah as if she's scared to spook him. "He says he's a McKinley."

Recognition flashes over his face and my gut twists that he somehow knows my last name.

"Chevy," Violet says. "I think we all need to sit down."

"What's wrong with the car?" Isaiah asks, ignoring Violet.

"Spark plugs," answers Rachel. He looks over at her and holds her gaze. Just like me and Violet, they have an entire conversation without saying a word.

"Start the car," Isaiah says. "I want to listen to it."

"Tell me how you know my last name," I push.

"You walked into my garage, so I'm feeling like you already know the answer. As I see it, you've got two options—leave or start the car."

I pull Violet's keys from my pocket and keep the car door open as I start the engine. He calls for me to pop the hood. I do, and after a minute of him asking me to press the gas and then to take my foot off, he tells me to cut the engine.

"Spark plugs," he confirms as he keeps his eyes glued to the insides of the car. "My mother told me James McKinley was my father. Did you know him?"

Was. He's aware James is dead. "Not personally." Everything inside me warps and it's damn painful. "He died before my birth, and according to my mother, he was my father, too."

"Ain't life a bitch," he mumbles.

True. I have a brother and I'm not sure how I feel about that. Scratch that—I do and it tastes bitter like betrayal. "You have a family. A huge family. They'll want to know about you."

"What did you come here for?" Isaiah asks. "From the look on your face, it wasn't me."

He's right, but telling him about the Riot, about the police, about everything is a risk. "A detective told me to come here and ask for you. He knows I'm looking for answers about who my father was before he died."

Isaiah picks up a tool and begins to work on the car. "I don't know a detective and I'm sorry to disappoint you, but I don't know shit about James McKinley."

"Isaiah," Rachel breathes out almost in a reprimand.

"Fine, I know McKinley's buried in Louisville, belonged to some motorcycle club in a town south of here, and I know a few other ramblings from my mother that aren't reliable. She first told me dear old dad didn't know I existed, but then I took a good look at his gravestone. Mom fessed up that he knew I existed and that we lived with him until he died."

"How old were you when he died?"

"Less than a year," Isaiah says.

Which makes him slightly older than me. "Why did she lie?"

"Why does she do anything? Gonna be honest, it's hard to take the word of a woman who's spent most of my life in prison."

Lightbulbs go off in my head. "In prison for what?"

"Not your concern. My turn to ask a question. Why am I on the radar of a detective?"

This is how it's going to be. A give and a take, because he doesn't trust me. An explanation as to how the detective knows him won't help. "Do you know anything about the Riot Motorcycle Club?"

"I hear they deal meth and cocaine. They won't touch heroin and pot, at least not in Louisville, because there are stronger groups in the area that don't like to share profits. I also hear the Riot deal in prostitution, but that's just rumors. That's twice I've answered your questions. Time to answer mine. Tell me about the detective."

Every image I had of my father collapses. He had a child… a living, breathing child…and James kept him a secret. Just like James asked Mom to keep me a secret. "I asked the detective if my father was loyal to the Riot over my family's MC and he told me to come here and talk to you."

Isaiah straightens and tosses the tool onto the bench. "Right about now I'm betting you're figuring out it's not me you need to talk to."

He's right. I need to talk to the woman who lived with James. I need to talk to Isaiah's mother.

"Let's get a few things straight. I spent years in foster care waiting and wishing for someone to waltz into my life and announce they were my long-lost family, but I let those dreams go. One thing life has taught me—blood don't mean shit. I've worked hard for the life I have now. I've finally got a great job, a girl I love and a family. The best kind of family. It ain't blood, but it's tight.

"My mom isn't a part of that family. With that said, she may be a piece of work, but she's my piece of work. You bring problems to her doorstep, you're bringing problems to my doorstep. If you're here expecting to drag me into some gang war because we share DNA, you're sadly mistaken."

Foster care. I scrub my hands over my face. Why? Why

foster care? He had a family. A family that would have loved him, cared for him, worshipped him like royalty.

"Fuck it," Isaiah mumbles. "There's another garage four blocks from here. The guy who owns it is named Brady. Tell him I sent you and I'd consider it a favor if he switched out your spark plugs. Good luck on finding your answers."

Isaiah turns and heads back the way he had walked in. Rachel's head swings back and forth between me and Violet and my newfound brother. Doesn't take long for her to chase after him and reality hits me hard. I have a brother. A blood brother who grew up in foster care and he's about to leave.

"My father knew about me, too," I call out. "And my father's family didn't know I existed until after his death. He told my mom to keep me a secret. Only reason they know about me is because the Riot told them. Moment they found out, my grandfather Cyrus took me in. The moment he finds out about you, he'll do the same. He loves like that. Blood may not mean shit to you, but it's everything to Cyrus."

Isaiah pauses in front of the door, then rolls his neck.

"Our MC is a legit club. The Riot has problems with us because we don't grovel. My family is full of good people and you'd like them. You may not know it yet and my family may not know it yet, but you're wanted. You've always been wanted. We just didn't know to want you."

He pulls on his earlobe, just like Eli does, but keeps his back to me. "Why did James keep you a secret?"

"I don't know." Because he was part of the Riot? Because James wanted something different from the club? Because Cyrus couldn't stand that James chose something else? "Why did he keep you a secret?"

"Isaiah," Rachel says softly, in a plea, in a reprimand.

Isaiah shakes his head. "Mom could be full of shit."

"Maybe she is, but you should let him decide that. What if she's telling the truth?"

Violet comes up beside me and places a supportive hand on my wrist. Her touch is a reassurance I didn't know I needed.

Isaiah glances over his shoulder at me. "James McKinley didn't belong to the Riot and he didn't belong to your MC. His life took a different path."

Violet's hand slips down and she holds on to my fingers as his words crush me. James chose differently and Cyrus threw him away.

"Take your car to Brady's," Isaiah says. "You shouldn't be on the road long without new spark plugs." He pauses like he's internally fighting. "Give me a few days. Let me reach out to my mom. If you want the full story, she's the one to tell it, not me."

He's offering me answers, and I'm filled with sorrowful gratitude. Before I can say anything, Isaiah leaves, the door swinging shut behind him. Rachel watches where he disappeared and after a few beats she slowly turns her head in our direction. Gone is the beauty queen and in her place are two narrow slits of eyes.

"Isaiah hasn't just walked through hell, he's been chained to it most of his life. You offered him the chance at family, and if you were lying to him to get answers, I swear to God I will make you regret it."

"He's not lying," Violet says. "Isaiah has a grandfather and an uncle and an entire army of men who will claim him in a heartbeat."

Rachel yanks her cell out of her back pocket and offers it to Violet. "Put in your number and I'll call you when he's ready for you to meet his mother."

She watches me with a perfectly pissed cocked eyebrow.

I understand her wrath. Rachel's protecting someone she loves. She's protecting my brother.

"I'm not scared of you," she says to me.

"You shouldn't be. I'm not a threat to either one of you."

Violet offers her back her cell and Rachel sizes her up. "And I'm not scared of you either."

With a toss of her braid, Rachel turns her back to us and follows after Isaiah.

Violet and I stand next to her father's car and try to digest the newest curveball life has thrown. She squeezes my hand, looks over at me, and I'm confused by the ghost of a smile on her face. "Don't know about you, but I like them. They are definitely McKinley material."

Violet

Sitting at a picnic table outside the crowded clubhouse, I'm fidgeting every few seconds as if I'm being attacked by cockroaches. There's a huge crowd and I can't help but wonder if the Riot's spying on me.

To be honest, we're all a mess at the picnic table. Chevy's heartbroken and flips a coin rapidly around his knuckles, watching it like it's a crystal ball with answers. After what I'd thought would have been a glorious day of being reunited with Breanna, Razor's gone silent and internal, and Oz is observing all of us as if he's trying to figure out the messed-up puzzle that has lost 75 percent of its pieces.

It's official—eighteen blows. Happy birthday to me.

Oz's mom, Rebecca, my mom and the rest of the Terror Gypsies made my favorite foods: fried chicken, potato salad, baked beans and all the chocolate cake I could eat. They even made sweet tea that's so sweet anyone who drinks it is at risk of falling into a sugar coma.

Me: I'm depending on you to lock the doors tonight and flip the porch light. ☺

It's my written reminder to Brandon to do what I've been encouraging him to do every night since we've been home.

The party started off as a family one with tons of little kids running around like they owned the place, but at eight anyone under eighteen had to go. Mom kissed me on the cheek, packed up Brandon and left. I'm officially at my first adult party. I'm assuming they're letting Chevy stay because he'll be eighteen himself soon and they consider being kidnapped an age handicap.

Brandon: I feel better when you or Mom do it.

Me: I know, but you can do this. I have faith in you.

He needs to do it. Simple things can cause him anxiety, and the kidnapping backtracked a lot of progress we had made. He was locking the doors before my kidnapping, regressed, and we will re-win this situation.

Brandon: I'll do it. I promise.

I breathe out in relief. Brandon doesn't like to break promises. He's enough of a Terror boy that his words mean something. Me: I love you.

Brandon: Love you, too.

It's a cool night, but not cold. The type that makes it nice to sit and admire the stars. All three boys wear black leather jackets. Oz and Razor wear their cuts as well, and Chevy's football hoodie swallows me whole, but keeps me warm. The music is loud, the beer free-flowing, there is lots of laughter and stories being told and a part of me is sad that I can't find an ounce of energy to go enjoy this party the million ways I thought I would as I grew up a child of the Terror.

I'm lost. Chevy is lost. So is Razor. I glance up from my not-even-touched red Solo cup of beer and look straight into Oz's eyes. Oz and I share a complicated relationship. He's like a big brother to me, and with me being someone who doesn't like anyone telling me what to do, Oz and I have always clashed.

Oz is like his father, Man O' War. He's a huge solid wall of muscle and intimidating to those who threaten his family. He's also a big soft teddy bear to those he loves. By the way he's watching me, I can spot the spark of pain because he doesn't know how to help not only me, but also Chevy and Razor.

By blood, Oz is an only child, but we're his family. Chevy and Razor his brothers, me his sister. Isaiah had a lot of things right. Sometimes the best family is the kind that doesn't share blood.

I glance over at Chevy and Razor and they're both looking down at the table, the equivalent of crying into their beers without shedding a tear. Sadness is a bowling ball rolling down pins in my stomach.

This entire situation has become too big. The Riot, being kidnapped, being watched, being threatened, helping the detective and now Chevy finding out that the foundation on which he has been raised is crumbling.

Since Dad died, I've tried living life on my own. Thinking that if I did, it would hurt less, but I've been hurt anyway and all that's happened is me ending up lonely.

I'm tired of hurting.

I'm tired of being alone.

I'm just plain exhausted.

I can't do this on my own anymore. Neither can Chevy,

and by the way Razor is looking like he was run over by a truck, he's close to collapsing, too. I meet Oz's eyes again and mouth, *Help us.*

He blinks. I don't ask for help, and even when we were closer, I hardly ever asked for help from him. He rightly thought of himself as the leader of us and I used to constantly fight him for the position.

I'm not fighting now. I need a friend. So does Razor, and so does Chevy. We need someone who is thinking straight and God knows it's not the three of us. If Oz truly is our brother, our friend, our leader—he'll figure out how to shake us out of this stupor.

We were stronger together as a group and we need that strength again.

Oz slams his hand down on the table, causing it to shake and Chevy and Razor to snap out of their trances. "Enough of this bullshit. Everyone in the woods—now."

He swings his legs over the bench to stand.

"It's Violet's party," Razor says.

"Yeah, I got that in the text, but we're sitting here like it's her wake. Get up now and in the woods before I kick all of your asses."

Razor smirks, Chevy snorts and the first rays of hope blossom inside me. Chevy rises to his feet. "I'd like to see you try to kick my ass."

"Not try," Oz says. "I will."

"He's always had a big head," Razor says to Chevy as he stands, but then winks at me. "He thinks he's bigger and badder than us. I say we drag him out into the woods and kick the shit out of him. Birthday girl gets first swing."

"I'm game," I say, and just like when we were ten, we leave the party behind and fade into the woods.

"You guys talk a good game." Oz walks backward and

his feet crunch against the fallen autumn leaves. "But I'm not seeing action."

Chevy and Razor share a side glance that spells all sorts of trouble and within seconds they're on the balls of their feet and plowing into Oz. It's a mangled mess of arms, legs, grunts and laughter. A playful wrestling match that's half serious, half not, and, at least once, either Razor or Chevy pops up with Oz in a hold and they egg me on to take a swing.

I can't do much more than laugh as Oz always finds a way to slip out of their hold, but ends up back on the ground. It's eight all over again. Ten all over again. Thirteen all over again. Sixteen, too. It's every year, every age, three boys who are becoming men with just enough of Peter Pan in them to keep them young.

As they wrestle, we keep moving farther and farther into the woods. Into our playground. The place where we'd spend hours frolicking and playing and being as free as wild children let loose into the world without a care.

I reach the old oak first and brush my fingers along the rough bark. I close my eyes and I can almost hear our giggles as we ran around this tree, feel the wind blowing through my hair as I pushed myself to beat Oz in a race to touch this tree first. I remember the feel of the dirt under my bare feet as I made the hike from Olivia's to the pond so we could swim in the cold water in the hot summer sun.

All three boys laugh as they stumble to their feet and they're a mess of dirt and leaves in their hair, but what's important is that they're smiling. I miss this. I miss seeing them smile.

"Hey," I call out, and they all stare at me. "Not it."

"Not it" is shouted into the night, and like always Razor is last. He socks Oz in the shoulder as he announces how each of us sucks.

"Doesn't mean you're not it." I waggle my eyebrows and then go running off into the night. And as if I've never been weighed down, I fly. Feet barely touching the ground, not feeling the sting of branches as they catch my arm. My knee aches in warning, but I ignore it. I need a few minutes to feel free and my body needs to allow me this moment.

Laughter is everywhere. From Oz somewhere to my right, from Chevy somewhere on my left as they trade insults with each other and from Razor as he counts down using a new curse word in place of a Mississippi. The laughter is also from me. It springs from my throat, and there's this warmth and energy that originates in my toes and is flooding my system.

Hope and happiness and memories of better times being relived.

Razor yells out, "Ready or not."

My heart beats in excitement of the unsaid *Here he comes.* I flatten myself against a tree, and somewhere in the distance, Oz and Chevy discuss plans of jumping on Razor when he comes near and I swallow a giggle.

Footsteps in the woods. Twigs being broken. Leaves rustling. I hold my breath as it feels as if each and every inhale will give my hiding spot away.

Razor moves away from me and I choke on the giggles when Oz and Chevy leap from their hiding spots and tackle Razor.

"Go, Violet, go!" Chevy calls, and they're giving me my chance to reach the oak and be the winner.

Once again, I'm on the move, but this time with a limp and not nearly as fast, but the pure joy that rages through my bloodstream at seeing the old oak is enough to wipe away all the pain that's become layers of grime on my soul. Just a few more feet, a few more steps—

A hand around my waist. I swat at it and begin to playfully elbow when another hand covers my mouth and nose. The hold tightens, fear surges through me and I'm off the ground. My heart sinks. No, not again. Heat flushes my neck, my face, and a dry heave rocks my body.

My feet hit the ground again, my back and head rammed into a tree and flat eyes bore into mine. "Scream and I'll have one of my guys in the woods put a fucking bullet in one of your friends' heads. We lost you and Chevy yesterday after the game and now those of us who have been watching you are in trouble."

Us. There's more than one person stalking me.

His hand goes to my neck. It's not tight, but it's definitely a warning. "We've heard rumors your car was seen in the south side of Louisville today. Why would you have been there?"

My eyes flicker over his face. I don't know this man. I don't recognize him from the kidnapping. He shoves me again, into the tree, and a sound of pain leaves my throat. "Why were you in Louisville?"

"Violet?" Chevy calls, and there's still happiness in his voice. "Where are you?"

"We weren't in Louisville," I say. "We drove around waiting for the party."

"Liar," he spits.

"Violet!" Chevy yells out, and his tone has changed. There's concern, there's anxiety and soon Razor and Oz join him in calling for me.

"Do you have the account numbers?"

My body shakes, but I force myself to keep eye contact. "Yes."

"Sneak out tonight," he says. "I'll meet you outside your house and you give them to me."

"I'm only giving them to Justin and Skull. They started this. They're the only ones I trust."

He leans into me and I turn my head because I don't want his face so close to mine. "This is not a negotiation."

The Riot believe they have all the power, but I'm the one holding the cards. "I'll meet them tomorrow night at the place where we were kidnapped. I give the numbers to them and nobody else. You want Eli, I want peace. Tell me, how happy do you think Justin is going to be when he finds out you've shoved me against a tree. According to him, this isn't how our clubs are playing anymore, or is he reneging on our deal?"

As if my words were acid, his grip on me weakens, and as he goes to step back, there is a snapping of a twig to the right. It's Razor and he pauses long enough to blink and then he's a freight train.

"Duck," the guy says. "They're going to shoot."

Shoot. My heart stutters. "Get down! Razor, get down!"

The guy runs, Razor is barreling toward us, his hand going to the gun he keeps at his back and his eyes widen when I throw myself at him. A bang, Razor collides with me and we're rolling until we stop. His body over mine, gun in his hand, a hand over my head as if he could keep me safe.

"Violet!" Chevy yells.

"Are you okay?" Razor asks.

I press at his chest, but he's solid rock. "Yes, let me up."

"Not until I know you're safe."

I punch at his chest. "They aren't going to shoot me. You, yes. Me, no."

Razor leans up on his knees and draws me up with him. I try to ignore the gun in his right hand and how my hands shake. Oz slides on the leaves in front of us as he tries to stop. He's also holding his gun, but with both hands. "Which way?"

"The guy who had Violet by the throat ran to the right. Shot came high and from the left. That bullet was meant to keep us in place so they could escape."

"Violet, why the hell do you keep running in the direction of bullets?" Chevy's voice curls into a dangerous tone I never wanted to hear again and his form appears out of the darkness. It's eerie how he goes from shadow to being in the moonlight.

"Because I don't want the people I love to get shot. That's why. What else do you expect me to do? Let you get shot?"

"Yes!" all three of them shout.

Idiots. Every single one of them.

"I need to go home." I'm pleading with Chevy to rein in his temper and get us out of this situation without alerting the Terror we have problems. "Just take me home."

"Take you home?" Oz's expression says he's about ready to turn the gun on me or himself at the idea of how insane I sound. "Someone just shot at you."

"At me." Razor's extremely calm and that causes my head to tilt. "They were shooting at me. For the same fucking reason they shot at me before."

Chevy swears under his breath and Oz is the only one scanning the trees, scanning the horizon. "What the hell is going on?"

Chevy and I share a look. Razor's gone internal again. We had a few minutes of happiness, but our weights returned, crushing us.

"What the hell is going on?" Oz yells this time.

Nothing from any of us. I know what's trapping me and Chevy, but I have no idea what's bogging down Razor. Before the kidnapping, he had reached out to me, helped me with a problem with guys from school. Now he's drowning and I'm doing nothing but watching him sink from the shore.

But that has to be how he feels about me and Chevy. He asked me to come to him the night I stayed at Chevy's. I think of the pain in Oz's eyes and the pain that's still etched on his face as he waits for one of us to crack.

"We're a family, dammit," Oz says. "When are we going to start acting like one?"

"Now," I whisper, and I flash two fingers before standing. From the way Oz's head straightens and the narrowed way Razor's studying me, they both caught it. "I don't feel good and I don't think I can ride on the back of a bike."

We aren't safe out here and we need someplace safe to talk.

"You can crash at the cabin," Oz says. "Cyrus won't mind."

If you don't feel safe at home, the club will protect you.

"You look pale, Vi," Chevy pipes in. "Maybe we should get you something to drink first. I think I saw some Sprites in the kitchen in the clubhouse."

She's not safe at the cabin.

Razor finally rises to his feet and offers me his hand and helps me up. "Want us to take you home? I'm sure Chevy can lift someone's car keys."

Are you safe at home?

That gets forced chuckles as they're all trying to play along.

"I'd like that Sprite and I told Mom I'd be staying with Chevy."

No, I'm not safe at home and Chevy knows what's going on.

Razor leans in, pats leaves off my back and whispers, "Stay in the middle of us and do not break rank. Oz will take point, Chevy at your side, I'm taking your six. We stay that way through the woods, we stay that way through the party. I don't fucking care if God comes down and calls your name, you stick with us, do you understand?"

I nod and whisper back, "Where are we going?"

His blue eyes go ice-cold. "To the only place it's safe. We're going to Church."

CHEVY

Took Razor "accidentally" bumping into one of the food tables and flipping it to cause a diversion, but Oz, Violet and I made it to the stairway undetected and headed up. On the second floor, Razor leans against the wall and watches to make sure no one's coming up the stairs, while Oz watches the hallway to confirm no one is leaving the bedrooms. I pull the pick out of my belt and within two seconds the door's open.

I tilt my head and Violet walks in. The brace is still on her knee, but a slight limp replaces the severe drag of her leg. The running in the forest didn't help—at least not her knee, but for a few minutes, Violet had a light in her eyes and color in her cheeks.

Oz flicks on the light as he enters, and I close the door, relocking it once Razor strides in. When we were kids, Oz, Razor and I broke in here. Cyrus caught us and busted our asses. We were breaking rules and we knew it, but even back then, we didn't consider bringing Violet. A girl in Church was unheard of and we weren't willing to cross those lines.

Violet does a slow spin as she takes in the view. She didn't have much time to check out the decor the last time she was here. For all I know, Violet was the first woman to be in this room when she kicked down the door a few weeks back. Seems like a shame. There are some damn good women related to these men and she's one of them. I can see where she feels like not being able to be in here is, to her, a disrespect.

"Sit," Oz says to Violet. "Get off your leg and prop up your knee."

He drags a chair around for her once she does sit and I hand her a bottle of water I swiped on the way here.

"They'll kill you if they knew we were in here and more specifically if they knew I was in here," she says.

On the other side of the table, Razor flips a chair and straddles it. "Considering I've already been hit with a bullet and just had another one shot in my direction, I'm not worried about death. I'm feeling invincible."

Violet squishes her lips. "Fantastic."

Razor only grins, but it's short-lived. He lifts his finger and circles it as he points at the wall. "Soundproof. Whatever we say in here stays in here."

In case either my or Violet's cells have been bugged, Razor took our phones and left them in the kitchen. We're technology free and breaking rules. Oz takes the seat at the head of the table as I sit next to Violet. "I don't care who goes first, but someone needs to tell me what's going on."

Squeaks in the chairs as we shift and I meet Violet's eyes. She nods. Damn, this is going to suck. "I have a brother and he lives in Louisville. He's maybe a year older than me and looks exactly like James."

Razor's and Oz's heads snap in my direction.

"The Riot are trying to use me to put Eli in jail," Violet says within a heartbeat of my news. She knows me. Knows

I haven't processed having a brother yet and knows I'm not ready to talk. "I broke into Dad's office, swiped account numbers, and I have to give them to the Riot tomorrow night so they can frame Eli, but I'm working with that Louisville detective, wearing a wire for them, so the plan is for the Riot to go to jail."

Razor and Oz are now one million percent focused on her and so am I. My heart beats so slow it hurts. "Tomorrow night?"

"Yeah." She bites her lower lip. "We didn't get around to naming a time, since Razor came racing over, but we have a place."

Oz leans forward on the table. "You were the one the Riot were after?"

"Shocking, right?"

Oz doesn't listen to her as his questions have taken over like a steamroller. "Did you say you're wearing a wire with the Riot? Have you lost your mind?"

"Yes," she says plainly, "and yes. And before you think you're going to run off and tell Eli what you know, you should keep in mind I'm being watched and have been approached by the Riot at this clubhouse, Cyrus's cabin and my home. The only people I trust right now are in this room. If you tell on me, you're signing a warrant for my death and that'll sort of piss me off."

She's being lighthearted, but how the hell should we be handling this? She and I—we're beyond anger and sadness and tears. Maybe she's right. We have lost our minds.

Violet takes the bottle of water, opens it, then tosses the cap in Razor's direction. "Your turn, and I'm going to be honest, you're going to have to dig deep to beat my problems."

I laugh. It's bitter and short, but it happened. "I've got a long-lost brother."

"Yeah, but in the end, that'll be good news. You know, once you get past the whole my-father-slept-around-a-lot thing."

True on that.

Razor rests his arms on the back of the chair. "Dad's found someone willing to defect from the Riot to the Terror to testify against the Riot on how they killed my mom, and if we accept, it's going to start a war. It's my decision if we press forward or not. I already lived too many hours thinking I lost the two of you. I'm not sure I can stomach knowing my decisions were the ones that hurt people I love."

All joking and lightheartedness crashes to the floor as if someone dropped a glass figurine. Razor, because of his mother's death, is scarred eternally in ways none of us will ever understand.

"If you go forward with the defector, maybe Violet doesn't have to wear the wire," suggests Oz. "We bring the Riot down that way, because from what I'm hearing, we're already in danger."

She shakes her head. "I'm on a deadline and my time is almost up. The Riot has threatened me, my mom and my brother if I don't see this through. My part is a go regardless."

I pull a coin out of my pocket and begin to flip it over my knuckles. Doing this helps me think, helps me focus. "We want the Riot shut down for good, right?"

Agreement from all involved.

"The Riot's a big club," I say.

"But if the wire goes right," Violet says, "we take down not only all the guys involved in our kidnapping, but we also get their top two guys."

"With a huge amount of men behind them searching for retribution," Oz says.

Violet slams her hand onto the table. "So we lie down and

do nothing? I'm tired of this bullshit, Oz, and you have to be, too. I see how freaked out you are every time Emily steps on Kentucky soil. Her grandfather is Skull, the bastard who is the head of this. I can take him down. We need to show the Riot we aren't scared and that each and every time they come at us, we will throw their asses in jail."

"If what the defector told us is true," Razor says, "then the guys involved in my mother's death are big players. Big players who aren't Skull and his son. If we wipe out their board, if we wipe out their decision-makers, the Riot could fold."

"I think you're talking fairy tales," says Oz.

He's probably right, but Oz wasn't in a basement and I can't allow Violet to live in fear anymore. "What other choice do we have? Our fathers spent over twenty years dealing with the Riot and in the end not a damned thing changed. We're not kids anymore and this fight is on our doorstep now. I say we turn the tide and start causing problems for them. This is our time. I say we blow this shit up."

"Me, too," says Violet. "We do the wire, Razor gives the green light to use the defector and we bring down as many of them as we can."

Razor rolls his neck, then massages the muscles there. "How do I keep Breanna safe? She's a long way from Snowflake. Even better, how do we keep anyone safe? To say there won't be fallout from what we do is naive."

I understand how he feels. Understand the bitter taste of fear in his mouth, understand the nagging of the loss of control in his brain, but... "Do you want a phone call telling you Breanna's been locked in the basement with the Riot? I've lived that basement and it's going to haunt me forever. Not doing anything—it's not the solution. It's what our parents did and we need to be better."

From under the table, Violet squeezes my knee and the

irony isn't lost on me. I went from being the boy who didn't make the decisions to being the man leading the charge.

"At the end of all this," Oz says, "Cyrus and Eli will say it wasn't our decision to make. That we should have included them."

"We will," Violet says. "But after the wire. There's the possibility that someone is a traitor at the clubhouse and I can't risk anyone else knowing until that wire is done."

Surprise prickles along the back of my neck. "You're going to let the club in?"

She's slow to nod, but she does. "Oz is right. There's going to be backlash and we're stronger together than we are separate. It's time I start relying on my family."

Stunned silence. All of us are. I take her hand and wonder how many rules I'd be breaking if I picked her up, propped her up against the wall and kissed her until we couldn't breathe.

"Then let's take a vote," Oz says. "Let's make this official."

Violet gives a hesitant smile. "We aren't a real board."

"No, but we're family and that's what matters. Everyone for taking down the Riot?"

All hands in the air.

"Anyone opposed."

Not a one of us.

"Then let's take these bastards down."

Violet

The air I inhale feels very cold in my lungs, but my skin is hot and clammy. After a hundred abrupt U-turns to make sure we weren't being followed, and the switching of cars and routes and a million other things, I'm in what would be the back bedroom of a white trailer in the middle of a trailer park in the south side of Louisville.

This room is a makeshift office for the police department. It contains two chairs and a desk pushed against the wall. Like the other rooms, it also contains fancy computers and electronics.

I widen a hole in my jeans with my finger and wonder if this was the best outfit to pick. The detective said to wear whatever I'd normally wear, so I pulled my favorite pair of jeans and a purple T-shirt out of the dryer, then put on my tennis shoes, my bracelets, Dad's watch and his cross.

After I returned home from the party, I found another note from the Riot in my English notebook. It had a time for the meet and they selected a new meeting place. Guess they feel like their safe house is a loss now that the police are aware of its existence.

My skin crawls and I rub at my arms. I hate that these bastards were in my house, in my room...obviously in there while my mother and brother were sleeping. They were in my home.

My home.

Sorrow fills me and it's so heavy that I gasp as if I'm drowning. I didn't get to say goodbye to Mom and Brandon. They left the party with waves from across the crowd and they were still asleep when I left this morning. I had no idea when they left last night that I'd be meeting with the Riot so soon today.

I wish I could have seen them this morning. Hugged them both a little tighter and told them that I loved them. My knee begins to bounce. Maybe it's a good thing I didn't get to say goodbye. They'd know something was wrong.

"Tell me where you're meeting the Riot," Chevy says for the millionth time.

And for the millionth time I answer, "No. The detective and I agreed that telling you that information is futile. It's only going to cause you to want to go and your being there jeopardizes me and this plan."

"I just want to know," he says. "I've already promised to stay here. When I give my word, it's a done deal."

"Do you take me for a fool? If I tell you, you'll stay because you promised, but then you'll tell Oz or Razor and then they'll show."

Chevy only scowls.

"We have to trust the police on this. Period. Now, how are the Riot getting into my house?" I ask to change the conversation.

In the chair next to me, he's acting like he's relaxed with his legs kicked out and arms sprawled along the chair, but there's an underlying current of anger that's just as powerful as a live electrical wire. "We only have someone watching your house from the front. Once the club finds out about the wiretapping, we'll have them watch your mom, brother and house twenty-four hours from all sides."

"The club has holes." Black holes where the Riot is slipping through.

Chevy folds his hands over his stomach. "I know, and that's not going to go over well. Regardless, the safety of you, Razor and anyone close to the two of you will be the priority."

I nudge Chevy with my foot. "Listen to you being all decisive. Making decisions about stuff the club doesn't even know about yet. It's like you're a whole new man."

"I'm not playing when it comes to you and Razor. You're both putting yourselves on the line. Least we can do is back you up." Chevy takes in the small room and continues to speak before I can react and inform him that's he avoiding what I said. "It's smart."

"What?"

"For the police to have a place like this. If someone is working for them and they're being followed, then they can't go into a police station. But someone visiting a run-down trailer in the middle of a hundred run-down trailers? It's a good cover."

"We also have houses in middle-class neighborhoods and a mansion in a fancier place. We chose this place because it's closer to where you're going." Detective Barlow strolls in and, like always, he's in a white button-down shirt. "How are you doing, Violet?"

"I'm good." If good means on the verge of puking. "So how does this wiretapping thing work? What happens if they pat me down? Should I have worn something bulkier so they don't see the wires and stuff?"

The good detective comes close to smiling and that un-nerves me. This man is not the type who smiles. He rubs his knuckles against his jaw. "Did you bring what I asked?"

Yes, and I don't like the idea of this being in anyone else's hands beside me and my mother's. I reach into my pocket and extract Dad's watch. It's old-school. A Rolex my grand-father gave my dad the day I was born. Gramps told my dad that he had become a real man that day—bringing a child into the world.

The detective reaches for it and I curl my fingers around it, then bring it to my chest. "What are you doing?"

"We have a professional in the next room who is going to open the watch and insert a mini voice recorder. Once we're done, my guy will take out the recorder and return the watch to exactly how it is now."

"I already lost this watch once and it broke my mom's heart. She's keeping it in the curio cabinet. Do you know what that means? It's precious to her." It means it's her world.

"You wore this watch when you were kidnapped. They won't question it being on you again. I put another piece of jewelry on you or a button that doesn't quite match or any-thing else, they might jump to the right conclusion. This watch will give me the audio recording I need and will keep you safe."

Handing him Dad's watch. It's like he asked me to cut off my leg.

"You'll get it back," he says.

I better or he'll never be able to father children. With way more effort than it should take, I place Dad's watch in the palm of his hand. The detective holds it with an air of rev-erence and that one slight gesture makes me feel slightly less like slitting my wrists.

I'm like a jack-in-the-box that has been sprung and I jump

to my feet to pace the small room. Hands in my pockets, hands out of my pockets. Nausea in my stomach, knots in my throat. Vision clear, then fuzzy.

Hands on my hips and I'm spun into something very hard and very warm, and when I glance up, I'm met by the most beautiful dark eyes. "I've got you, Violet."

I melt. Every inch of me a puddle on the floor. His hold on my hips tightens, and as if I weigh nothing, he sits me on the cleared-off section of the desk. The mischievous grin on his face is ghostly mirrored on mine as he settles between my legs.

"We're in a police station," I say.

"Police trailer," he corrects. "We already kissed in the police station. Just seems wrong to not kiss here, too."

My heart aches as I drink him in. Chevy. Broad-shouldered, a waterfall of muscle, dark hair, dark eyes, perfection and beauty and every cell within my body calls out to him. A sharp pang of regret causes me to close my eyes.

"Violet," he murmurs. "What's wrong?"

I shake my head that I don't want to answer, but then fingers roughened by years of hard work raise my chin.

"Tell me."

My mouth dries out and I swallow to help. "I regret not making love to you the other night."

He tilts his head in understanding. "You weren't ready and that's okay. We'll know when it's the right time."

I suck in my lower lip as the ends of my mouth bend down and tears prick my eyes. "What if that was the only time we had?" What if I mess this up and don't make it out alive?

His body stiffens and he cups my face with both of his hands. "It's not. We are going to have plenty of time. Do you hear me? We're going to get through this. Next month, this will start to become a fleeting memory and I'll have to actually fill out a college application."

I laugh, but don't know why. Maybe because that sounds so normal and normal seems so obscure. I place my hands on his chest, lightly fisting his shirt and bringing him closer. "Tell me that after this is all over, we're going to have the most boring and normal life ever."

Chevy brushes his fingers along my side, and where there had been lots of fear and anxiety in my blood, there are now warm fuzzies.

"I promise—we are going to be so fucking bored."

My lips edge up at the idea that he's playing along. "I want normal. I want high school parties where people sing bad karaoke. I want pie at midnight at the diner. I want to make out under the bleachers during basketball games."

"That doesn't sound boring, Violet. That last one sounded like a fantasy coming to life."

Because I'm soaking in all that Chevy is, I ignore where we are and how we shouldn't be doing any of this. My fingers slide down to the hem of his shirt and sneak underneath to touch the curves of his abs. He sucks in a breath and a thrill runs through me that I can do this to him.

"Tell me you want to go to college."

"I want to go to college." His hands wander a bit lower and in a rapid movement he shifts me so that my body is sweetly pressed to his.

"Tell me we're going to go to the same college."

Chevy lowers his head and his lips whisper against mine as he speaks. "We're going to go to the same college."

The electricity building between us enters my veins as liquid fire. "Tell me you'll never leave me again."

"Never." And he brings his lips to mine.

I open for Chevy—my mouth, my arms, my heart, my

soul. It all belongs to him. I pour all that I am into this kiss and leave nothing behind. I revel in the perfect way that our lips move, the pleasing goose bumps that form along my skin as his fingertips glide along my thighs.

Everything about Chevy is heat and strength and every nip, every touch brings on a glorious spinning in my head. In this moment, I want more, I need more, but then there's a clearing of a throat and the warmth I'm experiencing this time is in my cheeks.

Chevy kisses my forehead, hugs me close and then helps me off the desk. He keeps an arm around my shoulders as we face the detective.

"Do you need a few minutes or are we good to go over how today's going to play out?" the detective asks.

Part of me wonders if he's teasing, but he appears as serious as ever. Guess I'm about to walk into the valley of the shadow of death for him and he probably thinks the least he can do is let me kiss my boyfriend.

"We're good," I say.

"Then let's go over the plan."

CHEVY

I squeeze Violet's hand and she gives me a faint smile as she goes into the bathroom and shuts the door. The moment reminds me a lot of when I put her into the bathroom when we were kidnapped. Like then, I feel like barricading the door and keeping her locked in until I can confirm she's safe.

The detective is in the room Violet and I have been in and he's going over the backup plans to the backup plans with the two undercover agents who will be in the vicinity of the house where the exchange is taking place.

I pull out my cell and text: Only two police officers watching her and they will be down the street. They won't have live feed because they're scared the Riot will have equipment to detect bugs. She's only wearing a recorder that they'll listen to later. Understand what they're doing, but this means we won't have ears on the situation if it goes bad. They feel there are only two routes to leave the meeting place, and if they take Violet, they can stop it. I'm concerned about the Riot taking her, but I'm more concerned about what happens when she's alone. Violet won't tell me where the meeting place is. She figured out I'd tell you.

Razor and Oz are in a restaurant a few miles from here. The detective doesn't trust me on not following, so he and I will be hanging here when Violet leaves. I can't tell them what cars to follow or what direction they went. The moment Violet walks out of this trailer, we'll be blind.

Razor: She figured it out because she knows us. I need you to lift the cell of one of the people going. Crack open the back and on the sim card is a 15 digit number called the IMEI. Get me that and I can track his cell.

Lifting cells. I've been doing it since I knew what a cell phone was and I've been lifting them off bikers to piss them off for years. Can't say I've ever lifted one from a police officer before, but there's a first time for everything.

Not as concerned on getting my hands on the cell as returning it. That's when life gets tricky.

I watch the men as they talk. The cell that looks the easiest to lift would be from the guy with the black hair. His phone is half poking out of his back pocket. The guy with the blond hair also has his cell in his back pocket, but it's dug deep. That's a hell of a pick, but possibly doable. No way in hell I'm going for the detective. He sees too much. Knows too much. He'd probably pull a gun on me if I get within three inches of him.

To narrow it down, I shift my weight, scraping my knuckles against the wall in the hallway, and watch. It's not a loud or sudden movement. Very subtle. The detective and guy with black hair both pause with the sound, but keep going. Blond-hair guy doesn't react to it at all.

He's my target.

Water runs in the bathroom. The knob turns and Violet emerges. She slides her hand along her jeans with nerves and blows out an unsteady stream of air. "I'll take someone up on that water."

Bingo. Blond volunteers and I don't move from the door, but only angle my body so he can get through the doorway in the tight, cramped space I created. He slides by, his body hitting parts of my arm. Fingers shoot out, snatch his cell and then I'm entering the bathroom.

Door closed, I pop the cell out of its safety case, crack open the back, and using my own cell, I text Razor the IMEI number. My cell vibrates.

Razor: Got it. Is the phone turned on?

I push on the screen and it comes to life. Me: Yes

Razor: Good. Get it back on his body. I'll start tracking now.

Me: We are only there as eyes and ears. That's it. I gave my word that we'd let Violet play this out. Eyes and ears only. Do you got me?

Razor: Loud and clear. You're starting to get as bossy as Oz.

I'll take that as a compliment.

I flush the toilet for pretense, turn on the water as I pocket my cell and palm the police officer's phone. I return to the office, but this time I lean my body half in the office and rest my other shoulder on the hallway wall so that there is room to go around without having to touch me.

Violet's in the chair the blond abandoned and she's listening intently and nodding along to Barlow's instructions again. They've gone over it a hundred times, and I'm fine with them going over it a hundred more.

Out of the corner of my eye, I spot the blond returning down the hallway. I keep my eyes and posture turned on Violet. He's got to think I don't know he exists. Because the opening to enter is wide, he doesn't shrink away from me.

In a movement so fast that I'm not even aware I'm moving, I use my foot to edge a box an inch in his direction and he stumbles on it. I react, grabbing his arm to help keep him from landing on the floor, and slip his cell into his back pocket, and as I help right him, I use the hand that had the cell to pat his back. "You okay?"

"Yeah." He glances down to the box full of paper to be recycled and kicks it out of the way. "Cramped spaces."

"I get it. I share a tight two-bedroom condo with my mom."

Violet glances up at me, oblivious to all that just took place. I wink at her for reassurance and she brightens before returning her attention to the detective.

She's leaving in fifteen minutes. Fifteen minutes.

God help the souls of the Riot if she's not back in my arms in an hour.

Violet

Drop the names Justin and Skull at least once, confirm with them what they are going to do with the account numbers, give them the account numbers, leave. The police will confirm I'm not being tailed, and the Riot will go off and hopefully try to use the account numbers the police tech people are now monitoring. Once the Riot do start to manipulate the accounts, the police swoop in, take the hard drives and make arrests.

It's simple. Simple, simple, simple.

Except I'm the one who is sticking my neck on the chopping block and the Riot love to chop with their sharp, shiny knives.

I expected the Riot to choose a warehouse, because that's what happens on TV. I also expected wires taped to me, but it turns out I'm wrong on both counts. The Riot chose a pick-your-own-goldfish fish store.

A fish store.

It's beyond odd.

A bell dings when I enter, and if it wasn't for the fact I'm scared to death, I'd probably be captivated by all the beautifully designed tanks that house hundreds of colorful fish. There's a girl behind the counter, college age maybe, with dyed purple hair. She looks up from her book and gives a salesperson smile. "Hi, can I help you?"

"I'm here to meet Justin and Skull." Points for me. I already dropped their names in the first words I spoke.

She hops down from her stool. "Wow, I haven't heard anyone call him Justin in a while. They're in the back and told me someone would be looking for them. Follow me."

I do and we weave past the filled tanks to the supply area. To the left I spot a few frogs. "Do they own this place?"

"Yep. Skull loves fish. Sometimes he'll come in and just sit and stare at them and not say a word to anyone."

Creepy, but whatever floats his boat.

She knocks on a door and after a gruff "Come in" she opens it and waves her arm for me to walk in. Justin sits in one of the chairs in front of the desk, and from behind the desk, Skull's working on a computer.

"Hey!" Justin smiles like we're old friends. "Have a seat. Dad and I were just talking business."

Who to kill next? How they should break into my house next time? "Okay."

"Thanks, Cindy." Justin winks. "Close the door behind you when you leave and make sure we're not bothered for a bit."

She sort of does this weird bustle of happiness at his attention and shuts the door with Broadway flare.

Justin stands and he takes out some sort of device. "Hope you don't mind, but I've got to sweep you for bugs."

"Paranoid much?" I say.

"Well, you did talk to the police. Arms out, please. This won't take but a second."

"To be fair, I only talked to the police because you kidnapped me." I work hard to keep my breathing steady even though my pulse pounds in my ears. Justin slowly moves his black device up and around my body.

Jake Barlow explained this would happen and that this is why we were recording only and not transmitting the conversation live for the detective to hear. He said the Riot would be searching for radio waves or something like that.

"Talking to the police, being around the police," I continue even though I'm aware if I'm busted these might be my last words. "Those things sort of happen when you take someone against their will."

"She's clean," he says to his father, then back to me. "Yeah, I see your point. As a side note, we're going to need you to recant your statement from the police, refuse to testify, something like that. Try to convince your boyfriend to do the same. We're going to do some work from our side, but we need those charges on our guys dropped."

My fingers curl because I want to kill him. "I thought you said they were going against your orders and deserved jail."

"They were, but they've served some time in lockup, since they weren't granted bail, and they are now ready to accept responsibility for their actions and have agreed not to disobey."

"Disobey, like not point a gun and shoot it at me."

"Like that. Why don't you take a seat? I've heard you've had a rough time with your knee."

Yep, and it'll hurt some more if I kick the crap out of him. "You know you're going to hell, right?"

"Sure do. By the way, it's not healthy to hold grudges."

I drop into the seat and move my wrist so that the recording device is pointed in their direction. The office looks like any other office. It's not formal and warm like my father's, but it's full of papers and stacks of folders and boxes. There are calendars on the wall and used coffee cups on the desk and many, many crumbs of something eaten hopefully recently.

"Sorry for the delay, I just finished paying an invoice and now I've got to finish this order. What type of fish do you like, Violet?" Skull asks while he keeps his eyes peeled to the screen. "Maybe we can stock it in your honor."

"Personally, I like mine deep fried and with ketchup."

They both laugh. I wasn't lying.

"Don't you have people who do this type of stuff? Order, pay invoices, launder money?"

Skull laughs hard enough that I earned myself a glance from him. "I have people who do things for me, but there are some things I like to do myself. Like with my fish."

A click of a button and I gain his entire attention. "And Eli. He's someone I don't like leaving to other people to attend to. He's hurt me and my family. So tell, do you have my account numbers?"

CHEVY

Waiting—not a virtue. Feels a lot like having my balls slowly cut away from my body. The only solace I have is that the detective who sits in the chair next to me looks just as happy as I am to be left behind. His radio is on, and so far, it's silent.

Violet went in and now we can do nothing other than wait for her to leave.

Waiting.

Damn, I hate that word.

Violet has at least two police tails in the area. I'm hoping there's more. As expected, the Riot have people hanging out, too. Oz and Razor have made them. The police have figured out a few, not all of the Riot involved, but as long as everyone continues to play nice, we've decided to keep quiet. If we tell, the police will learn I've got two unknown people on Violet's team.

In the police's defense, the Riot aren't wearing their cuts, but I'm disappointed. The Riot watching the store are big names and we know them by face and road name in order to stay safe. I'd think the police would have done their homework, especially with Violet's life on the line.

My cell buzzes and I expect it to be another text from either Oz or Razor asking if I've heard anything. The two of them are sitting at an outside table at a restaurant a few doors down from the fish store.

It's from Oz and it's a pic of Razor. I grunt-laugh because the kid is wearing a baseball cap, a polo shirt with a collar and Dockers. He's playing Halloween dress-up as a frat-boy preppie to throw off the Riot. Gotta admit, Razor looks like a stranger to me—except for the eyes.

Razor texts: Oz is wearing the same fucking thing. I'm saving my pics of him for blackmail later. I'm thinking he's buying beers for the next six months.

Me: Sounds good to me. Anything on Vi?

Razor: Nothing

Fuck me.
Another buzz.

Oz: I think we got problems.

I sit up straighter and the detective looks up from his own cell and watches me like a hawk on a mouse.

Me: What?

Oz: Few minutes before Violet showed, we noticed a blond guy pull up and plant himself at the coffee shop. Problem is— he watches the world more than he's reading his magazine and he's watching intently.

Me: Making Violet's tail is the problem?

Oz: No. The fact that the Riot are noticing him is the problem. They make him and Violet has major problems.

Razor: Riot on the move. Tell him to get the fuck out of there.

"Tell your guy at the coffee shop to get out of there now. The Riot think there's something wrong with him."

Detective doesn't even blink as he talks into the radio. "Kurt, you need to move. You are on the verge of being compromised."

Confirmation back and Razor texts me: Your guy is moving. Acting like he got a phone call and he's all pissed off his Tinder date forgot their meeting at the coffee shop. Riot backing off. Smooth move by the police, but now Violet's down a gun on her side.

If I was a weaker man, I'd be intimidated by the glare the detective's giving me. Good thing I'm a McKinley, because I see that type of look daily.

Other people radio in that they now spot the new-to-them Riot players and confirm the Riot were questioning the guy at Starbucks.

"Tell me how you knew that," Barlow demands.

"Oz and Razor are watching at the restaurant down the street. How about you tell me how you're going to keep Violet safe now that we're down a man."

"Your friends being there are putting Violet in danger."

"My friends just saved Violet and your cop. I'm going to ask one more time, how are you going to protect Violet now that you've lost a pair of eyes?"

Oz: I don't like this. She's been in there too long and some of the Riot are bugging out. Not all, but some. Do they have eyes on the back of this place?

That humming that saturated my brain after the kidnapping returns and it's hard as hell to not throw my fist into the wall to try to control it. Me: Police have it under control.

"You sure you know what you're doing? You have a guy that was almost made and there are Riot leaving the area."

The detective's on the radio asking for updates, telling people to watch, telling people to move around. I stand and kick the recycling box into the hallway. Papers fly everywhere. These people have no idea what they're doing.

Razor: What if they don't have it under control? I agree, she's been in there too long. Maybe we pull rank. Maybe we should end this bullshit now.

"What are they seeing?" the detective snaps. "Tell me who exactly is watching my men."

"Tell me who's taking care of Violet?" I shout back.

He doesn't bat an eye as he says, "I am and Violet agreed to let me be the person in charge of this. If you can't trust me, fine, but trust her. She agreed to all this and was dead set that you follow the plan. I'm down a man, you saved his ass and now I need help making sure everyone else stays in place. Tell me who else is watching that street."

Oz: I agree with Razor. We should move in on this.

My gut twists and I rub the back of my neck as I try to grab hold of my emotions. The humming grows louder and the only thought is that I want Violet safe. I want her safe and back in my arms.

"Chevy," the detective says. "Tell me who else is watching the street."

My cell buzzes again and a decision of which way I'm going on this has to be made.

Violet

My entire body buzzes with nervous anticipation. Skull just brought up Eli and that's what I need—him to admit out loud what he's going to do with the account numbers. "I have the account numbers. Some are for the security business. Some belong to the club."

Skull's lips twist into what I believe is a grin. "Excellent. Hand them over and I'll make sure that the Riot and the Terror live out the rest of their lives in peace."

But I don't reach into my back pocket. Those numbers are my only leverage. "What are you going to do with them?"

"We told you. With those numbers we're going to take care of Eli."

"Not sure if you remember correctly, but when everything was explained to me, someone you know had just tried to shoot me in the head. Details of anything after that are fuzzy." No, they aren't. They are so crystal clear I can smell the mold in the basement, taste the fear on my tongue and shiver with the coldness of the air.

"Are you having a change of heart?" Justin takes out a

pocketknife and makes a show of flipping it open. It's not a long blade, but from the glint I can tell it's sharp. He begins to clean his nails with the tip. The man's crazy. Utterly and completely crazy. But he's sending a message. A very loud and possibly violent message.

"I heard you had a heartwarming moment with Eli yesterday morning," Justin continues. "Involved pancakes and singing 'Happy Birthday.'"

I grow light-headed. I'm tired of being watched, tired of being put under a microscope by these men. And I thought the Terror were controlling. "You need to find a new hobby. Watching a teenage girl is a bit sick and perverted. Maybe you should stare at fish like your dad."

He doesn't find me funny this time and I'm okay with that. He is sick. He is perverted and someone should tell him because maybe he doesn't know.

"If you did your spying correctly," I say, "you'd also know that Eli and I can't share air for longer than twenty seconds without screaming at each other. He did the birthday thing so we wouldn't get into another public screaming match."

It's true, but that day we didn't fight and this will be a testament of how close Justin's men actually get to me.

"Eli is responsible for my father's death. If you and Eli didn't have this stupid feud going on, then my dad would still be alive because he wouldn't have been driving to Louisville to see you." I expect a twinge of satisfaction at saying the words I've believed for so long, but instead strands of guilt wrap around my heart.

I don't blame Eli anymore. I don't blame anyone anymore. Dad died. It was terrible and it was awful, but it just happened. He's dead and I'm still alive. I breathe out with the floating feeling of release.

"Do you blame us?" Skull asks.

Not really. Not anymore, but I have a hunch a man like this doesn't understand letting things go. "Yes, but I blame Eli more."

And I treated him badly for it. I treated the club badly for it. What's worse is that I broke Chevy's heart. That, I regret. I lower my head but then lift it back up. What I don't regret is standing up for myself. Don't regret becoming my own person. I don't regret at all who I am.

I am my father's daughter and I will end this war between the Riot and the Terror here and now. "Explain to me again what you're doing and I will give you the account numbers. By doing this, you agree to a lifetime of peace with the Terror, you stop watching me and my family and you will no longer hurt people I love. Do you understand?"

Skull's studying me and I'm studying him right back. He expects me to flinch under his scrutiny, but he's fucking with the wrong girl.

"I could have Justin pin you down and I could just take the numbers."

My fear. "You could try, but you'd be screwed considering they're in my head." A lie.

Skull relaxes back in his chair and gives a laugh that causes me to want to run screaming to the nearest hot shower and scrub my skin off with steel wool. "I agree to your terms because I like you."

At least somebody does.

"We're going to use the account numbers to frame Eli. Put money where it doesn't belong. Take money away from people who will be pissed it's missing. We will destroy his reputation with his clients, his friends, his club and his family. He will go to jail, and once in there, he will belong to me."

I swallow the knot in my throat. Eli survived prison once before, but he has a lot of scars due to his stay that he doesn't discuss. I thread my fingers through my hair and comb the tangles as I sort through as quickly as possible whether I have everything the detective needs, but there's this sense of urgency that's causing me to inch to the edge of the chair.

I've been in here for too long and my luck and their patience are about to run thin. Abruptly, I stand and it startles both men. With my hand in the pocket of my jeans, I take two steps back until my other hand hits the doorknob. "This is how it's going to work. I'm going to give you the account numbers and then I'm going to leave. You aren't going to follow. You are not going to follow me anymore."

"Sounds like a plan." Skull picks up a pen. "Give me the account numbers."

I turn the knob, and when it gives, I yank the piece of paper containing the numbers out of my back pocket and toss it onto the desk. "I not only memorized the account numbers, but I also wrote them down."

The door is open, I'm slipping past, Justin is on his feet, Skull is opening the paper, my heart is pounding in my chest, in my ears, a pulse that's dominating and shaking my entire frame. I'm running down the hallway, but the emergency exit is blocked with boxes and I skid to a stop so I can escape through the store. Then there's a hand on my wrist and Justin glares down at me. "You're not leaving yet."

CHEVY

The detective is waiting for an answer on where the Riot is positioned, Razor and Oz are blowing up my phone, but the only thing I hear is what the detective said to me moments before... *Trust her.*

Trust Violet.

It's what she wants. Violet wants me to trust her choices, her decisions, to back her up when no one else will. She is smart, she is capable, but how can she not understand this overwhelming need I have to protect her, to keep her safe, to keep her locked away in a bubble...to keep her confined in what she'd only see as a prison.

I slide my fingers across the cell, but this time put it to my ear. Oz answers halfway through the first ring. "Tell me you want us to move on this."

"You're not moving. She didn't even want you in this. I brought you in. Violet trusts the police, so we need to trust the police. I need you to get off the phone with me and text me every single Riot you see, what they're wearing and their location. That is how we're going to help Violet."

I hang up and toss my cell to the detective. It begins blowing up again, and after a few beats, he reads the texts aloud on his radio. Exact positions, what the Riot are wearing and people are answering back that they're moving to avoid detection.

Collapsing back against the wall, I bang my head twice, preferring the physical pain to the emotional.

"You're saving her life." The detective pauses while more texts from Oz and Razor come in. "You're doing the right thing."

God, I hope so, because I'm nothing without her.

Violet

Bile rises up my throat and sweat breaks out along my hairline. Justin's going to kill me. I know too much, he's figured out I'm recording them and they never intended to let me leave. "I gave you the account numbers. I did what you asked, now you uphold your end of the agreement."

Skull steps into the hallway and he's deadly serious. "She did what we asked. The numbers are legit."

Legit? My head flinches back. "You already had the numbers?"

"Some of them, but we couldn't get them all. That's why we involved you, but knowing a few of the account numbers lets me know if you were giving me bogus information or not."

Screw this. I kick Justin's kneecap, his body jerks and he loosens his grip on me and I yank away from him, then draw back. Like my father taught me, I keep my thumb tucked outside my fist and I punch the son of a bitch in the nose. Blood squirts everywhere and he yells out a curse. "What did you do that for?"

His words catch me off guard and I blink as I try to catch my breath. "You weren't letting me go."

Justin straightens as he pulls a handkerchief out of his pocket and holds it to his nose. "I was going to get you a fish to take home. Jesus, women are crazy."

Little dots appear in my eyesight and I sway with the fuzziness in my head, but then I laugh. A loud laugh. A weird laugh. A crazy laugh. A fish. He stopped me to give me a fish.

"Follow me." Justin goes out into the store as he continues to apply pressure to his nose.

Skull appraises me, and while I expect him to give me crap for hitting his son, he merely says, "Your father would be proud of you today—working to bring peace to your club."

"Yeah, he would be proud." But not for what he thinks. And with that, I leave.

CHEVY

My body is on fire. The blood pulsating through my veins is liquid fire. Violet is in my arms and she's soft and warm and smells so damn good I'm about ready to explode. While on my lap, she gives me this smoldering, under-the-eyelash look of seduction as her fingers playfully wander under my shirt.

She's going to kill me.

I lower my head, lightly brush my lips against hers, and when she gently presses back, my hands curl into her waist. Soft giggles from her and my temptress pulls back once again. "We have company."

We do and someday I'm going to kick Oz's and Razor's asses for not giving us time alone.

"It's not like you would find privacy anywhere anyhow," Razor says like he's reading my mind. "In case you haven't figured it out, Pigpen and Man O' War are on a ten-minute rotation of checking in on us. Their instincts are telling them that this is bigger and badder than their wildest guess."

The local police arrested Eli and Cyrus this afternoon on charges of speeding and resisting arrest. Neither of them broke either of those laws, but it's the only way Detective Barlow could talk to them without tipping the Riot's hand of what's about to go down.

I didn't know that was going to happen. In hindsight, I'm glad I didn't know. Not sure I could have seen this through thinking my grandfather and uncle would be sitting behind bars with their reputations on the line.

But then Violet shifts and her long, silky hair slides against my arm. I turn my head, nuzzle my nose behind her ear, inhale her sweet scent and brush my lips to her skin. She cuddles closer, which is almost impossible with how she's sitting on my lap.

Across the yard, the clubhouse is lit up against the black night and pissed-off. Pigpen's been tearing through the cabin, the yard, the clubhouse like a toddler on the warpath. No one besides me, Razor, Oz and Violet understands why Eli and Cyrus were arrested. Until the Riot make their move against Eli and are thrown in jail, no one can know why.

The four of us are in Violet's bedroom at the cabin. Oz and Razor sit at opposite ends of the window seat. I'm cradling Violet on the bed. Like a calming pendulum, she brushes her fingertips slowly up and down my arm. It's a reminder that she's safe, that we're alive, that we are together.

We've been quiet since Louisville. Violet wore a recorder, she got the information the police needed and now we wait for the Riot to mess up and the police to do their job.

Violet watches the fish Justin gave her swim in slow, methodical circles in the glass vase she placed him in when she returned to the police trailer. It was the only thing she could find in the cabinets that would work.

"Why are you keeping it?" I whisper in her ear, but Oz and Razor glance over. The room is too quiet and we're all too hypersensitive from today to not hear even the most hushed sound.

Violet lazily lifts one shoulder. "I don't know."

"Have you considered it's bugged?" Oz asks.

She smiles and one by one, including Oz, we all smile, too. It's been a long day and we're full of paranoia.

"Forget I asked," he said.

"Never," she replies. "I will remember and remind you of that question until the day I die."

Until the day she dies. I wrap my arms tighter around her and she places her head on my shoulder. There's no humming anymore, and as long as she's around, there won't be. "Seriously, why keep the fish?"

"Justin let me pick it out. There were over a thousand fish and this one spoke to me."

"That's a Siamese fighting fish," Razor says. "Those are highly aggressive. The males will kill one another. Females sometimes will, too. I had a buddy once tell me that if you put a mirror up to the tank that the fish will kill itself trying to fight its reflection."

From the slight tilt of her lips, she already knows all of this and I kiss her temple. Violet picked the fish that best describes herself.

"It's a reminder," she whispers to me, but she's aware Oz and Razor hear.

"Of what?" I ask.

"That there are some fights worth fighting and some fights that need to be let go. And that sometimes I need to really take a good look in the mirror before I react."

"I need one of those fish," Razor mumbles.

She giggles, then sighs. "Our English paper is due tomorrow."

School. Somehow that feels a thousand miles away. So do

football games and pep rallies, dances and homework. "Have you written yours?"

"Nope."

"You two mean you can't figure out which path to take?" Razor says teasingly.

I know what path to take, and the way Violet kisses my neck, she knows, too. It's not the one most travelled. It's not the one least taken. We don't need a path when we're confident enough to set our own course in the thick woods.

"Remember you promised me boring," she says. "And I think we should start with blueberry pie. I like blueberry pie. I want to eat it until blueberries are running through my blood."

"I, Chevy, do promise you, Violet, a life that is as boring as we can possibly create."

She smiles and I'd do anything right now to have her alone, roll her under me and kiss her in very not boring ways.

Rumbles of motorcycle engines and we don't move. Due to the arrests, guys from other chapters have been driving in all night and evening. Oz watches the yard, then he stands. "It's them. It's Eli and Cyrus."

Violet hugs me and I hug her back. She's aware, like me, that they're going to want answers.

Violet

After Eli stalked into the cabin and saw the four of us there, he raged out of the cabin and ordered every single person to leave. It didn't matter how long they had driven to get there. He didn't care who had what position on the board. He didn't care about anything. Eli came across like a man whose mental wires had crossed, causing a nuclear reactor meltdown.

Then after two hours of him stalking around the place to confirm there was nobody around, he yelled at us to go to Church and we did. All four of us scuffling over like puppies with ears back and tails between our legs.

It isn't lost on me that this is the first time I've been officially invited to Church. It isn't lost on me that I might be the very first woman to have that invitation extended. But I don't revel in the win, at least not now. Eli's a little too hotheaded and heading to crazy for me to do anything more than stare at the wooden table in front of me.

Eli yelled. A lot. The yelling I expected and could take. The extremely silent and intimidating stare from Cyrus unnerved me.

"Do you have any idea how much danger you were in?" This time I'm pretty sure he's shouting just at me and not at the overall group. "I thought you were smart. I thought you had enough common sense to keep yourself alive."

I'm not fighting back. None of us are. We went behind their backs, behind the club's back, but not one of us regrets it.

"Why, Violet? Why would you do all this? I understand now that you didn't feel safe. I understand that we've got a security problem, but why the hell didn't you find a way to tell me? Just me?"

Eli stops yelling and I glance up from my possibly hours-long stare at the table to meet his eyes. His questions until now have been rhetorical, but from the way he's standing with his hands on his hips and glare firmly planted on me, he wants an answer.

"Because you never would have allowed me to wear the recorder. You would have tried to find a way to fix this on your own and the only way this could work is if I did it. I want the Riot out of our lives, so I did what I had to do."

Eli grabs hold of the chair in front of him and his knuckles turn white under his grip. "You're damn straight I would have stopped you. I promised your father I would take care of you if anything should ever happen to him. Even if I didn't make that promise, I still would have and will do anything to protect you. I don't ever want you pulling bullshit like this again."

Hopefully, I won't have to pull bullshit like this again. "But I will…that is, if it means keeping the people I love safe. Eli…yesterday at the diner, you asked me if our relationship was worth something and I want you to know that it is. It was worth my wearing that recorder."

Eli's eyes snap shut, and for the first time since we entered Church, he drops into a chair. "The Riot have already started with the account numbers. The police could probably go in and arrest them now, but they want to keep handing them rope to hang themselves with. Cyrus and I have given them permission to keep doing what they're doing. I can't decide if I want to hug the four of you or strangle you and I'm too fucking beat to decide. All of you are staying here until I can figure out what the hell I'm going to do with my security problems."

Eli glares at me as if he's waiting for me to challenge him and that glare is rightfully warranted. A week ago, I would have been in his face, but I'm all angered out. "Okay."

Eli points to the door. "Go. All of you. We'll talk again in the morning."

Oz, Razor and I don't hesitate in standing, but Chevy stays seated. He and Cyrus are staring at one another. Chevy wants to talk to him—needs to talk to him. Cyrus has another grandson and Eli has another nephew. But even better, Cyrus is now aware Chevy chose a different path.

Not the one his mother might have wanted, not the path Cyrus would have picked. Chevy has gone rogue, is blazing a trail that belongs to himself. His worst fear is that by doing so, he'll lose his family.

"I can't talk to you tonight," says Cyrus. "I need to think this all through."

"Tough," Chevy says, and a shot of pride courses through me. "Because I need to talk to you."

CHEVY

Violet offers me a soft smile before she exits Church. The door closes and it's me and Cyrus. I've betrayed him. So have Razor and Oz and Violet, but with me it's been different. It's always been different. To be honest, there are times I've felt like the third player of a video game Cyrus has been playing and I'm the last do-over.

Cyrus first had James and James left the club, Snowflake, Cyrus and the rest of his family for the unknown in Louisville. Eli stuck with the club, continues to stick with the club, but went against them one time when he was younger for the woman he loved and ended up in prison for too many years.

Cyrus believes I'm his last hope and I didn't fall into line like he wanted. I can't help but wonder if I'm a disappointment.

"You could have come to me," he says in a voice barely above a mumble. "I understand why none of you went to Eli. He feels too much, loves you all too much. But I don't understand why *you* didn't come to *me*."

"I turn eighteen in two weeks. What happens if I'm not ready to join the club?"

Tonight, Cyrus looks his age. He's nearing seventy and I've never thought too much about that. Before this evening, he had an everlasting air to him. That he was ageless, defying time.

But sitting at the head of the table it's apparent he wears every year like an oxen wears a yoke. His hair and beard are gray. His dark McKinley eyes full of too many years of past pains and learned knowledge that I'm sure he wishes he could forget. His skin is weathered by tears, laughter, wind, rain and sun. The wrinkles around his eyes and mouth are cemented in by happiness and sadness.

My grandfather has seen it all, probably knows it all, yet at the same time he can control nothing. Like James, Eli and me.

"Do you not want to join the club?" he asks.

Last thing I want to do is hurt the man who stepped up to be my father when my own died. Each and every warm memory of our time together churns together in my stomach. "To please you, I do. To keep my family, my brothers, the bonds I've built here, I do."

"But?"

"My entire life, I've been James's son, your grandson, Eli's nephew. I've been the heir to a legacy I don't even understand. You don't talk about James after he left. No one talks about James—not even my mother…that is until this week. It feels like I've been raised up on a high horse supported by a house of cards and I'm one good blow away from falling."

A flicker of anger in his eyes. "What did your mother say?"

"That's not important. What is important is what you haven't said. Did you give up on James as a son when he decided he wanted something different from the club and is the same thing going to happen to me if I decide not to wear a patch on my back?"

Cyrus smooths out his beard, but shifts in agitation. "Do you not want to be a part of this club?"

"I don't know. I don't know who I am or what I want to do with my life. I'm eighteen years old and I should be worried about the paper that's due in English tomorrow. I should be wondering how to ask Violet to prom and if I have to rent a tux to match her dress. I should be losing sleep over playoffs and have my nose in a playbook memorizing routes. But I'm not doing any of those things.

"I love this club and I love you, but for fifteen fucking minutes, I'd like to be eighteen and I'd like to be eighteen without having to lose everyone I love in the process."

Cyrus falls back into his chair as if my words were a punch to the gut and the chair rolls back with the force. "Why the hell are you just saying this to me now?"

The anger at being in the middle all these years bursts through me. "Because any way I chose, I was disappointing someone. You, Mom, the club, Violet. I've been a damned knot in the tug-of-war rope my entire life and I thought it was my job to stay in the middle. Past few weeks have taught me that it's not my job. It never has been.

"Oz knows what he wants, Razor knows what he wants, Violet knows what she wants and I don't because I've wasted too many years of my life trying to please other people. I don't know if I want to be in the club. I think I do, but that patch will feel like a weight if I wear it before I know who I am."

I roll my neck to ease the tension building there, and when it doesn't help, I spit out the rest of the truth because it doesn't make a difference if I hold it in or not. "I want to go to college. I don't know what I'll major in or have the slightest clue where to go, but I want to go somewhere and figure myself out, and if I get my way, I want to do this with your blessing. I want to know that no matter what I choose, I'll still have a home here with you."

My throat burns, my eyes water and I quickly rub at my face to hide the emotions clawing at me to be released. I've done it. I've rolled out my soul for him to kick around.

Cyrus scratches at his head, then lowers it. "I don't know where I went wrong with your father. We were all close. Me, Eli and James. Eli and James especially. Even though James was older than him, James loved Eli. Like a big brother should, like a best friend."

This I've all heard.

"James went to college," Cyrus says, and that captures me. "He did fine for three years, but then everything started to fall apart when the Riot realized Eli was dating Meg. James would come home every chance he had, but then as the situation became more intense, he stopped coming home as much until one day he stopped coming at all."

Cyrus closes his eyes as if someone shot a person he loves through the heart in front of him. Close to seventy years old and something that happened over eighteen years ago still crushes him from the inside out.

"Why?" I ask.

He reopens his eyes and shakes his head. "I don't know. We never knew. One day I had him and then one day—I lost him. I lost my son before he died and I don't know why. I have my theories, theories you've voiced, but that's all they are—damned theories that only haunt me."

The Riot told Cyrus about me. The Riot told me James was a traitor and then I passed that information along to Cyrus. My grandfather thinks his son was a traitor and it's got to be killing him. Isaiah said James wasn't Riot, but other than the word of a guy I've got no attachments to other than genetics, I can't prove him wrong.

"Chevy." Cyrus's voice cracks, and when he clears his throat, my heart throbs in pain. "I don't fucking care if you become a member of this club. You are my grandson and I love you. This is your home, this will always be your home and I will take this vest off my back and set fire to it if that means you'll believe me."

I don't need that. I've never needed that. I just needed to hear him say I'll always have a home. I swallow to keep my throat from closing and stand because my mind's a mess. "I'm not James. You're not going to lose me."

Cyrus climbs to his feet and hugs me. Hands high in a show of respect as if I was wearing a patch. In the club, men hug. It's a show of affection, a show of brotherhood, but it's hard and it's fast. As my grandfather hugs me and I hug him back, we hold on longer because we're making a promise... we're never letting go.

Violet

I'm not sure how Chevy's able to stay awake when my eyelids close of their own volition every few seconds. Each drop into darkness is like a piece of heaven, but then when my body begins to drift toward the car door so I can sleep, I jerk and force my eyes back open. Chevy needs me and I need to stay awake so he'll stay awake and then we won't die in a fiery car crash.

"I don't feel like this is our brightest idea," I say. "We've already missed a ton of school and our mothers will be pissed. We've already got the club mad at us. Do you think it's wise to anger the moms, too? We've had plenty of awful ideas lately, so shouldn't we pull back on the bad ones for a bit?"

"We've also had some good ones." Chevy switches hands on the steering wheel. "Besides, I can't wait for answers anymore. I need to start fresh, and to do that, I need the truth."

James. He's talking about James and my heart aches for him. Chevy shook me awake at six this morning. I at least have had a few hours of sleep. I'm betting Chevy has had none, but he's awake due to freebasing caffeine.

Chevy was determined to meet Isaiah by just showing at his Monday through Friday job, but I was able to convince Rachel via text to push a meetup between Chevy and Isaiah this morning. I promised that Chevy would buy him breakfast. Pretty sure neither of them care about that.

The donut shop Isaiah picked is up on the right and I point it out to Chevy even though the GPS is giving instructions at the same time. Except for a Mustang and another car around the back, the parking lot is empty, and when we walk into the place, we find the same.

It's a quaint little place. Only one table with two chairs near the windows, but other than that there's a glass case holding lots and lots of frosted and not frosted donuts. The sight of baked goodness and the scent of delicious sweetness cause my mouth to water, but then I notice Isaiah talking in a low voice to a woman behind the counter and my appetite dies.

The woman looks over at us, and when she spots Chevy, she places a hand on her stomach like she was kicked. "You look like him. Not as much as Isaiah does, but you look like James."

Isaiah folds his arms over his chest and stays silent as the woman crosses the room to Chevy. She's not what I would have expected for Isaiah's mom, but then again, that's not fair. My mother wouldn't be the definition of a biker chick. Looks are often deceiving.

This woman is young—obviously old enough to have a son out of high school, but still young enough that I don't consider her old. Her long hair is blond with a slight curl and she wears a cotton dress with cowboy boots. Her earrings dangle and she has a soft country twang as she speaks. "I'm Isaiah's mom, Ruth. He told me you want to talk about James."

Chevy glances over at me and the anguish written on his face slays me. He wants to talk about James, but he doesn't. He needs this and he needs me. I link my fingers with his, he locks them tight and we follow Ruth as she leads us away from the front of the store to a breakroom in the back.

CHEVY

"I don't own the place." Ruth is a rambler. Hasn't stopped talking since we walked through the door. "I just work here, but the owner feels like I do a good enough job that he lets me take care of the place after nine on my own. We get real quiet after nine, but I don't mind."

Ruth peeks over at Isaiah as if she's searching for his approval and she twists her hands together. Odd how she's the mom and he's the son, but he's definitely the more mature of the two. Isaiah leans against the wall as Violet and I sit at the breakroom table.

"Are you going to get into trouble for having us here?" Violet asks.

"No. I called and told my boss and he was fine with it as long as I don't make a habit of inviting people in. I told him that my son needed to speak to me and he knows that Isaiah and I don't meet often."

Isaiah's lips thin out. "Why don't you tell them about James, so I can get to work."

"Okay, but it doesn't feel right. James never wanted anyone else to know and I promised him I wouldn't tell. I broke way too many promises with James and I wanted to be able to keep one."

"You told me," Isaiah says with strained patience.

"Because you're my son and I've made mistakes with you and…"

The bell at the front rings and the expression of relief on her face makes me feel worse for her and for me. I just want the truth, but I don't want it if it causes her a mental breakdown.

"I bet you it's him." She brightens.

Isaiah narrows his eyes on her. "Him who?"

"Him." She jumps up and touches Isaiah's arm. "He'll tell them and I won't have to break this promise to James. He's a good man. I disappointed him when I…" Her face turns red. "When I made mistakes, but he helped me as much as he could then, too. Just wait right here."

She leaves. Isaiah pinches the bridge of his nose, then cracks his head to the side. "I'm sorry about this. My mom tries too hard when I'm around."

"Moms can get that way," I say, but I honestly don't know. My mom has always been a rock.

"I'm sorry for calling you in," Ruth says, "but I thought about how you used to help me some after James died because of Isaiah and that maybe you wouldn't mind."

"Why don't you tell me what's wrong?" The familiar voice causes my body to jolt as if struck by lightning and Violet reacts the same way. We both turn our heads to the door and we're met by the rising eyebrows of the detective.

"This is Detective Jake Barlow. Isaiah, Jake knows who you are because he met you as a baby, but he doesn't know Chevy. Jake, this is James's other son, Chevy. He found Isaiah recently and had questions about James. I thought it would be best if you told him."

A muscle in the detective's jaw jerks. "Why couldn't you have told him?"

Ruth's face falls and the detective nods like he understands. "Everyone but Chevy needs to leave."

Isaiah doesn't push away from the wall. "So what Mom said about him wasn't full of shit?"

"If she told the truth, then no."

Violet stands. "You know he's just going to tell me everything anyhow, so I might as well stay."

The detective tilts his head to the door. Because she respects him, she follows Isaiah and his mother out. He shuts it, then takes Isaiah's place at the wall.

Fuck me, I need a beer. "So you knew my dad."

"Yeah, I knew your dad. He's the reason why I've spent the past eighteen years of my life with the gang task force."

Maybe I had it all wrong. Maybe my first instincts were right. "Because he was a member of the Riot?"

"Because he went undercover in the Riot."

All the scattered thoughts in my brain disappear. "What?"

"Your father was a cop. He graduated a year early from college with a degree in criminal justice. He told your family he was in liberal arts because he didn't know how to break it to your grandfather quite yet. He always intended to go home and work on the force in Snowflake, but then things heated up between the Riot and the Terror and he asked the right people if he could find a way to legally bring the Riot down and they put him undercover. It was dangerous, it was risky and it's because of his work that I'm able to build a RICO case against the Riot. With what you, Violet and Razor have given us and what your father gave to me years ago, there are members of the Riot who will die in jail."

"Why didn't you tell me? Why not tell Cyrus or Eli or anyone?"

He crosses his arms over his chest. "We kept it secret to preserve the integrity of the case. Plus he was scared if it got out, even if he died, it would cause problems for the Terror, but mostly he was scared of the repercussions for you and Isaiah.

"The Riot knew about Isaiah because James's life here in Louisville had to be an open book to the Riot. They knew Ruth was his girl and they knew she had his child. After James died, Ruth and Isaiah meant nothing to them. They were never associated with the Terror or the Riot."

I rub at the slow throb in my temples. "The Terror would have taken them in."

"I know, but I was also scared sending them to the Terror would paint a bull's-eye on their backs."

"You've been toying with the Terror all year. You fucked Razor up royally with the bombshell you dropped."

"I needed him to talk to me."

I open my mouth to argue, but he holds up a hand. "And it worked. He's talking, they're all talking and the bad guys are going to jail. Isn't that what we want?"

I scrub my hands over my face. "He was a cop."

"He was a cop. And so you know, he'd be proud of you for lifting that cell so you could track my officer."

A short chuckle leaves my throat. "You saw me do it?"

"No, I guessed. Only explanation I could come up with for how your friends found Violet. Your dad was good with his hands, too. Could read people like you, as well. It's what made him good at his job. Ever think of becoming a police officer?"

"No." Can't say it ever crossed my mind.

"Think about it. We need more people like you." He

pushes off the wall. "Here's the thing. I didn't tell you any of this. Until after the Riot are arrested and the trials are over, I didn't know your dad, got me?"

He extends his hand, I shake it, and for the first time in my life, I feel like I might have some purpose for my future.

Violet

"I got an A!" I sing as I dance my English paper in front of Chevy's face. He tries to snatch it from me, but I dart around him and giggle as I skip ahead in the back field of my parents' land.

"My name is on that paper, too," he calls out.

But I take great pains to point to my name. "See, right here my name is on top and your name is on the bottom. Therefore, I get the A and you get the plus."

Chevy flashes that dimpled smile and my breath catches in my throat. "Is that how it works?"

"Yep. That's how it works."

I wait the few beats for Chevy to catch up to me, and when he does, I hold the paper out to him. He takes it and reads through our English teacher's comments as we continue over the dying winter grass and the new grass struggling to push through.

"Took her long enough to grade it," he mumbles.

True. "But it took us forever to turn it in. She didn't have to accept it from us, she didn't have to let us write it together and she didn't have to give us an A-plus, but she did."

Chevy and I landed an A in a class where people are happy to receive a B, all because we told her that the poem was complete bull and that we don't choose either of the poet's stinking paths. We decided to forge our own.

It's April—months away from this past fall's upheaval. So many people in the Riot have been arrested, including Skull and Justin. Two Reign of Terror members lost their membership to the club for their part in spying on me. Some of the Riot have made bail, some haven't. All are on the road to prosecution. So many things have gone right, some things have gone wrong. So many hearts have been broken, so many wounds are starting to heal. Overall life is moving forward. Each day away from the arrests brings another day of peace and each day of peace brings another level of confidence that there is such a thing as a future.

The people of the Terror can go back to riding their motorcycles without fear of the Riot and the next generation, including me and Chevy, are free to just be...free.

"Did you hear Eli's taking Brandon shopping today in Lexington?" I ask. It's killing me not to text Eli every fifteen minutes for an update. Eli and I have had several long talks about Brandon, and for the first time, Eli is listening.

The plan for today is to get Brandon new pants, since he's grown another inch, but the real goal is for Brandon to pick out the pants and buy them himself. Of course Eli will be there, but as an observer. Eli understands he has to be Brandon's advocate, not his enabler.

Chevy and I have both applied for and have received early acceptance to Eastern Kentucky University. We're both waiting to hear about financial aid and possible scholarships.

Once Chevy threw his hat into the college ring, he had

some interest from coaches. Eastern being one of them. They aren't a college with a huge football program with Saturday games on ESPN, but Chevy isn't interested in that. He just wants to play.

I've got good grades and more than decent test scores. I'll probably get something in scholarship help, but it won't be enough. Last week, though, Eli offered to help pay whatever I don't get in aid and scholarships. I'm probably going to accept because that's what family does—look out for one another and welcome the help when it's needed.

Chevy folds the paper in half and sticks it in his back pocket. "How's your knee?"

"Good." And it's not a lie. Every now and then when it rains, it aches, but other than that I'm fully functioning again. Still, this is the first time we've walked this far since the kidnapping. The winter was cold and brutal. The snow high. It was gray and it felt endless, but then we've been granted glorious days like today.

A warm breeze, a pink evening sky with the first stars starting to twinkle in the east. Another day is ending, the sun falling to its knees and giving way to night. It's almost easy to believe that every horrible thing that happened to us was a bad dream.

"How do you think tomorrow is going to go?" I ask.

Tomorrow, Isaiah is coming to Snowflake to meet Cyrus and Eli for the first time. They were shocked when Chevy told them about Isaiah and they wanted to meet him immediately, but Isaiah asked for time to process the idea of having blood family who cared.

Isaiah isn't the only one processing. Cyrus and Eli are trying to wrap their brains around the fact that James was an undercover cop. Chevy dropped that bomb after the arrests, but we're still keeping that secret contained to blood family. All this new information—a new member of the family, James's secret life—it's been a lot, but in the end, it's good news.

Isaiah and Chevy have met up a few times. Chevy said it's awkward, but they mostly play pool and talk sports. Sometimes, for guys, that type of conversation is heavy in emotional subtext.

Speaking of emotional subtext. "Did you know that Razor is taking Breanna to prom?"

"I heard."

My lips twist to the side and I try to push down the little flames of anger licking at my stomach. Prom is extremely close and everyone else I know has a date. That's not true. Addison doesn't, but I have hopes for her...a newcomer in the club has taken an interest in her. She just needs to take an interest back.

Point is, Chevy hasn't asked. I guess it's assumed, but he should ask because that's what boys should do. We promised each other months ago we would do normal and so far we've excelled at English papers and basement parties and late nights of eating pie at the diner, but I want the normalcy of prom and he needs to freaking ask.

"Oz is going to Emily's prom and Eli said she could visit the weekend of our prom so we can all hang out."

"I heard that, too." Dear God, I'm going to have to hurt him.

"Know what we should do?" he asks.

You should ask me to prom? "What?"

"You should bring Oz as your guest to the prom and I should bring Emily as my guest so we can all go together."

I stop walking, and while the idea is brilliant, I seriously want to kick him in the nuts.

Chevy swings around to face me and catches me by my belt loops. He drags me to him, and while that action typically melts me in ways that I wake up dreaming about at night, I'm a little too irritated at him for it to work.

"Don't you want Oz and Emily to go to prom with us?"

The mature answer is yes. The girl who has loved being boring as hell and just being eighteen is throwing a fit like a sleep-deprived toddler.

"It's not like Oz is going to dance with you. He and Emily can't keep their hands off each other for thirty seconds."

Extremely true. Begrudgingly I say, "Fine."

"Great." Chevy lets me go and starts walking again, but I turn to go home. My taking Oz as my guest is the right thing and so is Chevy taking Emily, and after all that we've been through, it's stupid to have my feelings hurt that Chevy hasn't asked, but there are some things in my life I've thought about since I was younger and prom is one of them.

But then I pause. This is stupid. Chevy has loved me, he has saved me and he has risked his life for me. This is the twenty-first century and I need to grow up. I spin around and say, "Will you go to prom with me?"

Chevy glances over his shoulder and blinks. "What?"

"Yeah, sure whatever, I'll take Oz, you'll take Emily, but will you go to prom with me?"

Chevy's expression darkens and he stalks in my direction. "You are the most impatient person I know."

Now I'm lost. "I'm what?"

Chevy bends and I let out a yelp when he lifts me with his shoulder, turns and continues to walk toward our section of the field. I'm laughing, I'm yelling at him, I smack him on his back and laugh harder when he tickles my side.

Finally, Chevy sets me on my feet and holds my shoulders as I get past the dizziness of all the blood that has gathered in my head returning to my limbs.

I blink a few times, and when I lean affectionately into

Chevy, he strokes my collarbone with his thumb. "A few months back, I promised you boring. I promised you college, I promised you a future, I promised to never leave your side again. I've got you, I'll always have you and we're going to have the most exciting, boring prom with all of our friends, but sometimes, I don't like sharing you."

Chevy twirls me and I suck in a breath. It's our spot. Our place in the field. It's where we played as children, it's where Chevy and I shared our first kiss. It's where he first told me he loved me, it's where he carved our names on the tree to the right. It's where we explored each other's bodies, it's where we explored each other emotionally.

It's the one place in the world that has brought me such joy and right now it's close to bringing me to tears. There are poles set up in a circle and hanging from them are lights. In the middle is a blanket with a picnic basket and surrounding the blanket are lit candles on wooden boards.

Chevy walks around me and hooks his cell phone up to portable speakers. My favorite song plays and Chevy extends his hand to me. "I once promised you dancing at midnight in our field. It's not midnight, but it will be in a few hours, so want to dance with me now and then dance with me again later?"

Yes. So much yes. But dancing isn't what I want. Not right now. We will, but there are other things we need to do first.

I walk over to Chevy, and when he gathers me into his arms, it's like the entire world stops. It doesn't spin. It stays as perfect as it is in this moment.

"I love you," I whisper. "I can't remember a time when I haven't loved you."

The right side of his mouth tips up. "You sure about that? You've given me a few looks that could strike me dead."

I laugh, then sigh. "Even then I loved you."

"I wouldn't have it any other way. We're like fireworks, Violet. Beautiful separate, but phenomenal when put together. Of course, you can't have all of that without a few explosions."

"You promised me boring," I whisper.

"I promise we will have nothing but boring explosions."

Boring explosions. I can live with that. Razor throwing pie at Oz at the diner, Chevy and me arguing over comma placement in our English paper, then ending up in the hottest kiss of my life, making out under the bleachers during a basketball game and then serving detention for a week after being caught.

I can handle each and every one of those beautiful, boring explosions.

"Remember a few months ago when you were giving me orders as we were about to kiss?" Chevy asks.

I do. It was in the trailer and Chevy was helping me with my nerves. "Yes."

"I feel that turnabout's fair play."

Eager to see where this is going, I nod in agreement. "Within reason."

"Within reason," he repeats. Chevy feathers his fingers along my neck and I love the ticklish sensation. "Dance with me, Violet."

Chevy weaves an arm around my waist, pulls me to him until we're body to body. My arms go around his neck and his eyes darken with lust as I lightly run my fingers along the strands of his hair near the base of his neck.

He leans down and his hot breath tickles my skin. "Head on my shoulder. You know how to do this right."

Head on his shoulder and I become liquid in his arms. His body moves to the beat and I follow along, closing my eyes as I enjoy each and every way our bodies connect. The way his fingers trace up and down my spine. The light brushes of his lips on my neck. His strong hand on my hip and his finger that's keeping time with the music.

A beat, another, and it keeps going until that beat is in my blood. My own hands begin to wander. Along his strong shoulders, down his back and along his arms.

"Violet," he whispers again, but this time his voice is rough and strained.

"Yes?"

"Lift your head."

I do and he cups my face. Heat encompasses me and so does the feeling that I belong, that I'm loved, that I'm his and he's mine.

"I love you," he says and his lips come so achingly close to touching mine. "And will you grant me the honor of going to prom with me?"

I'm beaming. Beaming. There's no other word for it. "Yes."

"Now, will you kiss me?"

Yes, a million times, yes.

★ ★ ★ ★ ★

ACKNOWLEDGMENTS

To God: Psalm 112: 7–8 NIV: They will have no fear of bad news; their hearts are steadfast, trusting in the Lord. Their hearts are secure, they will have no fear; in the end they will look in triumph on their foes.

For Dave: Thank you for teaching me that I don't have to choose the paths set before me. That I'm free to create a brand-new path no one has traveled down before. I love you, always.

Thank you to…

Kevan Lyon, Margo Lipschultz, Suzie Townsend, Colette Ballard, Angela Annalaro-Murphy, Kristen Simmons, Kelly Creagh, Bethany Griffin, Kurt Hampe, Bill Wolfe, my parents, my sister, my Mount Washington family and the entire McGarry "Madness" clan. It takes a village and I thank you for the support.

*Look for Katie McGarry's next compelling
and unforgettable novel SAY YOU'LL REMEMBER ME
from Harlequin TEEN.*

*When a politician's daughter who's spent her life obeying the rules
meets a guy who's best known for his stint in juvenile
detention, two worlds might be turned upside down.
Read on for an exclusive sneak peek…*

Ellison

The red light in front of me flashes, bells ring and I raise my arms in the air, savoring my victory. I even mimic the dance I performed in my limited and excruciatingly failed days as a cheerleader for peewee football by slightly swinging my hips side to side.

I split my "v," I dot my "i," I curl my "ctory." Peewee football cheer taught me I not only lacked rhythm, but I lacked enthusiasm for my team when it was thirty degrees and raining. But in my defense, how many six-year-olds do?

The group next to me tosses their padded mallets onto the game. Only one groans as if their loss was monumental. The rest laugh and good-naturedly tease each other. They've been fun to beat. For three games in a row, these two rugged guys and two girls have hung with me. Three times digging into their pockets to ante up, three times we've trashed-talked the other in ways that are only done on fair midways, three times each one bites the dust.

Whack-a-Mole is not for the faint of heart. This game is for the serious and only the serious win and I'm a serious type of girl when it comes to carnival games and hard-won stuffed animals. Someone's got to play and win, and it's going to be me.

For a few minutes, I forgot I had to be perfect and just being me felt great.

"Good game." One girl of the group offers me her fist and the multiple bracelets on her wrists clank. She's my age, with curly black hair in tight rings and friendly dark eyes. Her clothes, I love. Tight jeans, a tank that ends at her midriff and a jeweled chain around her stomach that's attached to her belly-button ring. She has a daring grin and style. Both I admire.

I'm not the type to fist-bump. Mom calls it low class, and by how long I've hesitated she's aware this is out of my territory. I fist-bump her back because I'm not only highly competitive, but I rarely back down from a challenge. For those reasons alone, it's amazing my mother lets me out of the house. "Good game."

Her grin widens, and I hold my breath as she tilts her head in that familiar déjà vu. I silently pray for her to shake it off, and when she does, turning so she can talk to her friends, I blow out a relieved breath.

Most of her group appears to be the same age as her, about the same age as me, except one guy who I'd guess is in his twenties. By the way they all listen when he talks, it's apparent he has their respect.

I watch them longer than I should because a part of me envies the way they all seem to belong to each other. My cousin Henry is twenty-four and loves me, but about the only thing we have in common is our parents, so I envy people like this.

The carny clears his throat, and I'm drawn back to the sound of people laughing on rides and the scent of popcorn. I offer the pink-and-black-striped medium snake to him and motion with my index finger that I'm on the hunt for the massive, big-daddy snake that could wrap around my body a few times. To the victor goes the spoils.

The carny doesn't accept my medium snake and instead hands me a green-and-black-striped small one. "You have to win four times in a row in order to get the big one."

Four times. Good God. At five dollars a game, I could have bought five of these hardened toys, but that's not the point. Winning is the actual prize.

I pull my cell out of the small purse I have crossed over my body to prevent someone from doing a dash-and-grab with my stuff. I ignore Andrew's "Where are you?" texts and check the time. I've got an hour to make it back to the convention center, change and be ready for Dad's press conference where it is my job to sit, smile and "look pretty."

If I'm really careful, there won't be time for my mother to berate me for taking off without Andrew. She allowed me to go to the midway with the understanding that I was to tag along with him. But I don't like Andrew and Andrew doesn't like me, so I walked right while he walked left and neither of us looked back to see if the other was following. Maybe Andrew will rat me out for leaving him. Maybe he won't. Either way, I'm happy with my choices.

Any way I look at it, I have time for at least one more game. I flip my blond hair over my shoulder and give a tempting grin that's meant to rub it in that I not only won, but won three times in a row. "You know you guys want to play again."

You know you hate being beaten by me.

From the expressions of the guys, I have pegged all of them correctly. The girls I could totally become best friends with because they knowingly laugh at their expense.

"I'll play." It's a small voice belonging to a child and my grin falls. Long unruly ringlets over a chubby preschool face. She stands on her tiptoes to hand money to the carny, and he accepts it without giving her a second glance. "I'm going to win this time. I have to. Daddy says it's my last game."

The aforementioned daddy hands another five dollars to the carny worker and picks up a mallet next to his daughter's spot. Ugh. Knife straight to the heart as he throws me a pleading glance. He wants her to win. He needs her to win. He wants me to help her win.

I totally hate being conned, but if I'm going to lose, it will be to a five-year-old.

"Are you going to play?" the carny asks me because it's his job to make money. I want to answer no, but because I was once five and my father did the same thing for me, I fork over my five dollars, then tilt my head in a princess-worthy stare over at the boys.

It takes four to play, and I need one of them to lose so this kid can win. They glance over at one another, waiting to see which one is going to man up.

"Your ego can handle being beaten by a five-year-old," I say.

A guy in their group who had been hanging back strides up. "I'll play."

For a second, there's a flutter in my chest. The lightest touch of butterfly wings and I secretly wish this guy would chance a look in my direction, but he doesn't. Instead, he hands the carny five dollars and claims the spot next to me.

Wow. I'm definitely okay with this.

He's a few inches taller than me, jeans, a white T-shirt stretched against broad shoulders and gorgeous. Drop-dead gorgeous. The defined muscles in his arms flex as he switches the mallet from one hand to the other, and I've stopped breathing. His blondish-brown hair is shaved close on the sides, but the top is wild, longer tufts of hair, and his face is freshly shaved. He has an old-school 1950's look with a modern-day twist and it works well. Very well.

I'm staring, I need to stop and he's also aware that I'm staring and haven't stopped. He turns his head, our eyes meet and those butterflies lift into the air. Warm brown eyes and that's when I'm finally scared into having the courage to glance away. But I peek back and sort of smile to find he's now looking at me like he can't stop.

For the first time in my life, I like that someone is looking. Not someone—him. I like that he's looking at me.

"We let her win," I whisper.

He nods, and I lift my mallet. It's tough not to get into position. To be poised and ready to strike. I love this game, I love winning and losing to be nice is all fine and good, but I have to fight the instinct to go full throttle.

"You're good at this," he says.

"I play this game a lot. At every fair and festival I can. It's my favorite. If there were an Olympic event for Whack-a-Mole, I would be a gold medalist several times over."

"Then I'm in the presence of Whack-a-Mole royalty." The laughter in his eyes is genuine, and I watch him just long enough to see if he knows who I am. Some people do. Some people don't. I've learned to read the expression of recognition and he's not wearing it.

My body relaxes. "Totally."

One corner of his mouth edges up, and my mouth dries out. That is possibly the most endearing and gorgeous grin I've seen. He twirls the handle of the mallet around in his fingers, and I'm drawn by the way he makes the motion seem so seamless.

This fantastic humming begins below my skin. To be brutally honest, I'm not sure what attraction is. My experience with boys has been limited, but whatever this is, I want to feel it again and again and again and in every level of my being.

The bell rings, my heart jumps and I inhale when the

worn plastic moles pop up from the holes. The instinct is to knock the hell out of them, but the tinkling laughter of the little girl farther down causes me to pull back. I hit one. Then another. I have to score something. She needs to think we at least tried.

The guy next to me hits a few moles, but in a rhythm. A crazy one. A catchy one. One that my foot taps along with.

The bell rings, the little girl squeals and my hopes of winning the large snake die.

A chirp of my cell, and I immediately text back my mother: Still at the midway. Heading back now.

Mom: Hurry. I think we should curl your hair for the event.

My hair, my outfit. That's what's important to her. I squish my lips to the side. It took her an hour this morning to decide she wanted me to wear it straight and it took her another hour to decide what I should wear on the midway, in case I should be recognized, but so far I haven't been. It then took yet another hour to decide what I should wear to the press conference.

When I look up, disappointment weighs down my stomach. The boy—he's gone. Not really gone, but gone from beside me. He's rejoined his group, standing with them and belonging. I will him to glance my way one more time, but he doesn't.

That's okay. I'm just a girl on a midway and he's just a boy on a midway and not everything has to end like a daydream. Truth is, once he found out what my world is really like, he'd have taken off running.

But I have to admit, it would have been nice if he had at least asked for my name.

PLAYLIST FOR
LONG WAY HOME

Theme:
"The Sound of Silence" by Disturbed
"With or Without You" by U2
"Too Close" by Alex Clare
"Immortals" by Fall Out Boy

Chevy:
"Down the Road" by Kenny Chesney with Mac McAnally
"John Cougar, John Deere, John 3:16" by Keith Urban
"Somewhere in My Car" by Keith Urban

Violet:
"Out of the Woods" by Taylor Swift
"Ghosttown" by Madonna
"Wonder" by Natalie Merchant

Chevy on Violet:
"Whatever She's Got" by David Nail

Violet, Chevy, Oz and Razor in Church:
"Renegades" by X Ambassadors

Chevy and Violet's Future:
"Where It's At" by Dustin Lynch

Don't miss this moving and utterly unforgettable
story of true love in the face of overwhelming odds,
from acclaimed author

KATIE McGARRY

When Drix was convicted of a crime—
one he didn't commit—he thought his
life was over. With the Second Chance
Program, the governor's newest pet
project, Drix knows this is his chance
to get his life back on track.

As the governor's daughter, Elle can
open doors with her name alone. But
the expectations and pressure to be
someone she isn't may be too much
to handle.

Drix is not the type of boy Elle's
parents have in mind for her, and
Elle is not the kind of girl who can
understand Drix's messy life.

But sometimes love can breach all barriers.

www.HarlequinTEEN.com

Find Harlequin TEEN on

HTKM21237TR

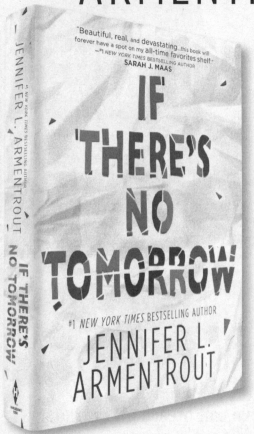

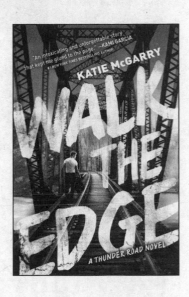
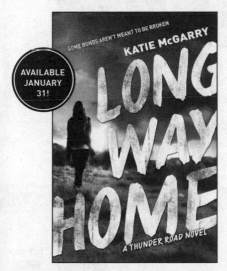